A HERO TO HOLD

Sheri Humphreys

www.BOROUGHSPUBLISHINGGROUP.com

A HERO TO HOLD
Copyright © 2016 Sheri Humphreys

ISBN 978-1534662-29-2

To Elnora King, who made me believe it could happen

CHAPTER ONE

London, May 1857

Four straight hours of smiling had given Charlotte Haliday an ache in her jaw. The corner of her mouth began to quiver, forcing her to bite the inside of her cheek. Pure stubbornness propelled her around the periphery of the room from one group to the next of society's elite, talking and feigning interest in the ballroom conversation. Sheer willpower kept her pretending ignorance of the skeptical, assessing eyes and whispers that trailed in her wake.

She kept her shoulders back, chin up, eyes level. The sound of the orchestra barely penetrated, coupled with so many conversations, the melee of whirling silk dresses and the aromatic fragrance of ladies and gentlemen turned out in their finest. Instead Charlotte concentrated on the faces—the reactions—of the people around her. She had a reputation to repair. She'd waited out eighteen months of mourning in the country. Now she intended to right the injustice that had been done her.

Those closest suddenly turned and watched as if she were about to offer them a treat. An icy little shiver grabbed the back of her neck and streaked down her spine. As casually as she could, Charlotte glanced around.

Her breath caught. A glorious blaze of yellow silk swayed a short distance away.

Lady Garret.

The woman lifted her brows and canted her head. A smug little smile just tilted the corner of her mouth. Charlotte struggled not to show any reaction, but tightness spread deep across her chest and into her throat. Her gaze locked with that of the baroness. The woman's amber eyes gleamed with amusement—and disdain.

Blast! How easy it was for the old pain to slip in. But this time Charlotte refused to be prey. She squared her shoulders and snapped her black, folded fan against her palm then answered Lady Garret's look with one of her own.

The baroness stiffened, lips tight. Good. She'd correctly interpreted Charlotte's look as a challenge.

The golden skirts shifted and Lady Garret started forward, the pugnacious jut of her chin like a spearhead. Charlotte waited until the last moment to swivel her head and break their locked gazes. She was finally ready to stand up to the ruthless woman, but she wasn't about to do so in the middle of Lord and Lady Elliott's ballroom.

She turned and headed with alacrity for the door to the veranda. Glancing over her shoulder, Charlotte saw Lady Garret halted by a gentleman who must have asked her to dance, but the baroness shook her head and resumed walking. Ahead of Charlotte several couples exited onto the veranda, effectively depriving her of it. Her only option for confronting the evil shrew in private was a shadowy alcove that had been all night offering weary dancers an opportunity to sit and rest.

It would have to do. At least the palms arranged at each side of the nook nearly obscured the interior.

Sweeping into the alcove, Charlotte found a solitary man seated on a tufted velvet divan. Disappointment kicked hard before determination forged in. The man would just have to leave.

He looked at her, his eyes narrowing a bit, and Charlotte was taken aback by the intensity of that gaze. With a stern expression upon clean male features, his was a commanding rather than handsome visage. Fine lines radiated from the corners of his eyes and made her think this a man accustomed to gazing at distant horizons. The ruffled look of unpomaded red-gold hair showed a disregard for fashion. A wide, expressive mouth sat above a chiseled chin dented by a masculine dimple. His apparel—finely tailored black and white evening dress—was unexceptional, though the breadth of his shoulders set the gentleman apart. Charlotte's gaze dropped to his hands. Encased in white kid, she couldn't tell if they held the same strength as the shoulders.

He scowled, and Charlotte realized she'd been gazing upon him far too intently. Now he returned the favor. His eyes swept slowly from her elegantly styled black hair to the hem of her purple gown, on the return trip hesitating for the merest second on her bosom. The pause stole her composure and left her fumbling for words.

"Sir, how do you do? I apologize for my forwardness, but I fear I…I must have a private conversation here. Now. Would you mind…? Would you be so gracious?" She couldn't believe she was asking him to leave. It was incredibly brash of her, and rude as well, but she had no choice.

He did not speak for a moment, his cold blue eyes making her stomach clench. But, blast it! She had to use the alcove. She braced herself to stand up to the iron-hard will she sensed behind that wary and disapproving look, straightened, adopted an expectant mien and tapped her toe impatiently.

"I'm afraid that's not possible."

He didn't even make an attempt to smile or be apologetic, and impatience overwhelmed Charlotte. In tandem with her tapping foot, she slapped her fan against her skirt. Despite appearances to the contrary, this was no gentleman. Why, he hadn't even attempted to introduce himself—!

Suddenly, all Charlotte's vexation drained away to be replaced by something else. Perhaps he knew who she was, had heard the rumors about her. Perhaps he was offended by her peremptory attempt to confiscate his quiet corner. Mayhap her appearance—unescorted—had shocked him, and her intrusion confirmed to him that the speculation he'd heard was true. Perhaps he felt she merited none of the courtesy he'd show any other lady.

After all she'd borne at the hands of society, Charlotte had thought herself immune to insult, but for some reason this man's failure to show her the most basic courtesy cut sharp. A lump lodged in her throat. Then his gaze went past her. She'd run out of time.

She turned to find the baroness. Everything about the woman glowed: her satiny dress, her golden hair, the breathtaking necklace of yellow diamonds at her throat, even her amber eyes. Charlotte and Lady Garret were of similar height, yet the woman's aura left Charlotte feeling dwarfed. This was the witch who had destroyed her marriage, made her a pariah among her peers, fabricated a despicable persona that all of society now assumed was Charlotte herself. It had been almost two years, but it seemed like yesterday Lady Garret penned her novelette, published and distributed it amongst her acquaintances. Those pages had left Charlotte blackballed from society.

"Lady Haliday, what a pleasure."

The malicious edge of humor in the baroness's voice made her words a parody, and resentment speared Charlotte. "You're a poor liar, Lady Garret, and you really needn't expend the effort. I'm immune to your poison."

The baroness noticed their silent companion, whose gaze was fixed upon her. "What, no introduction, my lady?"

The man did not react in any way. Well, Charlotte decided, at least he dealt out rudeness impartially.

The man shot her a look, brows lifting as if in question—as if he knew her and was silently communicating. Following blind instinct, Charlotte settled herself next to him on the empty half of the settee. She felt immediately and impossibly steadied.

Lady Garret's mouth firmed, and her attention returned to Charlotte. "I'm surprised to see you here, my lady. Especially tucked away in a corner with a gentleman. It's been a mere eighteen months since your husband passed. I'd go so far as to say this makes a mockery of his memory."

Charlotte schooled her expression to one of polite interest. She *would not* show Lady Garret even an inkling of distress.

"I'd guess your actions will provide society with some entertainment," the baroness continued. "A bit of a scandal is always appreciated. At least, it amuses me. It might even inspire me to pen another novel."

A slow smile curled her enemy's lips, and a quivering beset Charlotte deep inside. She kept her vision fixed on the baroness's glittering eyes and wrapped her hand around the edge of the divan seat, anchoring herself. Over and over, for the past year she'd imagined this meeting. God willing, she would prevail.

She leaned back against the divan and forced her shoulders to relax. She had to appear confident, so she concentrated on keeping her voice composed. "I'm no longer that naive young woman you manipulated and tried to destroy. This time I won't stand by while you spread lies about me. I'm not afraid of you, and I won't crumble."

The gentleman beside her turned his head, the chilly look gone from his eyes. Like heat from the sun, waves of quiet strength radiated from him and emboldened Charlotte. She marshaled her thoughts, leaned forward just enough to lend emphasis to her words, and continued with a harder voice. "You tell lies about me again, and I'll make sure all of London is familiar with your machinations and your wicked soul. Until then, I'll leave you be."

Lady Garret's eyes narrowed to mere slits. "How dare you threaten me?"

Charlotte did not look away. Didn't this woman understand that she had already been consumed by the fire of scandal and risen from the ashes?

"You can say whatever you like about me," she vowed. "You can tell all of London you saw me walk naked down the center of Regent Street. I don't care. If it happens again, this time I won't hide myself away—and I'll make sure no one believes you."

She felt the man sit straighter beside her, and a sudden desire to do something actually outrageous overcame Charlotte. To do something worthy of gossip, possibly even scandalous, and to do it without a care for the watchful eyes of Lady Garret. The thought left her giddy, and Charlotte closed her eyes to steady herself. Such an act would prove beyond all doubt that she had no fear of the baroness.

The gentleman beside her still radiated waves of quiet heat. His hand rested on the divan, and before she could consider the wisdom of her idea, Charlotte found herself caught up in it. She placed her hand atop his and laced their fingers. He tensed, and her heart began to race. What was she thinking? And yet, her daring thrilled her as nothing ever had, and when Charlotte looked at Lady Garret and saw the baroness struggling to hide her surprise, suddenly she was sure.

"At least *this* time," she announced, "what you write will be based on truth instead of falsehood."

In the grip of something foreign and reckless, Charlotte turned to the gentleman, gazed into his eyes and curled her hand around the back of his head. He resisted a bit as she drew him near, but she couldn't afford to hesitate now. She didn't relent.

A little shock ran through her as their lips touched. She felt his hesitancy and tightened her hold, some part of her still aware. Then his lips moved, and what had started out as the softest touch became firm.

A tremor took up residence in her marrow as she returned the pressure of his mouth. She'd kissed no man but Haliday, and she'd thought one kiss must be much the same as another, but this man's kiss was…different. Even the smell of him—the starch of his shirt, the enticing aroma of citrus and cloves and maleness—was unique. For a long moment Charlotte was lost in his solid heat, in the slide of his gloved hand along her jaw. Then, in the periphery of her awareness, she heard the rustle of skirts. Lady Garret was leaving.

Too dazed to feel triumphant, Charlotte placed her hand on the strange man's chest and gently pushed until their lips separated. She stared into bottomless blue eyes that brimmed with warmth, felt the tension in him, knew his breathing came as hard and fast as hers. Then his hand gripped her waist and pulled her back. His lips dragged over hers, nudged hers apart, and he captured her again in a warm, luscious kiss that burst upon her senses with a completeness that obliterated everything else.

She was lost. She'd been married four years, but never had desire swept over her like this. It confused her, frightened her even, but soon all thought fell away and Charlotte was left to revel in sensation. The man's hands slid up her back and brought her breasts and hip hard against him. His chest was broader and firmer than her husband's had been, and she nestled into his arms as if she'd been made to fit there. His tongue stroked hers, and her breath caught and heat ripped through her.

A confused, distressed little noise escaped her. The man abruptly pulled away.

Trembling, gasping, Charlotte looked into a shuttered face and humiliation crashed down. What had she done? What had she been thinking? She didn't even know this man's name. Fiery heat enveloped her, and her face burned. She thought she might expire of embarrassment. How could she have done such a thing?

"Oh!" She pressed her fingers to her lips, staring.

If Charlotte thought the man looked unhappy before, he now looked absolutely thunderous. Lips narrowed to a grim line, he held his shoulders rigid like a soldier standing at attention.

"Oh!" She jumped to her feet and saw his eyes flare. She had to leave, find someplace quiet and try to figure out what had happened tonight. She opened her mouth to ask the man's name, to tell him hers and apologize, but the ridiculousness of the situation stopped her. The man had spoken no more than one sentence in her presence. Perhaps if they remained strangers she could pretend this event hadn't occurred. She didn't even know if he was married!

She backed toward the doorway.

"Wait."

The grim command in his voice made her pause. His hand reached out, but she whirled and broke from the alcove. She headed straight for the veranda door, wanting only to escape into the dark night until she could compose herself.

She attracted some attention from the way she hurried, weaving her way around the revelers, but finally she gained the solitude and deep shadows of the veranda. Her chest heaved as if she'd run a footrace. The cool night air soothed her heated cheeks, but inside emptiness twisted, left her aching.

He could have come after her, but he'd not.

CHAPTER TWO

David Scott clenched his hands. A strong urge to hammer his fists against his thighs arose, but he held himself rigid as anger and lust seared through him equally. Sweat broke upon his forehead.

With a vicious curse, he damned himself and the reckless Viscountess Haliday. He hated her for filling his head with her rose and jasmine scent, her violet eyes, and the feel of her body pressed against him. Then she'd abandoned him and left him struggling to keep from impotently pounding upon his useless legs.

He took a deep breath, willing his fists open. At least her impulsiveness had resolved one pressing fear. When she'd drawn him to her, lust pooled low in his body. In spite of his physician's reassurance, he'd thought that part of him dead, but Lady Haliday made it clear that was not the case. The wakening of his sex brought overwhelming relief—but it brought anguish, too.

He let his head fall back. He had nothing to offer any woman of his class. No title, no fortune, no property. With the right lady it might be possible to overcome those things, but one last issue could never be conquered.

Get a hold of yourself, man. He looked down at his still, carefully placed legs. He'd already shed his tears, indulged in bouts of anger to vent his despair. Nothing would change what he'd finally, after months of mourning and struggle, accepted. He didn't have an intact body to offer a prospective wife. He wasn't paralyzed, but his crushed legs wouldn't permit him to stand or walk.

A flash of regimental dress drew his attention to the alcove's arched entry. Major Lord Miles Wakefield stood there in the crimson pants and dark blue coat of David's old regiment—the 11th Hussars, the Cherry Pickers. Even after all this time David still experienced a jolt when faced by this man. They'd been school companions, fellow officers and best friends, but their current relationship baffled him.

"Here you are," Wakefield said, looking about the small space as if it deserved his keenest attention. "What are you doing?"

Wakefield needn't know he had spent the entire evening in this alcove. David had made arrangements with Lady Elliott to arrive early so he could gain the ballroom without the benefit of watchful eyes; then he'd expected to situate himself at the outskirts of the ballroom or in the card room. Unfortunately, his wheeled chair left him feeling more conspicuous than he'd anticipated; drawing eyes because he sat in a wheeled chair was still something he wasn't wholly comfortable with. So he'd had Boone lift him from his chair and set him on the settee in this secluded locale. He'd taken the coward's way out. Ironic that, since he was soon to be one of the first recipients of the newly created Victoria Cross, now his nation's highest award for valor.

"The ballroom was a bit too much of a diversion. I thought I'd seek refuge here for awhile. The friends who knew I planned to attend have found me," David added, "and I've seen any number of others who decided to seek a little quiet."

"Encounter anyone looking for a tête-à-tête?" Wakefield asked, flashing the dimple he trotted out with the reliability of a calling card.

David considered telling Wakefield about the confrontation between Lady Haliday and Lady Garret. He trusted Wakefield to keep it confidential, but a strange reluctance to reveal any of what had happened held him silent. Of course, if Lady Garret spread the tale, his name would be on every lip. All of society would think he'd had an assignation with the scandalous Lady Haliday, whose supposed affair had filled the papers along with her husband's murder by a footpad. Anger flared at the viscountess's selfishness. He had enough complications in his life without becoming a target of silly conjecture.

"No."

Wakefield sauntered over to the settee. "You're missing the excitement. The infamous Viscountess Haliday is here. And can you believe it? Lady Garret is in attendance, too."

David grimaced. "Well, the world doesn't stop, does it? Why would it? My legs may be shattered, but all that means is one less gentleman to help fill a dance card."

Wakefield stiffened and half-turned. His eyes went to the palms blocking dancers waltzing past outside.

Damn! David tightened his lips to hold back the vile curse he wanted to spit out. Why had he let loose with such a self-centered, uncaring remark? He hated when he started feeling sorry for himself. He'd vowed not to do so any longer, no matter what the provocation—as if having a few people eye him at a ball qualified as provocation at all. He hadn't thought before he spoke, and his statement couldn't help but needle his friend. Even though David didn't consider the man responsible for crippling him, Miles Wakefield blamed himself.

Feeling worse than shabby, David cast about for a change of subject. "You heard of my new position?"

Wakefield spun back with a relieved smile. "Yes, congratulations. How is it?"

The tightness inside David eased a bit. "A welcome challenge. The charity was created two years ago, but it needs more organization. And being named chairman of the Royal Patriotic Fund Executive Committee solved my biggest problem—how to support myself so I won't have to rely on my brother's generosity."

"I'm pleased for you. Especially given the work you'll be doing."

"Assisting Crimean War widows and orphans? A cause close to both our hearts," David agreed. "Are you still stationed at the War Office? Durham's staff?"

Wakefield nodded. "We may be dispatched to India to give Campbell a hand. What a bloody mess that is."

David studied his childhood friend with curiosity. Just last week they'd gotten news of the Siege of Delhi. He had campaigned with Miles and knew what a fine officer he was, but the man held a title now and was unmarried. Wakefield had to feel some obligation to sell his commission and attend to his duties as viscount. He'd never intended to stay the course for life.

How contrary life was, that Miles was the one still in service to the Crown. David, crippled, Peter, dead... Of the three friends, they two had wanted to make the army their life. Part of David still yearned to do just that, to lead troops and defend his country. Another part of him remembered too vividly the aftermath, the dead and wounded strewn across foreign dirt. And of course he no longer had the choice.

David pushed his thoughts away, careful to school his expression. "You'll let me know if you get orders?"

"Yes. Of course."

For a moment quiet reigned, then Wakefield cleared his throat and dropped onto the settee beside David. He leaned forward, forearms on his thighs, hands clasped between his knees. "The thing is, I don't feel the same resolve I used to."

A sudden unwelcome thought held David immobile. "Please don't tell me your misplaced guilt about me has affected your ability to command."

"No. It's not that." Wakefield's gaze turned ferocious. "Balaclava—that whole cursed debacle—changed me, David. I know it affected you, too. It changed your whole life. You lost the use of your legs, and we both lost our idealism. Now... We shouldn't be in this mess in India." Miles fell silent, and the sounds of the ballroom floated in. When he spoke again, his voice was a raspy whisper. "I've seen too many men dead who shouldn't be."

Ah, yes. David dreamed about those same men. Peter was the first and dearest friend lost, but there were many.

"What you're feeling, Miles...I understand," he finally said. "And so do our comrades." Both living and passed.

They listened to an entire polka before either spoke again.

Wakefield stood. "Shall I fetch your man? Is it Boone?"

David was suddenly unbearably weary. Leaving would require maneuvering around the ballroom in his wheelchair, but by leaving early he'd be able to enter his carriage without a rash of onlookers watching. It took great effort to summon a weak smile. "Would you? Tell him I'm ready to go."

Wakefield nodded.

The man's exit brought a surfeit of relief but also an emptiness that invaded David's very bones. The ache spread, twisting fingers of numbness turning warm flesh to cold. It seemed so long ago that he'd stood alongside Wakefield at the front, easy in their friendship and in his own physicality. At the time he hadn't valued his body's effortless strength, the energy that could sustain him for days on the battlefield. He'd taken it for granted, accepted it as his God-given right. Now that joy he'd never fully appreciated was lost to him.

He raked his fingers through his hair and tried to regain his equilibrium. He'd contemplated this evening with anticipation, planning to renew old acquaintances and make fresh ones. Those looking for a few moments of peace or quiet conversation had regularly appeared in his alcove, and until the arrival of Lady Haliday he'd managed to forget his initial discomfort and enjoy himself. He'd even managed to make a decent number of contacts for the Fund. With work to sustain him, and having figured out a way to get himself in and out of his coach, he was moving about London and beginning to think he would be able to fashion a satisfactory life for himself. He might not be able to stand, but he could certainly take his place in society as a capable and independent gentleman. Yet Lady Haliday's kiss had revealed how very far from satisfied he really was.

Was it possible he still smelled her scent? He took a deep breath, and the lingering odor of rose and jasmine caused a resurgence of the lust that had been such a surprise and great relief. If only his newly forged confidence hadn't been wrested from him so quickly and easily when she fled and he was unable to pursue her.

Would he see Lady Haliday again as he left? He dropped his head against the back of the divan and sighed. His first society gathering since his injury, and he'd been faced with a woman who seemed to represent everything that was now outside his reach.

Why his manhood had roared back to vigorous life now, and with this particular lady, he didn't know, but he supposed the event was welcome. It had been nearly two years since he'd lain with a woman, and right now he thought just such an act might go a long way toward making him feel like himself again. This wasn't the first time he'd felt the urge, but it hadn't been strong enough before to risk the complications and embarrassment he knew he'd encounter. Even a high-priced bawdy house, which repelled his every sensibility, would need a bedroom on the ground floor. Any other would necessitate Boone and Pickett carrying him upstairs and depositing him in the lightskirt's bed, and he'd be damned if he'd be carried in and presented for service. He also supposed he must do the deed without removing his trousers. He'd not expose his legs, even to a whore.

His other option was to set himself up with a mistress, but how was he to find one? Was he to pursue an actress and join the queue backstage? Even then, how exactly how was he to persuade one of those ladies to accept his protection? He hadn't money enough to set such a lady up in the kind of circumstances that were typical of such liaisons. What he needed was a poor widow.

His Patriotic Fund work, he suddenly realized, would soon make him acquainted with any number of poor widows.

Disgust filled David. Just the thought of using his position in such a way was abhorrent. He rubbed the back of his neck. Every possibility was intolerable. Worst of all, while a bedding might satisfy his body, he wasn't sure that any other woman would obliterate his desire for the beautiful Lady Haliday's lips.

CHAPTER THREE

As soon as Charlotte returned from the veranda she saw Jane Todd, now Lady Etherton, a few yards away with her husband. Charlotte could have dropped to her knees and given thanks.

Tonight Jane wore a fashionable pale green gown. Violets swirled through the fabric of the skirt, and the bodice and sleeves displayed intricate purple embroidery. Since her marriage, Jane's elegance, regal bearing, and confidence had won society's admiration, but in spite of her social success Charlotte knew that Jane was inside the same serious young girl who'd been the only person at Mrs. Brewster's School for Gentlewomen to befriend a frightened, untitled, and lost, if supremely wealthy, girl. Most of Charlotte's other schoolmates hadn't liked her father purchasing her entrée to society.

"Jane." She reached out for her friend's hand and pulled her aside. Etherton followed along behind.

Jane started to speak but abruptly stopped and lifted her eyebrows. "What's wrong?"

Turmoil whirled like a spinning top inside Charlotte's chest. Her emotions quivered, ready to splinter apart. The kiss in the alcove was in large part responsible for her agitation, but she couldn't imagine talking about it here. In fact, she might never want to share that event, not even with Jane. She needed to get home where she could think about what had happened.

"Lady Garret and I…exchanged words. The entire night has been harder than I expected, and I'm exhausted," she said. "I'm going home."

From behind her spectacles, Jane's concerned golden-brown eyes studied her. "Are you all right, Charlotte? Where's your father?" Jane shot her husband a look. He turned, put his back to them, and surveyed the dancers. His broad shoulders effectively shielded them from prying eyes.

"Father's in the card room."

"Phillip will get him."

Charlotte shook her head. "He left me alone the entire night, Jane. The first time I've been out in society since Haliday was murdered, and he left me alone amidst the whispers and stares."

"Oh, your father!" Jane's brows bunched in a ferocious frown, transforming her delicate features. She gave her glossy, brown-haired head a shake. "I'll never understand how such a hard-hearted man as Matthew Shelby sired such a wonderful daughter."

Yes, he should have stayed by her side tonight and lent his support, Charlotte agreed, but as usual her father had left her to make her own way. He browbeat his way through life, manipulating people in order to achieve his ends, and whether or not they found the manipulation unpleasant or contrary to their own desires was none of his concern, not even when the person in question was his daughter. Charlotte had never been anything more to him than another asset for obtaining what he wanted, so right now she'd do anything to avoid her father's usual inquisition. She'd take his coach home and then send it back to await him.

Charlotte smiled and gave Jane's hand a squeeze. Her friend's concern and support had chased away some of her tension, as it always did. "I'd just as soon leave without him. He'd only want a report of every conversation and dance partner."

"Why don't Phillip and I see you home?" Jane raised her voice a bit, and her handsome, black-haired husband turned at the sound of his name and joined them.

Charlotte shook her head. "Thank you, but it's not necessary."

"Jane wanted to be home early," Etherton said. "This is a good time to leave, and it will give the two of you an opportunity to talk."

Of course Jane wanted to leave early. The past several days she'd devoted herself to comforting their youngest daughter. She'd sent a note explaining that two-year-old Nora was fussy with an earache, crying and clinging, and even though the girl had improved her mother would want to be home with her.

Jane touched Charlotte's arm. "You've been in London three days, and this is the first opportunity we've had to see each other."

After being rocked to her toes by Lady Garret and that kiss, being with Jane was like wrapping up in a warm velvet cloak. Charlotte steadied. The little quivers vibrating deep inside her stilled.

"All right," she agreed.

"Good," Etherton said. "I'll have my carriage brought 'round, find Shelby, and tell him you're leaving."

Charlotte gave the earl a grateful smile. Since his marriage to Jane, Etherton had become her friend. When the storm of gossip and notoriety surrounding her became a tempest, his support and friendship had been as steady as his wife's.

Charlotte and Jane found Lady Elliott and said their goodbyes. Once they reached the entry, Jane led Charlotte to a corner distant from the footmen stationed at the door, and away from the press of people more of Charlotte's tension eased. It wasn't until she no longer needed to guard herself that she realized what a heavy burden her emotional shield was. After tonight, she was uncertain she'd done the right thing in returning to London. Except, Jane was here.

"I'm glad Nora's feeling better," she remarked.

Jane spread her hand over her heart. "Much better, thank goodness. My poor girl was miserable." Her hand dropped, and her upper body leaned toward Charlotte. "Now tell me what happened."

"Lady Garret chased me down, accused me of sneering at my husband's memory, and threatened to publish another novelette about me."

Jane huffed. Her narrowed eyes glittered. "The little baggage. She still wants to torment you? It's been eighteen months since Haliday died. How can her intense jealousy have persisted?"

"She loved him." Charlotte shrugged. "I never understood it. *She* held Haliday's heart, not I. She had no reason to be jealous." Charlotte had been the one with the right to feel envious, but the infidelity never caused that. It just broke her heart.

"Except you held the position she wanted—that of Haliday's wife." Jane's voice was low and fierce, like a gamekeeper confronted with a rabid animal. "She considered you her enemy. Nothing else explains the horrible things she did."

All too clearly, Charlotte remembered the day Jane brought her Lady Garret's novel. Hand trembling, Jane had extended the book. Charlotte knew from her friend's pale face and tear-bright eyes that, however unlikely, the publication held misery.

"You must read it," Jane had said. "Lady Garret is gifting copies to her acquaintances. She wrote it herself, had it printed and bound." Her face twisted. "Please forgive me, Charlotte. I can't bear for you to know, but I can't bear for you to not know. Many are using discretion in their conversation, but the book is being discussed at every gathering. It's being taken for thinly veiled truth about you, Haliday, and Lady Garret. The wife in the novel—*you*—is heinous, Charlotte."

The physical descriptions of the three characters in the book matched Lady Garret, Haliday, and Charlotte herself. Suddenly Haliday's late nights, previously explained as evenings he'd spent deep in card play, seemed suspect. Charlotte had actually seen her husband and Lady Garret at dinner parties and soirees, heads close together.

"She ruined your reputation and made you an object of ridicule," Jane said, drawing Charlotte's attention back to the present.

"She did," Charlotte agreed, "because most people believed her novel to be true."

She gripped the hand Jane extended. "They wanted to believe it because I'm not one of them. I'm just the daughter of Matthew Shelby, a common tradesman who became one of the wealthiest men in England." She gave Jane's hand a squeeze and let it drop. "Why did I forget that the blame for what occurred didn't rest solely on Lady Garret and Haliday? Why did I think I could come back and I wouldn't be watched and pointed at?" All evening, she'd been the target of suspicious eyes and subtle and not-so-subtle expressions that ranged from cautious to annoyed.

"Because it's been eighteen months since that footpad shot and killed Haliday," Jane said, "two years since that witch created a scandal and placed you at the center. If they pointed, it's because you've just returned. It's your first appearance in society. The scrutiny will die down. I don't know why Lady Garret came after you tonight, but rumor has it she has a new lover." Jane planted her hands on her hips. "You're Haliday's widow and a viscountess, and you've every right to engage in society entertainments."

Her friend appeared so outraged and righteous delivering her defense, Charlotte would have hugged Jane if they'd been more private. She wanted to think Jane was right, too, that the stir she had caused was sparked due to surprise at her appearance and not disdain. She had received several invitations, after all.

"I stood up to her," she announced, and if she'd said it to anyone but Jane she would have been embarrassed by the pride in her voice.

A huge smile lit her friend's face. "Oh, I'm so glad. Please tell me you outdid her."

"Oh, yes. I got the better of her." Though Charlotte hadn't flustered Vivian Garret as much as she herself had been taken aback by the stranger's kiss.

Etherton entered the room, and he, Jane and Charlotte moved as a trio to the doors. Should she ask him if he knew the identity of the gentleman in the alcove? Charlotte wondered, and curiosity consumed her. Who was he? Would she end up looking for him everywhere she went?

No. It was better to put the stranger from her mind. He was one more person who found her scandalous. Otherwise he'd have come after her.

It was raining. Footmen waited outside with open umbrellas, ready to escort them to their carriage. Etherton snatched an umbrella from one of them and moved close to his wife. Hand to her waist, he guided her to the coach. Charlotte followed, a second footman keeping her dry but getting wet himself.

They didn't tarry getting inside. Etherton boarded last and took the rear-facing seat. He peered outside as the carriage began to move.

"I'm glad we left early. I'd rather my men and horses be warm and dry rather than standing in the rain."

"You'd have made an excellent army officer," Jane replied, a light, teasing note in her voice.

Each streetlight they passed lit the coach's interior for a few seconds—enough to make out Jane, and Etherton, who smiled at her. "Good officers don't worry about rain, dearest, except to the extent it affects engaging the enemy." He leaned toward his wife, appearing to study her. "You've collected a few raindrops."

He slid Jane's spectacles from her face and drew a snowy handkerchief from his coat. After polishing the lenses, he slowly slid the eyeglasses back onto her. His thumb stroked down his wife's cheek and across her lower lip before he leaned back.

Though there wasn't enough light to see Jane's color, and though eight years had passed and four children born since Jane became Lady Etherton, Charlotte knew her friend would be flushed. During Charlotte's absence they'd exchanged letters, and Jane's love for Etherton had diminished not one iota. It was good to see them together, to see small expressions of the deep, abiding love her best friend and husband shared. Few were so lucky. Charlotte's ill-fated choice had proved her luckless, but she took solace knowing that Jane was one of the fortunate few.

CHAPTER FOUR

Vivian Garret leaned against the ballroom wall and applied her fan, hoping to lessen the uncomfortable warmth her rage had stoked. The confrontation with Lady Haliday hadn't gone at all as planned. She'd wanted to upset the woman. Instead, *she* was the one struggling to catch her breath and still the awful churning in her stomach. Her last association with Lady Haliday had ended with her fearing for her sanity, too. What if those dark thoughts took hold again?

An icy chill slithered up Vivian's spine, twined down her arms, and turned her fingertips tingly. Devil take it all. She wanted to go home.

As if conjured from the very air, her escort, Stephen Endsley, Earl of Radcliffe, appeared before Vivian and swept her into the swirl of dancing couples.

"I believe you promised this waltz to me."

He knew very well she hadn't, but she didn't have the verve required for their usual repartee. At least she needn't think of her footwork with Radcliffe partnering her. He was as masterful on the dance floor as he was in the bedroom, and the distraction he afforded allowed her to prevail over her turbulent emotions. What might her life have been like if she'd married a man like this instead of Garret, who, though seventy-eight years of age, had still managed to initiate her to the duties of a wife?

She nearly stumbled as Radcliffe negotiated a complicated turn. He pulled her close until she regained her footing then stiffened his arms to place an acceptable distance between them. The way he towered head and shoulders above her, he could probably pick her up off her feet if he had a mind to. It amused her now, to think she'd once wondered if the difference in their sizes would affect their lovemaking.

"Should I be insulted? Your thoughts seem to be elsewhere."

He didn't like her preoccupied. Perhaps a partial truth would appease him. "I just encountered Lady Haliday." She stared at his blinding-white shirt. The fingers at her waist tightened.

"Vivian."

Startled by his familiar address, she looked up, registered his frown, then realized he'd spoken too softly to be heard by others. No one but Radcliffe had ever looked at her with that possessive gleam. Part of her reveled in it, while another part wanted to extinguish that dazzling glimmer.

"Did she upset you? Would you rather leave?"

His voice had deepened. Did he know that particular timbre made her weaken and forget everything but him? That he rarely used it outside the bedroom? His eyes narrowed and made warmth swirl low inside her. She wanted to press against him. Wanted to taste the skin that rose above his collar.

"You could make me forget my distress, my lord." Much better to concentrate on Radcliffe and put away all thoughts of Charlotte Haliday and their secret connection.

The hint of a smile curved up the corner of the earl's mouth. He gripped her elbow and pulled her aside to the edge of the dance floor, placed her hand atop his forearm and headed for the door.

It was so like him to not even wait for the end of the waltz. She'd wanted Radcliffe because of his wealth, and he hadn't disappointed; tonight she wore his most recent gift, the yellow diamonds. She'd had to take his compelling, domineering character as well, which was something she still grappled with.

As much as he excited her, she hated the power he exerted so effortlessly. Her overbearing father had doled out a surfeit of iron-fisted control, and when she'd left his heartless household she vowed she'd never again be under a man's thumb. Neither Garret, her husband, nor Haliday, her lover, had been able to employ masculine influence over her, but more and more Radcliffe enthralled her. His influence was altogether different than her father's, but it was no less commanding.

They reached the vestibule, and with a few concise words Radcliffe ordered his carriage and their cloaks. He strode forward, thrust his head into the cold air, and seemed to inspect the rainy night.

Vivian shivered. She couldn't be falling in love with him. Even considering such an impossibility made her sizzle with alarm. The feeling that accosted her when she was with him…it couldn't be anything more than a manifestation of desire. She wouldn't let it be anything more than that, because loving Radcliffe would only result in a broken heart. It would take a unique lady to hold his regard. Vivian might maintain her own household, be a daughter and a widow of barons, but she was far from the special woman Radcliffe would consider as a potential spouse. And even if Vivian were that woman, his pride would never accept someone whose name had once been bandied about in society.

Radcliffe's coach pulled up. The warm softness of her velvet cloak enveloped Vivian as the earl settled it upon her shoulders. Briefly, his hand swept down her spine and pressed against the small of her back.

She glanced up and found his questioning brown eyes fixed upon her. He bent his head and she caught the scent of starch, fine tobacco and bay rum.

"Would my company be more welcome another evening?"

His breath against her ear sent heat shuddering through her. She moistened her lips. "No. You're welcome tonight."

He lifted his chin and wordlessly directed her out the door. Footmen stepped up, umbrellas held aloft. Tonight, Radcliffe would drive away Vivian's dark thoughts. She'd think about how to solve the problem of Charlotte Haliday tomorrow.

#

Charlotte arrived at Lindley Square and went up to her bedroom. Employing the usual cheerful efficiency, her maid Rebecca had her in a night-rail within minutes, wrapped with a shawl, covered with a warm throw, and ensconced on the chaise lounge.

"Here's your chocolate, then, my lady," Rebecca said, extending the tray upon which sat a steaming mug.

Charlotte took the cup of sweet chocolate and wrapped her hands around its sides. "You'd best get to your own bed now, Rebecca."

"Yes, my lady." The maid moved to the door and bobbed a curtsy. The blonde curls protruding from under the ruffled edge of her cap bounced with the dip of her head. "Goodnight, my lady."

Once the door closed, Charlotte set her chocolate aside, stood, and pulled her shawl tight. As her feet left the protection of the woolen rug and made contact with the cold boards of the oak floor, she rose onto her toes. She walked on them the rest of the way to the ornately carved mahogany chest, knelt, and slowly raised the lid. She'd wrapped the object of her search in an old petticoat and hidden it at the very bottom.

Pushing her hand under folded garments, Charlotte burrowed through silk and lace until her seeking fingers touched the hard edge of a book cover. She jerked back as if she'd been pinched but then grasped the thing, pulled it to the surface and peeled the petticoat away. That hated little book of Lady Garret's.

Retreating to her chaise, every sense homed in on her repulsive burden and no longer caring about the chill floor, Charlotte sat, curled her legs up beside her and tugged her gown over her feet. She dragged a fingertip over the rich green fabric cover, opened the book, and stared at the title page:

A Marriage Most Awkward: a novel by Lady G_____.

How many hours she'd spent, thinking of all the lies, laid low by the pain. Then she'd finally accepted she'd given her heart to a man who never existed.

Haliday's infidelity was just the first in a series of life-altering discoveries. He didn't love her. Never had. He'd wanted her for his wife, but it had been her father's deep pockets and her status as heiress he'd loved. The one thing he'd wanted from her was a son, and once Charlotte knew about Lady Garret he preferred not to pretend at an affection he didn't feel. He also didn't care that she subsequently found sex with him abhorrent.

She hadn't needed to ask him how he felt, actually. When she confronted him with the novel, he'd bluntly explained the state of their marriage. When she asked why his mistress had gone to such effort to expose their private lives, he'd shrugged. When she persisted and asked why the woman told vicious lies in order to manipulate society and destroy the good opinions people held of her, he'd smiled a little. Said Lady Garret was a complicated and fascinating woman. When he'd finished explaining it all, Charlotte understood betrayal. In the place her heart belonged, a cold, hard, achy lump now resided.

After eighteen months in the country, living in the dower house at Hazelton Park, Charlotte had thought society would have forgotten the scandal—or at least stopped caring. She'd half expected Lady Garret to ignore her completely. But, no. Even after all her hard-learned lessons, Charlotte had let naïveté rule her.

Well, no more.

She rewrapped the book, pulling the gauzy white fabric tight around it. She'd never understood why she kept the revolting thing, but now she knew. It made her strong. The chest, this book sitting at its bottom, existed to remind her. *Do not grow complacent. Do not leave yourself open to hurt. Do not forget.*

Happiness is fragile.

CHAPTER FIVE

For two days Charlotte debated whether to tell Jane about the kiss.

Her plan to forget the stranger wasn't working. Both days she'd been spurred from sleep by images of glinting blue eyes and firm lips. That impulsive kiss had released something locked up since the early days of her marriage. Charlotte didn't like it. She didn't want this warm, curling anticipation that unfurled each time she thought—or dreamed—of her stranger.

She finally decided her feelings were too confused to share, even with Jane. A visit with her friend would be a welcome distraction, though. And she needed her intelligent friend's help.

Following their usual practice, Charlotte sent a note and then went to Jane's at eleven o'clock, ensuring they wouldn't be interrupted by other callers. Just being in Jane's private sitting room made Charlotte feel better. The room connected with Jane and Phillip's boudoirs and contained two cushioned chairs and ottomans, a settee, several small tables, and a small desk.

In a pale blue gown trimmed with cream lace, her light brown hair arranged in a high, braided knot, Jane looked stylish and confident. She and Charlotte took the facing cushioned chairs and grinned at each other.

"It's so good to have you back," Jane said. "I missed you horribly. Have you reconnected with anyone, now everyone knows you're in London?"

"I've had several invitations to dinner parties and soirees, but very few callers."

Jane frowned. "I'm sure it's the pompous, critical ones who are avoiding you. Just like those pretentious girls at school."

Charlotte shrugged. "It is the same as at the ball. I sense most people are curious to see how I'm faring. My title makes me an acceptable guest at an entertainment, but I suspect most ladies aren't eager to resume a more personal association. I can think of no other reason to not have callers."

A flash of pain twisted Jane's face before she firmed her lips and squared her shoulders. "That can't be it. They're all just embarrassed at the way they treated you. Once they see how sincere and delightful you are, you'll be deluged with callers."

Charlotte didn't bother to remind Jane how that had never happened during the four years of her marriage. She had Jane's friendship, though. And remaining a parvenu upstart didn't bother Charlotte so much except for the unfairness of those judgmental opinions about her. She'd done nothing wrong. She'd planned to have children, to be a fine hostess, to support charities. She wanted a fulfilling life. Last night she'd done needlework and listened to the tick of the mantel clock.

During the past eighteen-month mourning period she'd gathered her tattered self and sorted through her hurt and confusion. At Hazelton Park she'd read, taken long walks, and worked in the garden. Eventually the stubborn streak that had kept her head high during the worst of Lady Garret's campaign nudged her to return to London. Her pride had brought her back; a compulsion to stare them all down and the desire to lead an active, rewarding life overrode her remaining humiliation and pain. The one thing Haliday had always admired about her was her pride. He'd said she held herself like a princess royal.

"Jane…?"

Her friend's head tilted, and the space between her brows creased. "Yes?"

"I don't care if they don't want to associate with me. The only thing I miss having is respect. I deserve respect."

Jane's lips pressed together, and she nodded. She looked sympathetic and unsurprised.

"I've nothing here to keep me occupied," Charlotte continued. "I was content at Hazelton Park, but you know I love the city. I have as much right to music and art and diversions as any other lady."

"You deserve to enjoy yourself," Jane agreed.

Charlotte fingered the teardrop of jet that dangled from her earlobe and glanced at the row of jet buttons adorning her gray pleated bodice. "I'm in half-mourning now. I can be out in public and attend social functions, although something smaller than a ball for my social entrée would probably have been wiser. But I hate pretending, and I'm sure everyone knows I'm merely following proper etiquette."

"You've secluded yourself long enough."

Charlotte leaned forward. "Jane, I'm so afraid of becoming useless and bitter, of having an empty life."

Her friend bounded up from her chair. "That's not going to happen." Frowning, she stalked to the window then whirled and stalked back. "You just need something to keep you occupied."

"I'm sure you're right. Only, what? You know I have no talent for painting or studying." Both of which pastimes Jane enjoyed.

Jane hugged Charlotte and dropped back onto her chair. "This is why you're here today, isn't it? We need to find you something to do." She squeezed her eyes shut and shook her head. "No, no, not 'something to do.' Something to occupy your *mind*." Her face cleared. "Do you know Sidney Herbert?"

"I've met him."

"Well, Phillip knows him well, and Herbert is Chairman of the Royal Commission on the State of Health of the Army."

Jane's husband was generally thought to be the most brilliant Member in the House of Lords. Etherton was actually a fully qualified civil engineer who'd worked as railway engineer and railway bridge designer before he inherited the earldom. Jane always said his hobby was mathematics, although Charlotte had never understood how mathematics could be a hobby. Charlotte also knew Sidney Herbert had been Secretary of State at War during the war in the Crimea and, until recently, Secretary of State for the Colonies. Both he and his wife were well known philanthropists.

"I'll have Phillip talk to Herbert," Jane declared, gave an emphatic nod and continued. "I'm sure Herbert will be happy to make use of you, and you'll know the work you're doing is important." She paused, and one brow rose above the rim of her spectacles. "That is, if you want to do it."

"Yes," Charlotte said. It was exactly what she needed. She'd have no time to dwell on Vivian Garret. Better yet, she'd be far too busy to worry about a stranger who'd kissed her as though she belonged to him.

CHAPTER SIX

Vivian exited the dressmaker's shop and waited for her maid who had gone off to secure a Hansom.

"Lady Garret."

The deep vocalization emanated from a nearby coach, its open door held by a finely dressed footman, and a mysterious pull drew her toward the unidentified voice. One look at the shadowed face of the man inside transfixed her: Lady Haliday's father, Matthew Shelby. Rich. Powerful. A beast. Vivian put so much hate into her glare she was amazed he didn't melt.

"Send your maid home," Shelby said, "and get in."

Vivian stared. Four years ago, the last time she'd spoken to him, she'd cradled hope in her breast and still believed in the future. Only, instead of the most important day of her life, it became the most disastrous—not including the day of her dear Georgie's death. Nothing could ever be worse than that.

Looking at Shelby's imperious face, want erupted from an unknown fountainhead deep inside. It shocked her. She'd lain awake in bed, aching with this same want: the desire to be held, reassured, loved.

You're not a child, and he doesn't hold the slightest affection for you. Nothing he might say or give you matters now, she reminded herself. It was too late for apologies, belated acknowledgment, or even fortune to matter. Yet, drawn like a child offered a sweet, Vivian gave Mary a few coins and told her to go home, stepped into Shelby's coach and eased down on the cushioned seat across from him.

The door snapped closed. The coach rocked as the footman climbed aboard, and with a jangle of a harness it moved away. Vivian clasped her hands and tried to hold herself together. She fought down the unexpected wellspring of yearning and focused on a more comfortable, familiar sentiment.

Hate.

It had always existed for him in varying degrees. Shelby had generated many emotions in her, but finally Vivian had grown up and put aside such childish notions as the longing that unexpectedly assailed her today. She'd even attained a sort of peace until Georgie became ill. Desperate to help her two-year-old son, she'd sought Shelby's help. Seen him face-to-face. And that day he'd killed every other emotion she'd ever felt for him.

Surging back, that hate filled her with relief. These days it was her one constant, the single thing that kept her going. She wanted to say something that would hurt Shelby, destroy him, but all she could think of was her son's gray, pinched face as he gasped his last breaths.

Shelby's eyes narrowed. "What are you about?" he growled. "Why are you intent on causing my daughter distress? She's no threat to you."

Anger blazed up and burned away her vision of Georgie dying of consumption. "It's true I spoke to Charlotte at Lady Elliott's ball. But why shouldn't I?"

Shelby's lips drew back in a wolfish snarl, and satisfaction snaked through her. "I told you before," he said, his face dark. "I won't be blackmailed."

Vivian managed to shrug. "I have no interest in your money."

"Of course you want money. It's the only thing you've ever wanted."

Maybe once.

"Four years ago I did want money. Not for myself, but for my son George. You remember him."

She'd pitched her voice to taunt, a needle-sharp sliver to slide under Shelby's remaining composure, and a fleeting expression passed over his face. It disappeared too quickly to be deciphered, but the rigid set of Shelby's shoulders loosened. "I heard about your son. I'm sorry. But you should have gone to your father, Baron Clery, or your husband's heir for money."

The bastard. He had ice for a heart. If only she had the strength to choke him. She'd show Shelby how Georgie must have felt as he stared up at her, teary-eyed with fear, and whispered, "I can't breathe, Mama."

It took all the strength she could muster to force the bitter words from her constricted throat. "They wouldn't give me any money. My father hates me. I'm proof he was cuckolded. And Garret already had eighteen children when he married me. His eldest son had nothing to spare beyond the small annual portion I was given." That always-simmering anger and hurt roiled in Vivian's stomach. "While you own half of London."

"Brehmer is making a name for himself now," Shelby pointed out, "and his sanatorium is becoming well-known for its success in treating consumption, but four years ago, expecting some expensive hospital high in the Prussian mountains to perform a miracle seemed the worst sort of hopeless folly. My physician assured me there was no cure." He dragged his hand across his mouth. "I thought it mad for you to take a sick child there."

The anger Vivian struggled to contain erupted. "His. Name. Is. George."

Shelby's eyebrows shot up, and he reared back, alarm on his face. Some part of Vivian knew she was red-faced, spittle flying on puffs of hot breath. And, oh, she didn't want him to see her like this, weak and overcome by emotion. Tears blurred her vision, and she blinked furiously. "You thought you knew best? That's why my Georgie died?" Also, perhaps, because Shelby didn't want any kind of connection between them.

"Well…"

The man's eyes squeezed shut, and his fingers went to the throbbing pulse in his temple. Vivian recognized that look. Now, when it was too late, he doubted? Why were men so arrogant? Shelby's money and power had only made him more so. Oh, she wanted to destroy his confidence. She'd love to serve him even a small portion of the hurt he'd dealt her. When she thought of their connection… She shivered.

His hand fell and his shoulders squared. "It was never about the money."

"No? Then what was it? Afraid of the gossip? You let my son die in order to protect your name? Pity, then, that in spite of your efforts your dear daughter Charlotte has become the object of every wagging tongue."

CHAPTER SEVEN

Charlotte's hired carriage turned off Birdcage Walk onto Queen Anne's Gate and stopped. The Executive Committee office of the Royal Patriotic Fund was just across the road from St. James's Park.

Charlotte took a deep breath, striving to quell the fluttering in her stomach. She still couldn't believe she was to work for the Royal Patriotic Fund. Queen Victoria's newly created, government and private donation–supported charity assisted widows and orphans of Royal Army and Navy of all ranks who'd lost their lives in the Crimean War. Sidney Herbert had accepted her offer and placed her on the Patriotic Fund's Executive Committee, which was responsible for the day-to-day affairs of the Fund. He'd looked at her kindly, his tired brown eyes direct, and calmly offered her the position. He'd said a woman on the committee would help in dealing with the widows and charitable ladies' groups. Of course, as much as Charlotte wanted to apply herself to meaningful work, she didn't know if she'd be of any use to grieving women and children. The fear that she wouldn't know what to do or say had kept her wakeful most of the night.

She stepped from the carriage and stood for a moment breathing in the cool air of the overcast day, looking at the gray stone of the building. For the moment excitement overcame her trepidation and nudged the rabble of butterflies in her stomach. They swarmed off, leaving her breathless, a wide smile pulling at her lips. She couldn't think when she'd last felt like this. Long before Haliday's murder, certainly.

Her feet took the steps as though they wore dancing slippers. Beside the door, a brass plaque read ROYAL PATRIOTIC FUND. Inside, situated to the left of an empty reception area, she found a large room filled with clerical workers. Several of them wore military uniforms. Another plaque directed her down the right-hand hallway to the administrative offices. There she found a studious-looking young man behind a large desk.

He stood immediately, giving his drooping glasses a firm push onto the bridge of his nose. He smiled, his dark eyes sparkling even through the barrier of his lenses. "Ma'am?"

What a relief to find someone who didn't know her. Sometimes she thought herself infamous throughout London.

"I'm Lady Haliday. I believe Mr. Scott is expecting me?"

"George Chetney, my lady," the young man said, giving a quick bow.

She admired his bearing and proficiency. Only the merest blink indicated his familiarity with her name. Then his brows lifted.

"I don't have an appointment scheduled." A flush pinked his cheeks. "Perhaps it's a personal matter and he didn't inform me of the appointment?"

The serious young man's discomfort increased Charlotte's nervousness. "Sidney Herbert was to have sent a letter of introduction."

Chetney's face cleared. "Ah, yes." He turned his attention to the desk and riffled through a stack of papers. "Yes." He held up an envelope. "This arrived today."

Obviously, it hadn't yet been opened. Why ever had she been in such a hurry? She'd seen Herbert only yesterday. Why hadn't she waited to permit communication between Herbert and Scott, the chairman?

Because I'm so anxious to occupy myself with normal things. Or perhaps because I feared something would happen to ruin this opportunity.

"This way, please. It happens Mr. Scott is available...."

Herbert's envelope in hand, Chetney stepped toward what appeared to be an adjoining office. Charlotte never heard what else Mr. Chetney said, because the man behind the desk looked up and met her eyes as she stepped into the room.

Oh, God. It was her stranger.

In her entire life, Charlotte had never once fainted. Not when she learned of Haliday's affair, not when he was shot and killed. But suddenly she felt hot and weak and dizzy. Alarm flashed in her stranger's blue eyes, and then everything fell away.

#

David's heart lurched as the viscountess collapsed.

"Chetney!" he barked.

His secretary jumped, dropped the envelope he held, caught Viscountess Haliday and laid her down on the small, upholstered divan. David watched, never more aware that he was unable to stand and capture the lady himself. Even after nearly two years, he was not fully accustomed to others acting in his stead.

"Get some water," he instructed as he wheeled himself toward the divan.

The viscountess seemed unnaturally pale. David removed her hatpin and hat and brushed wavy dark hair from her forehead. Her cold, clammy skin worried him. He'd seen bleeding men shiver, seen their teeth chatter, and he associated such pale, cold skin with serious infirmity. He glanced at her narrow waist, wondering if he should loosen her corset. To do so would necessitate removing her bodice, and he certainly didn't want to do that.

Her eyelids fluttered, and relief eased his tension as they lifted to reveal those incredible violet eyes. In the days since the ball he'd convinced himself he must have imagined their color, since he'd never seen anything like them. But they were just as beautiful as he recalled. They were also a bit hazy and unfocused.

He tugged off one of her gloves and happily found her skin dry, though it remained cool. He held her hand and rubbed his thumb across her palm. "Lady Haliday?"

As if following the sound of his voice, her head turned. He remembered the hunger of her mouth on his at the ball. This woman had populated more than one of his dreams since.

"My lady? Are you all right?"

Her chest rose; her fingers wrapped around his thumb. "I feel so silly," she murmured. "I didn't eat today. My stomach was just too jumpy."

She blinked, and gradually her expression sharpened. Her gaze rose to his face, fell to his wheelchair, and returned to his features. She was too shocked to hide her feelings, he realized, and he clamped his teeth together. Of course, she had a right to be surprised. He hadn't been in his chair at the ball.

Her fingers grew lax and released his thumb. She sat up, swinging her feet down in the same motion. "You've been injured?" she asked.

He slowly shook his head. "Two years ago. I'm unable to stand or walk."

He caught a glimpse of stark pain in the viscountess's eyes before her gaze dropped. Her fingers, trembling, pressed against her mouth, and silently David swore. He'd yet to sicken a female with his useless legs, but Lady Haliday appeared to be the exception.

"Chetney," he yelled. Where in hell was the man?

Chetney hurried in, a glass in one hand and what looked to be brandy in the other. The two men exchanged looks.

"I don't know where you got it, but it's not a bad idea. See if you can locate a biscuit or two also, would you?" David took the glass from Chetney and offered it to the viscountess. The brandy should get her blood flowing and warm her up. "Drink a little of this. It should make you feel a bit stronger."

She took the glass, obligingly swallowed a sip, and blinked. "I'm sorry to cause such bother."

Her eyes lifted, and the compassion he saw in their purple depths almost knocked him over. Anger gripped him, and David rolled his chair back, putting a couple of feet between them. The first woman who'd breached his defenses, and she pitied him? How *dare* she?

She took another drink—a larger one this time—and coughed.

"What are you doing here?"

"If you're Mr. Scott, then I'm to work for you." She took another drink of the brandy. "You've a letter from Sidney Herbert."

David nearly cursed but managed to hold it in. Hadn't he already borne enough disappointment and hardship? His legs had been crushed. He'd be damned if he was going to work with this woman who passed out at the sight of him. He felt a hard laugh fighting to escape. At the ball she'd made him forget he was different from other men. That made the hurt so much greater now.

"That's impossible," he remarked. "It's obvious we don't suit."

In the subsequent silence, Chetney returned with a biscuit that he turned over to the viscountess.

"Do you know anything about a letter from Herbert?" David asked.

His secretary bent, retrieved the envelope he'd dropped and offered it. David opened it and unfolded the letter inside. He read it while the viscountess nibbled on her biscuit. The letter confirmed that Herbert had indeed placed Lady Haliday on the Executive Committee.

Frustration rose in a wave. Herbert had assured David that, as chairman, he would have control over the workings of the committee. Yet Herbert had given the viscountess a position without checking with him. This wasn't a society lady's charade, either. Herbert expected the viscountess to be a working member of the group!

With a wave David directed Chetney to leave the room and close the door. Having a committee member dropped in his lap without having any say should have been his primary concern, but the words that spilled from his mouth were about another issue entirely. "You know, I don't appreciate being used as a pawn in whatever game you're playing with Lady Garret."

The viscountess flushed but held his gaze, which David appreciated with a grudging respect for her mettle.

"This is so awkward," the woman muttered. Her eyes implored him to understand as she straightened.

"I apologize for my actions. I was desperate to get rid of her, and I acted impulsively. I don't expect you to believe me, but I've never done such a thing before." Lady Haliday stopped talking, picked up the glove he'd removed from her hand, and began wringing it. The way she was going at it, the poor glove would probably be ruined. "In future, I'll behave with nothing but the most proper conduct."

David couldn't keep the surprise and disapproval from his voice. "Are you saying you still intend to work for me?"

She seemed startled. "Why, yes," she said, her face turning even pinker.

David sighed. Lady Haliday seemed to bring his every buried doubt surging to the surface. In addition, she distracted him in a most unwelcome way.

Alarm flashed across her face. "Please, can't you forget what happened? I want to do this." She paused, and he imagined he saw desperation in her eyes. "I *need* to do this."

Damn it, but she made him feel the sorriest blighter, and even though he didn't want her there, he sensed that turning her away would be an act of cruelty. He felt compelled to agree to her request, even knowing her presence would make him uncomfortable.

"All right," he said, and immediately her stiff posture eased. "For today I think you'd best go home and rest—and *eat*." Not only had she fainted, but she'd drunk a fair amount of brandy. "Is your carriage out front?"

"I took a Hansom. I don't maintain a stable."

"I'll take you then." The words were out of his mouth before he could pull them back. He knew he should just let Chetney accompany her, but he wanted to make sure she got home safely. He also needed to give her an eyeful. The surest way to destroy all his ridiculous desire for her was to make sure she saw him as the cripple he was.

Chetney collected Boone from the back room, and after a small wait David was being wheeled to his waiting coach down the ramp that covered one side of the front steps and gave him access in and out of the building. Lady Haliday trailed behind.

Boone positioned David's chair beside the coach door, and David busied himself with sliding the transfer sling under his buttocks. The apparatus was of his own design, and it enabled him, by pulling on a rope, to hoist himself out of the wheeled chair and into the vehicle. He thought he'd grown accustomed to being stared at, but Lady Haliday's gaze made him as self-conscious as that first ogling pair of eyes had. He became warm, and sweat broke across his forehead.

Keyes, his coachman, handed him the hook and rope, and David slid the sling's two large end rings over the hook. The rope fed through a pulley attached to the inside top of his carriage. Hand over hand, David raised himself. Boone had only to guide his legs as David swung himself inside the vehicle. He realized he'd been less than a gentleman when he decided to let Lady Haliday wait outside the coach until after he transferred himself, but he also knew it afforded her the best view of his broken, useless legs. Once inside, David would loop the rope in a figure eight around a metal hitch and use his arms to boost himself onto the seat. He'd then release the sling's end rings and use his arms to pull in and position his legs.

The day the idea first burst upon him he'd been ecstatic, and the first time he'd maneuvered himself from chair to coach unassisted he'd felt a flash of pride the likes of which he hadn't known for over a year. The reverse transfer, coach to chair, was accomplished in the same way, only with David letting out the rope while Boone guided David's legs. The arrangement was reasonably efficient and gave him the mobility he needed to be independent. He'd been able to obtain meaningful work and an income after that, which ensured he'd not have need of his brother's coin.

Today, the pleasure of his design didn't register. Instead of making short work of the task, as he usually did, David ignored Boone's surprised regard and took his time. He planned to watch the viscountess's face. Whatever expression she either showed or tried to hide would likely butcher the burgeoning attraction he felt.

One quick glance had him struggling to swallow against the lump in his throat and gazing everywhere except at Lady Haliday. *Charlotte.* Herbert's letter had given David her full name. He'd become familiar with all kinds of looks—pity, horror, morbid fascination—but the viscountess's face bore none of those. Pain glinted in the depths of those purple eyes.

That one glance was all he could bear. Not because of the hurt he saw, but because of everything else: the surprise, admiration and curiosity. He steeled his own face, made it expressionless, while inside confusion and hope warred with anger and despair. Why in bloody hell must she look at him like that?

Huffing a bit, he swung himself into the coach and turned to getting himself settled. Charlotte Haliday made him feel things he'd thought locked up and buried deep, made him forget he was different from other men. And there, he knew, lay danger.

A minute later she joined him, dark skirts rustling as she sat across from him, the coach filled with her rose and jasmine scent. She appeared to have recovered from her swoon.

With a jangle of the harness and a slight lurch, they began to move. Her hand darted up to grip the handhold.

"Are you all right?" David asked, in spite of his reluctance to engage her in conversation.

#

Charlotte nodded, although she was pretty sure she was *not* all right. A dull ache throbbed in her head, and she couldn't seem to tear her eyes from David Scott.

Deep inside, she trembled. What kind of man was this? Her heart had nearly stopped as he pulled himself into the coach, the look on his face so full of pride and defiance it made her ache. The courage he must have, to face the world day after day. She knew what it took to do that. She'd been hiding for the past year, while David Scott had been carving out a life for himself.

He relied on other men to push his chair and lift his legs; the impressive physical strength he'd displayed didn't relieve him of that necessity. The patience the man must have... Charlotte couldn't imagine. She'd always been sorely lacking in that virtue, as evidenced by her appearance here less than twenty-four hours after her conversation with Herbert.

He'd accepted her apology for the kiss, but what must he think of her? In spite of everything, he'd been altogether considerate.

"You're very kind," she declared.

"I wanted to make sure you got home all right. I wouldn't have been easy not knowing."

She'd meant the way he overlooked her behavior and agreed to let her work for him, but she didn't correct his faulty assumption. She couldn't have borne going back to Sidney Herbert as a failure, begging for a different position, and to not go back, and to give up...? What would have become of her then? Scott had saved her from that.

"So I may start tomorrow?"

"Just be sure and eat first."

His tone was friendly enough, but he sounded weary, the words forced from his mouth. The blue of his eyes darkened, and she knew he didn't want her working for him. She thought of their kiss, the moment he'd pulled her closer and she'd lost awareness of everything but him. Could she really see him every day with that between them? She looked down at her hands. The glove she'd mangled was no longer fit to be worn.

A glance at Scott's face found all trace of hardness gone and a new, intense look in its place, as if he contemplated a puzzle. Street noise filled the silence, and neither of them disturbed the truce. Charlotte kept her gaze on the passing scenery, and gradually the tension in her shoulders eased. She didn't look at Scott again until they reached her townhouse.

"Good day, Lady Haliday. Please take care."

Such a serious man. Did he ever smile? How would he look with the corners of those well-shaped lips curved upward and his eyes warm as a summer sky?

The sudden jolt of desire had Charlotte nearly scrambling down from the coach. But the relief her escape afforded lasted only until she crossed her townhouse threshold. Her father, the very last person she wanted to see, waited in the drawing room.

CHAPTER EIGHT

The slightest inflection of her father's deep, smooth voice had always had the power to lift or twist her. Today, it seemed, he intended to chastise.

"Charlotte."

Tall, broad-shouldered and straight-backed, he stood at the window overlooking the street. The plate of sandwich remains resting on the serving cart nearby nearly stopped Charlotte short. He'd been there a while, and he didn't have the time or disposition to wait for her.

"Hello, Father. What a surprise. I'm sorry I wasn't here when you arrived." She covered her unease by removing her hat and handing it to her butler, followed by her gloves. "We'll have tea, Walters, and more sandwiches, please." Scott had been right about her needing to eat, and she certainly didn't want to faint again while her father watched.

She headed into the sitting room.

"Whose coach was that?"

"Mr. David Scott. Are you familiar with him?"

"Of course I am."

His answer was a surprise. "You are?"

Her father shot her a puzzled look. "I read everything *The Times* prints."

"What was in *The Times*?" Charlotte asked, feeling ridiculous.

"He's to receive the new Victoria Cross from the hand of the Queen."

"Oh?" Suddenly woozy, Charlotte sat down on her green brocade chair.

"How on earth could he escort you home and you not know that?"

She'd never understand how her father could become so suddenly impatient and perturbed. Even though she was now grown, a widow and a viscountess, even knowing how unfair he was and had always been, he still had the power to sweep away her confidence.

"I'm to work for the Patriotic Fund under him."

Her father's lips tightened. "So, the rumor is true. Charlotte, what are you thinking? Have you lost your mind?"

His dark blue eyes glinted with sharp accusation. She wished he'd sit down. With her sitting and him standing he seemed even more intimidating than usual.

The tea arrived. Thank God, Charlotte thought. At her inquiring glance, her father shook his head impatiently, so she poured tea and selected sandwiches for herself then waited to answer until she'd taken a sip. She'd become good at pretending unconcern, although doing it with Father was always the most difficult. Carefully she balanced her cup, keeping liquid from spilling over the rim.

"I'm breaking free of society's cage. I'm going to keep busy and do something worthwhile."

He snorted—a harsh, deprecatory sound he saved for ideas or people for whom he felt true disgust. Charlotte lifted her cup, blew gently across its contents and pressed the fine china rim to her lips.

"You're actually planning on working? Good God, girl. You're a *viscountess*." Her father jammed his fists into his jacket pockets and rocked forward. "Do you have any idea how hard I labored, how much money I spent, to achieve that end?"

Charlotte struggled to keep her back straight, but inside she cringed. She knew some of it, but she didn't know just to what lengths her father had gone in order to build his fortune. He'd amassed so much money he'd gained access to the highest levels of society. She suspected there were times he'd bought up debt in order to gain control of a particular titled debtor, but gentlemen wanted to borrow from him and invest with him nonetheless. Many of them depended on Matthew Shelby for their lucrative incomes—like her husband, which was why he'd married Charlotte.

Her father clasped his hands behind his back. He stood flush-faced, straight-browed and tight-mouthed—all signs of high temper. "Well, my girl, you're not going to sabotage everything I've worked for with your foolishness. I won't have it."

His domineering pronouncement set her own temper erupting with the force of Vesuvius. Anger burnt away all prudence. "You've already lost. I may be a viscountess, but I'm a childless widow. You'll never realize your dream: your grandson an aristocrat. On top of that, your daughter's considered scandalous. Father, nothing I do now matters. Don't you realize that? Why would you want to stop me from finding some happiness?"

"Happiness? Please, Charlotte, don't be a ninny. You're meant to be the wife of an illustrious man, and I intend to make sure that's what you become again."

He'd stunned her into silence.

"Society's memory is short. You were always smarter than the rest of those haughty misses you were educated with, and you are my daughter after all. You're as fine as any of them and your manner is more regal. By marriage you *are* one of them. You've only to wait to be accepted back into the fold. Working for this blasted charity won't achieve that end and won't make you happy."

He had the certainty of a man who'd gained his fortune through shrewd intelligence and fierce determination. She'd always known she was but one more chess piece on his board—the queen perhaps, but still something to be used to his advantage. On the surface, their relationship wasn't that different from those of her titled classmates and their parents. Those girls were also expected to make advantageous matches. Charlotte's father just lacked titled ancestors.

"You can't make them accept me, Father, and they never will. I'm not spending the rest of my life begging their favor." She'd had enough society-dictated emptiness, but a wrenching sadness squeezed her chest. No matter her feelings, her father would stand adamant. He always believed himself right.

"If you actually work with those widows and orphans, you'll make yourself a laughingstock."

"It couldn't be any worse than what I've already been through," she pointed out. And while she truly hoped to be of use to the needy women and children, she cast about for a way to appease him. "I promise to restrain conversing about my work. And I'll still be able to accept evening invitations."

His straight brows bunched together, and her father peered down his hawkish nose. "I hope you've managed your money wisely, because as long as you pursue this ridiculous notion I don't intend to support you."

Charlotte clamped her teeth together. She knew this was no more than a reasonable consequence to him, but he'd couched it as a threat. As if she'd ever asked for money! Haliday had left her a small income in his will. Other than gifting her the townhouse, her husband's successor hadn't provided anything additional—even though it was thanks to her there'd been a fortune for him to inherit.

She couldn't make free with expenditures, but she had enough to survive.

"I believe my dowry was the last time your finances were used on my behalf," Charlotte pointed out, her words sharp.

"And I'm quite happy to do so again. You're still young enough to bear children, and there are lords needing both money and heirs."

"Blast it, Father." Charlotte put down her tea, stood and faced him, arms crossed. "Why don't you just auction me off in *The Times*?"

The infuriating man grinned, softening his granite-hard visage. "I've made no secret of my designs. And I've never forced a thing on you. You couldn't wait to wed Haliday."

That was only too true. She'd been completely infatuated, a besotted fool. "Well, I have no intention of marrying again."

"Charlotte, you're a woman meant to have children. You'll marry again."

His gentle certainty both warmed and pained her. Her own mother, the youngest daughter of a gambling-ruined earl, had died when Charlotte was a girl. Father rarely spoke of her. But his prediction reminded Charlotte he often reminisced with great fondness and admiration upon his own mother and had compared Charlotte's looks and character to hers. Charlotte didn't mention that she thought herself incapable of bearing children. In four years of trying she'd had only one pregnancy, which she'd miscarried almost immediately.

Her father grasped the loop of gold chain resting on his embroidered silk waistcoat, ran his fingers along it and pulled the attached watch from its pocket. He checked the time. "I'd best leave," he said, returning the timepiece to its home. "I've been here far longer than I planned or wanted to be gone. I suppose I must accept your involvement with this charity. Of all the traits you might have inherited from me, I don't know why you acquired my stubborn nature. I hope you remember your promise and keep your work as private as possible."

She nodded. "I will. Good-bye, Father."

Charlotte heard him collect his hat from Walters, then the sounds of his leaving.

As soon as she knew he was gone, she asked for every discarded *Times* in the house. The pile of newspapers Walters brought wasn't large enough to give Charlotte hope she'd find what she wanted. She had no idea when the article about David Scott had appeared, so she perused each page. Halfway through the stack, the headline she sought leapt out at her. Charlotte took a quick, sharp breath and scanned the text.

Victoria Cross to be Awarded to Crimean Hero

A new medal is taking its place as England's preeminent award for valor, and today the War Office announced that David Scott would be among the recipients when Queen Victoria presents the first medals, 26 June, following a parade in Hyde Park. The Cross, made from Russian cannon captured at Sevastopol, is cast of bronze in the shape of a cross patté and ensigned with the Royal Crest and the words 'For Valor.'

Major Scott, brother to the Earl of Bridgewaite, will be awarded the Cross for conspicuous bravery before the enemy, 25 October, 1854, at Balaclava. One of Lord Tennyson's noble six-hundred, Scott's actions in the 'Valley of Death' that day two-and-a-half years ago make clear he deserves the honor. With Her Majesty's troops overwhelmed by the Russian guns, again and again Major Scott rallied the 11th Hussars and led them against the enemy force. When finally ordered to withdraw, he brought up the rear and stopped to assist a wounded officer struggling to stand under the onslaught of three Russian cavalrymen. Scott engaged the enemy soldiers in close-quarter fighting and ordered the injured major back to the British lines. Scott overcame his Russian combatants but took a saber to his shoulder. Wounded, he headed for the British lines at a full gallop, but his mount was struck by a killing shot and he was thrown underneath the horse as it fell. Unconscious, legs crushed, presumed dead, Major Scott lay on the battlefield throughout the night. It wasn't until the next day, when they cleared away the dead, that he was found to be alive.

Major Scott's injuries necessitated his medical discharge, but he is now the Executive Committee Chairman of the Royal Patriotic Fund. The courage and fierce tenacity of this man and the other sixty-one recipients will be recognized by all Britain when the Queen pins her nation's highest award—the Victoria Cross—on their chests.

Charlotte filled her shaking hands with fistfuls of skirt. A great ache threatened to choke her, and she forced herself to swallow against it. She imagined Scott lying under his dead horse, blue eyes staring up at the stars for endless hours of the night. Or perhaps smoke from the guns had settled in the valley and left him staring at a night sky devoid of light. He must have been in great pain, possibly wondering if he would soon die. What demons must have tortured him as he lay on the ground, surrounded by dead comrades and enemies? Such a night would drive some men to madness.

Scott's determined, proud face filled Charlotte's mind, his expression as he pulled himself hand-over-hand into his coach. A tear left her eye, and she reached up to dash it from her cheek. He'd told her he could not stand or walk. That was the physical cost of what he'd experienced that day, but what of his spirit? It might have been as crushed and crippled as his legs, yet he'd managed to build a new life for himself.

He'd been in the cavalry. That meant he'd been able to ride well, likely as though he were part of his horse. She could imagine him stretched out over the neck of his galloping mount, felt his heart fill with the joy of it… And now that feeling was lost to him. It seemed too unfair to bear.

A sense of failure and guilt rose in Charlotte, followed by a self-directed prick of anger. How long had she been obsessing over Haliday's betrayal? Two years. She pressed her fingers to her lips. Until Jane encouraged her, she hadn't even considered she might help herself. One month from now Scott was receiving a medal for valor on the battlefield, and surely he'd needed just as much courage each and every day since. She'd felt sorry for herself, while Scott's losses—and challenges—were so much greater.

She took her hand from her lips and cupped the teapot, its sides bringing welcome warmth to her fingers. She poured another cup and watched the steam curl up. It was easy enough to drink a bit of tea and infuse oneself with warmth, comfort, and a bit of vitality; if only she could as easily imbue herself with strength. Somehow, she needed to put some steel in her spine.

Perhaps David Scott, who probably sweated steel, would show her how.

CHAPTER NINE

Pleased that her determination seemed to have ousted her nerves, Charlotte felt steady if not confident when she arrived at the Fund offices the next day.

She started briskly up the front steps but slowed. At the top, a young woman attempted to maneuver a baby carriage, a toddler, and the front door all at once. Her heart-shaped face glowed red with the effort.

"May I help you?" Charlotte asked, stepping onto the landing and automatically reaching to manage the heavy wooden door. The toddler, bouncing on sturdy legs, had much-mended hose and bright, large brown eyes. Brown curls poked from beneath her cap, framing a round, red-cheeked face, and the little girl chose that moment to sit, her seeking hands reaching out for the braided trim on Charlotte's skirt.

"Oh!" exclaimed the young mother, obviously flustered. "I'd be so grateful if you could just get Betsy."

Charlotte released the door, bent and scooped the child into her arms. The moppet squealed and immediately reached for the satin ribbons of Charlotte's bonnet. Charlotte laughed and pulled the door open with her free hand, allowing the young mother to push the perambulator into the building.

The group paused just inside. Little Betsy blinked, expression wary as she took in the sudden dimness and chill of the entry. Her pudgy fingers tightened on Charlotte's ribbons, and Charlotte patted her back.

The harassed-looking mother reached out and took the cherubic Betsy into her arms. "Thank you for your kindness, ma'am. I'm Mrs. Charles Merriweather. You're already acquainted with my Betsy, and this," she added, indicating the infant inside the carriage, "is Charles junior."

Charlotte gazed at the sleeping baby, who appeared to be under a year old. "I'm pleased to make your acquaintance, and that of your delightful children, Mrs. Merriweather. I'm Lady Haliday."

The young mother's eyes widened, and she bobbed a curtsy.

"Are you heading for the Patriotic Fund office?" Charlotte asked. Such would make sense. Mrs. Merriweather would have been quite attractive but for appearing a shade paler and thinner than was fashionable. Her black dress was clean but had seen many washings, and the narrow band of lace at her collar had been carefully mended.

A relieved-sounding sigh escaped the woman. "Yes. Is it down this hall?"

"It is. I'm headed there myself."

Charlotte took Betsy back into her arms. She was suddenly very glad the gown she'd chosen was not only seasoned but one of her plainest. The only embellishment on the brown frock was a bit of amber braid.

She led Mrs. Merriweather directly to George Chetney's office. The man stood immediately, adjusted his glasses and smoothed his mustache.

"My lady. Ma'am. Good morning," he said, giving them a quick bow. "Mr. Scott is expecting you, Lady Haliday."

As if on cue, the baby began to cry and Charlotte's new acquaintance bent over the perambulator and lifted the infant into her arms. Charlotte certainly couldn't thrust the toddler at her, too, and it was doubtful that Mr. Chetney's glasses would survive if the toddler were handed into his care.

"This is Mrs. Merriweather," she said quickly. "I think she'd best come with me."

Then Charlotte strode through the doorway, trusting the others to follow.

#

David Scott watched as Charlotte Haliday sailed in from the outer office. She carried a child and accompanied a young woman in mourning garb who held a crying infant.

Since he'd heard Lady Haliday's voice, he was expecting her. What he wasn't expecting was the entourage. The sight of her with hat askew nearly undid him. A grin escaped before he hastily pulled it back.

The viscountess blushed, put one hand up to straighten her hat, and gave the child a couple of bounces. The blush and the way her arms tightened around the little girl gave David pause. Yesterday she'd been defenseless, waking from her faint, her eyes unfocused, her fingers clutching and trusting. Charlotte Haliday might present an image of aloof control to the world, but he'd seen her vulnerable and she wasn't cold at all.

How many people had seen her at such unguarded moments? Not many, he guessed. For a moment he remembered the warmth of her in his arms, the softness of her mouth. Definitely *not* cold, yet she chose to present herself as impervious. He understood concealing one's vulnerabilities and presenting a stalwart face to the world. He supposed that dissembling was as automatic for her as it was for him.

"Good morning, Mr. Scott." She turned toward her companion. "Mrs. Charles Merriweather, may I present Mr. Scott? Mr. Scott, this is Mrs. Merriweather and her children. We happened to arrive on your doorstep at the same time."

David acknowledged the introduction to Mrs. Merriweather, trying to keep his gaze off the viscountess. She easily coped with the fussy children, but that didn't convince David that Charlotte Haliday would be of use to him.

He waved to the chairs in front of his desk. "Please, sit down."

Charlotte. Just looking at her proved her unsuitability. She'd probably tried to dress plainly, but the quality of her clothing made it obvious she belonged to the upper echelons of society. She'd lit up the room when she entered. Wouldn't such élan make the Fund's clients feel inadequate?

He turned his attention to Mrs. Merriweather. The poor lady appeared nearly done in, so he smiled, hoping to put her at ease.

"What regiment was your husband with, ma'am?"

#

Charlotte rubbed Betsy's back and, sound asleep, the child exhaled a mighty sigh and rested her head on Charlotte's shoulder.

Charlotte could tell the interview was nearly over. Mr. Scott had been absolutely masterful as he questioned Juliet Merriweather. He'd listened to the widow unhurriedly, reassured her, and Charlotte had listened, stunned, as Juliet Merriweather confided in him. Then Scott had written out a bank draft. He'd made an appointment for Mrs. Merriweather's return visit the following month.

How proud the widow was, Charlotte mused. What it must have cost her to reveal her deplorable circumstances to two strangers! Yet Juliet Merriweather appeared to have the kind of backbone Charlotte admired. She'd disclosed her situation in a straightforward manner, chin lifted, eyes steady. Twice, though, the young woman paused as if gathering her thoughts or strength and glanced over at Charlotte, and as unlikely as it seemed, Charlotte thought her presence helped the widow continue.

David Scott's voice and direct gaze showed only respect for Mrs. Merriweather. How different his demeanor than with Charlotte herself. Her very presence seemed to irk him, and each time his gaze swung to her she felt him taking her measure. He didn't want her working for him, and she really couldn't blame him. Seeing him, even thinking of him, brought back the memory of their kiss. No doubt his recollection was just as clear. And he must believe the scandalous rumors about her to be true.

Mrs. Merriweather stood.

"Chetney," Scott called. His secretary appeared in the doorway. "Roust a boy to run down to the corner for a cab, would you?"

Chetney nodded. "Right away," he said, and left.

Charlotte stood, careful not to disturb Betsy. "I'll walk out with you."

Mrs. Merriweather stepped forward and took the bank draft that Scott held outstretched. "How can I thank you?" she asked. Her voice was thick, and Charlotte recognized the tone of withheld tears.

"I merely manage the Fund," Scott said. "Your allowance is based on your husband's rank and the number of children you have. I wish we could do more. Your husband gave his life protecting the Crown."

Perhaps Scott's matter-of-factness bolstered the widow, because she straightened and carefully placed the bank draft inside her reticule. "God bless you, Mr. Scott," she said, her voice once again firm.

David Scott's gaze fell, and he busied himself with papers on his desk. Charlotte almost thought him embarrassed, but she couldn't quite believe the possibility.

She and Chetney accompanied Mrs. Merriweather to the street, where a hack waited. Chetney paid the driver and oversaw securing the widow's pram to the back of the carriage. The transfer of Mrs. Merriweather and her children wasn't as easily accomplished, necessitating handoffs between Charlotte and Chetney until the widow was settled inside with a sleeping child in each arm.

What, Charlotte wondered, would happen at the end of this journey? From the interview she knew mother and children lived alone in two small rooms. Juliet Merriweather had dealt with the death of her husband, the birth of her son, and the necessity of moving to less expensive lodgings all in the space of four weeks. Charlotte couldn't imagine coping with such events. She'd always prided herself on her abilities, but the intricacies of managing a successful dinner party seemed as nothing compared to what Juliet handled.

"Is there someone to help you when you arrive home?" she asked.

"Yes. My neighbors. We all help each other. My lady, I hope I'll see you the next time I come?"

Charlotte considered the family before her. Juliet's dark gray eyes held a friendly sincerity, and watching the sleeping Betsy and little Charles wove a ribbon of warmth through her heart. Her decision to work for the Fund had been impulsive. She'd wanted to be useful and busy. She'd never expected such work to make her feel good in any but an abstract way, but it did, and Charlotte suddenly realized the constriction in her chest that had been with her for so long had eased.

"You certainly will," she said. She very much wanted to see them again.

CHAPTER TEN

She gave Juliet a final wave and returned to the offices, walking straight through to David Scott. "How much money does the Fund have? Can we help them all that way?"

He looked up from what appeared to be a ledger book. "There's a generous amount in our coffers, but we need to keep raising money. I could use your help procuring donations, planning fundraising balls and acting as liaison to local fundraising committees." The warm, expressive face Scott had shown to Mrs. Merriweather was gone, and he sounded reluctant. "You can do that, can't you?"

Charlotte stiffened. Could she meet with small charitable groups and plan balls? The temptation to throw a tart remark back in response was too strong to resist.

"The Prime Minister seemed to enjoy my dinner parties and soirees well enough. *He* always accepted my invitations."

David Scott raised his brows. "What finer affirmation could a hostess receive?"

The infuriating man was mocking her. Wasn't he? But not a glint of humor shone in those considering, clear blue eyes. If anything, he suddenly looked resigned, and overcome with the desire to fidget Charlotte sank onto a chair.

Scott set his pen down next to the crystal and brass inkwell and folded his hands. "Although there are nearly forty prestigious commissioners, including the Queen and Prince Albert, the Executive Committee is the day-to-day working branch of the Fund and consists of you, me, Chetney, and Mr. Downy, who's usually traveling. Our committee helps organize local fundraising committees around the country and provides assistance to them. We monitor the schooling and circumstances of our orphans. We have seven clerical workers. We estimate nearly two thousand widows and three thousand children need help, and we're getting over one hundred applications each week. We're busy, and I'll need you most days. If you can't commit to that, then I'd rather not have you. I must be able to depend on those who are here."

Charlotte widened her eyes, trying with all her might to maintain a look of innocent inquiry. Was he hoping she'd quit? He made it so plain that he didn't want her. That truth was like a sharp wasp sting.

Scott sighed and rubbed his chin. "Sometimes I visit orphans to check on them. I'd hoped to find a nursemaid or governess to go with me, but I guess it will have to be you."

They'd be working that closely together? Charlotte remembered how she'd felt sitting with him in his coach, and a nervous feeling crept into her stomach. She took a deep breath and thought of Juliet Merriweather's backbone.

"Mr. Scott, I am committed. I'm happy to plan balls, happy to correspond or meet with local committee members. I'm happy to lend assistance in any way I can. You have only to ask."

The man leaned forward, placing his palms flat on his desk. "Then I'll call for you at ten o'clock tomorrow. There's a family of five orphaned children I intend to see."

Charlotte's bravado fell away. Given the grim tenor of Scott's voice, she might have been accompanying him to a funeral. Images of five Betsy Merriweather-like, hollow-cheeked children with dirty faces crowded her mind. What was she to do with them? She had no experience with children, orphaned or not. The lingering pride from her recent successful encounter vanished, and a cold shaft of fear streaked through her. What would she say to them? What might they expect of her? Apprehension tightened her throat.

Scott's gaze moved past her to the doorway. His firm mouth eased into a grin, and the corners of his eyes crinkled. The smile transformed his face, filled it with warmth, and the change was startling. Charlotte's heart leapt then thumped hard. Suddenly, she wanted to be the recipient of that smile. The inherent strength of his face had attracted her, but until now this man had not stolen her breath.

Oh, Lord. Was she certain she wanted to work for him?

Behind her, she heard Chetney and another male voice. Charlotte turned and found a tall, sun-bronzed man in a military uniform of navy jacket and cherry pants standing in the doorway. A servant with a large basket stood behind him.

"Scott?" the golden-haired officer said. He paused then strode into the room at the hand motion he received. When he reached across the desk, the two men didn't so much shake hands as grip them. They exchanged grins. "I hope you're free for luncheon. I thought I'd take advantage of my proximity to you. I brought everything with me." He gave Charlotte a quick look with warm brown eyes. "Unless you have other plans?"

"Not at all," Scott said. "We've been working, but we just finished. My lady, may I present Major Lord Wakefield? We served together in the Crimea. Wakefield, this is Lady Haliday."

Wakefield bowed too quickly for Charlotte to analyze his expression. "I'm honored."

She acknowledged the introduction with a nod. There was an obvious camaraderie between the men, and it warmed her to think the two had remained friends through the upheaval Scott had undergone.

Wakefield looked back and forth between her and Scott, as if he were sizing up their connection. His gaze held a glint of admiration when it returned to her. "Won't you join us, Lady Haliday? I've brought plenty."

Charlotte's gaze immediately sought David Scott's. She found him watching her, his smile gone. He didn't want her joining them. That previous sting of hurt pricked a little sharper.

Charlotte looked again at Lord Wakefield, who radiated self-confidence—and interest. But that didn't assuage her disappointment regarding Scott's expression. Whatever appetite she might have had was gone.

She steeled herself. It was extremely important that Mr. Scott not guess how attuned to him she felt, and how much his opinion suddenly mattered. She intended to work for David Scott, and she wanted to prove herself to him. She might find herself unable to change the conviction of her father or society, but suddenly she wanted more than anything to change David Scott's opinion of her and she knew intuitively that he would admire neither indecisiveness nor weakness.

"I'd be delighted," she said to Lord Wakefield. Then, somehow, she mustered a smile.

#

David backed his chair away from his desk and pushed its wheels toward the folding table Wakefield brought. The viscount's servant was setting up a feast, complete with starched tablecloth.

There was cold chicken, egg sandwiches, a fine cheese, bread and butter, cold asparagus, and gooseberry tarts. It was a tempting selection of food, but rocks resided in David's belly. His friend and Charlotte were chattering together, oblivious of him. And, blast! He was thinking of her as Charlotte again. Perhaps that particular sea-change had occurred as she comforted the sleeping Betsy in her arms. He'd found it difficult to keep his eyes off her and the child.

The entire situation was untenable. He didn't want to give Wakefield a reason to speculate about his reaction to Charlotte, but he wasn't sure he could manage to monitor his speech and expression and conceal the strain of her presence. Not when he had to mind his interactions with his friend, too. He didn't blame Wakefield for what had happened with his legs, and he'd told him so, but the man's eyes were always a bit watchful, and David knew Miles analyzed his every intonation.

Of course, his friend certainly seemed relaxed now, offering Charlotte lemonade and leaning toward her each time he smiled— which seemed to happen with regularity.

In spite of the superb food, David noticed only Chetney ate much. The secretary loaded a plate and took it off to his desk, while Wakefield, Charlotte and David sat around the collapsible table in David's office. But Charlotte's apparent lack of appetite wasn't affecting her ability to converse. She kept up a running conversation with the attentive Wakefield throughout. It was even determined that Wakefield knew her father.

Near the end of the meal, Wakefield turned. "I'm selling my commission," he said.

David stilled. *He wants my permission. I wish he didn't need it.* "I think that's fine. You've made up your mind, then?"

"Time to think of settling down and securing the inheritance." Wakefield's lips twisted. "So far, I've been lucky." A subsequent thought seemed to leave him stricken, and he fell silent.

"I'm glad for you, Miles," David said quietly. He knew exactly what the thought had been.

Wakefield's head came up, and he stared into David's eyes. The stiffness of his shoulders eased, and he drew in a great draught of air. "Well." He stood. "I'd best let you get back to work. My lady, might I see you home?"

Charlotte had been quiet and watchful. David thought she understood that something more had transpired than the obvious.

"That's very generous of you, Lord Wakefield. Thank you." Charlotte looked at David. "Unless there's more I might do today?"

David shook his head. "I'll get Chetney organized so he can explain your duties tomorrow."

Wakefield's servant arrived to clean up the remains and collapse the table, and within moments David was alone.

His office gave him a view of the street. When the room was quiet, outside noises easily reached him. David went back to his paperwork but found it impossible to concentrate until after the sounds made by Wakefield's barouche faded away.

CHAPTER ELEVEN

At precisely ten o'clock, Scott's man called at her door.

The servant towered over her, a strapping tree trunk of a man. Charlotte's nerves crawled from her stomach to her throat as she approached the waiting clarence coach, her mind jumping between the unknown orphans and Scott. She'd tried telling herself his steady blue gaze wasn't responsible for the acute awareness that assailed her in his presence, but she knew the truth of it. She'd barely slept. Come morning she'd felt queasy, but remembering her recent faint she forced herself to eat a little breakfast.

A small cart attached to the back of Scott's coach held his wheeled chair. Scott didn't use the usual heavy, high-backed type Charlotte was familiar with. Instead, his chair appeared very like a regular sitting chair. Contoured and low-backed, made of cane and mahogany, the chair's seat and armrests were padded and upholstered with green velvet. In addition to the added footrest, the chair had been modified by removing its legs and securing the seat to two large wheels. Given the chair's lesser size and weight, Scott was able to roll himself about. Charlotte thought the larger, traditional wheeled chairs required someone to push them. This chair gave Scott a measure of independence.

She had no idea of their imminent destination, of how long they'd be confined together. The state her nerves were in, how would she manage a lighthearted conversation?

As she stepped up into the shadowed interior of the coach, she accepted Scott's extended hand. He wore an impeccable dark blue jacket and cornflower blue vest that seemed rather conservative by the current fashion. His tie matched his vest and his white shirt nearly glowed. She'd seen Lake Lucerne, and it was the same clear blue as his eyes.

Heat rushed up her arm and fanned through her. She sat beside him, looked into his shuttered face, and the nearness of David Scott overwhelmed her. Uncomfortably warm, and fearing he might sense her unease, she lowered her gaze. Blast. She hadn't felt this keen awareness of a man since her days as a young bride, and as much as she didn't want to admit it, her awareness of Haliday was never this potent.

Realizing their hands remained linked, she pulled hers away. Her cheeks burned. Pressing her back against the coach seat, she concentrated on keeping a small space between herself and Mr. Scott. She could have wailed. She didn't *want* to be attracted to this man. As honorable as he seemed, she never again wanted to entrust her heart to another.

But Haliday wasn't a trustworthy man, and Mr. Scott is.

As far as she knew, he'd been honest with her. He hadn't hidden that he'd been disturbed by her forwardness at the ball nor that he didn't want her working for him. Yet he'd been kind as well.

The carriage gave a small jerk and began to move.

"Good morning," Charlotte said, busying herself with her ash-gray skirt.

"You're on time."

A quick glance revealed an expression that complemented his surprised tone.

"Of course."

"There's no 'of course' about it. At least in my experience, ladies are rarely punctual."

She knew his assessment correctly applied to too many ladies of her acquaintance, those who intentionally made gentlemen wait. She'd always detested such nonsense.

"Well, you needn't expect me to keep you waiting," she asserted.

Oh. Wait. Charlotte was suddenly taken aback. Could one of the ladies he referred to be a *wife*? Why had she assumed he was unmarried? Her chest tightened as if someone had tugged hard on her laces. The way he'd kissed her, she'd assumed... But...oh, no. She really couldn't breathe.

"Is your wife the lady who makes you wait?"

Scott's head jerked. "Wife? I'm not married." His jaw went tight. "I'm...crippled, Lady Haliday."

"Why would that matter to a woman who loved you?" In Charlotte's experience, it was the inside of a man that was important. She supposed she still believed in love, at least in regard to Jane and Phillip. "Unless you can't—"

She gasped, and her hand flew to cover her mouth. They stared at each other. No. She *hadn't* almost just asked if he were able to perform as a man.

The tension in Scott's face released, his lips parted, and a choked sound emerged from his mouth. Laughing? He was laughing at her! Charlotte frowned, hating the way his smile made his eyes shine and her breath catch.

His face smoothed, except the curves at the corners of his mouth. "I could marry, but I hardly think it'd be fair to my wife. By necessity I live a restricted life."

Charlotte pressed her lips together, determined to withhold all further comments.

Scott turned to the window. She wanted to look down at his legs, but she didn't. She'd die of curiosity before she let him catch her staring at his crippled appendages.

They rode in silence for long minutes. No morning haze existed to dampen the pale brightness of the sky, which appeared nearly white. Charlotte squinted out the window until her tired eyes began to tear.

"How far are we going?" she asked.

Scott turned. "To Gray's Inn Road in North London. There's a family of five children, aged between three and twelve, in temporary lodging. We'll check on them, make sure their circumstances have been acceptable. I've managed to find permanent situations for them."

Charlotte welcomed the renewed formality in his voice.

"I'll be overseeing the construction of an orphanage built with Fund money, and once it's available it will make things easier. Until then we'll try to find acceptable prospects for the orphans."

"You found a home for five children? That's wonderful."

"Not together," he amended. "No one would take all five Butler children. There's a couple willing to take the two youngest girls, and I can send the boys to boarding school. I couldn't find a family to take the oldest girl, so I obtained a good position for her to go to, not yet having a Fund orphanage. They'll all have comfortable situations. The Nelsons expect to adopt the two little girls, and Hiram Nelson owns a successful import business."

Charlotte heard satisfaction in Scott's voice, and he had every right to be proud. She couldn't help but be impressed. London held so many orphans. More and more, journalists wrote of the unprotected children who populated much of the city's workforce. She had only to look out the carriage window to see children at each street crossing sweeping refuse from the paths of the genteel. A vision of others hunched over factory worktables rose in her mind. Rather than surrendering his orphans to such fates, Scott had managed to arrange something more agreeable.

Without warning, wonder rushed through her. Gooseflesh rose on her arms. *She* was part of this now. She was going to comfort and help children who'd lost their fathers and women whose husbands had died in service to the Crown. Excitement fluttered in her chest, yet at the same time she realized fear resided there, too. How she met this challenge would affect other lives. Nothing she'd ever done had felt like this.

The coach stopped, and the activities of those outside told her they'd reached their destination. A moment later Scott's herculean servant handed Charlotte down from the carriage into a working-class neighborhood, and she stood aside and watched as together he and the less imposing driver retrieved Scott's wheelchair. They brought it to the open door, and Charlotte realized they were going to assist Scott from the carriage. She knew she should probably step away and turn her back to the scene, but all she could do was stand and watch.

Scott appeared in the carriage door, suspended in his sling. Within moments he'd lowered himself into the wheelchair. His giant, whom she heard called Boone, held Scott's lower legs as he descended. Watching the effort in Scott's face and the care Boone took, Charlotte was struck again with a sense of observing what should by rights be private, yet she couldn't tear her gaze away.

The entire transfer was accomplished quickly and efficiently. Scott positioned his feet and legs just so and gave his waistcoat and coat a couple tugs. Boone moved behind the chair, and Scott's sharp gaze met Charlotte's eyes. His mouth tightened, and heat rushed to her face.

Oh, Lord. What is wrong with me, staring at him this way?

"Shall we?" he asked.

Boone maneuvered Scott's chair so his back was to the five waiting steps. "Simpson," he called, and then the driver positioned himself in front of Scott. With calm deliberation Boone tilted the wheelchair back. Simpson pushed the chair from the front, Boone pulled from behind, and they slowly rolled the chair up the steps.

Their knock at the door was met promptly, and a faded-looking maid led the party to a small parlor. The worn rug and divan gave the room a neglected air, in spite of the abundance of porcelain figurines perched on every surface.

The woman who next appeared resembled a life-size version of one of her own miniatures. Curls that had once been blonde but were now nearly colorless tumbled about her lined, middle-aged face. Layer after ruffled layer cascaded down the skirt of her pale blue dress and foamed from her neckline and elbow-length sleeves. She needed only a chip straw Pamela bonnet and a basket of flowers to completely duplicate one of her figurines.

Within minutes, Scott had introduced their hostess as Mrs. Russell and tea was served. Simpson returned to the carriage. Boone somehow melted into the corner of the room.

"It's been an adjustment," Mrs. Russell said in a burdened tone.

"And how are the *children* adapting?" Scott inquired.

Flounces swayed as their hostess straightened. "They've managed fine, as children are wont to do. They should be grateful, as burdensome as they are. Truly, I've not the stamina to care for five. The strain would have buckled me if I'd been less determined. It's lucky the oldest miss is capable. She's helped a bit," Mrs. Russell admitted with a sniff.

"I believe you've been compensated enough to put mutton or the like on your table," Scott said. Many tables in London couldn't boast of meat, and Charlotte suspected there had been times in the past Mrs. Russell had gone without.

"You give me enough to feed them. Don't think I'm getting wealthy."

Charlotte looked back and forth between Scott and Mrs. Russell. They'd only exchanged a few words and both were bristling like hedgehogs. Scott was glowering, and Mrs. Russell's nose was so high in the air that Charlotte worried she might tip over. How in the world could the woman have such a horrid attitude and be employed by the Fund? Charlotte hoped Mrs. Russell wasn't typical of the foster mothers being used.

Afraid the two combatants might explode, she spoke up. "You provided a safe haven and allowed them to stay together. We're grateful for that. Caring for five children must be quite difficult."

Mrs. Russell's head canted. "I had five of my own, but they didn't come as close together as these. They're three, four, five and six. 'Course, the older girl, she's but a half-sister to the rest of them. There's six years between her and the six-year-old."

"I'd like to see them," Scott said in a milder tone.

Mrs. Russell's tense shoulders eased. She left the room, dress aflutter like an armada of ships with luffing sails, stopped at the bottom of the stairs and called up. "Miss! Bring them down. The Queen's man is here." When quiet was the only response, she called again, voice pitched high enough to carry all the way up the stairs. "Eleanor! Come down here, miss."

There came sounds of shuffling feet overhead, and Mrs. Russell returned to the parlor. Then thunder rolled down the narrow stairs. The two boys, appearing to be the five- and six-year-olds, arrived first. One glance established them as brothers. They had nearly identical, round, apple-cheeked faces and bright red hair. The small girl who came next literally raced to the door of the parlor and stopped.

The three children stood poised in the doorway. Charlotte glanced at Scott. The children obviously weren't permitted into the parlor and complied with that edict by stopping at the door.

"Missy!" Mrs. Russell scolded. "If you don't slow down, you're going to break something. And that had best not happen."

Three pairs of green eyes widened. The girl took a step back, but a narrow, fine-boned hand came down on her shoulder.

"You needn't worry, ma'am. Hannah knows not to come in here." The slim, dark-haired girl suddenly behind the other three wasn't a child and wasn't yet a woman. The blue dress she wore, faded and several inches too short, revealed a body just beginning to bud into womanhood. She wore glasses and carried a younger, female version of the two boys—a round-faced little cherub with plump, cherry-red lips and the clear, pale skin of a redhead. The spectacles looked too heavy for her delicate face.

"Eleanor, I'm Mr. Scott. I've come to see how you're faring here."

The quiet timbre of Scott's voice conveyed the utmost kindness. It reminded Charlotte of the soothing way he'd spoken when she fainted.

The moppet curled a pudgy hand around her eldest sister's neck and laid her head on Eleanor's shoulder. Eleanor pushed her drooping glasses to the bridge of her nose and said, "We're doing just fine."

Scott nodded once. "I believe I've found homes for you."

The glasses didn't reduce the sudden heat of Eleanor's gaze. Fierce green eyes surveyed the group, and the arm that held the moppet tightened. "Together?"

"No. But I swear they're good situations."

Eleanor's face revealed nothing of her thoughts. "Can't we stay here, then?"

"For now you can. But it's not a permanent situation."

The three younger children stared at their older sister. They'd each drawn closer to her, and Hannah's hand twisted in Eleanor's skirts. The child looked up at her sister, lower lip quivering. "Ellie?"

Eleanor waited so long to answer, Charlotte wondered if she hadn't heard. Then she saw the bright gleam of tears in Eleanor's eyes.

"There's no decision to be made," Mrs. Russell said. "The sooner the better, I say."

Scott kept his gaze locked with Eleanor's. "I knew your father," he said.

Eleanor blinked and caught her lower lip between her teeth. "Truly?"

The words had captured the two boys' attention, too. "You knew Father?" the youngest asked.

The barest sort of smile curved Scott's lips. "Not well, but yes. John Butler was a brave soldier and a fine sergeant major. I'm honored to assist his family."

For a moment ephemeral warmth shimmered, as if the children's collective sighs hovered in the air.

"What are your names?" Scott asked.

"I'm Joshua, and this is Thomas," the taller boy said.

"And that's Hannah and Amelia," Thomas supplied.

"Well, Joshua, could you take charge of the girls while I chat with Eleanor?"

Joshua's chest seemed to expand before Charlotte's eyes. "Yes, sir," he said.

"Why don't you go outside and look at the gentleman's horses?" Eleanor suggested. "Just stay on the steps."

Eleanor set Amelia down, and Joshua took the little girl's hand. The four youngest trooped toward the front door, the boys adjusting their pace to match their smallest sister's. As soon as the front door closed, Eleanor spoke.

"We want to stay together, even if it's in an orphanage." Her hands fisted; her narrow chin tipped. "I'll take care of them, and as soon as I can get work I'll make a home for us."

Charlotte cringed. As determined as the girl was, there was no way she could support them all. But Scott nodded as if the plan was sound.

"That's several years away. What if I send the boys to boarding school for now?"

"School?" The yearning in the girl's voice was clear.

"This one's a dreamer," Mrs. Russell accused. "Always drawing pictures or staring off into space. Don't seem natural, if you ask me."

Charlotte stiffened, insulted for the girl, but Eleanor's only reaction was a firming of her mouth. Charlotte admired the restraint. During her school years she had often been called different, at first because of her lack of social standing and the wealth of her father, later because of her unusual education. She'd received a lady's instruction, but when she'd shown an interest and aptitude for subjects more typical of a boy's schooling, her father had her tutored in math, literature, history and several languages.

For a long moment, Scott gazed at Eleanor. "I believe I've found a good home for the girls."

Eleanor's face remained blank. "And what of myself, sir?"

Scott hesitated, but only briefly. "I've found a place for you in service, below-stairs in the home of Mrs. Prescott-Hughes."

An involuntary gasp escaped Charlotte. Scott sent her a questioning look then returned his gaze to Eleanor.

"It's a suitable position for you. And your brothers and sisters will have good situations."

Everything in Charlotte shouted *no*. She knew Mrs. Prescott-Hughes, and it would be difficult to find a meaner gossip. The woman perpetually looked as if she'd just sucked on a lemon, and her pursed lips took every opportunity to criticize the world around her. Her daughter Frances had come out the same year as Charlotte. Frances stammered and was miserable at social gatherings; around her mother she maintained downcast eyes and slumped shoulders, her pale fingers invariably twisted together. Charlotte had actually seen Mrs. Prescott-Hughes publicly harangue her painfully shy daughter, and Charlotte had no doubt the entire Prescott-Hughes household cringed in just the same way Frances did. The steady-eyed Eleanor simply could not go there.

Eleanor's face was unreadable, but Charlotte saw almost imperceptible tension filling the girl's body. She had already lost both parents. This plan would leave her alone, out of contact with the brothers and sisters she'd cared for and protected. How could Scott ask that of her?

"Well," Mrs. Russell remarked, her voice laced with great satisfaction. "That's settled, then. Miss, you should be mighty grateful to Mr. Scott."

Eleanor started. Her eyes looked fever-bright. Her gaze moved between the three adults, then, pleading, returned to Charlotte. A moment later, Eleanor's gaze dropped to the floor.

Something inside Charlotte dropped, too. This couldn't be the best option. There had to be something else that could be done, some way to keep the children together. Scott's solution had seemed fine before she met them, but now…discontent gripped her. She didn't want to believe Scott was satisfied with this arrangement, either. She wanted to be alone with him, close enough to look past his restrained expression and seek the emotion—the caring—she sensed he kept concealed deep inside.

A slight movement drew her gaze to his hands. Curled around his chair's armrests, his fingers pressed into the wood until they blanched.

"What if," Charlotte began, "you went into service in my house instead?"

Eleanor and Scott both jerked their heads toward her.

"We'll make sure you have opportunities to see your brothers and sisters as well."

As the words flew from her mouth, Charlotte watched the tension leave Eleanor's slim body. Certainty settled within her. This would keep Eleanor safe, and perhaps in time something better could be arranged. She couldn't tell what Scott thought, though. His momentary expression of surprise had refashioned to a businesslike blandness.

#

David wanted to chastise the viscountess for her impulsiveness, but he could hardly do that when gladness filled his heart. He'd been sick when he couldn't find a way to keep the Butler children together. The oldest girl's situation no longer seemed so distressing.

He arranged to pick up the Butlers the next day, and they all said their good-byes. Eleanor bobbed a curtsy, a wary but hopeful look on her face.

As soon as the coach was underway, he felt Charlotte settle her gaze on him. The set of her mouth was pure stubbornness, but her eyes...her eyes were like distant stars.

"You know you can't take them all in," he found himself saying. "Kind as it was."

Her mouth curved, and the stars ignited a blaze in his chest that shocked him, so caution rushed in to temper the flare. It was difficult to believe that his acceptance of her decision meant so much, but the evidence was right before his eyes. His chest grew tight. The urge to shake her was no less strong than the urge to kiss her, damn it!

"But I can take *her* in."

"Would Mrs. Prentiss-Hughes have been so terrible?"

"Actually, yes. I know the lady."

"Ahhh. I didn't realize. I thought it would be a good position. In the future...well, I'm not sure how we can determine unacceptable billets."

Charlotte's eyebrows rose. "We? You're going to let me work with you then?"

"You already knew that."

"But you don't want me."

He nearly groaned. If she only knew how much he *did* want her. His wanting was at the root of most of his objections. Today she'd shown generosity and compassion, and her eyes told him how much this position meant to her. Somehow, he must ignore his unwanted emotions. Failing that, he'd hide them. She deserved his acceptance.

"You've convinced me. You were good with the children both yesterday and today."

Her reply was nearly a whisper. "I didn't expect them to touch me the way they do."

And David hadn't wanted to know her like this, but it was too late. He had already seen that she was a warmhearted, caring woman.

A strange look came over her face, as if she wanted to say more but couldn't. Then words came out in a tremulous rush: "Eleanor especially. She's the same age I was when my mother died."

David couldn't help himself. He reached for her hand, and Charlotte gripped his in return. Her purple-blue eyes were dark pools. He'd never wanted to hold a woman as much as he wanted to hold this one now, but…

"You'll be able to protect her," he said. "Take care of her."

Her eyes lightened, dispelling the shadows. The aloof expression so often in evidence was absent, and instead, her face bore an open vulnerability. "Yes."

A tremulous smile curved her lips. For an instant her fingers tightened on his, but then they slipped away.

An ache rocked up from the depths of David. He'd thought her not only tenacious but arrogant, the way she'd stood up to him and insisted he let her work, the way she'd confronted Lady Garret. He'd been wrong. She had perfected this look of composure, but with him her mask slipped. Again and again he'd caught glimpses of the real woman: the instant she realized he couldn't walk, the moment she'd lost herself in his kiss, and now, with this young orphan. Charlotte Haliday was a woman of deep feeling. Last year's gossip must have been torment for her.

He quickly admonished himself. She'd already aroused his desire, and now the viscountess was garnering his admiration? This time he'd excuse himself, but he'd not let it happen again. He turned his head away and hardened his will. For however long they worked together, he would show the same mastery of his emotions he'd always shown on the battlefield.

He swore it.

CHAPTER TWELVE

For the first time in two years, Charlotte felt reasonably comfortable in a ballroom. Tonight she was attracting no undue notice, and she could focus on her cause. Her tension was nowhere near as keen as it had been at that first ball where she met Scott.

This ball had a purpose—to raise capital for the Patriotic Fund. Jane and Etherton had been extraordinarily helpful. They rarely entertained on such a scale, and nearly all their invitations had been accepted. Charlotte hoped Jane's generosity would be just the beginning. If this was successful, others could be expected to host similar gatherings. Having the charity endorsed by Queen Victoria and Prince Albert helped, too.

Charlotte looked to where Scott sat deep in conversation. He had no sense of social hierarchy! She imagined it stemmed from his years in the cavalry. She knew his brother was the Earl of Bridgewaite, but Scott had absolutely no attitude of superiority about him. She couldn't think of another gentleman who'd converse with a footman the way Scott was doing now, and his face, alight with vitality, stirred something deep inside her. She wanted to be closer, wanted to be the recipient of that smile and the warm regard in his eyes.

She strolled toward the men, watching animation play over Scott's face, but curiosity slowed her steps at the footman's words.

"My brother was in the Grenadier Guards. He fell at Inkerman."

Scott angled his head, and his carefree expression fell away. A look of pain replaced it. "We lost too many fine men at Inkerman, and the Grenadier Guards took more casualties there than any other regiment. They wouldn't stop—just kept pressing on."

"Billy wasn't one to give up. He would have been one to push forward as hard as he could."

"Did he leave a wife? Children?"

"No. But it's good to see this ball benefitting the loved ones left behind." Without relaxing his stiff posture, the footman reached inside his coat and withdrew several coins. He extended them to Scott. "Might I make a donation, sir?"

Surprise stilled Charlotte. A servant making a donation? She'd never heard of such a thing. But why not? Why hadn't she realized that this cause touched all hearts? And she suspected the coins this footman offered represented a far more generous, open-hearted contribution than the much larger donations expected later tonight from wealthy guests.

Charlotte moved up next to Scott's chair as he accepted the footman's coins. This close, she couldn't deny his presence affected her in extremely disturbing ways. Each day at the office she attributed her awareness of him to a desire to prove herself and be regarded as an asset, but tonight she was unable to evade the truth.

She wore a new gown of deep purple silk and lace, beautiful in spite of its adhering to the etiquette of half-mourning, and she'd allowed Rebecca to spend extra time dressing her hair, twining a rope of pearls through the shining black knot at her nape. The maid had been most pleased with Charlotte's sophisticated appearance, but Charlotte hadn't been able to take more than one quick look in her mirror. The reflection had seemed that of a poised woman whose flushed cheeks and jewel-bright eyes revealed underlying excitement. But how would Scott see her?

His gaze swept over her, and Charlotte's nervousness intensified into a fierce quivering in the pit of her stomach. At work his straightforward, uncritical demeanor allowed her to concentrate on learning her duties. Only tonight, as she donned silk stockings and scented her skin with perfume, had she allowed herself to imagine him seeing her as a desirable woman instead of as an associate.

Almost immediately, Scott looked away. "Thank you, Herbert," he said. "Your money will be put to good use."

She'd seen him before in evening dress, but the events of that night had obscured everything but the look in his eyes, the feel of his arms and lips. Now, in the light of the ballroom chandeliers, Scott appeared the epitome of refined masculine elegance. His starched white shirt, white waistcoat and tie, coupled with black tailcoat and trousers, were the standard eveningwear of gentlemen, but he made it all look remarkable. The severe color scheme emphasized the chiseled strength of his face, the sloping breadth of his shoulders.

"Good evening."

Next to her, Miles Wakefield bowed then straightened and grinned. Charlotte managed to conceal her surprise. She'd been so intent on Scott, she hadn't even noticed the footman moving away and Wakefield approaching.

"When do you muster out?" Scott asked, indicating the regimental dress uniform the other man wore.

"Less than a month—the end of June."

It had been a couple of weeks since Wakefield announced he intended to leave the Queen's service, though the time had passed extremely quickly for Charlotte. She had been busier than ever before in her life, learning the workings of the Fund. Most of her time was delegated to correspondence with local fundraising committee chairmen and women all over England. In addition, she met with women and children who came to the office requesting assistance. She'd even grown easy talking with them.

"My lady, might I have the honor of the next dance?" Wakefield asked.

Charlotte stared into his nutmeg-colored eyes and felt the weight of Scott's blue gaze upon her as well. Was it difficult for him, watching every other man in the room doing what he could not? Had he liked to dance? She expected Wakefield to be an accomplished partner, but it was Scott she yearned to waltz with. Even knowing it was an impossible and futile desire.

"Thank you," she said. "I'd be delighted."

Wakefield stayed close, and the two men talked. A short time later a new set began. At the first strains of the waltz, Wakefield offered his arm.

It had been almost two years since Charlotte danced, but her partner made it effortless. For a moment she was aware of watchful eyes around her, and Charlotte wondered if they were monitoring her scandalous self or Wakefield's golden beauty, but then he distracted her.

"How is Scott? How is he really?"

Unfailingly correct, she almost answered as Wakefield led her through a particularly deep turn. She wasn't sure exactly why he was asking. His frown gave an impression of worry.

"He's very even-tempered," she replied.

"Does he laugh?"

Only once. And with few exceptions, his smiles held no real humor. They were—pleasant.

"He smiles, but he doesn't laugh."

"Impatient?"

"Not at all."

"Well, I guess I'd expect him to be patient with you. What about Chetney and Boone? Does he get short with them?"

"No."

"He's got all the hatches battened down, then." Wakefield swung Charlotte through another deep turn. He gave a small jerk of his head, indicating the room. "He must hate all this. It wasn't intentional, but being the spokesperson for the Fund cast Scott in the figurehead role of brave, indomitable warrior."

"He's not a figurehead," Charlotte said. "He's being presented with the Victoria Cross next week. People are honored to speak with him. I've seen how they react. And he's always gracious."

Wakefield grunted. "David doesn't care about all that hero nonsense. He hides it well, but he's not happy."

Those words made a boulder land inside Charlotte's chest. She'd wondered if Scott's circumstances ever made him angry or depressed, but he didn't volunteer such confidences.

"David was always a man who laughed," Wakefield continued. "I've no doubt he enjoys his work, but a man's life should be more than his labors."

Charlotte wished her partner would slow down; the man waltzed at a gallop. "He never makes excuses for himself. He's very matter-of-fact about being crippled."

"He's a strong man." Wakefield's mouth tightened. "A better man than I am. Yet I'm dancing and he's in that damnable chair."

Ah. So Wakefield felt Scott's circumstances strongly. Charlotte gave his hand a quick squeeze. "It's not for us to question God's plan. Your friend seems to be managing well enough."

Right there on the dance floor, Wakefield stopped. Charlotte's momentum carried her into him, and her breath left her with a soft *humpf*. The lord major put his hands on her shoulders and steadied her.

"I didn't see much evidence of God's plan on the battlefield, and *I'm* the reason he's in that chair."

For an instant shock held Charlotte immobile, then she pulled Wakefield to an empty spot at the side of the room and struggled to recall what the *Times* article had said. Scott had stopped during a retreat to assist an injured officer. It was after he'd gotten that officer headed toward safety that he suffered his injuries. So, Wakefield was the injured officer Scott had rescued?

She pulled him with her and put her back to the wall. Facing her, his expression was hidden from the room's other occupants.

"You mustn't blame yourself." Charlotte pitched her voice to sound as fierce as she imagined a commanding officer might. "I don't believe Scott does. He hasn't ever made you feel he blames you, has he?"

"I told you, he's a better man than I." Wakefield's face and body were taut as pulled wire. "If it had been the other way round I'd have detested him."

Charlotte stared at Wakefield's tormented expression, lost for words that might comfort. She finally just squeezed his elbow. His head dropped forward, and he took several deep breaths.

They'd attracted some attention. Charlotte hated the inquisitive looks but ignored them. If this conversation resulted in a re-shredding of her reputation, then so be it. Wakefield's unjustified shame had finally overcome him and prompted him to reveal his deepest feelings. He needed solace. This was too important to censor because of appearances.

"No. You wouldn't have hated him," she said after a moment. "And you'd have done everything in your power to reassure him. I think if Scott knew how you felt he'd be very disturbed."

"He knows I feel remorse. He just doesn't know the degree of my guilt."

"You hide it from him," Charlotte murmured.

"I try to, but it's not easy." Wakefield gave her a narrow-eyed look. "He knows me too well. We were put into the same house room at Eton, and we've been the best of friends ever since." His mouth tightened. "Scott always knew he was for the military, and I decided to follow him. We managed to purchase commissions in the same regiment."

He paused and his lids dropped, effectively shielding his eyes. Charlotte just waited.

"That day...David survived the battle and would have been safe behind our lines if he hadn't come back to help me. *I'm* the reason he lost the use of his legs." Wakefield's head came up, and he searched Charlotte's face. "Night fell, and he was left for dead on the battlefield. I can't even imagine the hell he went through until I found him the next day." Wakefield took a great breath, and a short, harsh laugh erupted from his chest. "He's so bloody independent, he won't let me do anything to help him. He won't even let me talk about it!"

"He lets you be his friend," Charlotte said. "And you can talk to me whenever you like."

Wakefield smoothed his mustache and gave his head a little shake. "Well, I don't know why I chose now to give vent to my guilt, but I feel better having told someone."

#

Charlotte and Wakefield. David couldn't stop watching them, though he knew he should. Yet, why? It was not as if he should worry his attention would draw them additional notice. They certainly weren't attempting any discretion themselves, cozied up next to the wall and engaged in some obviously intense private conversation. A number of other guests showed interest, as evidenced by pointed nods and whispers.

Equal parts shock and chagrin warred within him. Charlotte had convinced him of her sincerity. He'd felt sorry for her, rot it! And here she was, making a spectacle of herself, drawing eyes and conjecture. Perhaps she was indeed as scandalous and cold as the gossip made out.

His body steamed, his tie cinched his neck, and he'd have given anything, *anything*, right then, for legs to carry him out of that stuffy damned ballroom. Or better yet, across to Wakefield and Charlotte so he could ask them just what they thought they were doing, engaging in an intimate conversation in such a public place. Their faces were intense and they stood too, too close. What was wrong with Wakefield anyway? As a gentleman he should be aware his actions would result in criticism and Charlotte would catch the brunt of it.

David swiped the edge of his hand across his mouth. Tonight's guests were here for a charitable purpose, and he hadn't detected any animosity toward Charlotte among them. He'd been watching, and men and women alike had been convivial and respectful. So what was Charlotte doing? Were she and Wakefield now so enamored of each other that they'd lost all propriety and care for Charlotte's patched reputation? Did they care for nothing but their attraction?

"I don't know what put that scowl on your face, but I'd hate to be the cause of it myself."

David looked up to see Lady Etherton's tentative smile. Her lips and cheeks were as pink as the roses that littered the silk of her gown.

He knew the woman to be Charlotte's good friend, and she had been more than gracious to him as hostess as well, so he looked pointedly in the direction of Charlotte and Wakefield. "If your friend the viscountess is really concerned about regaining the good opinion of society, she should take better care of her actions."

Lady Etherton stiffened. "Charlotte wouldn't engage in unseemly behavior. You don't know her."

David was immune to the reprimand. He knew the viscountess better than Lady Etherton appreciated, and more than that he knew Wakefield. Miles was irresistible to women. His golden, Greek-god looks drew them like iron shavings to lodestone. And yet, as much as Miles enjoyed females, David had never known his friend to take unfair advantage of one. He drew in a long breath and centered himself.

"Regardless of how things *are*," he pointed out, loathing the fact, "it's how they're perceived by society that matters. I'd say Lady Haliday knows that better than most. Or should."

He didn't give a damn about society, but that didn't make his pronouncement any less true. Lady Etherton's pained expression confirmed her agreement with his opinion. Then her face cleared. A quick glance showed that Charlotte and Wakefield were making their way back.

Lady Etherton turned. "If you're ready, we'd like to introduce you to the assemblage now."

The plan had been for Lord and Lady Etherton to introduce him as Chairman of the Patriotic Fund's Executive Committee, and David would in turn make a short speech thanking the guests for their donations. All evening he'd been girding himself for this. He wasn't just David Scott any longer, and Lord Etherton would be introducing him as a hero of the highest order. Next week he was being awarded the Victoria Cross. All eyes would be on him, the crippled hero in his wheelchair. He'd best get accustomed to that.

The thought made him grit his teeth. He had his share of citations and medals, but none of them had garnered the kind of attention this Victoria Cross did. He'd seen tears fill the eyes of soft-hearted women. The young just stared slack-jawed and speechless while battle-hardened veterans regarded him with respect. The *Times* touted his bravery on the battlefield and also had the appallingly bad taste to commend him for his current life. Then and now, he only did what he must. He wasn't anyone special. The real heroes were still there, resting under the muddy fields of the Crimea.

Well, perhaps the medal would help him get more donations for the widows and orphans of those brave men. If it did, he could bear being a person of note.

He looked up at the waiting Lady Etherton. "I'm at your service," he said, using the opportunity to practice a smile he didn't feel.

Lord Etherton arrived at the same time as Wakefield and Charlotte. David shot Miles a look and was gratified to see his friend flush. He had every intention of having a few words with Wakefield about his inappropriate tête-à-tête. It was none of David's concern if there was something between his friend and Charlotte, but he'd be damned if he'd watch them at it.

He ignored the surge of hurt that welled up in him. When she'd started working for him she'd managed to rouse his sympathy, but if tonight was representative of her behavior he'd been premature to excuse her. Why in bloody hell had he believed her when she tried to explain away their kiss as something out of the ordinary? Because, he admitted with reluctance, he'd desired her in spite of knowing better. He was as gullible and foolish as Wakefield now appeared. He'd best mind his obligation to the Patriotic Fund instead. If Charlotte began to jeopardize what he was trying to accomplish, he'd simply discharge her. He didn't need the distraction or the aggravation.

The thing of it was, as reluctant as he'd been to take her on, the past few weeks Lady Haliday had proven herself, always prompt and showing nothing but compassion and kindness toward the women and children they were helping. He'd expected arrogance and defensiveness, but she'd shown none—perhaps because she came from new wealth rather than the aristocracy. He didn't know exactly how her father had obtained his seed money, but it was common knowledge he'd started as a laborer.

Yes, that must be it.

"Well, it appears we're ready," Lord Etherton said.

With a wave of his hand, David summoned Boonc over to push his chair to the end of the ballroom. Etherton kept pace.

"I've had a number of people express a desire to meet you, Scott. I suspect your Patriotic Fund coffers are going to see significant growth after tonight."

"I appreciate everything you've done," David replied. "I've had several people indicate an interest in hosting similar festivities."

"Well, it was Lady Haliday who got Lady Etherton to do it. Your thanks are best addressed to her."

David nodded, but he was disinclined to praise Lady Haliday. He had no intention of complimenting her. She had other admirers aplenty.

CHAPTER THIRTEEN

David hated Sundays. The Patriotic Fund offices were closed and the day stretched long and empty in front of him. His brother Julian, his wife Anne, and their children, Edmund, Simon, and Sarah, would be at church services this morning.

The earls of Bridgewaite and their families had worshipped at the Tenbury Wells church for generations, and lingering over his morning coffee David imagined his brother and family sitting in the earl's pew, Simon on the end, fingers tracing the initials that David had carved in the wood so many years before. Julian often joked that Simon took after him. David's nephew admired and often imitated him, certainly. The boy was already a fearless rider. But watching Simon galloping his pony, wooden saber extended as he bellowed with a child's version of blood-curdling yells, didn't make David laugh as it did Simon's mother and father. David didn't want Simon automatically following the drum as the second son frequently did, yet he couldn't find a way to explain his feelings to the others.

He missed the children, Anne, and the comfort of Summerbridge. He even missed Julian, although his brother's worry was enough to drive him to Bedlam. When he'd first arrived home from the Crimea, Julian's protectiveness was welcome, but it became stifling as David's body healed and he struggled for independence. Finally, against Julian's wishes, lame and with little money and no income, David had taken himself to London.

He'd experienced as much trepidation as he'd ever felt facing the enemy. His father had long ago given up the Bridgewaite London townhouse to settle a debt, so David didn't even have the benefit of a family residence. Julian was still struggling to right the muddle in which their father left the estate, and David had been determined not to add to his brother's responsibilities. So the Patriotic Fund

Executive Committee Chairman position was heaven-sent, and with stringent attention to his limited funds David was able to eventually secure a small townhouse and coach, both necessary for his independence. He'd been right to come to London, but days like today made Summerbridge seem very far away.

He heard indistinct voices, the sound of the front door closing, and a confident stride coming down the hall.

"Scott."

"In here, Wakefield," David called.

Miles appeared and tossed a small book down on the table beside him. "Look what a street boy left at my townhouse this morning."

Even before he opened the slim, bright green publication and gazed at the title page, David knew. *A Marriage Most Awkward by Lady G.*

He snapped the book shut and tossed it back on the table, then looked up at grim-faced Wakefield. "It appears you provoked someone who wants to make sure you know who you danced with last night."

"Whoever sent it is vindictive as hell," Wakefield said. "It's been nearly two years since the book first appeared. Of course, since we were in the Crimea, I'd never actually seen it."

"We knew all about the commotion it caused from the newspapers, though."

Wakefield poured himself a cup of coffee and sat down. "I hope the long conversation I had with her last night didn't bring any of this back for anyone. I know I appropriated her attention, but I didn't think we attracted undue notice."

"You must be joking." David struggled to rein in his temper, but he couldn't deny that Wakefield's guilt gave him a little spark of gladness. "What were you thinking, cuddling up with her like that? The two of you are probably the topic of discussion at every breakfast table this morning."

Wakefield straightened. His rising coffee cup reversed course and hit its saucer with a clink. "We weren't 'cuddling up.' We had a brief conversation and were completely decorous."

David clenched his fists. "It appeared inappropriate to *me*, Miles, and now someone's seen fit to dredge up all the gossip about her, at least to you." He indicated the novel with a jut of his chin.

Wakefield turned away, and David watched a muscle tic near his friend's eye. Miles looked like a man who'd had too much champagne and not enough sleep.

Clouting Wakefield further probably wasn't warranted, but oh, David wanted to. "Just where did you go after the ball last night? Not to bed, I daresay."

Wakefield turned back, his brown eyes razor sharp. "I took the viscountess home then went to a club."

Something hard and base ran through David. He pictured Charlotte and Wakefield together in a private coach before he claimed to have left her and gone to a club. What kind of club? A gaming club? Or was 'club' a euphemism for a bawdy house? Had Wakefield found a whore with black hair and blue eyes and imagined Charlotte's face and arms? *Christ!* An icy sliver twisted deep into David's core.

He laughed harshly and tunneled his hand through his hair, then found himself saying, "She works for the Fund, and I don't want her scandalous history dragged up again. You'd best treat her like your grandmother when you're in public."

Wakefield's eyes narrowed. "I'll tell you once more. There was nothing improper about the conversation I had with Lady Haliday."

"Well, it *looked* improper as hell! If it was so innocent, why did you look so guilty afterwards?"

"Because we were talking about you!"

Taken aback, David stared. "About me?"

Wakefield scrubbed his face with his hands then raised his head and took a big breath. "I told her a bit about you, about how you were injured."

That intense conversation had been about *him*? David wanted to grab Wakefield and shake him until he spewed forth every exchanged word. Instead, he forced his fists open, spread his fingers and wiggled them, encouraging blood into the digits.

In all honesty, he wasn't surprised or angry that Charlotte and Wakefield had talked about his crippled legs. Early on, he realized people were curious about him. But David clamped his teeth together. He *would not* ask if Charlotte had expressed pity. Bad enough to think of Wakefield and Charlotte discussing him, which brought back the lack of confidence he'd worked so hard to overcome after his injury.

He stared Wakefield down and felt a dull satisfaction when Miles averted his eyes. "You'd best go," David said. "I don't want to know any more."

Looking grim, Wakefield went.

\#

David's stomach growled, and he rubbed his hand over it. They'd been busy with their individual duties since arriving this Monday morning and it was past time for luncheon.

Ordinarily, the Fund staff all ate together around Chetney's desk. It had become a highlight of David's day over the past weeks, even though the respite provided equal measures torture and delight. He'd been having the devil of a time keeping his eyes off Charlotte's lips—hardly gentlemanly behavior, especially given his position as her superior. He was usually able to drag his eyes away, but invariably they landed on her eyes, her bosom, her hair, her neck… Oh, blast! There wasn't any part of her he didn't want to look at. He'd been successfully hiding the fact, but it was difficult always being on guard. It certainly didn't aid his digestion.

He looked up when he heard the rustle of her skirt. Charlotte's smile hit him like a cannon shot to the chest.

"I'm thrilled," she announced, "with the donations pledged at the ball."

It pleased David, knowing Charlotte so enjoyed participating in the administration of the Fund, and he was inclined to forget all the annoyance he'd felt at the ball. After all, the talk had been about him. Better yet, she seemed relaxed and comfortable these days. He recognized the easy camaraderie they'd acquired over the last few weeks as something to be treasured. He didn't think he'd ever really had a lady friend. Not a close one, anyway, whom he saw and worked with every day.

Friend? his brain mocked. If only his *too* friendly, rather carnal thoughts weren't continually calling him out as a liar.

"Your hard work paid off brilliantly," he said, deciding she deserved praise after all. He couldn't deny everything she'd done to make the ball a success.

"I think ours is becoming a very popular cause. Not surprising, since the Queen and Prince Albert were the first patrons."

"Just as important, it's worthy," David pointed out.

"Yes, it is, and I'm so proud. I wanted to do something valuable, and this *is*."

Her lashes swept down, and the crests of her cheeks turned rosy. Probably she felt embarrassment at sharing her feelings. David quashed his smile. "I feel the same way. One can always be proud of working hard and doing one's best, but knowing your work has helped improve someone else's life…? There's a very special pride in doing that."

His own words gave him pause. When he'd first landed in this damnable chair, he'd thought he faced an ineffectual life. He'd almost given up on everything. Thank God he was a stubborn son of a bitch. He'd been so wrong. This work made him as proud as anything ever could.

"You're right." Charlotte nodded, looking easy again. "I'm so thankful to be here."

He hadn't wanted her. Forced to hire her, he'd been infuriated. Now, the other night's frustration aside, he couldn't imagine life without her. She was wonderful in the office with the women and children. Which reminded him…

He waved her forward. "Come in and sit down. I need a bit of help with something, if you have no objection."

She settled into the chair just in front of his desk, and he caught a tantalizing whiff of roses and jasmine. He inhaled deeply.

"What can I help with?"

He retrieved the uppermost sheet of paper from the stack atop his desk and slid it across to her. "A Mrs. Peter Carroll would like to make an appointment. She intends to give us a rather nice donation, and she has a few questions about how the funds will be used. Would you mind meeting with her?"

Charlotte picked up the paper. She looked puzzled. "You always see the donors."

Until now, he had.

"Mrs. Carroll has requested that she meet with someone other than myself." Even though he'd once sat at her table, shared laughter, food and friendship with her and Peter. But that was before Peter secured his promise to keep a brotherly eye on Edith and died in his arms. It was a promise David was having the devil of a time keeping, since Edith would have nothing to do with him.

Charlotte made a little noise. "What? What do you mean?"

She sounded highly offended. For him. That eased a bit of the strain thinking and talking about Edith always caused him. David sighed…and found he wanted to tell her everything.

"Peter Carroll, Wakefield and I met at Eton. All three of us were younger sons of titled fathers and immediately became fast friends. We did everything together." From sports to studies to practical jokes, it had been always the three of them.

"When we finished school, we banged around Europe a while then joined the army. We couldn't believe our luck when we found three cornet commissions available in the Eleventh Hussars. We'd desperately wanted the cavalry but never dared dream we'd find places in the same regiment." The occasion had necessitated a celebration, during which a state of thorough drunkenness was achieved and never again surpassed.

"Settling into the cavalry was like settling into our favorite old saddles. Miles and I made good officers. Peter was in a class unto himself. The men under his command adored him. He said it suited him as nothing ever had.

"Then he met Edith. I stood up with him at their wedding, and I'd never seen a happier couple. Edith didn't like army life, but she knew how much Peter loved it and for a while everything was fine. We were stationed at Hounslow then, escorting the Queen. Nothing really changed after we moved to Norwich. We were gaining experience and rank. Peter was an extraordinary officer and leader, and clever. Everyone knew he'd have an exceptional career."

"What happened?"

Charlotte's question pulled David from his cache of memories. Thank God. From here on he'd best just recite the facts, or there was no telling what he'd end up doing and saying.

"We received orders for Dublin, and Edith didn't want to go. She wanted Peter to resign and work for her father in his import business. The arguments were endless, and Peter was miserable. He didn't want to sell out, but eventually he reconciled himself to it." David paused as the all-too-familiar cloak of guilt settled over him. "I talked him out of it."

He barely registered Charlotte's little sound of distress. He'd been aghast that Peter would give up the life he so loved, and what promised to be a phenomenal career. It didn't bear considering that the army would lose such a man. Only, he should have minded his own business. Peter hadn't survived their first big battle. Edith had accused him of playing God when, months after her husband's death, David went to see her. It was his first time out in public in his chair, the first time he left Summerbridge. He'd only managed it because he'd felt compelled to see her. Edith hadn't even invited him in. She'd stood in the doorway, oozing bitterness and anger, and blamed him for her husband's death. Every moment was torment.

"He fell at Alma. We'd landed at Varna only three months before."

David wasn't really aware of Charlotte moving until he felt her hand on his shoulder. Then he looked up into her eyes. The pain that had risen with his recollections drained away.

"Edith hates me, of course."

Charlotte squeezed his shoulder, and warmth spread through him like drinking hot mulled wine on a bleak winter day. "Of course I'll meet with her," she said. Her tongue darted out and moistened her lips before she added, "I-I didn't know Peter, but he wouldn't have stayed in Her Majesty's service if he hadn't wanted to, would he?"

No. Peter had wanted David to change his mind. Of course he had. Even after he'd made the decision to stay and had an unholy row with Edith, he'd been smiling and good-humored. He'd said he'd shed an elephant from his back.

"But he wasn't supposed to die," David said.

"No, he wasn't," Charlotte agreed.

CHAPTER FOURTEEN

David received his own copy of Lady Garret's little novel in the Tuesday morning post. Chetney brought it in, a pained look on his face, one hand still clutching the paper wrap he'd removed. David accepted the silk-covered volume, anger springing to life. The sender could only want him to think badly of Charlotte—as the sender had likely wanted with Miles.

He certainly would have hidden it if he'd heard her, but his secretary had not yet turned to leave when the rustle of her skirts alerted him to Charlotte's presence. She glided through the doorway and stopped, eyes wide and riveted on the slender book in his hand. Her gaze lifted to his face, and David's stomach fell.

"It arrived in the morning post." He dropped the book onto the far side of his desk and held Charlotte's gaze. "You can take it if you like."

Charlotte backed up a step. "No." She opened her mouth as if to say more but then shut it. She glanced away, blinked, then looked back and studied him, a tiny furrow between her brows. "Who sent it?"

Chetney handed over the wrapping and retreated to his office. David glanced at the brown paper and then held it up for Charlotte to see. It bore only his own name and address.

#

Charlotte stared at the dark, angular script, trying to make sense of the book being here. Heat enveloped her; her heart pounded and threatened to overwhelm her senses.

She raised a shaky hand to her throat but quickly lowered it. Scott would think her feeble if he noticed her trembling. Was there never an end to her shame? A few days ago she'd been unbearably tense as she waited to see what kind of greeting she'd receive from the Patriotic Fund ball patrons. The relief at their lack of attention had been staggering. She'd thought society was ready to consign her scandal to the past, but here was evidence of the false reprieve. Lady Garret wasn't done meting out torture.

She stared at the mocking, bright green cover, tingling as if the baroness had slapped her. A deluge of anger drowned out everything else. She wanted to grab *A Marriage Most Awkward* and bash it against the wall. It was so unfair! She'd done nothing—*nothing*—to deserve Lady Garret's destruction of her reputation.

"It was Baroness Garret?" Scott asked.

Charlotte's very marrow recognized Lady Garret's hand in the direction. "Of course it was."

"Ah. Wakefield got one, too."

Charlotte heard quiet sympathy in Scott's voice, and she wondered if she could contain the fury that boiled through her. His face bore a pained look, and that helped. She felt his kindness cooling her rage.

"Were you expecting this?" he asked.

Expecting the baroness's little book to make another appearance? "No."

She hadn't expected the devastation she felt when she saw Scott holding it, either. How foolish she'd been, thinking the armor she'd forged in the country strong enough to protect her.

She sat down in the empty chair facing Scott's desk, and an irrational desire to tell him the whole story swept through her. Jane was the only person she'd confided in, and even Jane didn't know *all* of it. Charlotte had been too humiliated.

The surge of longing was foolish. Even if David Scott's strength could easily encompass and support her, she couldn't bear to reveal how meek and half-witted she'd been. How could he hear her story and not think less of her?

#

David wished she'd do something: curse or cry or grab the damned book and tear it to pieces. Instead she sat with hands clasped tight, her full lips pressed into a thin line, spine straight and unsupported by the ladder-back behind her.

Her countenance was so composed that it made him ache. Only her eyes were not. They spoke of confusion and hurt, and much as he wanted to ignore their message David found he couldn't. He understood how it felt to be helpless and angry. Once home from the Crimea, he'd cursed, thrown things, and piled abuse on Boone. There had been a time of drunkenness and despair, of blaming God. He'd thoroughly frightened his brother, but Julian had refused to let him go to Hades and he'd worked his way through it.

The tense, contained woman before him needed to work her way through this, maybe even by confiding in him…but he knew she wouldn't. He couldn't expect her to either, not when he'd never shared his own trials. Charlotte had no way of knowing he still found each day a struggle. Just getting into the building required effort, and his prospects for true happiness… What would she think if she knew how he resented Wakefield's flirting and dancing with her?

He reached forward and picked up the little book. "I've never read it," he assured her as he smoothed his hand over the silken cover.

The look of defeat in her eyes smote him as effectively as the saber he took at Balaclava. Helplessness assailed him.

I must do *something*.

He opened the book, grasped the first few pages, ripped them out and tossed the paper into the brass waste receptacle beside his desk. He kept going, and it didn't take long to work his way through the book and turn it into a heap of tumbled trash. Next he located a cache of matches in his desk drawer and extracted one. As soon as it flared, he pitched it into the waiting pile. The flames soon licked up the sides of the receptacle and fully devoured the contents.

Chetney came in, saw the situation and began waving his arms about in an attempt to dissipate the thickening smoke. He went to the window and after a brief struggle raised the sash. Then he began waving at the smoke.

"Couldn't you have waited until you got outside?" he asked.

David heard Charlotte chuckle. He looked up and found her fingers pressed to her grinning mouth, eyes alight. He grinned back, and suddenly they were both laughing, huge, belly-shaking laughs that made ebullience swell his chest near to bursting. The encounter left him gasping, and quite certain that Charlotte Haliday's eyes were as lovely as spring bluebells.

#

At last. She was home.

Charlotte did no more than nod to Beckham and hurried up the stairs to her bedroom. Rebecca followed, but Charlotte dismissed her.

She'd never seen Scott grin or laugh like that. She'd been unable to tear her gaze away. Her buzzing awareness of him had only increased, and all day his laughing face kept coming back and making her smile. How it had transformed his visage! And there was more. She hadn't offered him any explanations, yet without hesitation or qualification Scott had championed her today. The way he'd immediately destroyed that book, his obvious outrage that Charlotte had been subjected to such a thing… She'd grown so warm, once she returned to her desk she had to apply her fan. Scott *believed* in her. Believed her a person of value.

She remembered his laughing face, his blue eyes glinting, the corners of his eyes crinkling, and her own persistent, humming awareness. She feared she had come to think of him in a manner most like a lover, and that wasn't what she wanted, even if she did feel an excitement in it that was completely novel. Completely hopeful. David Scott made her feel renewed and left her breathless and lightheaded, the way she imagined she'd be if she could actually waltz with him, dance and twirl while holding him so close she could feel his heat. But she didn't think she still believed in love. Not for herself. She couldn't imagine offering up her heart to anyone. She wasn't brave enough.

Scott seemed such an admirable man, but he was still just a man. She would never again succumb to the whimsy of romance. It was mostly insubstantial.

She did believe in friendship, however. And though she'd never had a man as bosom-friend, she couldn't help but think she and Scott might develop such an unusual attachment. A close connection with Scott would have substance, would make it possible to bear the tribulations of this senseless attraction.

Love might be no longer possible for her, but perhaps happiness was.

CHAPTER FIFTEEN

"My lady?"

Charlotte kept her attention on the letter she was penning. She spent a portion of each day writing to Fund widows who lived outside of London. She'd already acquired a fondness for a number of her correspondents, and her small, spartan office with its modest desk was becoming a place of pleasure. Today she'd sat down, swept her gaze around the unadorned room and wondered at the sense of contentment it gave her.

"Yes?"

She expected the secretary to offer tea, but when he remained quiet she lifted her head. He slid through the doorway and closed the door. Placing his palms flat on the desktop, he leaned forward, stretching across the scarred wood surface.

"It's the Earl of Bridgewaite, my lady. Mr. Scott's brother."

Surprise and curiosity brought Charlotte to her feet. "Did you tell him Mr. Scott's not expected until later?" He was attending the Patriotic Fund's Royal Commission meeting, and they didn't expect him at the office until afternoon.

"Yes, but I thought you might like to meet him," Chetney said. "And I don't know if you'll have another opportunity. I asked him to wait in the reception area."

Charlotte gave the secretary a grateful smile and made her way to the front.

Unexpectedly, the sight of the tall nobleman brought her up short. It was oddly hurtful to see him, a man so like Scott in appearance, standing. He was older yet presented a more carefree appearance. His light brown hair was tousled, his face unguarded. Charlotte wondered if the brothers were of a like height. Even as tall and robust as the earl was, Scott's shoulders were broader.

Bridgewaite smiled, removed his hat and gave her a little bow. A sudden catch in Charlotte's throat had her clearing it. Instinctively she knew the earl's self-assured grace had been shared by his brother.

"Lady Haliday?"

"How do you do, Lord Bridgewaite? I'm afraid Mr. Scott isn't here."

"Yes, Mr. Chetney was kind enough to inform me."

"You're here for the ceremony tomorrow, of course." Scott had been closed-mouthed about the medal presentations, but the *London Gazette* and her own father had provided details. A vast amphitheatre of seats had been erected in Hyde Park. The Queen herself would present the newly created medal to the sixty-two recipients at a grand ceremony. Twelve-thousand attendees were expected.

The earl nodded. "I don't often get to London, but I've brought the entire family for this. The children are excited beyond belief. We're all very proud."

"Oh, children? How old are they?"

The earl's eyes sparked with pride. "Edmund is ten, Simon is eight, and Sarah is four."

"I believe there'll be seating near the front for recipients' families. You should have a good view of the proceedings. I hope I'll be able to obtain a good seat, too."

An unexpected dart of anger made Charlotte look away from the earl. Her father would be seated in a section reserved for Members of Parliament, but she herself had received no special invitation—surely thanks to the damage Lady Garret had done to her reputation. She planned to go early and obtain the best seat she could. She wanted to see the Queen pin the medal on Scott.

"But you must join Lady Bridgewaite and myself, Lady Haliday."

Charlotte started. It would certainly be enjoyable to have the companionship of Scott's family during the proceedings. Had Scott discussed her with his brother? Did the earl know of her reputation and it simply did not matter to him? Not by voice or expression did he betray the slightest hesitation.

"Oh, that would be delightful! If you're quite sure?"

"Of course I am. And you must join us afterwards. You and Mr. Chetney. We're planning a little celebration at the hotel. We've invited Lord Wakefield, too."

Bridgewaite indeed seemed very certain. Within a few minutes they had the details settled, and Scott's brother took his leave. As he did, the loneliness and touch of self-pity Charlotte had been feeling were completely dispelled. She couldn't recall the last time she'd felt such anticipation. She wanted David Scott to see how grateful his queen and his country were. It was only right for the assemblage to recognize him as a true hero.

#

David sat at attention, waiting his turn. Bloody hell, but he hated this. Hated being on display. They'd wanted him back in uniform for the presentation. He wore the colors easily; his very bones knew the weight of them. And at least he was surrounded by comrades, and even another Cherry Picker, Lieutenant Dunn.

They were calling up the Navy and Royal Marines first, and then they would move on to the Army. David's regiment, the 11th Hussars, was third in order of precedence. It wouldn't be long.

He scanned the family seating, looking for Julian, Anne and the children. Lady Haliday was with them. He'd almost given up when... *There.* They sat near the top of the closest section of inclined seats.

As if he could tell his uncle's eyes were on him, Edmund waved. David nodded and turned back to the proceedings.

A colorful spectacle of waving flags, military men, horses and observers stretched in every direction. The smell of gunpowder from the artillery's royal salute still drifted in the air. As Lord Panmure read each name, the men were summoned forward to the Queen, who sat a good-looking roan, her red coat, black shirt and plumed hat distinctive and stylish. A small table, draped with a scarlet cloth, held the medals. As each man came forward, the Queen bent from her saddle and pinned the Cross to his chest.

In the past David had participated in a military review for the Queen, but he'd never been this close to his sovereign. He'd certainly never known her touch or had her pay homage to him. Today that was happening in front of thousands.

Lord Panmure suddenly called out, "Major David Scott, Eleventh Hussars," and Boone pushed his chair forward. But a problem was immediately apparent. Seated as he was, the Queen couldn't reach his chest.

"Please excuse us," she said, and looked at her husband. Prince Albert gave his wife a kind look and dismounted. He took the Cross from the Queen's hand, looked David square in the eye, pinned the Cross to his chest, and saluted. The Queen extended her black-gloved hand. Stunned, David took her fingertips and bowed his head.

The next man in line was called, and Boone wheeled David away to the accompaniment of cheering and applause.

He was glad he'd worn his uniform. He was a military man. The Cross was meant to hang on his uniform coat, eclipsing every brass button, every other medal and every bit of braid by sheer presence. David rubbed his fingers over it, the crimson ribbon and curved metal relief, thinking of the captured Russian guns that had been melted down for the bronze. Quite possibly this medal had come from the very cannon that had fired upon him.

David let his hand fall and looked out to where his family and the viscountess sat. He'd be waiting through the remaining medal presentations and the parade of troops. They'd assembled what looked to be four thousand men behind him. He expected there'd be additional band music, too.

So, here he was, a cavalryman who could no longer sit a horse. The act he'd been decorated for—which had saved Wakefield's life—he'd done without thought. He felt no more a hero now than he had before. Danger was inherent in battle. When under fire he didn't weigh risks before acting, and he hadn't before going back for Wakefield, either. It seemed odd, knowing others considered him one of the bravest of men.

How did Charlotte Haliday see him? Thinking of her, the words on the Victoria Cross seemed mocking. Shouldn't a man capable of earning such a medal face all risk with bravery? He should be the kind of man who didn't give up. Yet when he looked at Charlotte, Viscountess Haliday, David acknowledged there were parts of his life he had definitely abandoned, that he'd been far too unsure to pursue.

Was it for the best?

#

This is what a family is like.

Charlotte gazed about the dinner table with a sense of wonder. She couldn't recall ever sharing a meal with a child, but Scott's brother made it clear he wanted his progeny present at the family celebration. The three children's faces were alight with excitement, and the adoration for their uncle was easily observed.

Bridgewaite and his family had taken a suite at the luxurious Cavendish Hotel, and the earl had arranged for the use of a private dining room. Bridgewaite and Scott sat at opposite ends of the table. Lord Wakefield, Mr. Chetney and Charlotte sat on one side, the countess and the children on the other. Every few minutes one or more of the three erupted with laughter.

The quivering shimmer of the chandelier seemed to have taken up residence inside Charlotte. She'd never seen Scott as happy as he appeared tonight. Just watching him filled her with a marvelous sense of rightness. His eyes crinkled at the corners, and masculine slashes scored his cheeks. His whole person seemed to smile.

He wore his uniform, which increased his unfamiliarity. Charlotte tried not to stare, but even with her most concerted efforts she couldn't drag her gaze away for more than a few seconds. Rather than the red coat she was accustomed to seeing troops wear, Scott wore the navy coat and scarlet pants of the 11th Hussars. His Victoria Cross dangled from its crimson ribbon, dominating a chest already heavy with decorations. His blue coat intensified the blue of his eyes, and each time their gazes met, confusion swamped her. She found the serious, contained man she worked with each day immensely appealing, but this new, laughing Scott left her giddy.

"Did the Queen smile at you, Uncle David?" asked Simon, the middle child. With his straight posture and auburn hair, the boy resembled his uncle. And if Scott had given the same smile he was flashing now, how could the Queen have resisted?

"She didn't smile at me," Scott replied, "but she did favor Prince Albert with one."

Simon's eyes widened. "He saluted you, Uncle David."

"The Prince bestowed a great honor upon your uncle and the others," said Lord Wakefield, who had also participated in the parade. He too was in uniform. "I'm glad I was a part of it—one of the last services I'll perform before mustering out."

"The Queen honored you today, but it's the nation that paid homage," Bridgewaite spoke up.

Scott nodded. "I'll try to spread a bit of the tribute I received to the families benefiting from the Royal Patriotic Fund."

Charlotte smiled. He was already doing that. She couldn't recall a single person who'd left the Fund office not feeling better and prouder than when they arrived. She'd watched widows and children transform before her eyes. Haliday had killed her trust of humanity, yet each time she looked into Scott's eyes Charlotte saw a man without equal. He made her feel things to which she feared giving name.

Somehow, the four-year-old Sarah's saucy voice managed to pipe out louder than all the adults. "Why do you keep staring at Uncle David?"

Everyone stilled, and Charlotte froze. She didn't have to look to know the little girl's eyes were trained on her. Embarrassment swamped her, and she'd have melted away if not for Scott's steady regard, his dark eyes full of a kind of lightness that eased a good deal of her mortification. Little Sarah's announcement hadn't discomfited him. He'd *liked* it.

"Sarah." The censure in the little girl's mother's voice caused Sarah's head to whip around. "Apologize to Lady Haliday at once. It's impolite to accuse ladies of staring."

The little girl's mischievous look disappeared. Her little white teeth crimped her lower lip and she bowed her head. "Please excuse me, my lady."

Oh dear, she had to say *something* to excuse Sarah. Even better if she could move them past the awkward revelation.

"It's just," Charlotte began, "that I'm not accustomed to seeing him in uniform, Sarah. He looks rather splendid, doesn't he?"

Sarah's head came up, an expression of relief replacing her worried frown. Her gaze swept the table and, apparently satisfied she was no longer in trouble, the child giggled. Then the next course arrived, which served to distract everyone.

Determined to keep her gaze off Scott for the remainder of the evening, Charlotte dared one quick last look. His direct regard startled her. His eyes narrowed, his attention so intent that everything else faded away for Charlotte. He wasn't making any attempt to be discreet; he just looked. Her heart gave a thump and began racing.

His face tightened, and she recognized what was happening. They'd both been hiding the attraction they felt, and now they'd recognized it in each other. Warmth stole through her and became a heaviness that settled and grew into a physical yearning.

Oh, blast. That fire had been banked, smothered into a mass of glowing embers, but this exchange had fanned it back into a blaze. She was at a dinner table, surrounded by people, and her body was responding in the most sexual way to Scott's look.

Scott drew in a deep breath, and his chest lifted, making several brass buttons glint. Charlotte tore her gaze away and swept it around the table. The children were absorbed in their meals. The rest were being entertained by watching her and Scott. Wakefield was frowning. Chetney looked ready to burst with joy. Bridgewaite smiled, but his wife looked stunned and not particularly happy.

Charlotte tore a piece of bread from the slice before her, popped it into her mouth and then wondered if she'd ever be able to swallow. She took a sip of wine, peeked up and…found everyone looking natural. Scott's attention had been captured by his two nephews, and on each side of her, by design or providence, Chetney and Bridgewaite ignored her.

She'd weathered many dinner parties and soirees as the center of speculation and gossip, and she'd survived. Lately she'd thought the experience might actually have made her stronger. But none of that had exposed her the way she'd felt exposed tonight, captured in the grip of Scott's fervor. Tomorrow, when she saw him, she'd be meeting a man she'd not known before. The thought of it excited her and filled her with trepidation.

Then she remembered he'd be seeing her differently, too. Now he knew her secret.

CHAPTER SIXTEEN

The next morning, Charlotte arrived at the Fund office just as Scott's carriage pulled up. She hadn't slept well, her body too restless to relax, her mind full of images of him. She hadn't intended to divulge her admiration at dinner, but she'd revealed that and so very much more. No matter how she'd tried to ignore the attraction she felt these past few weeks, she hadn't been able to get their kiss out of her mind. And after last night, she had reason to think Scott felt similar.

Which just made the situation worse. Scott deserved better than a woman incapable of love. And knowing he wanted her made it all the harder to resist seeking what happiness she could.

She hesitated as Boone retrieved Scott's wheelchair. Would Scott feel self-conscious if she stood and waited for him as he lowered himself into it? Would he find her rude if she went inside and didn't wait?

The urge to watch him maneuver between coach and chair was strong. The look of strength and determination that overtook him at such times fascinated Charlotte, but it also lodged a rock-hard knot in her chest. She found it impossible to look away from the bulges of his arm and back muscles, and today she feared more than ever what her face might reveal.

She turned and stepped briskly toward the entrance. A small, scruffy black dog sat squarely before her, impeding her progress.

Charlotte grasped the door handle and pulled a little bit, but the dog didn't move. She couldn't open the door without hitting him.

"Hello there. Might I go in?"

The dog did not respond. Warily, Charlotte pulled the door even more until it bumped against the rump of the beast...who did not appear offset.

He appeared friendly, at least. His alert brown eyes peeked up at her through a cascading tangle of hair, his pink tongue displayed as he panted. The moment she'd spoken, his tail began wagging. The longer she looked, the faster it wagged.

She pulled a little harder on the door, and then he did move, standing up on his back legs, his front legs pawing the air. He barked twice, a surprisingly deep, husky bark for such a small dog.

"Yes, you're very funny," she muttered, "but this won't do at all."

The dog made an appealing picture in spite of his tangled coat. His upright ears, covered with drooping hair, gave him a comical appearance. And, there went the tail again.

A sharp whistle rent the air, and the dog responded immediately, darting away.

"Having trouble?" Scott asked from behind her. He sat in his chair at the foot of the ramp, Boone behind him. The dog now stood close, sniffing his leg.

Scott extended his hand. After the dog sniffed it, he rubbed the beast's head. Boone pushed Scott up the ramp, the dog trotting alongside.

The animal seemed well-behaved, but Charlotte had no doubt he was homeless. Perhaps Chetney would have a biscuit or two they could give him. Even the stray's long hair didn't hide how lean he was.

"Boone, if you'll grab the dog, the viscountess can hold the door and I'll push myself through," Scott said.

"I thought I might find something for him to eat," Charlotte said.

"Her."

"What?"

"She's a bitch." Scott frowned and contemplated the dog, which sat looking between him and Charlotte, who reached down and ran her hand over the beast's dark coat, finding it as matted as she'd suspected. Under the hair she could feel every rib.

"She's starving," she said. "The poor thing."

Scott's frown grew into a scowl. "Well, she can't come in. If we feed her, we'll never get rid of her." He must have seen Charlotte's surprise and flushed a bit, but his mouth firmed. "There are ten homeless dogs for every person in this city. This one's not even a decent ratter, or she'd have some meat on her bones."

Scott's rejection made Charlotte want to hug the lonely-looking dog. "I like her."

"Well, she's a fleabag." He rubbed the top of the dog's head again, and suddenly he seemed more resigned and regretful than disapproving. "She looks like she's got Skye Terrier in her, but she's a mongrel. No telling where she came from—or where she's been. Definitely not a dog for you."

Charlotte could tell from his expression and tone he expected their conversation to end there. And, no doubt he was right. Viscountesses owned purebred dogs. They obtained them from breeders, not from the streets of London. Yet Scott was making a rather large—and wrong—assumption about her.

She opened the door to the Fund offices. "I guess you've forgotten I was born the daughter of a tradesman, a man some consider a scoundrel. I don't require a carefully bred, pampered dog. I like this one just fine."

Funny thing, too. She hadn't wanted a dog before now. But something about this beast's watchful expression made her want to care for it.

Scott looked up at her and sighed. "Then you'd best see if Chetney has something you can feed her."

He signaled Boone to push him in. Rather than enter alongside him, the dog brushed against Charlotte's skirt and looked up at her.

"It appears it's your lucky day," she said. And hers too. The dog had served as a distraction. She'd been able to greet Scott without embarrassment. He'd seemed just as determined to ignore what had transpired between them last night. Of course, the relief she felt didn't completely dispel her uneasiness.

Tail wagging, the dog kept perfect pace as Charlotte followed Scott inside. Within minutes Chetney had produced a water bowl and a biscuit that was quickly crunched into oblivion.

Charlotte went into her small office to finish the correspondence she'd left. Her first appointment was at one o'clock. As soon as she settled behind her desk, though, the dog came straight to her side. Charlotte rubbed its silky head. She fondled the dog's furry ears and nearly laughed as its canine eyes drifted closed.

"Hello again, sweetie. You need a name, don't you?"

As soon as she stopped rubbing, the dog slipped under Charlotte's desk, circled, lay down atop her toes and gave a great sigh. No doubt the rug there had attracted the animal, but Charlotte found the warmth of the dog's body wonderfully comforting.

#

David considered his watch then tucked it back in his waistcoat pocket. It was nearly time to close the office. He couldn't recollect a longer day, listening to Lady Haliday speaking in dulcet tones to that flea-bit little minx. She'd found a length of twine and taken the beast outside several times, and if he wasn't mistaken, at noontime she had purchased it a meat pie.

He couldn't get yesterday out of his mind. No matter how hard he tried to concentrate on his work, memories of the viscountess's face and form kept intruding. He couldn't be wrong about the regard he'd seen in her eyes.

He knew widows who engaged in discreet affairs. Society turned a blind eye, preserving the ladies' reputations, and after yesterday he dared think Lady Haliday might accept if he made such a proposal.

He'd never considered himself a man beset with daydreams, but since yesterday his lustful imaginings had crowded out everything else. He'd wrestled with his desire since he'd first looked into her wondrous eyes and realized her boldness hid determined bravado, and yesterday evening that desire metamorphosed into a craving impossible to ignore. Listening to her coo to the dog wasn't helping.

Damnation! Scott closed his eyes and leaned back against his chair. Exactly how did one conduct an affair when unable to walk? Thank God for his one intact femur. At least he was capable of getting into bed and undressing himself. The problem was putting a woman in the bed. There was no such thing as discretion when his arrival and departure required orchestration by attendants. So he couldn't go to her.

And she couldn't come to his residence. Such a thing would be considered brazen, and society would never turn a blind eye to that. He could rent a small cottage for liaisons, but how exactly did he invite her there? It sounded presumptuous and awkward beyond belief.

He rubbed his hands up and down his legs. His right thigh was strongly muscled, but below that and his whole left leg were anything but attractive. Although they had a small amount of movement and had retained much of their feeling, his appendages appeared as weak and useless as doll's.

Well, he'd simply not remove his trousers. If he had the opportunity, that was.

Even keeping his legs hidden, she might still find him repugnant. His arms, chest and shoulders were heavily muscled now—far more so than was fashionable. Rather than portraying the refined look of the gentleman he was, his torso had the bulk of a man accustomed to heavy labor. Still, after last night he was willing to risk her rejection, even her revulsion at his condition. She might feel differently when faced with intimacy, but right now…well, he knew desire when he saw it. And his family did too. Last night every person at the dinner table had seen the connection between Charlotte and himself.

Would she find the offer of a liaison insulting? Maybe with another man, but he wasn't fit to offer marriage and she should know as much. As hard as he strove to be independent, he wasn't and never would be. Any woman he wed would find herself shackled by his limitations. Even Lydia, whom he knew had loved him, couldn't face life as the wife of a cripple. He'd just arrived home from the front, in the grip of despair and pain, when she broke their engagement. He didn't blame her.

In the outer office someone was speaking to Chetney, and David began rolling his chair toward the door. Who could be making an appearance at this late time of day? Whoever it was, the voice was deep and unfamiliar.

By the time he reached the door, Charlotte had joined Chetney and the visitor. The tall, well-dressed gentleman turned, allowing David a view of intense dark blue eyes under a broad forehead and a proud beak of a nose in a chiseled face.

"Mister Scott, may I present my father, Matthew Shelby? Father, this is Mister David Scott. And this," the viscountess continued, extending her hand, "is Mister Chetney."

Shelby gave the secretary a nod then stepped forward to shake David's hand. "I'm delighted to meet you, Scott. Congratulations. I was at yesterday's ceremony."

Of course he would have been. The man was a prominent member of Parliament.

"A pleasure to meet you," David said. "I'm fortunate to have Lady Haliday working with me. She's a great help."

Instead of the pleased look David expected, Shelby's expression shifted to distinct annoyance.

"I can't say I'm happy with the situation," the man said. "I'm sure you're doing wonderful things here, Scott, but my daughter shouldn't be part of them. Since she hasn't yet come to her senses, I came to get a look at the place."

David stifled the urge to make a biting retort. Shelby had been sharp as fresh rhubarb, but that didn't mean Charlotte would approve of a challenge. Her face, which had turned pink with David's compliment, now flushed red. She stiffened like a wary pupil before a stern headmaster.

David turned back to her father. Although Lady Haliday wasn't doing the typical aristocrat's charitable work, he doubted anyone in society knew exactly what she did here. So, why did her father object? The work pleased her. She came early and stayed late. Despite her title, she had a way of putting women at ease and comforting them. Perhaps David's biggest surprise had been the way their faces calmed after talking with her.

With a bark, their disheveled canine guest scampered into the room. Everyone watched as it plopped down beside Charlotte.

Shelby frowned. "What the devil is that mongrel doing here?"

"She's my dog." Charlotte's expression didn't reveal a thing, but the defensive edge to her voice conveyed much.

"Charlotte, are you addle-pated? The beast looks infested with creepers."

The viscountess crouched down, gathered the dog into her arms, and stood. "I only just found her today. She needs to be bathed and brushed."

David got Chetney's attention and jerked his head toward the door. The secretary looked fascinated, but as far as David was concerned the man needn't be privy to an argument between Charlotte and her father.

Chetney looked down, muttered, "Excuse me," and left.

Shelby stepped forward, towering head and shoulders above his daughter, and gazed down his nose at her. Charlotte stood her ground but was forced to tilt her head back to meet her father's eyes. David itched to give the man a healthy shove.

"Are you doing this to taunt me?" Shelby asked.

Charlotte pulled the dog closer to her chest. "My dog has you that upset?"

Shelby snorted. "Don't pretend to misunderstand. I don't appreciate it. You know very well it's this ridiculous position you've put yourself in. Coming here each day and acting the part of...just who are you pretending to be, Charlotte? A woman like the ones you help, who've lost their loving husbands defending the Crown? Or a woman consigned to working in order to provide food and shelter for herself? Perhaps you're joining the sisterhood next? You're purposely turning your back on the life I dedicated myself to giving you."

David gripped the wheel rims of his chair. Shelby was known as a ruthless businessman whose methods had reaped a fortune. Obviously, he was just as hard-hearted with his daughter. Bad enough that Shelby would say such things to Charlotte, but to do it while being watched! If Shelby's words weren't proof enough of his selfish disregard for her feelings, his conduct was.

Charlotte's gaze darted to David, settled on him, and the wealth of feeling he glimpsed there left him in no doubt of her pain. She held his eyes, seemed to muster herself with a deep breath that lifted her shoulders, and then looked back to her father. "I've lived my entire life as you liked. Now I intend to just live."

With great gentleness, she bent and set the dog back on its feet.

Shelby frowned. "You have survived till now with what your husband's will provided and what his heir settled on you, but don't fool yourself into thinking you don't need my support. And don't forget you're still my heir. That makes you a very desirable unmarried woman!"

David was trapped. He considered wheeling back into his office, but he didn't want to leave Charlotte alone. What was the bastard doing, talking to her this way in front of him? She'd be mortified.

Charlotte pulled back as if catching scent of something foul. "I have no desire to acquire another husband. One libertine was enough." Then she rasped, "I've never wanted to be at odds with you. Why can't you stand behind me this one time?"

"You must live as you were meant to," Shelby replied. "Thanks to me you're a viscountess. I didn't give you schooling equal to that of any titled lady—hell, any titled *man*—to have you associate with downtrodden women and meddle in their affairs."

"I'm not meddling. I'm helping good, deserving women."

David ached for Charlotte. She stood stiff as a trooper undergoing a general's dressing-down. There weren't too many women who'd be able to stand up to such a strong-willed man as Shelby, either. She must have a backbone of iron.

Shelby made a disgusted, dismissive noise and turned away, shaking his head. "Well. I can only hope you'll come to your senses."

He'd addressed himself to his daughter but looked at David, too. David looked back, and whatever Shelby saw in his eyes seemed to enrage the man. He turned and stormed out the door.

Charlotte stood immobile, staring straight ahead.

David checked the regulator clock on the wall behind Chetney's desk. "Boone and Simpson should be out front. Get your dog and I'll take you home."

His quiet words seemed to rouse her. She spun and hurried into her office to collect her things.

#

After getting her dog, reticule and shawl, Charlotte avoided Scott's gaze and preceded him out the door. She passed Chetney, returning from wherever he'd disappeared to lock up the office.

Somehow, she and the dog managed to gain the interior of Scott's carriage. She settled the dog beside her and sank against the padded seatback, thinking. How could she continue to work with Scott after such a scene? She'd had enough criticism and humiliation from Haliday to last a lifetime, and now her father was heaping another measure on her. What must Scott think? Her father had as much as admitted to a life-long scheme to obtain a title and social standing for her.

What would she do if Scott dismissed her? In just a few weeks this work had become her bedrock. Ironically in tune with her father's complaint, the eyes of her widows reflected an unfamiliar image of herself. They valued her, and it filled her with satisfaction. She had meaningful work and felt proud of what she was accomplishing. She liked that feeling. Why shouldn't she have the opportunity to grow accustomed to it?

Evidently Scott was ready to hoist himself into the coach. Boone hopped in, threaded a rope through the pulley attached to the ceiling, and stepped down.

She'd never watched from inside the coach while Scott pulled himself in. She'd always observed from outside and entered after he was settled. Now, from his chair positioned in front of the door, he pulled himself in while Boone supported his lower legs. Scott maneuvered onto the rear-facing seat, grasped his legs and arranged them with knees bent and feet on the floor. Then he pulled the rope from the pulley, causing the sling under him to flatten. He gave his coat a tug and nodded to Boone, who shut the door. The coach rocked as Boone climbed aboard and settled beside the coachman, and a moment later they began to move.

Charlotte looked at the dog, which lay beside her, head resting on its paws. She removed one glove and sank her fingers into the soft fur of the beast's neck and ears. Rubbing brought an unexpected comfort.

"Are you all right?"

Charlotte had focused on the dog to avoid looking at Scott. She didn't think she could bear to see the disgust and pity he surely must feel, but oh, no. He wasn't going to ignore what had happened. Why couldn't he just pretend he hadn't witnessed that abysmal exchange between her father and herself?

She kept her gaze on the dog. "Yes, of course. I'm accustomed to such discussions with my father."

"I'm sorry for that. It must be incredibly difficult to stand up to him. He wouldn't have achieved all he has if he weren't ruthless. I suspect it's the only way he knows."

Scott's insight surprised Charlotte, and he surprised her more by continuing.

"The things he said were hurtful. I hope you intend to disregard him and stay at the Patriotic Fund."

It looked like he meant it, too. His mouth was compressed, and he looked furious for her. Charlotte's heart expanded and filled her chest. She struggled not to reveal how deeply these words and this support affected her, but the relief of having Scott champion her was nearly overwhelming. Only Jane had ever understood and been on her side before.

"He wants me to marry another peer. He won't rest until he has a titled grandson."

As soon as the words were out, Charlotte wanted to snatch them back. How could she have revealed that? To make it worse, her last few words had wobbled.

Scott stretched out his arm, slid his hand behind her neck, and drew her to him. Charlotte didn't think, didn't resist, just leaned forward and met his mouth with her own.

She'd feigned not wanting him, but now all pretense fell away. It was as if they were merely continuing from where things had ended all those weeks ago at Lady Elliott's ball. Scott's lips pressed firmly against hers, and his tongue slid along the crease of her lips. Charlotte opened eagerly. He held her face, offering up deep, drugging kisses that drew her ever closer to him until she was perched on the very edge of her seat.

Drunk on the subtle scents of clove and citrus and starch that clung to him, she gave herself up to the heat and passion of his mouth. Heart racing, she slid her ungloved fingers through the cool silk of his hair until they met the heat of his scalp. He grabbed the ceiling pulley and leaned into her. His other hand stroked down her back, tightened at her waist, and almost before she realized his intent had swept her across to his seat.

He gathered her close and pressed against her, chest to hip. She hugged up to him, running her hands over the hardness of his shoulders and back. She felt the breadth and strength of him, his arms as rock-steady as she knew his heart to be. So she tightened her embrace until she was flush against him, tingling breasts compressed by his chest.

Desire swamped her. Every stroke of his tongue sent a burst of heat shivering through her veins. It settled low in her pelvis, an emptiness so acute she ached with it.

His mouth moved along her jaw and settled into the depression below her ear atop her hammering pulse. Against her skin, his mouth curved into a smile.

"Ah, Charlotte," he murmured, "you are the softest, most divine-smelling woman."

She leaned back and searched his eyes. They looked as bright as when he was full of laughter, as intense as when he considered a weighty problem. His color was high, his breathing quick. Charlotte drank him in. *She'd* put that look on his face.

He drew her back into his embrace, held her hard against him. She met his seeking mouth with her own, let his arms support her and wished she could lie beneath him, feel all his weight pressing against her. Wished her decorous dress and corset were gone. She longed for his hands, wanted them on her breasts, her belly, all her secret places.

Her hands slipped under his coat, explored the ridges of his back, skated down to his narrow waist. As impossible as it seemed, he drew her even tighter against him. When he released her mouth and his lips nudged aside her collar, she couldn't hold back a moan. His teeth captured a bit of flesh at her neck and his tongue laved it, making her want to commandeer a part of him in return.

They were tilted a bit, Scott canted on one hip. Charlotte smoothed her hand over him, boldly curling her fingers along the curve of his buttock. He pressed against her, angling her farther backward, and her hand slid away from his hip and grasped his left thigh. The bone suddenly rocked in a seesaw motion.

Charlotte gasped, jerked, and suddenly Scott no longer held her.

She straightened. For a moment, before his head turned away, she saw stark pain and anger.

Oh, God, what had she done? Had she hurt him?

"David, I'm sorry," she said, contrite. Helplessness assailed her. He seemed much farther away than the small space that separated them. He sat stiffly, looking at his legs. His hands, fingers spread, gripped his thighs.

Though he appeared deeply disturbed, he didn't seem to be in physical pain.

"David..." She touched his arm then jerked back when he turned toward her, face fierce, eyes glittering.

"Leave off, Charlotte!"

Oh, why had she reacted that way? She knew his legs had been crushed, knew his bones were in pieces, but the unexpected shifting of his thigh had startled her.

He tunneled his fingers through his hair, and she realized at some point he'd shed his gloves. She found them on the floor, retrieved them, and smoothed the soft deerskin on her knee. He sighed gustily and looked at her. His cool, distant expression was startling. Where had all the fire gone? How could he extinguish all that intense emotion?

"My lady, I apologize. I'll understand if you no longer want to work with me."

Fury overrode all else. "Don't you dare. Don't you dare act stiff and formal with me, David. I have no intention of pretending this didn't happen."

Thank God, that's all it took for her to fan the embers in his eyes into fire. But his words were bitter and made her heart twist. "I'm certain you've noticed. I'm not able to offer either marriage or an *affaire de coeur*."

His blunt words snuffed out her anger. Was he afraid his manhood had been affected by his injuries? She didn't think so. His body had been hard and impassioned. He'd *wanted* her. She dared a quick look at his trousers. No, there was nothing wrong with David Scott's manhood.

"If you think your being lame makes you unattractive or undesirable, you're wrong," she pointed out.

He gave her a long look.

The coach rocked, and Boone suddenly appeared at the door. With surprise Charlotte found they'd arrived at her townhouse. And she wasn't done with this conversation, but Boone was opening the door.

"Oh, blast."

Deliberately, she laid Scott's gloves on his thigh and gave his leg a little squeeze. Then she scooped up the raggedy dog and, ignoring Boone, hustled out of the coach.

CHAPTER SEVENTEEN

"I can't believe it's the same dog," Eleanor Butler said.

Charlotte's amazement echoed the girl's. Eleanor had bathed the dog and then at Charlotte's insistence dried her in front of the sitting room fire. Charlotte's housekeeper, Mrs. Jones, donated a brush that was missing more bristles than remained, and Eleanor was doing her best to work through the dog's tangles, but the canine had begun to dodge her ministrations.

Charlotte knelt beside them with her needlework scissors. Round-eyed, Eleanor straightened.

"My lady?"

Charlotte set the scissors down and reached toward the brush. "You hold on to her while I brush her. I'll snip out the worst of the tangles."

Eleanor obeyed, securing the dog with lean, long-fingered hands. Charlotte took a moment to rub the dog's soft, upright ears, then tackled her dark fur as gently as possible, brushing out what she could and using the scissors where the fur was impossibly knotted.

"How are your sisters and brothers faring, Eleanor?"

Since Charlotte had brought the girl home from Mrs. Russell's, her cheeks had acquired a pinkness that added to the overall charm of the girl's appearance.

"Very well, my lady. The boys are happy at school, and I see Amelia and Hannah every week. I go with Mrs. Lipton when she goes to market. They're not too far from there, and the lady caring for them doesn't mind my visits. She's been good to the girls. I miss them all something terrible, though."

"And how are your own studies going?" Charlotte had found a school attended by the daughters of successful tradesmen and enrolled Eleanor. Five days a week the girl attended until early afternoon. Then she reported to Mrs. Jones, who kept her busy with household tasks until the evening meal.

A warm smile stole over Eleanor's face. Charlotte had noticed it came quicker and quicker as the days passed. "I never dreamed of such good fortune, my lady. How can I ever thank you?"

"No thanks are necessary. Are you using the library as I instructed?"

On more than one occasion Charlotte had caught the girl standing in the doorway, gazing at the shelves of books, front teeth crimping her bottom lip. Charlotte had told her the books were hers for the reading, but Eleanor had only stared back with huge, apprehensive eyes. Charlotte puzzled over it for several days, why the girl, who so obviously yearned to read, wouldn't even browse. Perhaps the books, with their smooth leather covers and their fine white pages, seemed too fine. So on impulse Charlotte had asked Mrs. Jones to make Eleanor responsible for maintaining the room. She was to keep it clean, neat and organized. She was to inspect the books for torn covers or other damage that necessitated repairs. And she was expected to confine her studying for school to the room. Now Eleanor could frequently be found in the library. Whether on the ladder returning a book to its resting place or nestled in a chair, captivated by a story, the girl always looked as though she belonged there.

"I suppose I need a name for her," Charlotte said of the dog after Eleanor nodded. Her long black coat was getting a considerable trimming, especially along the belly and legs. The little beast seemed to have resigned herself to their attentions, but Charlotte still took care to be gentle. Each time her hand drew near the canine's mouth, the dog's pink tongue lapped at it in tender reassurance.

Charlotte set down the brush and scissors. The dog's bright eyes peeked out from behind a veil of feathered hair. "I dare say she's beginning to look quite appealing."

"I think she's relieved to be here," Eleanor said, petting the beast's head. "She looks happy."

Charlotte stifled her smile. "Well, her belly's full and she's safe. Those are happy circumstances for any stray."

The dog pushed a head under Charlotte's hand, soliciting another rub.

"It's been a long time since you've had either. Hasn't it, little stray?"

The dog, perhaps understanding Charlotte was finished, sat and began to pant, tongue lolling from between white teeth.

"How about *Piccola Persa* for a name? That's Little Stray in Italian," Charlotte remarked. She smoothed her hand over the dog's back. "Or perhaps just Persa."

The dog looked back and forth between her and Eleanor as if aware they were discussing her. Her tail wagged madly, and Eleanor giggled.

"I think she's telling us she likes it," the girl said.

Considering Eleanor and Persa, Charlotte's chest filled with gladness. She quickly got to her feet and, mumbling something about putting the scissors away, headed for her room. She hurried up the stairs and arrived out of breath. This tension wasn't unlike the feeling just before succumbing to tears, only she knew she wasn't about to cry.

She sank onto the chaise. What was happening to her? The tenderness she'd felt just now, looking at Eleanor and Persa, was shocking. She suddenly seemed to be teeming with emotion at every turn. Scott's kiss had unlocked something crucial within her. Something soft and generous that went far beyond her feeling for him. He made her experience things she'd thought excised from her person. Not love. Certainly not that. But she couldn't look at him without wanting to touch him. Strange, that she'd never realized she'd buried more than her desire for a husband and family.

Each new day brought the anticipation of her work and of seeing Scott. Today they'd each revealed their vulnerability. Their desire had been exposed. And then she'd repulsed him with her reaction to his leg.

She pressed cold fingers to her hot, heavy eyelids. She'd hurt him. She'd give anything to have that moment back.

Her desire was all-consuming. She'd thought she knew desire in the early days of her marriage, but now Charlotte saw that had merely been a longing to be loved. This…craving she felt for David Scott, she'd never before felt anything of its like. Perhaps unintentionally, Scott had today revealed that he wanted her just as much as she did him. She was certain of it. But he'd also made clear he wouldn't pursue an intimacy with her. Strange to think a man as commanding as Scott could doubt himself. He kept his insecurities well-hidden.

Charlotte sighed. Before today she'd been satisfied with her decision to never pursue love or marry again. Yet didn't she deserve some small measure of physical pleasure? Was it so terrible to want Scott's arms around her? The gratifying, independent life she'd planned now looked wearisome and solitary. The satisfaction she'd gained through her work seemed insubstantial. A great yearning had taken up residence within her, and she feared she'd never again know peace.

#

Charlotte followed Jane's maid into the private sitting room. She'd preceded her arrival with a note asking if she might visit, confident her friend would welcome her. Jane's unexpected reply had been, *Yes, please come now. Hurry.*

Her plan to confide in Jane and ask advice about David Scott died the moment she walked in and her friend's head lifted. Jane's face bore all the earmarks of a prolonged cry: red, puffy eyes, a flushed, damp face and such an expression of hurt that Charlotte knew doom had fallen. And she still wore her nightgown and wrap.

Charlotte hurried to the chaise her friend occupied and grasped the hand not clutching a wilted handkerchief. "Jane? What is it?"

Her friend pressed her limp handkerchief to her eyes and took a deep, shuddering breath. "It's Phillip."

Oh, God. Charlotte sank onto the chaise. "Was there an accident? What's happened?"

Etherton simply had to be all right. Charlotte squeezed Jane's hand and waited. Dread tightened her throat, making her work to swallow.

Jane bent her head. Her chest heaved several times as she took in great breaths. "He has a mistress and a son," she croaked, the last word a mere whisper.

"What?" No. Jane must be wrong. Phillip adored his wife. It was because of Jane and Phillip that Charlotte still believed real, lasting love was possible. "Are you sure?"

Jane nodded. "We...we argued. I want another child. Phillip doesn't. He insists he doesn't want me taking the risk."

Shock held Charlotte silent. Eight years of marriage, six pregnancies, one miscarriage, and four healthy daughters. The last birth—a stillborn son—had been frightful, with Jane nearly dying of hemorrhage.

"Phillip needs a son to secure the succession, but he won't even consider another child. He says he's fine with the title going to a distant cousin." A crease appeared between Jane's brows. "Mr. Jonathan Mattingly. Do you know him?"

Charlotte shook her head.

"He already has a son."

"Jane…" What did this have to do with Etherton having a mistress and child?

"He says there's nothing to discuss, that he's happy with our family. I know how he loves our sweet girls, but if I can't give Phillip an heir of his blood I'll fail him. I'll let the whole family down."

"Jane, you nearly died." Her friend had been unconscious, but Charlotte remembered Phillip's ravaged face, how he grieved over the loss of their child and how he prayed for his wife, never leaving her bedside.

Jane retrieved her glasses from the side table and shoved them on. "He wouldn't listen to me. Didn't care that it was what I wanted. We had a terrible row. I don't understand how it happened. He kept telling me I wasn't being *sensible*. I got so angry. I was determined to sway him and kept saying I wanted to give him a son. Finally, he shouted that he already has a son."

Too late to stifle her gasp, Charlotte's fingers flew to her mouth.

"Phillip didn't mean to tell me. But since he had, he went on and told me everything. They live in the village and he sees them whenever he's at Friar's Gate. Charlotte, he *loves* the boy."

Of course Etherton loved the boy. That was the kind of man he was. Yet something was missing from Jane's tale. How could Etherton have been unfaithful when every time he looked at Jane or their daughters his eyes filled with such warmth?

"When did this happen?" Charlotte asked. Her friend, the most intelligent girl at Mrs. Brewster's school, the one who could reason her way through any situation, was floundering. Charlotte wished she could do something other than sit, a helpless spectator to Jane's pain. She wrapped an arm around her.

Jane slid her fingers under her glasses, pushed them up, and buried her face in her hands. "Last night."

"No, not the argument. The affair. When was the affair?"

"It happened before we met. Phillip said he ended it when he realized he cared for me. He swore he's been faithful and doesn't feel anything for the boy's mother but a fondness." Jane raised her head. "The boy is nine years old."

Charlotte was confused as to the problem. "This boy won't inherit the title. You know that, Jane."

"But Phillip loves him. He told me so, Charlotte. He's schooling him. He supports them."

"Of course he supports them. Etherton is a responsible, generous man. This doesn't diminish his love for you or your daughters."

"But it feels like he's given this child something that belongs to me. That boy...that boy will always remind him of what he should have had. What I failed to give him!"

Jane's eyes were so earnest that Charlotte straightened, giving her friend's clasped hands a squeeze. She wanted to sympathize but couldn't stop the little voice in her mind that said Jane hadn't been betrayed. Jane truly thought she and her girls owned all her husband's love and loyalty? Still, she had suffered a terrible loss when her son had been delivered stillborn. Jane and Etherton both had. It had been more than a year, but that wound would still be raw. Perhaps it was affecting the way Jane was managing the situation.

"All the love he's giving to his bastard... That's love *my* son is supposed to have."

Charlotte didn't understand. Jane didn't have a son. How could Etherton be depriving a son he didn't have? And Jane was a mother. She knew the love you gave one child wasn't stolen from another. Your heart simply expanded to include the additional children. Etherton loved Jane and had accepted not having a son to inherit the title. He didn't blame or resent Jane. He only wanted to protect her.

Her friend was usually so sensible, but in this instance she was being irrational. Charlotte didn't know how to help.

"Jane, are you angry at Phillip...or yourself?"

Jane's eyes flashed. She stood, strode to the window and looked out. After a minute, she whirled about. "I admit I'm jealous. But please don't tell me I have no reason to be."

Charlotte wanted to say as much, but she didn't. At least she understood the jealousy. "Let's have some tea."

She found Jane's worried-looking maid standing just outside. After ordering tea, she pulled Jane away from the window and made her sit in the upholstered chair positioned in front of the fireplace. She wrapped a shawl around Jane's shoulders and tucked the ends around her friend's cold hands. Then, with Jane looking comfortable and in control, Charlotte took the opposite chair.

She hated to ask about something so private, but she suspected there was another hurt at the heart of Jane's distress. "If Phillip is determined not to risk your bearing another child, how are you preventing pregnancy?"

Jane tightened the shawl. Her face flushed. "He…withdraws. I don't like it, but…"

But there was nothing else to do other than complete abstinence.

"How did your argument end?"

"He went into his bedroom and slammed the door." Jane drew a deep, jerky breath. "He *never* sleeps in there."

"Perhaps it was smart. He allowed you time to think. Now the two of you can have a rational discussion."

"How can we have a rational discussion? He's not a rational man. He's held this secret from me since before our marriage. Of course, the servants at Friar's Gate know. The entire village knows." Jane threw her hands in the air.

Charlotte had experienced the bite of a revealed secret, and the sting of casual acquaintances and servants knowing something private and hurtful. Seeing her friend suffering with the same pain made her stomach squeeze. "I'm sorry, Jane. But please let Phillip have his say. Listen to his explanation. He'd never intentionally hurt you. I'm sure when he decided not to tell, he thought he was sparing you."

Jane gazed at her for a long moment and then shook her head. "All these years he's kept them right under my nose."

The tea arrived, fragrant and steaming. Charlotte poured and placed a plate with a fresh cinnamon bun beside Jane. Jane swallowed a drink of tea and winced.

Charlotte raised her cup and gently blew across the surface of the liquid. She remembered the hard, aching knot that had lodged in her chest the day she learned of Haliday's affair. It had lived with her for weeks before ebbing away. How could Etherton have hidden the existence of his son for so many years and then told Jane in such an awful way? How could he have been so cruel or thoughtless? Etherton wasn't a man who lost control. Yet since he had told Jane, why couldn't Jane at least try to understand? How would their love survive if she couldn't forgive him? Jane didn't need the additional burden of Charlotte's disillusionment and anger, but Charlotte couldn't help but feel some anger at both of them. Didn't they value what they had in each other?

Or, maybe she'd been wrong and their love wasn't ever as strong as she'd thought.

No. Charlotte recalled the way Etherton looked at Jane. He'd never hidden his feelings as he regarded his wife. Damn it, this just wasn't right.

She set down her cup. "Where is Etherton now?"

Jane shrugged. "He went to his club. Said he'd come back home when I was ready to be reasonable—"

Her voice broke.

So, after all of that Etherton had left Jane to cry and fret. His actions left an uneasy, heavy churning in the pit of Charlotte's stomach. Abandoning his wife after such a revelation was downright beastly and not like the man at all. She could only assume he'd had a complete loss of temper and control, even as unlikely as that seemed. Still, she maintained her position that he was a trusted friend. In spite of how he'd retreated, she could never just reverse her opinion and think him in the same league as Haliday.

"I'll stay as long as you like," she said to Jane, and was rewarded with something approximating a wobbly smile. "I can tell you didn't sleep last night. You need to rest or you'll make yourself ill."

Her friend's passivity as the wrap was removed and she was put to bed told Charlotte how dispirited Jane was. Charlotte pulled the covers around her friend's shoulders, Jane closed her eyes and curled her arms and legs in close to her body.

Settling into a chair, Charlotte tried to relax. How could men feel no compunction when they hurt their wives? It was hard even to imagine Etherton keeping his bastard a secret for all these years, financially supporting his son and spending time with him all behind Jane's back. Was Charlotte being foolish to cling to her belief in

Etherton's love for Jane? He hadn't been unfaithful, but he'd hidden an important part of his life from his wife.

Charlotte closed her eyes to subdue their burning. For a moment the face of David Scott swam before her. She couldn't imagine Scott acting dishonorably. Yet, why should he be any different than any other man when it came to pleasures of the flesh? Jane had learned a hard-taught lesson today from her husband. Charlotte had firsthand knowledge of it, herself. Under their guise as protectors, men controlled women. When they couldn't, they left. Charlotte's father was actually even trying to reassert his authority. He'd best think again. She'd make her own decisions. She wasn't about to live under his thumb again. Not his or any other man's.

What must it feel like to be a man? So confident, so certain your every action would be tolerated, your every dictate obeyed? A man's reputation was unaffected by all but the most grievous acts. Women, the opposite. Jane had little choice but to eventually accept or ignore what Etherton had done, or she would spend the rest of her marriage miserable.

Charlotte's friend shifted and mumbled, lost in the oblivion of sleep. Charlotte hoped it was deep enough to be dreamless.

Wriggling her shoulders, Charlotte twisted until she found a position where she could let her neck and shoulder muscles slacken, then she closed her eyes and thought of Haliday, Etherton, and finally Scott. If a man could engage in dalliance and remain free of guilt and stigma, why not a woman? Especially if the woman had no husband and the man no wife to betray.

Why not indeed, Charlotte decided. Such a liaison would hurt no one.

Such a liaison between Scott and herself would hurt no one.

CHAPTER EIGHTEEN

Monday, Scott had a meeting with the Fund commissioners and wasn't expected at the office until early afternoon. Charlotte returned from walking Persa with her energy somewhat renewed. She'd spent much of the past two days with Jane, and it had been draining.

She entered the administration offices door and found Scott, a long roll of papers across his lap, talking with Mr. Chetney. When she crouched to remove the leash from Persa, Scott grinned down at her. For a moment everything but him faded away.

The grin deepened the crinkles at the corners of his eyes and made his clear blue irises shimmer. Smile lines appeared in those lean cheeks and emphasized the masculine dimple that marked Scott's chin. She didn't know if his red-gold hair had been tossed by hand or wind, but it looked exceedingly attractive.

Dragging her gaze away, she released Persa and stood.

"We're moving forward with the girls orphanage-school project," Scott said. "Since it will in effect be a shelter, it's to be called the Royal Victoria Patriotic Asylum. Mr. Hawkins has completed the architectural plans, and the Queen will lay the foundation stone in Wandsworth Common on July eleventh. There's to be a ceremony of sorts. Tomorrow I'll travel to Essex to show the plans to our master builder, Mr. George Myers, and give him the updated timetable. He'll need to get back to London to go over the diagrams with Hawkins."

"You're going to Essex tomorrow? By train?"

How exciting to think their orphanage and school would soon be taking shape. She'd ask Scott to show her the diagrams.

"No, I'm taking my coach. It will be a long day, but I'll leave very early to ensure I arrive home before dark."

She'd never before considered it, but obviously traveling by train would present a number of difficulties for Scott. And he'd not only have trouble getting aboard a train but any hired conveyance.

After the past two days, leaving the city sounded wonderful to Charlotte. "Oh, I wish I could go with you. I'd love to get some fresh country air."

Scott took no more than a moment considering. She hadn't intended to sound so wistful, but her regret disappeared with his reply. "Come along then, if you don't have appointments tomorrow. There may be times you'll need to visit the building site to see Myers. It won't hurt for you to meet him."

One corner of Scott's mouth quirked up, and a little quiver passed through Charlotte. She'd be in the coach with him for several hours. She'd never had the man to herself for such a length of time, and it was even more appealing than the anticipated sojourn through the countryside.

"Thank you," she said.

Some of her delight must have communicated itself to Persa. The little dog barked, and her tail began wagging madly.

"Where are we going in Essex?" Charlotte asked.

"Audley End House in Saffron Walden. Baron Baybrooke is considering some renovation and wanted Myers to take a look."

"I've been to Audley End House. It's a beautiful estate." Charlotte's gaze dropped to the papers balanced on Scott's lap. "Would you mind showing me the plans? I confess I'm curious what architectural diagrams look like."

A flicker of surprise passed over Scott's face. "Not at all, my lady. Shall we open them up on my desk?"

She followed him into his office, where he rolled the papers flat and weighted down the corners with an inkwell, a small statue of Wellington, and his hand.

"Get that corner," he said, indicating the remaining curling section with a nod.

Charlotte complied and discovered her hip in close proximity to Scott's shoulder. This close, she could smell the clean, masculine scent she now associated with him. She did her best to ignore it and stared determinedly at Mr. Hawkins's diagrams.

The school, built in the gothic style, would be huge. The building stretched away from a large central tower, with each end capped by a shorter tower. Scott pointed out dining hall, cloister, infirmary and chapel.

"There'll be a statue of Saint George and the Dragon at the entry," he added.

"It's huge. And so modern."

"Amazing what can happen with the backing of the Queen and Prince Albert, isn't it?"

Charlotte couldn't seem to keep her gaze off Scott's face for any length of time. "It's exciting. I hope the commissioners allow us some influence when the asylum staff is chosen. Our Fund orphans need skilled teachers and compassionate caregivers."

Scott blinked, and a subtle change in his expression warmed her like an unexpected gift. She'd seen him regard her with caution. At different times he'd looked at her with dislike, confusion, desire or challenge, but right now she saw true liking and approval. She was seeing a friend.

"They do. Perhaps I can convince you to give the students lessons in deportment. They'd learn from the best and you'd show society what a paragon of correctness you are."

#

At his words, Charlotte's huge and unaffected smile caught David and held him suspended. For a moment he felt the same exhilaration he'd known during a full gallop on the back of Alynore. Then Charlotte giggled, sending surprise and delight flaring through him. A moment later they were both laughing.

Charlotte held her hand over her mouth as if she wanted to suppress her merriment, but that didn't diminish David's pleasure. Her flushed skin, breathy mirth and quivering bosom were affecting his body to the point of pain.

He looked away and began rolling up the plans. What had he been thinking, inviting her to accompany him tomorrow? He hadn't thought beyond the sudden impulse to please her with a country journey. The day would likely be torture.

He extended the rolled plans toward her. "Would you mind giving them to Mr. Chetney?"

She grasped the opposite end of the plans but didn't pull them away. Her laughter died. Her eyelids fell and hid her gaze.

"Thank you," she said, "for giving me a chance, back when I started. And for believing in me now."

"You're welcome." David caught a flash of her violet eyes as she tugged the plans from his hand and turned away. Then she left his office, her little dog trotting behind.

David recalled that first day, when he'd been forced to accept her as part of his staff. He hadn't expected to ever value her assistance, but he did. He valued it now greatly. Each day brought examples of Charlotte Haliday's kindness and compassion. She had a knack for knowing just how to approach the Fund's children and widows, and for working out what kind of assistance would help most. The emotion she'd just revealed made it clear how much all of this meant to her, too.

Strange, he'd never before wondered if ladies found their lives satisfying. He'd never thought them concerned with much beyond social connections and the trappings of society. He feared he'd done many a disservice.

Charlotte certainly hadn't been satisfied with her life. She'd sought something more. She'd overcome notoriety to do so, too. This work made her happy, and David wanted to keep her working here, wanted her happiness to continue. So, if he could help her stand up to her father or anyone else who stood in the way, he'd do that.

Somehow he'd ignore his lust—he had to admit that's what it was—and relish her joy.

#

The next day's plan was to stay at Audley End House only as long as necessary. Mr. Myers met them quickly, reviewed and approved the plans. Luckily Baybrooke wasn't at home, so David and Lady Haliday were saved the necessity of doing the polite thing. They consumed a light repast while Myers asked questions, and then they headed back to London. David considered resting the horses a bit longer, but unless he missed his guess the countryside was in for a nasty storm. The day had started overcast and windy.

He had never considered his coach as more than a way to achieve mobility, but now, here, seated beside Charlotte, David found himself in a cozy cocoon. This morning she'd entered it rosy-cheeked and smiling, and she'd settled beside him with a contented sigh, her brown and black striped skirt against his leg. There had been an ease between them, and David relaxed, contributing inconsequential remarks to match Charlotte's comments about the scenery and weather.

Since leaving Audley End House they'd spoken very little, but the long stretches of quiet were comfortable. Outside the window, dark clouds rolled toward the coach, blotting out the sun and turning the afternoon dusk-dark. The wind started to buffet the vehicle a bit, but David had instructed Simpson not to stop unless it became dangerous.

Lydia, who'd once been his fiancée, had not been so restful as Charlotte. Of course, he'd been a different man then, athletic and active. A good portion of his time with Lydia had been spent with the two of them on horseback. When he'd returned from the Crimea and she broke their engagement, bitterness briefly consumed him. Now he knew he'd loved the horses more than he had loved her. He thought of Lydia rarely now and without regret. Not so the sights, smells and sounds of horses. Those made him ache. In his dreams he was still a horseman.

"You seem pensive today," Charlotte said.

David turned and found her watching him. What expression had he worn, to earn him such a personal comment?

"Just thinking of horses." That was the truth in some measure, but still a safe topic.

"You were a cavalry officer."

It was a statement of fact rather than a question, and it was followed by silence. Charlotte waited, hands folded together and resting on her lap.

David looked out the window. *Hell*.

"For me, freedom is being on a horse. I miss having my own mount—one I can communicate with, that can read my body and hands. I always swore Alynore, my last horse, could sense my thoughts. Whatever I asked—he'd give his heart, he'd give everything. There'll never be another like him."

"Where is he now?"

Oh, God. Why had he mentioned Alynore?

"He died at Balaclava."

Thankfully, Charlotte remained silent.

Would the memories ever stop? Alynore, shot at a full gallop, falling as if the hand of God had picked him up and thrown him down, pinning David beneath. He'd never forget the screams as the stallion died. Finally, quiet and the long night had come, him lying crushed beneath Alynore's body. The images had come without warning, and David was again lying on the battlefield, wondering which would come first: death, daylight and rescue, or madness.

The coach jolted, and Charlotte gripped his arm.

"Don't be alarmed," David said to comfort her. "Simpson knows what he's about."

The rain started then, and in a few minutes it had reached torrential proportions. The carriage slowed and then stopped. Boone appeared and opened the door. Cold wind and rain gusted into the coach.

The man was drenched. He swiped his hand down his dripping face and leaned his head into the coach. The smell of wet earth swept inside.

"Can we make it to shelter?" David asked, raising his voice to be heard above the drumming rain. They might be forced to stop under a tree and bring Simpson and Boone into the coach until the storm passed. He'd prefer to get them somewhere the men could dry out and the horses could receive shelter, too.

"Hockerill crossroads is just ahead. I think we can make that, but it's bad out here, sir. The low-lying places are already beginning to flood."

"We can pull off the road and you can wait in here with us, or we can push on and get a roof over our heads."

"If it's all the same to you, sir, I think Simpson and I would just as soon have us a fire and a hot toddy." Boone shuddered and then adjusted his tricorn, pushing it firmly onto his head. "We can't get any wetter or colder than what we are."

David knew the man was miserable but didn't question his choice. "Very well. Let's try to make the Crown."

Boone shut the door, and as soon as he'd gained his seat they again got underway.

"At least it's not hailing," Charlotte said.

"I'm sure Simpson and Boone are glad of that, but it's unsafe to travel. We may be forced to spend the night at the Crown's Inn. The roads sound nearly impassable now. If it lets up soon, we may be all right. But if it continues, I think we'll have no choice but to lay over."

In David's experience most women would be hysterical by now, but Charlotte maintained her composure. She reminded him of some of the military wives he'd known, who followed the camps and matched their husbands' courage with their own brand of inner strength.

"I'm sorry, Charlotte," he said. She had no lady's maid and no nightclothes. "I know this will be a hardship. Hopefully the inn will have a servant who can act as lady's maid for such a predicament as this."

Her lips twitched. "It can't be helped. You don't need to worry. I'll manage."

Her words conjured up an image of her disrobing, garment by garment. With supreme effort David managed to pull his gaze from her lips, but it only fell to her bosom. He willed himself to stop, but her rose and jasmine scent wrapped around him and held him suspended. Since their kiss, he'd been influenced by even her subtlest aspects.

He had the devil's own luck. He'd been doing his best to ignore the attraction he felt for Charlotte, and now they most probably would be stranded out of town. It offered the perfect occasion for a liaison. They would have both opportunity and privacy.

Only, he couldn't face Charlotte with his broken body. She'd recovered quickly from feeling his fragmented bone move during their kiss, but she'd been horrified also. He certainly didn't expect her to regard his form as desirable, and he couldn't ask her to make accommodations for his inadequacies. As much as he wanted her, and as much as she would deny it, he knew she could never be happy with a man such as he.

Oh, she was attracted to him, David allowed. She'd been greatly affected by that kiss. But he'd given her respect and friendship at a vulnerable time. He also feared his damnable hero label might have influenced her. During that kiss he'd lost all restraint, but he would never let it happen again. Any kind of relationship with him would only complicate Charlotte's life.

Neither could he consider an attachment for himself. It was a man's duty to protect the woman he cared for, and he could no longer claim that privilege. Once he'd been able to put fear in a

man's eyes, but who would stand in awe of him now? Who would—
?

The coach slowed and stopped. A servant from the inn ran forward with an umbrella and opened the coach door.

"Go in and get warm. I'll join you in a bit," David said to Charlotte.

By the time he gained his chair, he would be soaked. At least he could remove his coat before leaving the coach and keep that item dry. And, he couldn't help but see a certain humor in the situation.

He needed a cold drenching, and nature was ready to oblige.

CHAPTER NINETEEN

Charlotte sat still, listening to the muffled sound of Scott and Boone conversing in the next room. She'd never felt less like sleeping.

They'd eaten in a private dining room, sitting close to the fire where the heat could warm Scott and dry his wet clothing. He'd discarded coat and waistcoat, leaving him in only a limp white shirt and leaving her distinctly nervous. Unfortunately, Charlotte's tension hadn't abated after she returned to her room. A bold idea had captured her and wouldn't turn loose. Here, away from the routine of their lives, they had privacy. They might engage in intimacy without anyone knowing. Not even servants.

Could she really do such a bold thing? She stood and began pulling pins from her hair and tossing them onto the chest. What would Scott think? She couldn't bear it if he thought less of her. She admired him more than any man of her acquaintance, and with good reason. If he turned her away... Oh, God, what would she do if he turned her away? She was mad to even consider approaching him. She sank onto the bed and raked her fingers through her hair. What if such an action jeopardized her ability to work with him?

She stood, stalked to the fireplace and extended her chilled hands. They shook. She pulled them back and pressed them to her hot cheeks, but she couldn't dispel the thoughts and excitement gripped her when she dared imagine them together. She yearned for David Scott, and one selfish, wicked notion refused to leave her mind.

Hadn't she earned the right to receive pleasure from a man's body? The very thought of engaging in intimacy with Scott made her weak. How many times had she lain beneath Haliday and submitted to his rutting? She'd done her duty because he promised to leave her alone until the end of her days if she'd give him a son. Now all the places that waited for David Scott's caress ached, as if to draw the touch of his hand and his manhood. Somehow she knew his loving would be nothing like her dead husband's.

She heard Scott's door close and footsteps retreat before all was quiet. Boone was gone.

Charlotte began disrobing, both cursing and glad of her lack of a lady's maid as she struggled with the buttons of her bodice, ties of her petticoats and hooks of her corset. She removed her garters and stockings and drawers. Finally, she stood in only her wrinkled chemise, her arms prickled with gooseflesh. She wrapped her shawl about her and curled her toes into the rug. Her heart thumped so hard it pulsed in her temple. Did she dare…?

She went to the basin, set aside her shawl and washed her face, then pulled off her chemise and washed the rest of herself. Clean and dry, she slipped the chemise back on. She had no perfume, no brush to smooth her hair. Studying her pale, bare legs and feet, she decided the bed cover would do better than her shawl. She gathered up the colorful quilt and wrapped it around her.

For long minutes she stood at the door, listening, searching herself and gathering her courage. She took the key, let herself into the hall and locked the door.

Please, God, let Scott's be unlocked.

The knob turned under her hand, and the door swung open. For a moment she couldn't move; then she stepped into the room, shut and locked the door before even taking her measure of the bedchamber. She stood with her back to it. A knot obstructed her throat. She couldn't swallow and didn't think she could speak, so she tightened her hold on the quilt and turned.

Scott sat near the fire, a blanket covering his lap and legs. His bare shoulders gleamed in the light. He stared at her, his face inscrutable, his gaze following the long sweep of her hair and dropping to study her bare toes.

Her teeth chattered and she clamped them together. His clothes—including his small clothes—were draped over a rope strung across the end of the room. A hard gust of wind rattled the window and Charlotte crossed to the four-poster, let her concealing quilt fall, and slid into Scott's bed.

Scott wheeled over and looked at her across the open expanse of mattress. The dim light made it impossible to make out more than the grim line of his mouth and the glitter of his eyes.

"As much as I want you," he said, "you must first know that I never intend to wed."

His words caused both relief and dismay. One part of her was glad at how he'd simplified everything, another part saddened that he planned a solitary life.

"Nor do I."

His jaw tightened, and his eyes narrowed. For a long moment he studied her. She held her breath.

"Are you certain, Charlotte?"

The husky timbre of his voice sent shivers racing through her. "Yes, David. I am."

He barely looked away as he repositioned his chair, turning and then backing it up alongside the bed. He threw back the bedcovers, adjusted the quilt across his lap and boosted himself onto the chair arm.

The quilt came with him but slipped. Charlotte had known he was naked, but seeing his bare hip shocked her. He boosted himself again, this time onto the bed, the muscles of his back and arms bulging.

The sudden rattle of the doorknob and knock startled Charlotte. She pressed her fingers over her mouth. Scott lifted his head.

Boone's voice came through the door. "Mr. Scott, sir? I found a book for you."

"I've changed my mind, Boone. I'm going to bed."

"Do you need some help, sir?"

"No, I'm all right. I'm already abed. I won't be needing you any more tonight."

Boone made no reply. There was only silence.

"Good evening, Boone."

"Yes, sir. Good-night, sir."

Charlotte and David waited and listened until Boone's footsteps became too distant to hear. David grasped his legs and pulled them onto the bed then, whipped away the quilt and tossed the covers over himself. It all happened so fast that Charlotte caught only a glimpse of the lower half of his body.

He turned toward her, all shoulders and sculpted muscle, curling red-gold hair arrowing from his chest to his abdomen and disappearing beneath the bedclothes. Charlotte didn't know where to look. Such a muscular form might not be fashionable for a gentleman, but seeing the evidence of his strength and masculinity made her all muzzy. She felt his warmth, caught his familiar scent and heard his quickened breathing. Her fingers curled around the edge of the covers. She wanted to reach out and feel him, but a sudden siege of nerves made her hold.

He plucked her hand from the covers and rubbed his thumb back and forth across the back of it. "This might well be a mistake. We could cause ourselves all kinds of hurt."

His words might have left her wondering if he even wanted this, but there was no mistaking the hot spark of desire in his eyes.

"You're right," she said. "But at least we'll have the bliss of tonight. No matter what the future holds, I want tonight."

"What if you conceive?"

She shook her head. "I won't. I...won't."

He frowned a moment then leaned over her, and she dared to put her palm on his chest. The cool, springy curls over hot flesh enticed her. Every small hesitation fell away. She slid her trembling hand up to his warm neck and rested it over his hammering pulse.

He reached under the covers, and his fingers skimmed down her sides. She sucked in her breath as he gathered her chemise, and in one smooth motion he drew it up over her head and upraised arms and tossed it aside. So already she'd experienced an intimacy with Scott that she'd never had with Haliday. She'd never been completely unclothed with her husband.

When his mouth brushed across hers, Charlotte thought she might combust. Desire gripped her, belayed her fears, and she pulled him toward her. He was already gathering her into his arms. They lay on their sides. His lips settled firmly onto hers, and his tongue slid into her mouth. She tasted him as her hands explored the breadth of his shoulders and slid up into the cool silk of his hair.

He slanted his mouth and deepened the kiss, and the part of her that Haliday hadn't destroyed—the purest part, nestled deep within Charlotte's heart—rose up to meet him. The demand of his mouth released her from all constraint. In response she aligned her body to his, rubbing against him with breasts and abdomen and reveling in the unyielding length of his manhood hard against her hip. Every touch ignited her passion. Her nipples were rigid and achy, and she pressed them harder against his taut chest, tantalizing herself by rubbing them against his curly hair.

Leaving her lips wet and far from satisfied, her breath sighing, he slid his mouth along her jaw and down her throat. He cupped her breast, teased her nipple with his tongue, then sucked hard before gentling.

Charlotte moaned. She ran her hands over his muscled contours and slid them down the straight ridge of his spine before she stroked lower to explore his narrow waist and the curve of his firm buttocks. A strangled groan came from him, and he moved to her other breast, his tongue and teeth working it to a rigid peak.

The acute sensitivity he'd fostered with his lips and teeth and tongue spread like sparks through the center of her. She wanted his weight pressing between her thighs, wanted his hard, swollen member filling her. It lay right over her most responsive part, building her craving as it rubbed.

She widened her legs and rocked against the silky, firm length of him, prompting his return to her mouth and a possessive kiss that robbed her of all thought. Calloused fingers trailed down her body, stole her breath and set her trembling. She clutched his back as his finger entered her, and his thumb rubbed the bulge of feminine tissue that lay just above her body's entrance. Acute tension flashed through her.

"David."

Her strangled voice squeezed out with the force of a sob, and a moment later his lips covered hers with as much hunger as if it were his first taste of her. His tongue thrust into her mouth as his finger slowly withdrew and once more penetrated her body, and she wrapped her top leg over his hip. Sexual tension built until she lay at the brink of something that her body instinctively strove to reach as she raked her hands up his sides and bit at his lip.

"David," she begged.

He rose, supporting himself with extended arms and his intact right knee. Cool air rushed over her damp skin. Every pore waited for his next touch.

He abandoned her mouth and trailed his lips down her throat. His breath sawed over her, ragged and hot, and Charlotte rolled to her back and stared up at him. She dragged in air as he reached down, hooked his left knee and lifted it over her pelvis, and his lower leg dragged over hers. Then he twisted his shoulders and with one hand adjusted the position of his shattered leg, while Charlotte shuddered with need.

Finally, he was going to claim her.

The thigh of the leg he kneeled on bulged with muscle. His useless left leg was thin and frail as a child's, but it wasn't repulsive. He turned back to Charlotte, face taut. She'd never forget his masculine frame poised above her, their mingled scents, his cock at the moist entrance to her body.

His flushed body radiated heat. Charlotte threaded her fingers through his hair, pulled his head down to hers and captured his mouth. He plunged into her with one powerful thrust and groaned.

Everything in her that had waited for David Scott opened. She tightened her legs and arms, held on to him and, gasping, buried her face in the curve of his neck. The rasp of evening whiskers pricked the side of her face, but her body held him tight and she felt every inch as he pulled out and drove into her again.

"Oh, God, but you're sweet."

They were the first words he'd spoken since their loving began. He seemed to grow even harder, and each thrust pushed her toward that looming pinnacle. He drew her hips higher, found a stroking rhythm that made it impossible for her to hold back a litany of begging, and impossibly then he drove even deeper, touching her in the most primal of ways.

His fingers found her nipple, and when he firmly squeezed, the masculine power that enveloped Charlotte grew ever more intense until she had no recourse but joyful surrender. Fire shot from the tip of her breast to her womb, and her body clenched. A madness born of passion seized her and flung her to a place at once unimaginable and so magnificent she could only cling to David, press her mouth to his shoulder and stifle her cry.

Moments later he too stiffened and shuddered. His head arched back, and a low, guttural moan erupted from his throat.

#

Still inside Charlotte, too enervated to move, David rested limply against her. Then she twitched, and he hooked his arm around her waist and rolled to his side. Somehow her knees ended up wedged between his, effectively supporting his shattered left leg in a comfortable position.

She nuzzled up against him and sighed, and the sound and feel triggered the release of his own breath as well. Here he was, in a strange inn and a strange bed, having loved a woman for the first time since his injury, yet it had never felt awkward. He couldn't recall when he'd last felt this perfect. Certainly it had been before his injury.

No, he realized, not even then. He'd never felt as contented as this.

His eyes began to burn, so he pressed his thumb and forefinger, hard, into their wet corners. He sniffed once and rubbed his hand down his face; then he sighed again, smoothed his hand over Charlotte's long, silken black hair, and gave himself to sleep. When he woke, it was to predawn light.

Charlotte, just a silhouette, sat on the edge of the bed with arms upraised, white chemise sliding down her body. She pulled her hair out from under the garment. It tumbled down her back, and regret stabbed through him. He'd slept soundly. He wished he'd woken in the middle of the night and loved Charlotte again.

He reached out and smoothed his hand from her shoulder to her elbow. The skin was so soft that he wanted to bury his lips in the warm bend of her arm. He wanted to press his nose to her neck and breathe in her fragrance. He'd not had enough, not nearly enough. Now their time was up.

She looked over her shoulder at him, and his hand fell from her arm. She stood, retrieved her quilt from the floor and wrapped it around her.

"I've got to get back to my room before the inn is awake."

He raised himself up onto one elbow. "What happens now, Charlotte?"

She went to the fire, knelt down and tossed kindling on the coals. Almost immediately the fire crackled, flared, and the resulting glow spread into the room, making her quilt sprout color. She rose slowly and turned.

"Can we discuss this in the coach?"

"We can, but I think you need to understand something."

She canted her head to the side and came near the bed, looking puzzled and a bit apprehensive. He crushed the unspoken reassurances he longed to offer.

"What?" she asked.

Even after last night, he still feared exposing his injured body to her eyes, but he couldn't make plans until he knew she understood exactly what an intimate association with him meant. He sat up and swept the coverings from his legs. "This is what you must understand."

He was half hard, but the state of his cock wasn't what concerned him. It was her reaction to his legs. They weren't deformed, just spindly-looking, excepting his right thigh. By contrast, it was bulky with muscle. He could move his feet and toes just a bit, but moving his legs required him to grab and lift them.

Completely exposed, he maneuvered closer to his wheelchair, which still sat at the bedside. That let her see just how his legs looked when he picked up the damned things and moved them. He didn't think he could bear it if she appeared revolted, so he didn't watch her. Instead he stared at his legs, every moment aware of her breath, of her tiniest movement.

She advanced one step. He could see the edge of her quilt from the corner of his eye.

"Do they hurt?"

"Usually not. Rainy days, like today, they ache a bit."

She astonished him by placing her hand upon his leg. "Can you feel my touch?" she asked.

He dared a glance at her. She didn't appear repulsed; instead her face bore a look of great concentration.

"Yes. I've numbness in a couple of areas, but overall sensation is normal. They're limp as noodles, though." And, depending on how they were placed, they could be crooked and floppy, too. "The surgeons wanted to amputate, but Wakefield wouldn't let them. I'm fortunate none of the bone ends pierced my skin, because amputation would have been a certainty."

Charlotte bent and kissed first one leg and then the other, and then she pressed her forehead against his knee. Her unbound hair fell across his thighs and its silky caress as she straightened made him shiver and harden. Oh, God, the feelings this woman raised. He hadn't even known he could be so full of them.

She turned brilliant bluebell eyes on him. "I'm so sorry for what you've suffered and lost, David, but this makes you no less a man to me."

For a minute he couldn't speak. He gave her a jerky nod, swallowed and dragged in a breath before he was able to respond, his voice embarrassingly husky. "You'd best hurry to your room."

She smiled, and he couldn't hold anything back from his own happy expression. He knew he was grinning ear to ear but he couldn't help himself. She bent and kissed him then—a kiss satisfying even given its brevity.

After she left, David sat for a long minute, captivated by their exchange, awash with something he couldn't quite identify but which felt suspiciously like joy.

CHAPTER TWENTY

Four days later, David asked Boone to wait outside and wheeled himself through the cozy, single-story cottage. Could he really embark on an affair with Charlotte and rent this house for their trysts?

He'd moved heaven and earth and been blessed with good fortune to find it so quickly. Small yet comfortable, its windows looked out on a compact but glorious garden. The home was private and within his meager means—probably the two most important considerations—but the low rent wasn't what drew him. He could picture them together in this informal setting, imagine Charlotte in the bedroom with her hand wrapped around one of the bed's cherry posts, gazing out the bay window to the riot of blooming rosebushes beyond.

He closed his eyes and let his head drop back. Was he really going to do this? Could he enjoy an intimate relationship with Charlotte, knowing its conclusion always loomed in the future? What if he fell in love with her? How would he survive when their affair ended, as he knew someday it would? He was no longer the tall, straight, self-assured man he'd been.

She had truly shocked him when she touched and kissed his legs. He didn't doubt she accepted the man he was—or rather, the man she saw. Broken but carrying on. Supposedly a hero. But she didn't know the real man. That one remained inside him, hidden.

Would he have been so anxious to purchase a commission if he'd known what his future held? He'd accepted the possibility of death but never considered he might be left dealing with a broken body. He'd been awarded the Victoria Cross for an act of bravery, but in his heart he truly wondered at his merit. If he'd known what fate had in store for him, would he really have returned to the battlefield to rescue Wakefield?

He heard the door open, the rustle of Charlotte's skirts and soft tread of her footsteps.

"David?"

He wheeled into the parlor. Seeing her pushed all doubt away. She fit into the house as if it had been designed to complement her. She wore a blue dress with a deep, shawl-like ivory collar. She'd brought the sky inside with her.

"You're wearing color." Color other than one acceptable for half-mourning, that was.

"You know my wearing somber colors is for appearances." One corner of her mouth curved up. "I don't mind being a hypocrite when I'm only disgusting myself, but I stop when it means risking your derision."

"I'd never criticize your decision to break from half-mourning."

She moved close, smoothed back a lock of his hair with her finger. Heat fisted low in his body.

"I know. Next month will mark two years and my mourning period will end. But today...today I wanted to wear something pretty."

For him. His heart expanded until it filled his chest, and he grinned. She was so much more than pretty.

She whirled then, paced to the kitchen and back, nodded approvingly as she looked around and asked, "How many servants will we need?"

"I should think one cook-housekeeper will be enough for a place this size. Boone will be available if we need him, too."

Charlotte went to the window that looked out on a gnarled oak and stood watching as two squirrels chased through the tree. She smiled. "It's a little jewel box of a cottage, isn't it?"

An apt description. And she would be the precious gem inside.

"It is," David agreed. "It's actually called Rose Cottage, no doubt due to the gardens."

"I'll make arrangements at the livery for my transport."

She didn't have her own coach, so she'd need to rent a conveyance. But she sounded distracted.

"Having doubts?" he asked.

She whirled, her brows drawn together. "What?"

He said nothing. She walked over and offered her hand. He took it and found her grip surprisingly firm.

"No. No doubts," she said. Her flawless ivory skin blushed pink. "May I engage the cook-housekeeper?"

David felt his own face heat. Although he'd never spoken of it, he guessed she'd realized his funds were limited and wanted to help offset these costs. As embarrassing as the concept was, he was grateful for the offer. "I'm sure you'll be much more efficient than I would be."

Her suggestion also made them partners in this venture. It settled his nerves a bit.

They were alone, and the front door was closed. He pulled her down and captured her mouth. Her warm, responsive lips moved against his and his every hesitation skipped away. Sometimes he forgot military service had taught him to live for today instead of the distant and uncertain future.

Without breaking their kiss, he grasped her narrow waist and tugged her onto his lap. Her skirt and petticoats foamed up and he found and gripped one silk-covered ankle. A contented sound escaped her, and she wrapped her arms around his shoulders and pressed herself to him. He thought he could be content staying like this forever, smelling and tasting Charlotte, cradling her in his arms. He angled his head and deepened the kiss.

#

"Jane, you needn't stay next to me." Charlotte frowned at her tenacious friend. "I don't need protection."

Jane had yet to leave her side as they mingled with perhaps thirty other guests in Lady Hamilton's music room. Charlotte loved that her friend wanted to encourage her, but sometimes she wondered if Jane believed she couldn't fend for herself. Although accusations and unsubstantiated innuendo had once wounded her, Charlotte had been proving for some time now that she no longer feared society gossip. The struggling widows she met at work had strengthened her determination to do so. They were persevering, and she had so many advantages they did not.

Also, before her every day was a man who met life without excuses. Charlotte's gaze went to David, who sat conversing with their hostess. His broad shoulders and straight back looked as strong as she knew the inner man to be.

He laughed at something Lady Hamilton said. Red glinted in his hair, and a warm, deep craving to sink her fingers into his shiny locks overwhelmed Charlotte. She'd pull his mouth to hers and...

She curled her fingers into her palms. She couldn't stand in the middle of a soiree dreaming about Scott, but she wasn't sure she could stop herself. Tonight would be their first night at the cottage.

Charlotte looked around to see if anyone was watching her face. No telling what her expression had revealed.

Jane's voice drew her attention.

"I'm not here to protect you. I enjoy your company," her friend said, chin jutting forward. For a moment she looked about to say more, but instead she gave a little shrug and turned her attention back to the room.

Lady Hamilton had been kind enough to host a soiree to promote the Patriotic Fund and the gathering was well attended. Everywhere she looked, Charlotte found cordial faces. Tonight she had a feeling of acceptance she hadn't experienced since before the scandal and Haliday's death.

"Thank goodness society seems to have acquired some common sense," Jane remarked. "Lady James and Miss Bettencourt both asked questions about you and your work. I think they're envious."

Charlotte wished she could relax, but she suspected she might always have a nagging distrust. "Hmm. I doubt that, but I can't deny they're friendlier." Everyone had been pleasant, but one person was glaringly absent. "Etherton didn't want to come tonight?"

She kept her tone casual. There had been no more talk of Phillip since the last time, so Charlotte was in the dark. Jane had been accompanied by her sister-in-law instead of her husband, and as accommodating as Jane had been this evening, something about her wasn't right. A too-bright smile stretched her lips. Flushed cheeks supplanted her creamy complexion. Also, Jane had lost weight and faint shadows darkened the delicate skin below her eyes.

"He's still at his club."

Jane and Phillip hadn't resolved their estrangement, and it had been a week! Charlotte chided herself. She had been so caught up in her own life she'd not checked on her friend. She had honestly assumed the pair would resolve their quarrel. It was a shock to find they hadn't.

"Jane, I've been a terrible friend. I'm so sorry. Are the two of you talking?"

"No." The look in Jane's brown eyes made Charlotte wish she hadn't asked, especially since they weren't in private. "Don't look so stricken. You know I'd send a note if I needed you. I've spent my days thinking, and I'm just as angry and hurt as the day I found out. Phillip takes the girls to the park every day, but he's yet to speak more than a few words to me."

Jane's shoulders lifted in an elegant little shrug, and her gaze wandered away. A moment later she looked back at Charlotte, eyes wide and dark with dismay. Charlotte turned to see what had disturbed her. At some distance stood Lady Garret, her molasses-gold dress several shades darker than her blonde hair, laughing up at Lord Radcliffe.

As if she felt Charlotte watching, Lady Garret turned, and for a moment their eyes locked.

Jolted by the baroness's bold, confrontational stare, bright with taunting amusement, Charlotte looked away. Would she *never* get over the stab of hurt she felt each time she unexpectedly encountered this Circe? The sight of her affected Charlotte much the same as a noxious odor—she had a strong compulsion to get away. Instead, Charlotte straightened her spine and plastered a smile on her face.

She hated that a mere glimpse of the woman could put her in such a state. Even though she'd successfully hid her reaction, she couldn't deny to herself that she'd had one. It was as if the baroness still held sway over her. Her eyes sought Scott. She caught him watching her and immediately felt better. His calm, steady gaze reminded her he admired and believed in her.

He said something to Boone, who stood behind him, and a moment later wheeled up beside her. Charlotte wanted to sink into his lap, the way she had at their cottage, and bury her face in the crook of his neck. She'd feel secure with his arms wrapped around her, and that certainty astounded her. When had she begun to equate total safety with David Scott, and what had happened to her determination of a moment ago to stand up for herself? Sexual attraction was one thing, but she couldn't let herself become dependent on a man. She'd been fool enough to do that once, but never again.

David isn't like anyone else. He'd never betray you.

Charlotte ignored the disturbing little voice in her head. They had been careful to make an arrangement that maintained their personal independence. It suited them both.

"What is *she* doing here?" Jane asked in a fierce whisper.

"I imagine she came with Radcliffe. He's Lady Hamilton's cousin. I believe the past month they've been seen in each other's company on several occasions—or so the *Times* has reported."

Pleased to hear her voice sound cool and pragmatic, Charlotte concentrated on maintaining an impassive expression. Beside her, Scott's gaze darted to Lady Garret and his eyes narrowed, giving him a dangerous look. A subtle tension stiffened his body.

He looked at Charlotte again, and his eyes roved her face, fiercely assessing. Oh, God. The feeling of safety he gave her... The icy strain caused by Lady Garret's presence had completely dissolved. A different kind of awareness thrummed through her veins. She wanted to kiss David, open her mouth and slide her tongue along his. Rub her breasts against him. Watch his blue eyes heat and become gas-lit flame. A warm, aching emptiness settled between her legs. An emptiness that pulled and tingled and begged to be filled.

Scott sucked in a sharp breath. "Come. Sit down. Lady Hamilton is telling everyone to have a seat. The pianist will begin in a few minutes."

Jane gave Charlotte's hand a squeeze and moved off to join her sister-in-law. Charlotte managed to pull her eyes from Scott's and force her feet forward. It was a relief to have the anxiety caused by Lady Garret driven from her mind, but Scott's power to do so was itself unsettling.

Charlotte moved to a chair that sat at the end of a row. Boone positioned Scott's chair next to hers and then went to stand near the wall. Lady Garret was behind her somewhere, so it was time to act like the kind of woman she was determined to be. Circe couldn't bother her unless Charlotte let her.

Awareness of Scott's presence beside her heightened all Charlotte's senses. Even though they weren't touching, she could feel him along the left side of her body, a sensuous heat that penetrated clear through the silk of her dress and her many layers of petticoats. She closed her eyes, inhaling the spicy masculine scent she'd memorized. Suddenly aware she was swaying toward him, she snapped her eyes open and straightened. He sat grinning at her, the gleam in his eyes bringing warmth to her face. She opened her fan and applied it vigorously, which only made his grin widen.

"I think you've spoken to most of the people here," he said. "It appears you're back in the good graces of society. They probably realize how ridiculous they were and feel guilty about it now. Time and distance brought them some sense."

"Mmm." It was sweet of him to try and distract her and make her feel better. She could agree with him and leave it at that, but a powerful desire to tell him the truth gripped her.

"I just can't trust it," she whispered. "I've had too many I thought friends turn away from me when it all happened. Lady Garret just reminds me of that. I still feel betrayed. How can they expect me to forget? Or to forgive."

David's jaw tightened. "I want to hold you," he said, his voice a low rasp.

Inside, she quivered with longing. Scott's arms would fill the emptiness that persisted even while she smiled and mingled. He would soothe the distress Lady Garret provoked—but not for much longer, she assured herself.

Most of the seats filled and the room began to settle, but a small flurry of activity drew Charlotte's attention to the back of the room. It was her father. Lady Hamilton drew him inside, directing all her attention and conversation to him. She drew him forward and up to the very front row, seated him, laid her fan on the chair beside him and went to stand at the front of the room.

Obviously, their hostess planned to sit beside him. Charlotte wasn't overly surprised. Her dynamic, handsome father had been attracting beautiful and savvy women for years. As one of the wealthiest men in London, it didn't matter if Matthew Shelby arrived late. It didn't matter that the huge, sparkling diamond stickpin in his necktie turned his elegant, correct attire flashy. His common beginnings no longer mattered. His wealth compensated for every failing.

The pianist strode to the piano, and Lady Hamilton began her introduction. Having heard the man play several years before,

Charlotte expected a commanding performance. He bowed in acknowledgment of the introduction, but as he straightened, his gaze landed on Scott's legs and the wheeled chair and then darted away.

Had Scott noticed? He hadn't moved or in any way indicated he'd seen that startled, assessing look, yet somehow Charlotte knew he had. She wanted to reassure him, to grip his hand and tell him how full he made her heart. But she couldn't do any of those things.

She leaned toward him, her mouth near his ear, and hid their faces with her open fan. She took a long, delicious breath that filled her head with the scent of David Scott and turned her insides to warm candle wax, and she could feel the stiff fabric of her corset pressing against the tender tips of her breasts. "I can't wait," she whispered.

His head turned her way. He studied her eyes and her lips, and his mouth curved.

As the notes of Chopin's "Heroic Polonaise" spilled from the pianist's fingers, Charlotte sat back against her chair and thought of the hours ahead.

#

"Good evening, Scott. Charlotte, I need a word with you."

Charlotte's father stood before them. Charlotte hadn't seen him since the day of their argument at her office. Lady Hamilton's guests were dispersing, and their hostess stood at the door, bidding them good-night.

"Will it take long?" Scott waited beside her. He'd escorted her tonight, so he would have to wait if there was a discussion.

Father's mouth tightened. For once, though, Charlotte didn't really care if he was perturbed. She'd waited all evening to be alone with David, and now Father was delaying that. Of course, if she refused he'd ignore her. When he had his mind set on something, he selfishly disregarded all but his own need.

He picked up her hand, wrapped it over his arm, gave Scott a nod, and led her away to a deserted corner. She had to lengthen her stride to keep up with his long legs. At least he didn't waste any time getting to the point.

"What was that woman doing here?"

Charlotte didn't need to ask to whom he referred. "I believe Lady Garret came with Lord Radcliffe." The couple had been among the first to leave.

"What is Radcliffe about, getting himself mixed up with her?" Shelby didn't wait for Charlotte to answer. "Did she approach you?"

That hard look in his eyes made men quake, but Charlotte was inured to it. "No. She didn't."

His expression shifted and his tension appeared to ease. The concern surprised her. On the heels of that, warmth unfolded at her center.

Her father nodded and headed them back toward Scott, who'd sat watching their exchange. "If she says anything objectionable, I want to know at once."

Ah. Suddenly, Charlotte understood. He hadn't asked a single question about her welfare. Hadn't spoken a friendly word. No, of course not. His concern was for her reputation, not her happiness. And while she'd shown no greater amount of caring for him, that didn't matter. Father liked it that way.

#

Vivian Garret held her breath as David Scott and Charlotte Haliday entered the cottage before her. As instructed, her coachman had stopped some distance down the street. She stared, hardly able to believe her eyes. Scott and Charlotte were engaged in an *affaire de coeur*.

She'd *known* it. It had been sheer luck that she and Radcliffe arrived at Lady Hamilton's fashionable townhouse just behind Scott's coach. She'd observed the couple as Scott lowered himself into his chair then sensed something in the way they looked at and spoke to each other. They hadn't known they were being observed, and so they'd not been guarding their reactions. There had only been one quick, shared look, but she'd recognized it.

Then, inside—what fun!—seeing the insipid Charlotte start after noticing her. Vivian had nearly laughed aloud. Hopefully her presence at the soiree had ruined the tedious ninny's evening. Vivian had wrangled the invitation from Radcliffe with that very intent, and discomposing Matthew Shelby as well had made things that much better. His presence had been a surprise.

Of course, Radcliffe had expected the evening to end with them enjoying themselves in her bed, but she'd avoided that by pretending a sudden illness. The genuine concern the earl demonstrated made her squirm with guilt, but she would make it up to him another night. At her residence she'd convinced him to leave her and then took a Hansom back to Lady Hamilton's. And, lo and behold, Vivian's speculation bore fruit. Scott and Charlotte had led her here.

Oh, what a delight! Hadn't the haughty Charlotte changed? She was Naughty Charlotte now.

Scott's carriage left. The lights in the front of the cottage went out, leaving it lit only by a distant glow from a back room. Vivian's appreciation faded. She rubbed suddenly throbbing temples, knocked on the cab's roof, signaling the driver to move on, then leaned back, madly blinking to keep brimming tears from falling from her eyes. How could Charlotte Haliday be meeting a lover? Quite unfairly, the forlorn widow was rising from her ashes like the Phoenix. She'd already lived a life of privilege and wealth. Her father had given her the education, clothes and jewels that most women could only dream of. She'd married a titled lord and become titled herself. And now she'd taken a lover, which meant she was happy. It was...not...fair.

Swiping at her eyes, Vivian stamped her foot. The satisfaction she'd recently found with Radcliffe seemed suddenly hollow. Radcliffe wouldn't marry her. She'd gained a reputation when she'd had her affair with Haliday and was no longer the kind of woman Radcliffe wanted for a wife, while if Vivian knew anything at all about Charlotte Haliday née Shelby, she knew the look Charlotte had shared with Scott meant she loved him. Somehow the lady had persevered through scandal and tragedy and found love. Why was she fated to have so much good fortune?

Well, it wouldn't last. Vivian didn't intend for Charlotte to triumph and marry a hero. No, indeed. Disaster had befallen Charlotte once before, and Vivian would make sure it did again.

Sniffling, Vivian tightened her wrap against the chill night air. She had meant only to fool Haliday into thinking his wife had hired a man to assault him, when in fact it had been herself. The ruffian was supposed to give Haliday a mild thrashing and warn him to stay away from her. Vivian had assumed Haliday would easily be convinced the attack was engineered by his wife. After all, wasn't a spiteful, spurned wife capable of almost anything? Only, something had gone wrong that night behind his club. She'd underestimated Haliday. The expected grappling had turned into a fierce engagement that ended with both men dead.

Hot prickles ran down her spine and skated over her skin. Even now Vivian could hardly stand to think of him as dead, and she refused to feel guilty. She'd merely wanted to make Haliday angry with his wife. Wanted to create more fodder for gossip. Wanted society to have more evidence that Charlotte was a scheming, jealous shrew, and in turn Matthew Shelby would have been incensed at the additional damage done to his daughter's reputation and marriage. It had all gone awry.

Now Vivian had been presented with another opportunity to crush Charlotte Haliday and her father, and this time, she vowed, nothing would go wrong.

CHAPTER TWENTY-ONE

Charlotte stood staring at the aromatic blooms that graced the table, unaccountably uneasy and not the least bit hungry.

Mrs. Penny, Rose Cottage's new cook-housekeeper, had left a cold repast for them. Boone asked if he might be of service but, dismissed by Scott, retired. The designated housekeeper's sitting room-cum-bedroom was unoccupied and available for his use since Mrs. Penny went home each night.

All day Charlotte had been in a state of anticipation, thinking of being here with Scott, so how could she now feel self-conscious and unsure of herself? *Oh, dear God.* At the inn she'd been bold, and excitement gripped them both. She knew he admired her newfound confidence at work and found her appearance pleasing. And, Scott would not desire a weak woman. He'd want a woman as confident and capable as he was—and there was naught of that in her tonight.

Her mouth uncomfortably dry, she licked her lips.

"Charlotte?"

She didn't know how long she'd been standing lost in thought. His low voice drew her, made her wish them past this unexpected awkwardness. Scott had poured two glasses of wine and moved onto the wide chaise he'd purchased for the main room of the cottage. "Wide enough for two," he'd told her, and indeed it was.

He invited her to the empty space beside him with a lifted arm. He'd removed his coat, waistcoat and necktie, and he looked brawny and altogether appealing.

She imagined she heard all kinds of things in his voice. Desire, most certainly, but she thought she heard concern and compassion in those deep tones, too. Just his speaking her name eased the tension knotted inside her.

He held out his hand, and she nearly stumbled in her haste to gain his side. When she reached out, he captured her hand and pulled her down into his arms. She pressed her cheek against the firm muscles of his chest and wrapped her arm about his lean waist. His warm hand rubbed up and down her back. Even though it was summer and too warm for a fire, the cool night air had chilled her during their drive to the cottage. They'd felt the first drops of rain as they entered.

"Not hungry?"

"No, not in the least hungry."

For some minutes the patter of gentle rain was the only sound in the room. Scott's body heat seeped into her, and she relaxed against him.

"I've a friendly ear, Charlotte. You can trust anything you say will be kept in confidence."

She sat up and searched his steady blue eyes. He hadn't needed to tell her that. She trusted this man. It wasn't indiscretion she feared.

Reaching for one of the glasses of wine waiting on the table beside them, Charlotte took a sip. Scott knew the conversation with her father had upset her. He probably guessed she was nervous, too.

She took another swallow of wine and returned the glass to the table. Scott spread his hand over the back of her head and pulled her toward him. The press of his warm lips against her forehead cracked something inside her chest and made her grow warm and soft there. Then he gently resettled her head.

One by one, he plucked the pins from her hair then combed through the long locks with his fingers. Her eyes filled with unrelated tears. *Oh, no. Please, no.* Charlotte squeezed her eyelids shut. Thank God David couldn't see her face. She could barely suppress the surging roil of emotion her father's reaction to Lady Garret had kindled. Why must it choose now to push its way to the surface? And why was it so impossible to force it back while nestled in this man's arms?

She fought back the urge to rise and escape. Did she want to explain how angry and empty her father made her feel? How she hated that, even knowing how he'd wronged her, she still caught herself trying to please him? Should she tell Scott everything about her marriage? Would telling him these things unburden her heart, or would it just shame her?

Scott had destroyed his copy of Lady Garret's novel, but he must know the basic facts of her marriage and its scandalous failure. All of London knew. Still, he didn't know everything. No one did, not even Jane.

Charlotte didn't know if telling him was the right thing to do, but the compulsion to do so, to release all the secrets and pain bottled up inside her was overwhelming. She'd not felt this longing with anyone else, but with David Scott the urge was too powerful to resist.

She took a deep breath and let it sigh out. Scott's fingers burrowed into her hair, combing and stroking, and her tension leaked away.

"Seeing Lady Garret upset me. When I expect to meet her I guard myself, but when she surprises me it is as if she steals all the air from the room. I'm paralyzed."

Scott's warm palm rested on her upper back, his hand rubbing and soothing her. She lay on her side, half atop him, his body hard and solid beneath. Simple peace flowed through her, and she released another sigh.

"When I married Haliday, I loved him. I trusted him. I thought he loved me, too, even though I knew my dowry had attracted his initial interest. He charmed me…."

She glanced up at Scott and found those red-gold lashes hiding his eyes. Did ladies discuss former lovers with their current paramour? His tension-free face and relaxed, wide mouth invited her confidence. She might worry about Scott no longer accepting her after she unburdened herself, but she couldn't find the slightest sign of apprehension about him. The way he held her, the way he listened, he looked unshakeable.

Oh, but she wanted to believe in that certainty.

"I was actually glad about the huge dowry. I knew he was desperate for money to repair his estate and his coffers. I was so glad I could help him."

"And now? You don't think he loved you?"

"He told me he didn't."

Scott inhaled sharply. "What a bastard."

It wasn't so difficult after all, baring her soul to David. It was somewhat liberating, in fact.

"He was always very contained, very self-assured and proud. He was fourteen years older. I never expected him to be demonstrative unless we were private. I suppose, having no experience, I regarded the act of lovemaking proof of deep feeling."

She paused. It seemed impossible now, that she hadn't realized his lovemaking was empty of all but the most base feeling. For four years she'd been happy. Haliday had been busy overseeing the repairs to his estate. He'd paid off his debts. Most evenings found them attending dinner parties or entertainments. She had done her part by renovating the interior of the London townhouse and Hazelton Park, his country seat. She'd enjoyed being his viscountess. After a lifetime of being socially inferior, she found it heady, using skills she'd spent her youth perfecting and being admired for them.

And, Haliday was a man with extraordinary looks, a sharp mind and a way about him that garnered respect from other gentlemen and caused women to envy her. She supposed she'd been too engaged by her new status and way of life to see that outside the bedroom she and Haliday rarely spent exclusive time together. They'd certainly never lain together as she and Scott were doing now.

"His visits to my bedroom became less and less frequent. He began staying out most of the night and told me he was enjoying pursuits at his club. I buried my unease and reassured myself."

Scott picked up her glass and wordlessly offered more wine. Charlotte raised herself up to accept, took a couple of sips then returned the glass to him before easing back onto his chest. The pause helped sort her thoughts.

"One night the frightened little voice in my head overcame my assurances and kept me awake until he arrived home. I mustered my courage and opened the connecting door to my husband's room."

She'd never done that before; he'd always come to her. She recalled how he'd looked, sprawled in his chair before the fire, his coat, waistcoat and shoes discarded, his shirt open, a glass of liquor in his hand. He'd shocked her a little. He'd looked...dissolute.

"I could tell from the glitter of his eyes that he'd been drinking. He was surprised, and I think displeased, too, when I entered."

"Ah, Charlotte," Scott murmured, as if he sensed the pain that was coming. As if he knew how she'd spent that evening preparing and needed reassurance from her husband and not a confrontation. She'd bathed in perfumed water, dried her hair before the fire, brushed it and left it hanging down her back. Her silk nightgown had been new, yellow as butter and seductive enough that Rebecca had hidden a smile when she saw it.

She pressed on. "I hurried across the room, knelt beside him, gathered my courage and laid my hand upon his thigh. I told him I'd missed him."

He'd frowned at her and sighed. She remembered that heavy, wordless expression of weariness as if she'd heard it yesterday. He'd tossed down the remainder of his drink, carefully set the glass on the table beside him and shifted in his chair, neatly dislodging her hand.

Charlotte realized she was clutching a handful of Scott's shirt in a fist. She forced her fingers open, stroked over the wrinkled fabric, felt the hard muscle of his chest below it, and continued. "He said he'd done his best to produce an heir. He didn't see the point in continuing to be so dedicated to it, since he'd pretty well given up hope of ever getting one from me."

The words had nearly smothered her with feelings of shame and inadequacy. She'd failed Haliday in the most basic and important way an aristocratic wife could fail. But that was not the end of the story.

"Then he laughed. Said what a joke it all was. He'd married me in order to repair the title, and now it appeared he wouldn't have a son to inherit."

The look in his eyes had made the world stop. She didn't know why she'd been so shocked. He hadn't been to her bed in weeks. And yet...

Scott's arms tightened around her. The slight change of position brought Charlotte's cheek over the muscular swell of his chest, and the steady beat of his heart filled her ear. Charlotte slid her hand up his chest until it rested against his warm neck, and her fingertips nudged into the cool silk of his hair.

"He said he thought it would be a relief to me that he'd found someone else to share his favors. After all, he went on, we hadn't been a love match. Foolish me, I couldn't believe he was being intimate with another woman. I was so naïve." Charlotte forced herself to breathe slowly. In, out. "I thought he'd fallen in love with me, just as I'd fallen in love with him."

She stopped and focused on Scott's heartbeat. If she weren't careful she'd break down much the same as she had on that horrid night. At least she'd managed to return to her bedroom and not collapse in her husband's presence.

"How did you learn his amour was Lady Garret?" Scott asked.

"Jane—my friend Lady Etherton—brought me the baroness's little green book. That was when I found out whose bed my husband was visiting. The rest of London found out, too."

That damnable book. At first Charlotte couldn't believe the baroness had meant the thinly disguised characters to depict herself, Haliday and Charlotte, but then the smirks and the outraged and pitying looks began. Society had taken the little novel for truth.

"It was nothing but lies," Charlotte whispered. "Lady Garret portrayed a Lady H___, who represented me, as a vindictive, evil shrew who dedicated herself to nothing but obstructing the two lovers, Lady G___ and Lord H___. They were more than mere lovers, the novel claimed. They were soul mates connected by the deepest of loves. I doubt society would ever have sympathized with the adulterers if I hadn't been assigned such a malicious persona. But it worked. And even after she published such despicable lies, Haliday continued to see the woman.

"I didn't understand, because at that time I still believed he had a heart. When I confronted him, he seemed genuinely puzzled. Told me it was just a story, no one took it for truth. He denied being scorned or criticized. And he didn't care if I was."

Scott's thumb rubbed up and down the back of her neck. "I know what a scandal it caused. I read about it in the papers. The society reporters seemed to follow the three of you everywhere. When Haliday was shot, they even suggested you as a suspect."

"I know there were some who believed I conspired against Haliday, but the detective inspector never did. He always felt it was a case of theft gone terribly wrong."

"I wish I'd known you then. That I could have been a friend to you."

She couldn't tell him—she simply *couldn't*—that a part of her had been glad when Haliday was murdered, when it all had come to an end and she was set free. Scott was such an honorable man. How could he possibly forgive that?

"Your belief in me now means more than you know," she said.

She hadn't intended to tell him all this. Not now, not for a long time. Maybe not ever. She'd started the evening aflutter with anticipation, but seeing Lady Garret and Father had stirred all the self-doubt she'd tried so hard to quell. Now she found herself regretting her honesty.

"You were kind to offer a friendly ear and let me unburden myself, but I'm afraid I've ruined our evening."

He cupped her jaw and tilted her head back. "You haven't ruined a thing," he said huskily.

He kissed her, and everything else fell away. Charlotte opened for his tongue and sought his warmth and strength, wrapping her arms around him and pressing tight against him. He tasted sublime, and the feel of his hard body made every feminine part of her warm and ache for more intimate contact. With his kiss, that hungry need, unlike anything she'd felt before, overcame her. He answered her with his mouth and tongue, heightening the desire and leaving her in no doubt that his feelings matched hers.

His lips slid away. Breathing ragged, he kissed her face, her eyes, her temple, then returned to plunder her mouth. She ceased to think. Feeling supplanted everything until Scott withdrew again. He looked at her, the creases at the corners of his eyes deepening and his mouth curving a bit, and she knew he wasn't smiling at her. This was a smile that spilled from the happiness he held inside. She felt it, too.

He pressed a quick, hard kiss to her lips. "Shall we adjourn to the bedroom?"

Charlotte nodded, rose and stood behind Scott's chair as he lifted himself on stiff arms and transferred from the chaise to his chair. He pulled his legs over and settled himself, and Charlotte bent over the back of the chair to embrace him. For a long moment they stayed thus, her arms wrapped around him, their heads together and Scott's strong hands resting on her arms. Charlotte wanted to thank him but found her words had dried up. So she straightened, picked up the lamp and followed behind as he rolled his chair into the bedroom.

Tonight was different in many ways. Their first time together had been impulsive and dominated by compelling, fierce desire. They'd already been undressed. Scott had been quite naked, in fact. Tonight could not have been more deliberate.

The bed was turned down, but they were both fully clothed. Charlotte set down the lamp and stood, hands clasped at her waist, not sure what to do. Would she need to play valet and help Scott remove his clothing? Would they watch each other undress? She'd always been wearing a nightgown and ensconced in bed when Haliday exercised his marital rights.

As he'd done at the chaise, Scott lifted himself out of his chair onto the chair arm, then over to the bed. Immediately he grabbed his legs and pulled them over. Bending at the waist, he stretched out his long arms and tugged shoes from his feet with ease then made quick work of removing his shirt and small shirt, and soon he was naked of all but trousers. He made merry with those, too, lying back to unbutton the front and push trousers and underdrawers down his hips at one time. Then he sat up again, stripped them off his legs and tossed them into his chair.

Charlotte still watched, feeling unaccountably shy and gauche. His beauty was the living embodiment of a Greek master's statue. The only thing to mar him was the puckered scar high on his shoulder. A saber wound. He'd made light of it when she questioned it at the inn, but its size and position were no laughing matter. A little lower and his lung would have been pierced.

She looked away from the uncomfortable reminder of his mortality. The rest of him was much more pleasant to gaze upon, like perhaps the kiss of sun and air that made his hair gleam the red-tinted gold of a copper penny, hair that dusted his chest and arrowed down his abdomen.

Scott met her gaze and made no attempt to hide the proof of his desire. His eyes narrowed. "Come here, Bluebell. You need a little help, don't you?"

Warm feeling crowded out her hesitancy. David, her matter-of-fact lover, would unerringly lead her.

She moved next to him and sat, presenting the row of buttons at her back. The first touch of his sure fingers brushing her neck as he opened one sent heat streaking through her. Under the many layers of her clothes, the tips of her breasts hardened.

"Bluebell?" she asked. The second and third buttons came free.

"Didn't you know? Your eyes are the exact purple color of bluebells."

His lips grazed her back, and a tiny moan escaped her. Her bodice fell open.

"No, I didn't know," she gasped. "They've always been compared to amethysts."

He drew her bodice down her arms and tossed it atop his clothing. His mouth captured her earlobe, his tongue and teeth took ownership of her flesh, and she quivered from head to toes. With a little tug, he released her ear.

"Amethysts are cold and hard, their fire forever locked inside. That's not you, Charlotte. You're vibrant and sweet and brimming with life." He paused, rested his face against her hair and took a deep breath. "And fragrant."

Hands at her hips, he urged her up and began pulling the layers of skirt and underskirt and petticoats down. She helped him, letting everything puddle around her feet. She held her breath as his hands wrapped around her waist and released the tie of her lacings. He urged her back down on the bed as he loosened them, easing the constriction of her corset, the fastenings of which came next. His warm breath fanned her back, his hands brushing her breasts in a purposeful way as he released each hook. He added her corset to the growing pile of clothes and wrapped powerful arms around her, pulling her back against him.

For so long she'd struggled to be strong and unbending. To be likened to a small, fragile yet enduring flower released the constraints inside her. She didn't need any protective barriers between herself and David. She needn't guard herself, and that knowledge went deep, to the very bottom of her, enfolding and holding her with the same strength as his arms. The discovery was momentous—and also alarming. She'd once felt that way about Haliday, and she'd been wrong. So very wrong.

But there's more caring in David's little finger than in all of Haliday's person.

Scott drew her chemise up and lifted it away. Her drawers followed.

Charlotte turned in toward his arms as he lay back, pressed herself against his heat and, still shy about showing her emotions, turned her face into the curve of his neck. She closed her eyes, staggered by the feel of his naked flesh against hers. The relief and desire and anticipation were so strong, the ache for him was nearly painful. She rocked her hips, rubbing his hardness against the acute sensitivity of her feminine flesh, and they moaned simultaneously.

"I can't wait, David. Please don't make me," she begged.

A choked laugh escaped him. "Ah, Bluebell, what am I going to do with you?"

Love me.

The thought rose up from nowhere, and Charlotte immediately discarded it, terrified. Then David effortlessly positioned her under him, adjusted his legs, and oh so slowly eased into her. She thought she might shatter, the already severe tension in her womb and between her legs rising. She felt every bit of him pressing inside her cunny.

His mouth captured the peak of her breast, and his teeth and tongue worried the contracted tip to a state of exquisite feeling. When he moved, the sweet stroke made her gasp.

"David."

He lifted his head. There was just enough light to see his eyes.

"*David.*"

The tension wound tighter. She was ensnared by his unhurried loving, every inch of her connected to him in an elemental way. Their bodies moved as if perfectly matched. Their breaths rasped, they sighed and moaned. She clutched him to her, intoxicated by his slow, powerful strokes and ardent kisses. Strong, calloused fingers smoothed her hair from her moist temples, and his lips and tongue tasted her face and neck.

Charlotte wanted it to go on forever. She moaned and he captured her mouth in a searing kiss that laid claim to more than just her lips. When the kiss ended, she was gasping and he was straining, and inside he was pressing in a new way. Her tension geysered, her body clenched around him, and she disintegrated like so much stardust flung into the furnace of the sun.

He, too, groaned and shuddered, gripped by release.

He collapsed against her. A minute later he roused and shifted them enough to ease his weight from her in a way that left them still entangled. For a time they simply breathed. His eyes were bluer than she'd ever seen them. She tried to keep her own eyes shuttered by her lashes, afraid of what he might see in their depths.

He gazed at her a moment and his lips curved the slightest bit, just enough to deepen the grooves at the corners of his mouth. He brushed his mouth back and forth across hers, kissing her softly. She'd never known anything so sweetly tender. And just like that, the yearning for him was back.

Her wantonness shocked her. Surely such strong desire marked her common origins? Jane didn't share the intimate details of the marriage bed, but Charlotte was sure ladies didn't have the appetites of harlots.

She moved away, and David's member slid from her body. Charlotte got up, pulled the covers up from the foot of the bed, and doused the lamp. She then rousted through their tumbled pile of clothing until she found her chemise, but pulling it on didn't lessen the desire that pulsed anew. Her nipples rubbed against the fine fabric and she shivered with the desire to rub them against him.

She returned to the bed, carefully maintaining a space between their bodies. Feeling decidedly cold and nervous, she wished she could snuggle up next to David again, and hated that she was now wide awake when minutes ago she'd been replete and drowsy. She turned away from him and sighed, and wondered if she shouldn't just go home. Then his arm came around her and pulled her back against him.

His heat enfolded her. His hand coasted down her belly, sank into her curls, and nudged her sex. She wiggled backward, pressed into him, and felt proof of his wanting her again, hard against the back of her hip.

His tongue slid across her shoulder, and his lips moved against her nape. "I didn't get enough. I want more."

His husky, seductive voice, his arousing mouth, his hand caressing her in a manner she'd never contemplated—they devastated her. He wanted her again. Again! An amorous relief twined through her. She hadn't even known it could happen again so soon.

She turned toward him and met his seeking lips. Their kiss was so deep, so powerful, it made her breasts heavy and the area between her thighs tingle. His fingers went there again, and she gasped.

"Do you like that?"

She did, oh, she did. She nodded and tried to tell him with her kiss.

When they broke apart, his eyes gleamed with an intensity that filled her with heat. He smiled, pulled her leg over his hip, and came into her.

CHAPTER TWENTY-TWO

David woke early, aroused and wanting Charlotte. He lay spooned against her relaxed and sleeping body, and he wished he could stay here, in Rose Cottage—in its *bed*—all day, but he couldn't. They'd agreed to leave for their respective homes early, before daybreak.

Slowly he adjusted the position of his arm so he could enjoy the gentle rise and fall of her ribs as she breathed. He hadn't before doubted his ability to work beside her without revealing their personal association, but now he wondered. Since his injury he'd discovered a not insignificant talent for concealing his emotions, but he couldn't imagine being able to hide what he was feeling now.

He loved her. There was no mistaking it.

He'd been a fool to think he could engage in an affair with Charlotte and not fall in love. He hadn't even made it through twenty-four hours without succumbing. He should have guessed. He'd been enamored even before the sex.

But oh, how sweet. Right now, lying beside her, the world could not get any sweeter.

Still, this moment would end, he reminded himself, as eventually their liaison would, too. It was fated to end just as he was destined to be alone. Charlotte deserved only the best of men as the husband and father of her children, and he was crippled.

He'd suspected he'd be hurt when the affair ended. Now he knew the pain would exceed every battlefield injury he'd ever sustained. He squeezed his eyes shut. He had borne pain. He could bear it again.

Somehow he knew she'd never before shared all she'd confided last night. Did she even realize how much she trusted him? If she did, she could rest easy. She might not acknowledge her faith in him, but last night it had become the cornerstone of his love.

He took a deep breath, inhaling Charlotte's distinctive rose and jasmine cologne mingled with the musk of their lovemaking. It had to be the most divine scent he'd ever smelled. He'd awakened hard, and this made him even harder.

Pressing against her lush buttocks, he swept aside her hair and dragged his tongue across the pale, delicious skin at her nape. So tender and so vulnerable, God, but he loved that spot. His hand moved leisurely up her chest, coming to rest with one nipple nestled in his palm. She rewarded him with a sigh, a languid shifting of limbs, and her body pressing into his.

For a minute he enjoyed the contours and textures of her breast before sliding his hand down to the juncture of her thighs. As if he'd commanded it, she quivered.

#

Afterward, watching Charlotte dress enthralled him. He wouldn't have thought it would be so. After all, she was covering up all that tempting flesh rather than revealing it. But David found that, having traced her curves with his hands, he regarded her in a totally new way. He now knew the fine shape of the legs hidden under all those layers of skirts and how they gripped his hips. He knew the almost translucent whiteness of her breasts, the dusty pink of her areolas, the taste and silky feel of her skin. And he knew how all of that was for him alone.

He kept one eye on her as he donned his own clothes and got into his chair. Then he gave her his undivided attention.

She'd gotten over her initial shyness and grinned at his scrutiny. Finally, she sat and presented her back to him. She needed his assistance to manage her buttons, just as she'd needed it the previous night to undo them.

Then he hadn't noticed, but today he saw each ivory button was a carved rose. He smiled and began slipping buttons through buttonholes. The activity gave him the perfect opportunity to broach an important topic. One that had been worrying him since their first time together.

"What if you begin increasing, Charlotte? Have you considered that?" She'd said not to worry, but if that happened she'd really have no choice but to marry him regardless of what either of them wanted.

The thought stilled his fingers, and she glanced back at him. "There's little chance of that happening. I was married four years. Haliday wanted an heir and applied himself to the task. To no avail."

He hated thinking of her with her former husband, most especially of the man exercising his marital rights. David clenched his jaw and resumed his buttoning endeavors.

"You were never with child?" he asked.

Her head dropped forward. Something about her vulnerable posture made him grasp her shoulders, as somehow he knew there was more.

"I...I was enceinte when he died. I hadn't yet told him."

He began gently kneading her shoulders and wondered how often Charlotte had chastised herself for that. "What happened?"

"I lost the child in the days after his murder."

"I'm sorry, Charlotte."

He slowly fastened the last three buttons. She stood and went to the mirror that hung over the bureau. Knotting her hair low on her neck, she quickly began inserting pins. The mirror revealed her solemn stare, straight into her reflected eyes.

"The physician who attended me said, since I'd gone four years without conceiving and then lost my first pregnancy within a few weeks, he felt there was little chance I'd ever carry a child the necessary duration."

She looked so miserable. Damn his useless legs! He wanted to stand behind her and turn her into his arms and hold her. Instead, he was effectively relegated to tugging at her skirts.

"I'm sorry. It's no consolation, but at least you won't have to worry about being forced into wedlock with me."

The remark made him feel rather cruel and cold when he'd meant to be reassuring.

Charlotte turned and gave him a wide smile that didn't reach her eyes. "Yes. I'm sure it's a relief to you as well."

It wasn't that he didn't want children. It was that he'd want them to have a better father.

He gave her a very direct look. "You will be sure and tell me if it should happen."

Her eyes widened. They looked especially dewy, perhaps suspiciously so, and he rolled his chair closer. She stepped back, then whirled and made for the door.

"Of course I will, David," she called. "We'd best hurry if we're to get home before sunrise."

He trailed behind, the conversation having left him uneasy. As much as he wanted this association, was it wise? What if she were wrong? The last thing he wanted to do was force Charlotte into a marriage she found undesirable, and how could it be anything but that when he was a shattered husk instead of the man she deserved?

He entered the cottage's cozy sitting room and found Boone conversing with her, a hack he'd engaged already waiting out front. She'd wrapped her velvet stole around her shoulders, and David rolled his chair close. He wanted to kiss her good-bye, but such an act was unthinkable with Boone watching. So, somehow they ended up holding hands. Charlotte's heightened color made David wonder if she wasn't a bit embarrassed.

He raked his free hand through his hair, and with the other he gave her fingers a gentle squeeze.

"You never wear a hat," she pointed out. "Or use pomade."

"I think my naked head draws as many stares as my wheelchair. I know I'm not fashionable, but top hats tend to fall off when I'm leaning forward, wheeling myself."

"And your lack of pomade or hair oil?"

"Habit. I've a habit of rumpling my hair when I'm thinking. Or frustrated. I guess I do it when I'm bored, too. I tried all the usual hair compounds, but invariably I'd end up with my hair sticking straight up."

"Well, I like it." With the tip of her forefinger Charlotte smoothed back a lock from his forehead. When her finger stilled at his temple and she smiled, it was as if he'd never sated himself last night or again a mere hour ago.

She glanced at Boone, blushed, and a moment later was gone.

#

Three weeks later, Charlotte stepped from her hack and waited for Persa to jump down. The little dog had become a favorite at the Fund offices, and Charlotte never tired of watching their younger visitors grin when Persa bounded up to them. Fur waving, the dog now leapt to the ground and raced to the Fund office entrance.

Persa's tail wagged madly as she waited at the door for Charlotte. Today the pet made things feel more routine when they were anything but. She'd left David, her lover, early this morning. In a few minutes she'd be greeting Mr. Scott, her supervisor, under the friendly eyes of George Chetney. So Persa was a welcome distraction.

The hack drove away, and Charlotte pressed her hand to her midsection, wishing she could quell the excited flutters that assailed her. They'd had the luxury of meeting at the cottage for three weeks now. She wouldn't have expected to still feel this level of excitement whenever she encountered David, yet she did. There was truly no reason for nerves, but her body seemed to have a different opinion.

She knew the skirt and bodice she wore were really too fine for the office, but she'd wanted to wear her favorite ensemble again. The deep purple-blue color most attractively complemented her eyes, and David called her Bluebell because of her eyes.

Thoughts of last night brought memories of David's caressing hands, and Charlotte felt herself warm. Aware she stood motionless and smiling, she pulled herself from her reverie and started again toward the door, focusing on Persa and laughing at the charming picture her pet made.

"You just want to see if Mr. Chetney has saved a bite of his breakfast for you."

The blow came from out of nowhere. It wasn't just a bump that unbalanced her and caused her to fall; it was a slam that knocked her off her feet and sent her flying. She landed hard on her left side then settled facedown, arms spread, the breath driven from her lungs. Stunned and struggling to breathe, she barely comprehended the presence of a man grabbing her reticule, roughly pulling its strap from her arm, and running away. Persa tore after him, growling ferociously. Then Charlotte was alone.

She managed small gasps and then larger breaths. She could hear Persa's bark becoming more and more distant, and worry for her dog replaced concern for herself. Her palms and knees stung and her left arm and hip throbbed. She'd smacked her chin and mouth, too.

She managed to raise herself onto her uninjured forearm and roll to her right side. Everything worked. She sat up but almost immediately a weak head and queasiness assailed her. Suddenly hot and sweaty, Charlotte reclined and stared up at the sky. The hard paving stones beneath her, still cold from the night, felt surprisingly comfortable.

"Lady Haliday!" Running footsteps stopped at her side, and Lord Wakefield knelt beside her. Concerned eyes swept over her. "Are you all right?"

She hurt. Her head spun. The buzzing in her ears nearly obliterated his words. And, Wakefield's appearance relieved her, but there was something wrong about him. He didn't look like himself.

She ran her hand down his lapel. "You're out of uniform."

He wasn't in his usual military attire but wore a top hat, dark green coat and brown trousers. His tawny brows lifted. "I'm no longer in the Queen's service, my lady. I've mustered out." He took her hand. "You're scaring me. What happened?"

Their brief exchange seemed to clear Charlotte's head. "I was knocked over and my reticule stolen. Please, can you see Persa? I think she ran after him."

"Persa?"

"My dog." Charlotte could no longer hear any barking.

Wakefield cast his gaze around. "I don't see her. Why don't we get you taken care of, and then we'll find Persa?"

She didn't care for his suggestion, but she sensed she wouldn't dissuade him. "I'm fine. I just got a little muddled for a moment. I landed pretty hard." She sat up and began gingerly rubbing her knee. The palms of her hands stung. She made to draw her legs close in preparation of standing, but a sharp pain in her hip stopped her.

"Stay still."

Without another word, Wakefield scooped her into his arms, rose and headed for the building. Startled, Charlotte wrapped her arms around his neck.

"Lord Wakefield! This isn't necessary."

"You're not going to spoil my fun, are you?" His long strides had them at the entrance. "Can you get the door?" He bent a bit, enabling her to grasp the door handle, and the moment she had it open he shouldered it back and carried her through.

As they entered, Chetney jumped to his feet. "Lady Haliday! What's wrong?" He hurried around the desk. "Mr. Scott," he called.

"My reticule was stolen and Persa went after the thief." She didn't want to talk about herself. Persa could be lost. "Mr. Chetney, please, can you go after her? They went in the direction of the park."

#

Hearing the commotion, David rolled to the doorway of his office. The unexpected sight of Charlotte in Miles Wakefield's arms took him aback.

"Bring her in here," he called. He rolled back into his office, but her anxious eyes implored him. "Chetney, go find Persa," he commanded.

Wakefield strode in, gently placed Charlotte on the settee then knelt beside her. It was the second time she'd lain there, David realized, recalling her first day at the office. He tried to get his chair close, but Wakefield, carefully removing her glove, blocked him.

Miles turned Charlotte's hand over, revealing a bright red palm already beginning to purple. Seeing Charlotte's slim hand in his friend's much larger one imbued David with a sense of impatience he recognized as possessiveness.

"Look out, Wakefield. Move out of the way," he said, not caring if he sounded short.

Wakefield gave him a surprised look but obligingly stood and stepped aside, allowing him to move his chair beside her.

"I'm fine, David."

Charlotte extended her hand, and he gently lowered it to rest, palm up, on the sofa before surveying her from head to toe. Her sleeve had torn at the shoulder seam and the white fabric of her chemise poked through. She looked decidedly pale and fragile reclining there, her fashionable hat knocked askew and one long black curl falling down.

He pulled the chapeau's ribbons, lifted it away and thrust it at Wakefield. Giving in to his strong desire to touch her, he held Charlotte's upper arm and rubbed his thumb up and down it. The contact eased his belly, which felt as if he'd swallowed a bag of lead miniés.

"What happened, Charlotte?"

"Someone knocked me down and stole my reticule."

David glanced at Wakefield and saw his friend's gaze locked on his stroking thumb. Well, Wakefield could stare all he liked. And he didn't give a damn what Wakefield thought of them using each other's Christian names, either. He had no intention of worrying about appearances right now.

He removed her other glove and saw the heel of that hand was likewise swollen and bruised. Charlotte moved to sit up.

"I'm fine, really."

"She landed hard," Wakefield said.

David gently pushed her rising shoulders back down. "Just rest a moment."

They heard the outer door open and close, and a moment later Persa, panting and tongue lolling from her mouth, ran into the room. The dog hurried to the settee and stood on her hind legs, her front paws resting on the seat cushion. David put his hand atop her head to keep her from jumping on Charlotte.

"Persa. Good girl," Charlotte exclaimed.

Chetney entered, breathing as if he'd done his own share of running.

"You found her, Mr. Chetney! Thank you."

"Did you catch the footpad?" Wakefield asked.

Chetney shook his head. "I was some distance behind. I followed the sound of Persa's barking and caught glimpses of him. She was right on his heels, but he ducked into a pub then apparently went out the back. I heard him yell as he went in, though. I think Persa gave the bloke a souvenir."

David gave the dog's head a rub, and she sat on her haunches. Charlotte began to sit up again. This time he assisted her, providing support to her back.

"I don't mind the loss of my reticule. There wasn't much in it. But oh, why did he push me so hard?" Charlotte grimaced and slowly lowered her legs. Once she had her feet on the floor, she stiffened her back and took a deep breath. "Well, nothing seems to be broken."

A good deal of David's tension eased away. "I want you to go home and rest. And don't come in tomorrow if you're hurting." She opened her mouth, so he added, "And no arguments." Her mouth closed and she blinked at him.

Blast it, he'd sent his coach away. Simpson and Boone would return late this afternoon to transport him home, but he couldn't very well deliver Charlotte to her residence without it.

"Let me see you home, Lady Haliday," Wakefield offered.

David tried to dismiss the irritation he felt. There was no sense in letting his friend's escort perturb him. He certainly didn't want Charlotte going home alone.

"What are you doing here, anyway, Wakefield?" he asked.

"Saving ladies in distress," Miles quipped.

David glared, and his friend's eyebrows rose.

"I just wanted to tell you I'm officially no longer in the service of Her Majesty." Wakefield started toward the outer office. "Let me whistle for a hack. I'll send my horse home with a boy."

As soon as Wakefield went through the door, Chetney following, David cupped Charlotte's cheek. "Are you really all right? Shall I send for a physician?"

She wrapped her fingers loosely around his wrist. "I'm fine. Just a bit shaken up."

"Send me a note this afternoon. I'll want to know how you're faring. I hate it that I can't be the one to take you home."

"I know."

Her smile dispelled a good deal of his vexation.

Wakefield reentered and positioned himself opposite from David. "Are you ready?" he asked.

Charlotte stood, Miles providing a steadying hand. She took one step then halted, favoring her right leg. "I believe my hip is quite bruised."

She bit down on her lower lip and stood on one leg, clutching Wakefield. Helplessness assailed David. He grabbed his wheels and began to turn his chair. He'd offer his shoulder for support, perhaps even convince her to sit in his lap and let him wheel her to the street. But before he could position his chair, Wakefield spoke.

"If you'll allow me?"

Then Wakefield bent and swept Charlotte into his arms again.

"Oh, please. You needn't carry me a second time. I can walk if we take it slowly."

Wakefield grinned. "You're not the least bit of trouble, I assure you."

David knew that smile. It was the one his friend often used to such good effect on desirable women. And the last thing David saw of the pair was Chetney ushering them out the door, Charlotte comfortably ensconced in Wakefield's arms, her hands locked behind his neck.

David rolled back into his office and shut the door. A flash of purple caught his eye, a button from Charlotte's bodice lying upon the floor. He picked it up and rubbed it between his fingers. It was round, silky smooth, and covered with the same fabric as her dress, which had nearly matched her eyes.

He slipped it into his waistcoat pocket and expertly maneuvered his chair behind his desk. Then he picked up his small brass desk clock and hurled it into the wall.

#

Charlotte tensed as the carriage bounced over a dimple in the road. Initially she'd been a bit dazed, but now that the shock of her assault had dissipated, with every movement she was becoming more aware of pain down the right side of her body.

Keeping her voice steady took effort. "Nothing like this has ever happened to me. I don't know why it's such a shock. Pickpockets and footpads are a menace all over the city."

Wakefield's golden eyebrows bunched. "But it's usually a child who's gone before you even know he's there. This was a man, and the swine had no cause to shove you like that."

Charlotte looked at Persa, who lay beside her on the seat, and she rested her hand on the dog's furry back. The little beast had been fearless.

She shuddered. "He was so bold." Her voice rang hollow, and she swallowed past the constriction in her throat. "Just my bad luck to cross his path, I expect."

Wakefield considered her. Something in his face made her tense. "And *good* luck to have it happen where Scott could take care of you."

She studied his expression. Cautionary, she'd call it.

"I gained the impression you and Scott have become good friends."

Charlotte's face warmed. Did Wakefield really think she and Scott were mere friends, or could he tell they were far more than that to each other? What had he seen pass between them?

"I do consider him a good friend," she allowed. "A confidant, even."

Wakefield's gaze swung to the window. He stared out for a minute then turned back to face her. His tea-brown eyes narrowed. "I hope I'll not offend your sensibilities with my brashness, my lady, but I'm compelled to ask you to be heedful of my friend's feelings."

"What?" Charlotte felt nearly as stunned as when the thief pushed her down. Was Wakefield warning her away from Scott? She didn't know the man that well, but she'd thought of him as a friend.

Wakefield's lips tightened. "Scott's overcome a lot, and he struggled to do so. Most men in his circumstances couldn't have done it. A failed...friendship might well jeopardize all his hard-won gains."

She wanted to slap him. Everything came down to trust, didn't it? And Wakefield didn't find her trustworthy. She'd thought him a lighthearted gallant, but by posing this now, while she remained overwrought and shaking, he'd proven himself as shrewd and determined as Scott. He'd placed her at a distinct disadvantage.

She wondered if Wakefield had considered that Scott's 'friendship' was a risk for her as well.

"I've no intention of hurting Mr. Scott. I have great concern for his well-being."

"Scott's fiancée broke their engagement when it became clear he'd never walk again. He hadn't yet accepted his circumstances, and then the woman he loved explained she no longer wished to wed him. I feared for his sanity. And now, this friendship with you... He's already borne enough hurt for any ten men."

Scott's fiancée. She barely heard Wakefield's other words. They swam in and out of her head, a tumult she could not grasp. David had been engaged.

He hadn't told her. She'd shared everything about her marriage with him. She'd told him how badly Haliday hurt her. She'd even told him about her miscarriage. And he'd never mentioned he'd had his own love thrown back in his face?

Hurt and confused, she suddenly didn't want to be there, enclosed in the carriage with Lord Wakefield. Oh, would this ride ever end?

She considered him. He looked both uncomfortable and determined. His color appeared flushed, as if he might be embarrassed. So, perhaps she'd been hasty in her judgment of him. Perhaps his motivation stemmed more from his concern for Scott than his mistrust of her. And suddenly she remembered what Scott had said that night in the inn, when she'd gone to his room. *This might well be a mistake. We could give ourselves all kinds of hurt.*

Ourselves? David knew exactly how a world of hurt felt, and he'd apparently borne it.

Charlotte blanched. Once he'd been in love and planned to marry. Had she done Scott a disservice? Had she selfishly pursued her own desire without considering his feelings? She didn't want to think so. She hadn't worried overly about an attachment stopping him from getting what he wanted because he'd said he never intended to wed. But how could she have been so focused on herself that she never considered that her affair with Scott could become a hopeless snare for him? What if he fell in love with her?

David should marry. He shouldn't let his legs prevent him from leading a life inhabited with a wife and children, even if I'm not the one to give him either of those things.

Scott had deep feelings for her. His loving left her in no doubt of that. They needed to talk.

A sudden picture of smiling, red-haired, blue-eyed children sent a pain tearing, twisting, stabbing through Charlotte. She had to use all her will not to reveal her distress to Wakefield, who continued to watch her, but the carriage was slowing, thank God.

"Thank you for telling me," Charlotte said.

"The thing is, I think if he isn't already in love with you, then he soon will be."

Charlotte froze. She wanted to deny Wakefield's assertion, but her deeply honest conscience wouldn't allow it. Part of her feared he was right. Another part, one she didn't want to acknowledge, spilled over with happiness at the thought.

She considered Wakefield. He looked deadly serious. And grumpy.

"I'm glad he has you for a friend," she said.

The man's eyebrows rose, but the coach stopped. Finally, they'd arrived at her townhouse.

CHAPTER TWENTY-THREE

Vivian hummed a popular ditty. Anticipation stirred her blood and sent it skipping in concert with the tune. She hadn't realized her masquerade would be so entertaining. She'd dressed in one of her housemaid's gowns, stuffed her hair inside a cap, and now trailed behind Charlotte Haliday's dog and the young servant girl walking the mongrel.

The girl crossed over to the central grassy area that sat surrounded with road and townhouses and slowed to a stroll. Vivian increased her own pace until she came abreast of the Haliday servant. The girl appeared tall for her age, which Vivian guessed to be around twelve. Her dark hair was secured in a long single braid, and round spectacles were perched on a nose too refined for the girl's position in life.

"Well, she's a noice one, ain't she?" Vivian asked, doing her best to mimic coarse speech. She sounded so authentic that she nearly ruined it all by laughing but managed at the last moment to contain her mirth. She figured the girl would take her grin as simple friendliness.

"What's 'er name?" she asked, pointing to the dog.

The smile the girl flashed was particularly sweet. "Piccola Persa."

"Blimey, what kind o' name is that?"

The girl giggled. "It's Italian."

"Is that a fact? Yer mistress must be quite a laidy."

The girl nodded. "She's a *real* lady—a viscountess."

"Sit 'ere a minute, dearie." Vivian waved her toward a nearby bench. The girl sat, and Vivian settled beside her. "Gor, it must be good to serve in a fine lady's 'ouse. I bet there's naught you need, eh, dearie?"

"She's educating me."

Vivian drew back and widened her eyes. She put as much envy as possible into her voice. "You've all yer 'eart desires, 'aven't ya?"

"Well, I wish I could be with my brothers and sisters, but I do get to see them, and they're all in fine places." The girl's chin firmed. "Someday I'll be able to provide for them and we'll be together again."

"Why, I bet you could do it now, dearie. Ya seem genteel enough. Can ya read 'n' write, then?"

The girl nodded and searched Vivian's face.

"There's a rich old woman right around t'corner 'at's lookin' fer a companion." Vivian pointed down the street. "I bet you'd do jest fine, love."

The girl frowned. "I wouldn't want anyone to know I was looking for another position. They'd think me ungrateful."

"Well, now. 'Magine bein' with yer proper family might make it so that's not so important. Why don't ya just hop along right now, then? If'n it don't work out, they'll never know a thing. Jest leave yer dog wi' me. Y'll be back in a trice."

"Oh." The girl was obviously undecided, looking from Vivian to the dog.

"What's yer name, love?"

"Eleanor."

"Well, El'nor, she's got near as much money as the Queen, that woman."

The girl's eyes widened. "Where is she, exactly?"

Ah. Vivian curled her toes and withheld her smile. "It's the 'ouse with the lion 'eads on the gateposts. Round the corner an' 'alfway down the block. Mrs. Stover is the lady's name."

Eleanor made a little kissing noise and patted her leg. The dog came near, and the girl bent and stroked the canine's head. "I suppose there'd be no harm—"

"Don'tcha worry yer 'ead, now. Ye can depend on Mabel Grey," Vivian said, reaching for the leash. Eyes full of trust stared back at her for another undecided moment, and then the girl capitulated.

"You're sure it's all right? You'll stay right here?"

"Mable Grey is as dependable as the cock's crow at daybreak. We'll be here."

Vivian took the leash, and after an encouraging nod the girl turned away. She soon disappeared around the corner.

Reaching into her pocket, Vivian stared at the dog. Its head was already raised.

"Aren't you the smart one?" she asked, abandoning her accent.

The dog moved closer and sat, tail thumping the grass.

Vivian unrolled a cloth, revealing three small balls of cheese. She quickly offered one, and the dog took it and swallowed in one quick motion. Those dark, gleaming eyes watched alertly for anything more.

Those bright eyes, that pink tongue, the long brown hair that blew aside with each movement of the animal's head... For a moment Vivian stared, rapt. Then the dog barked and stood on its hind legs, front paws resting on Vivian's knee. The canine's gaze locked onto the cloth in Vivian's hand, the dog barked again, and its gaze darted from the hoped-for treat to Vivian's face, then back to the food in her hand.

Heaviness blanketed Vivian's chest and constricted her breath. A stone dropped into her belly, and sickness rippled out in waves. Vivian swallowed, fighting back the bilious feeling. Why ever had she thought this would be easy?

The mutt shifted, front paws scrabbling against Vivian's knee. She pushed the dog away, forcing the terrier to drop from her hind feet to stand on all four, then looked at the two remaining offerings of balled cheese. Vivian reached deep, fishing for the determination that had sustained her when she'd finally abandoned her faint-hearted, impossible yearnings, faced reality and let her dreams die. This was *necessary*. It wouldn't harm Charlotte, technically, but it would greatly distress her, and hopefully Matthew Shelby would find his daughter's dismay equally upsetting. A man who liked to control everything and everyone he touched wouldn't like feeling so helpless.

Vivian held out the second cheese ball. The dog gobbled it down. Tongue dangling, the beast almost looked as if it was smiling.

As she picked up the last wad of cheese, another wave of sickness assailed Vivian and she struggled to fill her lungs with air, trying to quell the compulsion to retch. The leash fell to the ground. She left it and lifted a trembling hand to her hot face. Moisture covered her forehead, so she wiped it with the cloth that had held the cheese.

She didn't have to give the dog the third morsel, she decided. Two should be enough arsenic to make the beast sick. A third would make her severely ill or even kill her, and it wasn't Vivian's intention to kill the animal. But sometimes things went wrong. It hadn't been her intention for the man she hired to murder Haliday, either. She'd been sick for weeks after that catastrophe, even sicker than she was now. Which is why this time she'd made sure: when she'd hired a man to attack Charlotte, she'd made sure he understood he was to do no more than bruise her.

Vivian's stomach cramped. She clutched her abdomen and bent forward, the remaining cheese held in her fist. The dog—Piccola Persa, the girl had called her—nudged Vivian's fingers with her nose, licking heartily, continuing to sniff and nudge her nose around in hopes of more.

Had the dog already eaten enough to make her good and sick? Vivian licked dry lips and swiped the cloth around her sweating neck again. The aroma of cheese filled her nose, and her throat clamped shut so tight that a pain stabbed there. The girl Eleanor would return soon. Indecision added to the mix of emotions churning about inside Vivian, but there would have been no point in putting herself through this if she didn't do the job right.

For a moment she imagined Charlotte Haliday, still bruised from her assault, bending over her dying dog, and she felt another twinge of guilt. Should she show Lady Charlotte compassion? No. Vivian had never known a single person to show *her* mercy. Not her husband, her mother, or her father. A harsh laugh broke from her. Most assuredly not the man whose loins produced her.

Uncurling her fingers, Vivian opened her hand and exposed the little round of cheese. The dog snatched it up, swallowed, and swept its tongue out to capture any trace that might remain.

Okay. Vivian had to leave. She simply had to. She needed to get away from the dog, and she wanted to be gone before the girl returned, full of questions after not finding a Mrs. Stover residing in the house down the street. She grabbed the beast's leash, stood, and tied it to a nearby bush. Almost done. All she had to do was—

Vivian looked up just in time to see the girl round the corner. She waved and began backing away, as if she couldn't wait there any longer. The girl quickened her pace, and the dog gave a little yip, but Vivian turned and hastened away.

She heard the girl calling after her, but she pretended not to hear. She hated that the dog would suffer, but then, this was all for a good cause and couldn't be helped, could it?

#

Charlotte sighed and laid her book down, shifted and rubbed her aching hip. Since Wakefield's escort home she'd been resting in bed and trying not to spend every moment bedeviled by his disclosure.

She *liked* David. Liked and admired him more than any man she'd ever known. She'd envisioned them as friends who could engage in sensual delights to their mutual satisfaction without the complication of love. But why had she ever thought that such a warmhearted man would hold himself distant from his lover? Of course his feelings were engaged. David wasn't a man who did things by half measure. He wouldn't give a small part of himself and try to restrain the rest, as she had.

She'd lain under him, his body intimately linked with hers, and looked into his eyes. He'd filled his fists with her hair, pressed against her, kissed her mouth and tasted her. In those moments she'd known every part of him was present, and nothing was more important to him than being there with her. How could she have been so foolish as to think she could share her body with such an exceptional man and *not* have his deepest feelings affected?

This morning she'd seen his heartfelt concern for her well-being, too. He'd appeared downright murderous.

Yes, he'd told her he would not marry, but he'd not said he wouldn't fall in love. The thought of him loving her… Well, the responsibility frightened her. It gave her power over him, gave her the ability to hurt him, and she didn't want that burden. She owed it to him to make sure he understood. As much as she admired, liked and desired him, she could not allow herself to love him. And if he couldn't accept that…she didn't know what she would do.

Unbidden, memories of their last night together filled her mind. She'd experienced more pleasure then than she'd known was possible to attain in a man's arms. She wished she was there with him now, at their cottage, instead of lying here with too much time to think these unsettling thoughts.

She'd sent a note, reassuring him that she'd suffered no more than bruises and was resting. His reply had instructed her to stay at home tomorrow. She didn't want to do that.

She had to stop this. It made little sense. Three months ago she hadn't known David Scott. Today she longed for him with an intensity that didn't wane. Just his presence would have comforted her, but in lieu of that she would have taken one of those new photographs or maybe even a miniature of him, or a lock of his hair. She didn't love him, but she would admit she felt more for David than she had for any other man, including Haliday in those first days of their marriage. But love was not going to be possible for her, and it would be devastating to him.

A high-pitched little howl suddenly drew her attention to Persa, asleep on the rug. Her pet's body gave a series of jerks, legs stiff and sticking straight out in an unnatural way, so, ignoring her pains, Charlotte left her bed and knelt beside the dog. What she found was glassy eyes that were rolled up to reveal the whites of Persa's eyes. Jaw clenched and head extended backward, convulsions racked the beast's body. Foamy white spittle oozed from the terrier's muzzle.

"Persa!" Charlotte blinked away tears suddenly flooding her eyes. "Help!" she yelled.

The convulsion ended as suddenly as it began, leaving the dog unconscious and breathing heavily.

Rebecca hurried in. "My lady?"

"Something's very wrong, Rebecca. Persa had a convulsion."

The maid gasped, hand pressed against her chest. Mrs. Jones appeared in the doorway, too, and she strode to them.

Persa made a small noise. The dog blinked, her legs moved, and a moment later she was standing, her nose pushed under Charlotte's hand, tail waving slowly. Charlotte hauled her onto her lap and cuddled her. A moment later, Persa began to retch.

Charlotte set the dog down and watched helplessly as the contents of Persa's stomach splashed upon the rug. When Charlotte pulled her back up onto her lap, the little dog collapsed.

"Something's horribly wrong," she realized. "Mrs. Jones, is there anyone who can help?"

The housekeeper hurried for the door. "I'll ask Walters and Beckham."

Charlotte hoped one of them knew someone knowledgeable about dogs.

She stroked her hand along Persa's body. The feel of the dog's silky hair and solid little body was comforting, but Charlotte knew it was false comfort. And, suddenly, her bruises protested her position on the floor.

"Help me, Rebecca."

Charlotte transferred Persa to the maid's arms and slowly rose to her feet. Once back in bed she motioned for the dog to be laid beside her. Quiet, Persa submitted to the transfer. Beside Charlotte, she lay still, panting.

Eleanor appeared, her face white. She immediately knelt beside the bed.

"She was fine on our walk, my lady." The girl's voice shook, and a tear slid down her pale cheek.

Charlotte laid her hand atop Eleanor's head. "Sometimes illness strikes suddenly. There's no way for Persa to tell us when she's feeling poorly."

The dog's brown eyes, usually alert and full of affection, held a sad combination of misery and fear. It made Charlotte feel helpless, an emotion she particularly hated. She'd lived with it for too much of her life.

The ever-brisk Mrs. Jones returned. "Beckham went down the street to Lord Beamish's stable. One of his grooms is son to his kennel master."

"Thank you, Mrs. Jones."

Persa struggled to her feet and whined. An audible rumbling came from her stomach.

Eleanor stood. "Shall I take her outside, my lady?"

Charlotte nodded.

Slow and careful, Eleanor gathered Persa into her arms.

"When you come in, bring her to the kitchen," Charlotte instructed. There had been more than enough lying in bed. She could survive a few aches, as Persa would be better in the warm kitchen. There'd be no risk of soiling carpets, either, and the small grassy area behind the townhouse would be only a few steps away.

"Mrs. Jones, please have the floral chair and footstool moved from the sitting room to the kitchen. Perhaps Mrs. Lipton can put up with us in her kitchen for a day."

The housekeeper's eyebrows rose the merest bit, but she gave a quick nod and hurried off.

"Rebecca, get my old blue gown, the one I wore gardening at Hazelton Park." She saw Rebecca roll her eyes and smile as she turned away to the armoire, and Charlotte reined in her own smile. Rebecca had wanted to toss the dress years ago, but it was utterly comfortable and cut very loose. It allowed for freedom of movement on the days Charlotte sought the oblivion of digging in her garden.

Charlotte had just settled in a corner of the kitchen with Persa on the upholstered footstool when Lord Beamish's groom, Oliver Newton, arrived. It seemed her entire household followed, crowding into the kitchen. Eleanor, Mrs. Lipton, Mrs. Jones, Penny the kitchen maid, Walters and Beckham all stood in a circle around her chair and footstool.

A rather strapping young man, Newton knelt, murmured to Persa and examined her, his large hands gentle. Eleanor stood beside Charlotte's chair, her lower lip caught between her teeth. Persa whimpered as Newton pressed against her abdomen.

"Excuse me, my lady, but have her bowels run?"

"Just now," Eleanor said. "And she's vomited twice."

Eyes grave, Newton studied Eleanor. He nodded. Persa lay panting, and he opened her jaws, examined her teeth and leaned forward to sniff the dog's breath. Then he straightened and shook his head.

"I can't be sure, my lady, but the dog's condition puts me in mind of poison. Could she have gotten into the rat powder, perhaps?"

Startled, Charlotte looked at Mrs. Jones, who shook her head.

"No, my lady. We're careful to put it where Persa can't get it," the housekeeper said.

Newton stood. "All you can do is wait, my lady. Try to get some milk down her. You might have to drip it into her mouth."

After giving a few more instructions and receiving Charlotte's thanks, the man accepted the coin Walters pressed into his hand and left with assurances he'd return if summoned.

Poison? Charlotte believed Mrs. Jones, who was efficient and capable.

"How could she have gotten poison?" she wondered aloud.

Eleanor collapsed beside the footstool. Her hands gripped the stool's edge, her slumping figure the picture of despair. "It's my fault, m'lady. This morning in the park I left her with a stranger. Persa must've got into something while I wasn't there watching." Shoulders shaking, the girl began to cry.

Charlotte sat forward. "What? What do you mean? Eleanor, enough now. Take a deep breath and tell me what happened."

The girl's story tumbled out. In spite of all the advantages Charlotte had given her, it was obvious Eleanor was still desperate to be back with her brothers and sisters. Charlotte knew fine things didn't fill emptiness. She'd hoped the people in her household and Eleanor's studies would make the girl happy, or at least content. Perhaps with more time they would. Charlotte would make sure Mrs. Jones saw that Eleanor's visits to her brothers and sisters increased.

Of course, while she understood Eleanor's yearning for her family, the girl's decision to abandon Persa to a stranger hurt. But the girl looked so distressed...

"Hush, now. There's no reason to think Persa got into poison when you left her. There's no poison in the park. It's more likely that it happened while she was chasing the man who seized my reticule. Mr. Chetney found her sniffing all around the tavern the blackguard disappeared into."

Eleanor sniffled and wiped her wet cheeks with her fingers.

"We're going to take the very best care of her," Charlotte continued. "Why don't you get a bowl of milk and a rag? You can soak the cloth in the milk and see if Persa will lick it. If she doesn't, we'll do as Mr. Newton suggested and drip the milk into her mouth."

Thirty minutes later there was another convulsion, which caused Eleanor to break out into fresh sobs, but they settled into a routine that seemed to alleviate Charlotte's anxiety and eventually Eleanor's as well. Charlotte imagined none of her servants would forget those hours with their viscountess and her dog in the kitchen and Eleanor running Persa outside at regular intervals.

Persa seemed a little less miserable once evening fell. Newton returned to check on her and remarked at how pleased he was with her small improvement.

Knowing he was a groom, Charlotte pulled him aside. With everything possible done for her dog, she wanted to ask his advice on a subject she'd been considering for several days. Ever since David had spoken with such longing about riding, she'd wondered exactly why he couldn't still do so. Riding sidesaddle as she did, a rider basically perched atop a horse. Unlike men, who gripped a horse with their legs, women merely balanced, which was why most chose not to hunt or jump; the security offered by their pommels was minimal. But, couldn't David use a specially built saddle that secured his legs, one on each side of the horse?

Accustomed to being connected with his mount, the possibility of any other way of riding probably hadn't occurred to him, but a stable need only have the same pulley apparatus that he used to get in and out of his coach. To mount, he could position a horse under it and pull himself up. He'd need help swinging his leg over and strapping his legs down, but once settled he would be completely independent. He'd be able to give partial direction to the horse with his one strong upper leg, and since David had been an excellent horseman she guessed he wouldn't have any difficulty balancing on the back of the horse, especially one eventually trained for one-sided leg signals.

After consulting with Newton, Charlotte was even more encouraged, and she acquired the name and direction of an admirable saddle-maker. She'd surprise David, she decided. Giving him a way to experience the freedom and activity he so craved would be tremendously exciting. She couldn't wait to go riding with him and see his face mid-gallop.

Charlotte penned a note to David, even though she wouldn't be able to send it until the next morning. She explained the events of the day, excepting the saddle talk with Newton, and added a humorous bit about eating in the kitchen with her servants. Charlotte had thought Walters might not survive that, but they'd all managed to get through what she knew was an uncomfortable meal for them.

She hesitated at the conclusion of the note. *I wish we were at our cottage,* she finally wrote, *but just the thought of you gave me strength today.*

Remembering David's concern when the thief knocked her down had made a great difference as the wretched day progressed. David cared about her. Cared about Persa, as well. Knowing that had made the strain of the day easier to bear, even if it also reminded her of her obligation to protect him from a broken heart. Lord Wakefield had made that clear.

Charlotte sighed, wanting to be strong for David. They would have to talk about their future.

CHAPTER TWENTY-FOUR

Early evening shadows were beginning to darken Rose Cottage. David lifted his head, intent on the sounds of an arriving carriage. Finally.

The notes exchanged the past several days while Charlotte watched over the health of Persa had been a poor substitute for seeing her. He'd nearly gone out of his mind, worrying about Charlotte after the assault and unable to see her and assure himself of her well-being. He'd wanted to see Persa, too, as Beckham, serving as message carrier, thought the poor mite close to death. But as much as David wanted to be there, a visit would have necessitated his men carrying him up Charlotte's stairs like a helpless infant. He'd chosen to be satisfied with notes.

He set the carved figurine he'd been absently rubbing on the table beside him. The carving wasn't half-bad. Always before, his whittling had been done to while away nighttime in camp or amuse Julian and Anne's children. This carving was different. He'd tried his best to capture the look of Charlotte's dog. The beast was positioned upright on its hind legs, front paws held out.

He recalled the day Charlotte adopted Persa. He'd discouraged her, not wanting to add compassionate to the growing list of admirable qualities he'd observed, but kindhearted she had told him in no uncertain terms that she wanted the dog. That day he'd kissed her.

The cottage door opened, and Charlotte entered. All he could do was drink her in. Tension eased away and effervescent buoyancy took its place. A coachman deposited a bag in the entry, tipped his hat and closed the door as he left. Thank God Charlotte came to him quickly, her lips as eager as his.

It didn't take much pulling to convince her to settle onto his lap. By the time he released her mouth, they were both breathing hard. He buried his face in her dark, glossy hair and inhaled the glorious scent.

"David."

Her surprised, pleased tone made him smile. She'd seen the carving. He picked it up and handed it to her.

"But where did you find it? It looks exactly like Persa." Charlotte's elegant fingers explored the small carving. "I adore it."

"I made it for you, Bluebell."

She turned her head and looked at him. This close her eyes were amazing, their deep purple-blue color unlike anything he'd ever seen. Perhaps, on rare summer nights, as the first stars appeared the last faint glow of sunlight painted the sky that shade.

A delighted smile curved her lips. "*You* made this?"

"I started whittling during my army service and found I enjoyed it."

Charlotte held the figurine against her chest. "You couldn't have given me anything I'd like better."

He started to tease her, but seeing her eyes he held his tongue. She meant it. He guessed he could have offered emeralds and she wouldn't have found them any more appealing.

"How is she?" he asked of Persa.

Charlotte smiled, gave a breathy exhalation and shrugged. "She seemed fine today. Her appetite's not quite back to normal, but her eyes are bright and she's wagging her tail."

"That's good news. I can't wait to see her."

Charlotte set the figurine on the table. "And what is this? More presents?"

She'd seen the box. "Your father sent it to the office."

Her brows rose and she slowly pulled the box to her. She tugged the ribbon free and lifted the lid. "My favorite."

She sounded amazed, so David looked inside. The box was full of fudge, the color of cream and chunky with dried fruit. The sweet scent of almond and coconut wafted up.

"You're surprised?" he asked.

"He's never sent me candy. And I'm surprised he knows my favorite."

"Perhaps he's more aware of your likes and dislikes than you know. And perhaps he's more thoughtful. He must have heard about your misadventure."

Charlotte picked the box up, examined it, and looked at David. "Of course there's no note. He wouldn't take the time to write one. He probably didn't purchase the candy himself, either."

"But he did know your favorite," David reminded her. "A footman delivered it yesterday and said it was for Lady Haliday from Mr. Shelby."

Charlotte picked up a square of the candy and offered it. David shook his head.

She brought it to her mouth, bit it in half and began to chew. "Mmmm." Her eyes drifted closed. She swallowed, smiled, and moved close to him. She pressed moist, open lips to his, and when her tongue stroked his, sweetness flooded his mouth.

"Mmmm," he echoed, and sucked lightly.

This time, when their lips parted he pushed her from his lap, tilted his head in the direction of the bedroom and assumed a questioning expression. She stood and headed there, nibbling the remainder of the candy piece as she went.

He entered the bedroom as she sank down on the edge of the bed, a troubled look flashing across her face. She moistened her lips and twisted her hands together.

"I've got to talk to you first."

Unease oozed through him, and he rolled suddenly tense shoulders. A moment ago they'd been clinging to each other. Now she sat before him, stiff and reluctant. He wished she'd look at him, but her downcast gaze hid her eyes.

He moved his chair close and leaned forward, resting his forearms on his thighs. He reached out as if she were a trapped, injured animal, and he cupped his hands around hers. Then he forced his voice to sound ordinary, which turned out to be a Herculean task. "What's wrong?"

She took a deep breath and finally looked at him. Her eyes relieved him somewhat. Anxiety shone in their depths, but her desire hadn't abated.

"I wasn't planning to say anything just yet, but I…" She dropped her head.

The knot twisting his gut tightened. He hated seeing her so at odds, and just what in bloody hell was so difficult for her to say? He lifted her hands to his lips and kissed the knuckles. "How can I help, Bluebell?"

She seemed to gather herself. Her chin came up, and she faced him again. "We haven't spoken much of the future, and I think we should."

"You have concerns?" Clearly, she did.

"My feelings for you have grown deeper than I ever thought possible or expected. And I'm concerned you might feel the same way."

She was concerned he might feel... Thank God he'd had the good sense not to confess the love he felt!

Her words came out with a rush of air. "I'm worried you'll end up being hurt."

Of course he'd end up being hurt. He'd always known that. Straightening, he retained hold of her hands. "What brought this on?"

The space between her brows creased. She drew a deep breath. "Wakefield told me about your engagement. That you became despondent when it ended."

That hit him like a cricket bat to the chest. He released her hands and leaned back. "You've discussed this with Wakefield?"

"No. I mean—oh, he was only trying to help. We didn't fool him for a minute, and he feared I'd be careless of your feelings. It happened the day he took me home."

His jaw ached, the way he clamped his teeth before he forced enough relaxation to permit speech. "Contrary to appearances, Wakefield is not my mother." How many times had he laughed and said the same thing to Miles himself? But this was no joke.

Charlotte steepled her fingers and held them to her mouth. "A fiancée? Why didn't you tell me?"

David dragged his hand down his face. "Lydia and the end of our engagement is all wrapped up with my injury and being in this chair the rest of my life. In the beginning it was hell. All of it. Once I became determined to live—not exist, but *live*—I didn't want to dwell on what I'd lost."

"Is she the reason you decided not to ever marry?"

"Not in the way you mean. I'm not harboring a love for Lydia, but the way she changed when she realized I'd never walk again did convince me I wasn't fit for marriage.

Charlotte leaned forward, her expression impassioned. "You are. You *should* marry. You're such a good man, and you have so much to give." She slapped her palm to the armrest of his chair. "This won't matter to a woman who loves you."

Ah, Charlotte, little Bluebell... She was tearing herself up, worrying about him.

He spoke before she could add more. "I could say the same to you. You may doubt it, but I know you still have the capacity to love. I've seen you with the Fund children. You love them. And these deep feelings you say you have for me...you may not love me, but that doesn't mean you couldn't love another man."

She shook her head. "No. I don't think I can *trust* a man enough to let myself love him. I trusted Haliday like I trust the sun to rise tomorrow." She rolled her lips inward then released them. "He betrayed me. Broke something inside me. Others may be able to love without complete trust, but I can't. How can I surrender my heart? Give someone such absolute power over me?"

Her hands gripped together, fingers interlocked and squeezing. "David, you deserve my trust. There's nothing more you could do to convince me you are worthy. But I'm too afraid to surrender. And I know it's not fair to you."

She spread her fingertips across her forehead and rubbed. Her hands dropped and she shrugged. "I'm afraid you'll fall in love with me and be hurt when I'm unable to love you back. I'm ashamed to admit it, but in the beginning I wasn't thinking about you. Only myself. And now...well, I would die if I hurt you."

The cricket bat gave him another wallop. She didn't love him? And she couldn't trust him? No. Everything in him rejected that. He didn't believe it. She'd been too open, too giving. She *did* trust him. She just couldn't admit it. Which put them in a hell of a bind. She had just as much risk of being hurt by him.

Except, he wouldn't ever intentionally do anything to hurt her.

"Come here," he said. He grasped her waist and urged her over. She seemed a bit reluctant, but once settled on his lap she wrapped her arms around his shoulders and pressed the side of her face against his. He pulled her in tight.

She spoke, her voice steel under velvet. "Perhaps we shouldn't continue to meet."

David said nothing. Charlotte clearly wasn't ready to risk her heart again. But if her primary concern was hurting him…well, weren't his feelings his own affair? He had no intention of ending their liaison. Was it so impossible that two people who didn't wish to marry could find happiness living as he and Charlotte had for the past few weeks?

She was still waiting for an answer. He hugged her close. Christ, but she felt good in his arms.

"You don't need to worry, Charlotte. My heart's safe."

She sat up. Cupped his face. Studied him. "Promise me. Promise you won't fall in love with me."

Damn and blast! He was going to have to tell her an outright lie. How absurd this all was. He hesitated. She didn't think she could trust, yet right this moment trust shone from her. And he was going to be an absolute bastard and take advantage of that fragile, fledgling emotion. How could he not? It was what they both wanted.

"David?"

He grasped her head, pulled her to him and kissed her, hard. He mustn't let her see his face. He kept her close, rested his lips against her temple. "I promise, Charlotte. I promise."

They shared lusty kisses until the confines of his chair became too restrictive. Transferring to the bed, he opened his trousers, lifted her atop him, and gathered up her copious skirts. He helped her straddle him and ran his hands over her slim, strong thighs and curvaceous buttocks. Desperate, he parted the slit in her drawers and pressed his finger into her tight, slick heat. She gasped, clutched his upper arms and squeaked his name.

The compulsion to mate with her raged, a wildfire beyond control. There was no mistaking she'd never been atop her husband, but she understood his intent when he raised her, and she joined with him eagerly. Her eyes went wide, then drifted closed as she sank down and buried him in her depths. That wet heat gripped him and he nearly exploded.

Her eyes opened, dark with wonder, and she bent and delivered a searing kiss with a power he'd previously only guessed at. He ceded control of their lovemaking to Charlotte, but he held her hips and helped guide her. He capitulated to the bliss of that escalating passion which had them devouring each other's mouths.

Their clothing and hair grew damp, their coupling more forceful. He murmured her name and praised her, the marvel of their joining robbing him of rational thought. Her body rocked and surged until they both strained and blew like galloping horses. It took everything in him to hold back until he felt her go over, her body gripping his shaft with powerful spasms. He surrendered and let his release wring him until he was limp, and a lingering, soul-deep pleasure filled him.

#

Sometime later he watched Charlotte retrieve the bag she'd brought, withdraw a silk robe from its recesses and begin unbuttoning her bodice. Somehow the conversation about the sad state of their hearts had led to the most urgent lovemaking he'd ever experienced, accomplished without them even pausing to remove their clothing. It had been incredible.

David propped himself against the pillows and settled in to watch Charlotte. He'd also brought a small bag. They'd planned to stay this evening and all of Sunday while the Fund offices were closed. Charlotte had told her butler she was staying overnight at a house party.

David was enjoying the view of her corseted bosom when she slipped out of her bodice. A saucer-sized, dark purple bruise marked her upper arm.

He sat up. "Charlotte. My God. Come here, sweetheart."

"It's fine. It's just from my fall."

She came to the bed and stood before him in chemise, corset and petticoats. He'd known the footpad slammed into her, and Wakefield had said she hit the ground hard, but he'd never dreamed... "Are there others like this?"

Charlotte made a little grimace. "Hand me my robe?" she said as she untied her petticoats and let them drop. Her corset followed.

She untied her drawers and stepped out of them, leaving her in nothing but her chemise. Slipping her arms into the ruby-red robe, she left it open and then slid her chemise up, exposing one long, shapely leg. A huge purple bruise marked her hip.

Stunned, David berated himself for the vigorous lovemaking they'd just enjoyed. "Did I hurt you? Why didn't you say something?"

She let the robe fall and drew the lapels together. "No, David, you didn't hurt me. Not at all."

"Is that all of it?"

She nodded and tied the robe's sash. "Except for my hands." She held those up, palms out, displaying the purplish discolorations. He'd been aware of those.

She climbed back onto the bed. "Here," she said, starting to unbutton his shirt, "let's get rid of this." A moment later she pulled it over his head, drew it from his arms and tossed it aside. "There." She snuggled next to him. "That's better."

He slid down onto his back and pulled her close. "I knew you fell hard, but I had no idea it was forceful enough to cause that kind of bruising."

He ran his hand up and down her spine, his hand gliding over the silk. He couldn't help gently exploring the warm curve of her waist and buttocks. She was so finely made. He skimmed the pads of his fingers over the knobs that ran the length of her spine and the little valleys between her ribs. Damn it. He knew he should have gone to see her after the assault. What would it matter if he'd had to have Boone carry him in? He'd let his pride keep him away and hadn't even realized how badly she'd been injured!

Rage tore through him, and he closed his eyes. Sod the bloody bastard! What he wouldn't give to have hold of that bugger for five minutes.

"He must have smashed into you with an incredible impact." Why had he done that? Snatching a reticule off an unsuspecting woman's arm wouldn't require much strength. What if her head had hit the ground with that much force? It might have killed her. David hugged Charlotte a little closer.

"I believe he plowed into me with his shoulder. He grabbed my reticule while I lay on the ground."

That day she'd been pretty shaken, but her voice was matter of fact as she related the events. David began plucking pins from her tousled, half-fallen hair, and he said, "I'm surprised you weren't even more shaken than you were. To think you had to deal with Persa's illness later that same day!"

She stayed silent, her hand open, her palm resting over his heart. He closed his eyes and let the warmth of her seep into him. The feelings she'd shared today made him ache, but she'd warned him not to love her to prevent his feeling exactly like this. He burrowed his hand into her hair, rubbing her scalp.

"I'm sorry for discussing you with Wakefield," she said.

He needed to do something about Wakefield's tendency to step in, trying to manage his life for him. But perhaps Charlotte needed to hear more about Lydia. As great as that hurt had once been, those memories held no power over him now. He supposed he might have brought it up at any time.

"It's all right. I don't mind your knowing about her." He combed his spread fingers through Charlotte's hair. "I've known Lydia my whole life. Her father's estate borders Summerbridge. We grew up riding together, and she was as mad for horses as I was. I now realize we didn't have much in common beyond that, but at the time I thought she'd be the perfect wife for me. We'd always been good companions, you see, and she'd grown into a lovely woman.

"Once I obtained my commission and her father's leave, I proposed. She accepted but saw the wisdom in waiting to wed until after I'd established myself in the army. I received orders to the Crimea. She was willing to marry me before I went but agreed that waiting seemed the more prudent thing to do."

Charlotte raised up on her forearms and glared at him. "And when you came home wounded, she broke your engagement? How could she do such a thing? What kind of monster is she?"

A raspy laugh broke free as something inside his chest cracked. Meeting only slight resistance, David pulled her back down to him. "A very sensible kind, I imagine."

"I meant what I said. You'd be a fine husband and father."

Lately, the alternative future he'd settled for had been as close to satisfying as he'd ever dared imagine. He squeezed her arm and said, "It takes more than the ability to copulate."

Her head popped up again, and he saw his blunt language had registered. Her words were fierce when she said, "You have everything—*everything*—any wife could need."

Except the ability to protect the woman he loved or rescue her when she was violently struck down. He couldn't even go to her home easily to assure himself of her well-being! And yet, Charlotte didn't understand how that knowledge undermined him.

"Well," he said, "for the time being I've no need of a wife. I'm well satisfied with the woman I've got."

Charlotte shook her head, a slow smile curving her lips.

David grimaced. How could she be so determined for his marital bliss when she'd given up on herself? That damned Haliday. He remembered the man. Dark, handsome, and arrogant.

"I know this will reveal me as both selfish and immoral," he said, "but I'm glad Haliday's gone. I only wish it had happened sooner."

Charlotte was suddenly hugging the breath out of him. He eased her backward.

"You like that I'm selfish and immoral?"

A choked laugh escaped her. "You're not. And since you're not, perhaps I'm not, either. I've felt so guilty. I never wished him dead, but I've been glad to be released from him."

Understanding, David kissed her and gathered her close. Someday she'd be ready to love again. He didn't want to think he might lose her, though, so until that day he'd treasure this time and be grateful.

CHAPTER TWENTY-FIVE

There. There she was.

Relief swept through Vivian with the intensity of an ice storm blowing in from the North Sea. The girl Eleanor approached the park with the dog on a leash. The dog walked with head upright and a bounce in her step.

Vivian waved a boy over and pressed a coin into his hand, directing him to secure a cab. Minutes later she was settled inside a Hansom and on her way home. She closed her eyes but popped them open and blinked hard when she felt moisture gathering behind the lids. The dog was fine, just as Vivian had known she would be. This was the fifth day she'd kept watch in the park, waiting for an appearance of the girl and the dog. Now perhaps she could sleep. Worry she might have ended up killing the little beast had grown until she could think of little else. Egad, it was as if she suffered some sort of disease of the emotions!

Haliday's death had changed her, she admitted. She'd never be free of that guilt. She'd meant him to suffer a few bruises and a blow to his pride, meant him to blame his wife and be livid with rage. Instead he'd ended up dead. Now her nerves were so affected she couldn't even manage a little bad luck for a dog without falling to pieces.

She arrived home to find Radcliffe waiting. Somehow he'd gotten her servants to set him up in her sitting room and serve tea. That miffed Vivian a bit. She was the one who paid the servants, after all. He might have the status of a special guest, but this was still her household.

Long legs outstretched, the remains of his repast on the table beside him, the earl lowered the newspaper and lifted his brows as she walked toward him. His gaze lazily roved her, and inside her mind the clouds drifted away to expose the sun.

"So, my lady has finally returned, has she?"

Vivian couldn't tell if he was out of sorts with her, but she knew he'd come by on two other days to find her not at home.

"I'm sorry I was away. I hope you've been comfortable?"

He folded the paper and set it aside.

She needed time to collect herself. "If you'll excuse me a moment, Radcliffe, I'll just rid myself of this hat and make myself presentable."

She started to turn away, but his voice stopped her. "You're quite presentable as you are, Vivian."

He rose and advanced slowly, her entire body humming a warning. She could tell he wasn't angry, but something about him made her distinctly uneasy.

He removed her hatpin, lifted the fashionable little chapeau from her head and stabbed the pin through its crown. Strong fingers traced the brim and stroked the adorning feathers from quill to tip. A flick of his wrist sailed the hat into a nearby chair, and he sighed.

"Where have you been, Vivian?"

She didn't like how easily he could discomfit her. He had no claim here. She was an independent woman and had never asked for the slightest support from him. They were both aristocrats, which, she believed, put her in a different category from past mistresses. The expensive jewels he'd given her were gifts from a wealthy man to his lover, not any kind of payment. Ironic, how she'd planned his seduction in anticipation of those very gifts, yet now they were insignificant to her. Oh, how had her life become so tangled?

Trying to ignore his penetrating gaze, she focused on a shirt button, rubbing it with her fingertip. This close, her senses seemed ultrasensitive, poised and waiting for the brush of his fingers, the press of his lips. The combination of unease and attraction played havoc with her composure.

She looked up through her lashes. "I've been to the park. Every day."

He captured her nervous finger. "Hyde Park? St. James? Regent's? Why the sudden interest in taking the air? It's been a bit early in the day, and you're gone for hours."

Something about his tone made her examine his face, but his expression divulged nothing. She said, "Only a small park for the use of nannies and dog-walkers. You know I grew up in the country. I merely wanted to sit outside on a bench and watch. Sometimes it's nice not to be in a fashionable place."

Especially when those you passed went on to whisper about you.

He frowned, and she added, "Sometimes I read." His expression didn't change.

She didn't know what to do, and with every minute her nervousness grew more acute. He couldn't know anything about her secret activities, which, as unlikely as it seemed, left only jealousy. A powerful surge of hope supplanted her nerves. If she thought there were any possibility of his having real, deep feelings for her…such an event would eclipse everything bad in her life. Sweetness filled her, then Radcliffe released her finger and reality came sweeping back. Such a notion was fantasy. The earl was still frowning.

She couldn't think of a way other than seduction to distract him. She lifted onto her toes and ran the tip of her tongue along his jaw. "Come upstairs," she whispered. "I think we can rid you of that frown."

She'd thought herself too twitchy to feel desire, but with her lips against his smooth-shaven skin, the scent of soap and smoky, spicy wood filling her head, how could she not?

His hands clasped her shoulders. He stepped back. "As tempting as that is, I have another appointment."

Shock silenced her. She'd seen him dash off hurried notes and cancel appointments in order to stay with her. Now he was walking toward the door.

He turned. "Are you free tonight? For the theatre?"

"Yes."

He gave a short, decisive nod and left.

#

"Sir." A worried-looking Chetney stood at David's door. "A Miss Rebecca Marsden of Lady Haliday's household is asking to see you."

Alarm shot through David. For the past two days an empty, unsettled pit existed where his stomach should be. Today marked the third day Charlotte had not been to work. It had begun with her feeling unwell during their overnight stay at the cottage. By morning she'd decided to return home, and knowing she'd be most comfortable there, he didn't argue. The last two mornings a footman delivered a note telling him she felt too ill to come to the office. So a maid requesting to see him could not be good.

"Send her right in."

A moment later Chetney showed a young woman with curly brown hair through the door. David recognized the brown and black striped dress she wore as a castoff of Charlotte's, and his gut clenched. The frock distinguished her as Charlotte's lady's maid.

"Miss Marsden?"

"Mr. Scott?"

At his impatient nod, she spoke in a rush. "Mrs. Jones, my lady's housekeeper, bade me fetch you. She doesn't know what to do."

The urge to stand and pace made David fist his hands. "Is Lady Haliday very ill?"

"She's unable to eat and too dizzy to leave her bed or pen a note. She keeps asking for you, Mr. Scott, and won't let Mrs. Jones send for her father. The physician came yesterday but she's much worse today, sir."

David looked at Chetney hovering in the doorway. He barked the man's name, and the secretary stiffened in a first-rate imitation of a soldier coming to attention. David commanded, "Send a boy running to my stable. He's to tell Simpson it's urgent."

Bless him, Chetney immediately turned and hurried away.

David opened his desk drawer, extracted a sheet of paper and began penning a note to Harland Bliss, a physician he'd met in the Crimea. He'd heard Bliss, having left the army, resided in London. Chetney would find him as his very next task.

It took an interminable amount of time to leave the office, drive to Charlotte's home and get himself inside. The relief David felt upon arriving lasted only until a spare woman with thin lips and the dangling keys of a housekeeper faced him.

"Mr. Scott, I can't let you upstairs," she said, twisting her hands. Miss Marsden and three footmen stood in the small vestibule as well. Boone and Pickett waited behind David.

He could see the lady's distress and somehow held on to his temper. "She's asking for me, isn't she?"

The housekeeper nodded. "But she's not in her right mind, sir. She couldn't want you going up to her private room."

Etiquette demanded he wait. Mrs. Jones was only doing her best to protect Charlotte, and Bliss would arrive soon. The physician would inform him of Charlotte's condition. David going up to her bedroom was inappropriate by anyone's estimation.

But he had to.

He knew the housekeeper was the one person Charlotte confided her whereabouts on the nights spent at Rose Cottage. Hopefully the woman wouldn't send for the constable or order the footmen to toss him out, because he would have no intention of going.

"Boone. Pickett. Let's go."

His two men stepped forward and scooped him from his chair. He perched between them, weight resting on their linked arms. He'd gotten up the outside steps to the front door this way, but he'd been in his chair when shown inside.

He looked at the heftiest footman nearby. "Bring the chair," he ordered. Then he tapped Boone and Pickett on their shoulders. "Up."

Miss Marsden hurried ahead, leading the way. Good. He wouldn't have to search through every room because the housekeeper wasn't helping. And by the time his chair was on the upper floor and he was ensconced in it, Mrs. Jones relented. David had Boone and Pickett wait in the hall while she showed him to Charlotte's room herself.

All rational thought left him at his first glimpse of her. He was barely aware of the lady's maid pushing him closer. Shock, anguish and panic coalesced as his heart galloped in a chest ready to explode.

"My God."

Her eyes opened, and she lifted her hand. He grasped her fingers but also smoothed tousled strands of hair away her face. Her skin was cool. Pale.

No fever, then.

"David," she rasped.

Cold fear gripped him. This was far worse than facing the Russians outmanned and outgunned. Her dull, unfocused gaze drifted past him. Her cheekbones seemed more prominent, her eyes sunken. Her collarbone, exposed above the neckline of her gown, stood out sharply. How could she have lost so much weight in just three days?

He kissed her fingers. "Sweetheart, I've sent for a doctor. He's good. Superior. He'll help you." Where the hell was Bliss, anyway?

One corner of her lips curved the tiniest bit, and her eyelids drooped. "I'm glad you're here."

He looked up at Mrs. Jones, who stood wringing her hands. "Why didn't you send for me sooner?"

"She wasn't this bad yesterday, and the physician visited twice."

David clamped his back teeth and tried like hell to hold on to his temper. Charlotte's lips were colorless and chapped, her mouth so dry she had to struggle to speak. "A lot of good he's done. Have you even given her water?"

Mrs. Jones chewed her lip. "She has a horrible thirst and begs for water, but even a sip makes the retching begin. This morning she's been half out of her head and too dizzy to sit up."

David almost expected his jaw to crack. Bellowing at the housekeeper wouldn't help, and he could see the woman was distraught. The sight of Bliss striding through the doorway brought a modicum of relief. At least now something would *happen*.

The physician's unruly brown hair needed a trim and contained more gray than David remembered, but Bliss's direct gaze still conveyed the intelligence and steadiness the man was respected for. The physician nodded and set down the sizeable leather case he carried.

"Scott. Good to see you."

David released Charlotte's hand and leaned back in his chair. Bliss wrapped his fingers around her wrist. His eyebrows rose.

David drummed his fingers on the arms of his chair, tension squeezing his throat.

"Heartbeat's a bit fast," Bliss muttered. He glanced at David. "Give me a few minutes, will you?" The physician smiled at Miss Marsden. "Can you stay?"

David gripped his chair wheels. It was the proper thing to leave while Bliss examined Charlotte, but everything in him wanted to stay. He backed up, his gaze upon her while Bliss felt her forehead, speaking softly, gently pulling her eyelids up to study her eyes. From his bag the physician removed a tubular device for listening to the chest. Using the earpiece, the doctor applied its trumpet bell-shaped portion over Charlotte's heart, but when he straightened he shot an annoyed look at David.

David acknowledged Bliss with a hike of his chin. He turned his chair toward the door and called for Boone, who waited in the hall. After wheeling out, the second interminable wait of the day began, but it came to an immediate end when Charlotte cried out. Even through the closed door, the distress in her cry sent an icy wave through him.

"Boone, get me in there!" David pushed hard at his chair wheels. Boone turned a deaf ear to Mrs. Jones's objections and obeyed. He took David straight to Charlotte's bed.

Knees drawn up, face pinched, she clutched her abdomen. Her long, low moan sliced through David's heart, and he stroked his thumb across her wrist and turned on Bliss. Christ, his fear had him all tangled up. He could barely think.

Bliss folded his arms across his chest and pressed his lips together. "She's got a very tender abdomen. Dry mouth, extreme thirst, confusion. Severe headache. Frequent regurgitations. Dysentery." He looked at Miss Marsden. "And it started suddenly?"

"Yes," David said.

Bliss's gaze whipped around. His brows rose.

"We had dinner together, but she ate very little. She went home right after the meal, feeling sick."

"And she felt fine before the meal?"

"She seemed to. She ate some candy and didn't complain."

Bliss turned toward Mrs. Jones, who stood near the door. "Anyone else in the household sick?"

"No, sir."

He dropped his chin and stared at the floor with narrowed eyes. Just when David thought he couldn't bear to wait any longer, the physician lifted his head and looked at the maid.

"Miss, is she a lady who uses arsenic for her complexion?"

"Arsenic!" David ran his hand down Charlotte's arm and gripped her now relaxed hand. "You suspect arsenic poisoning?"

Bliss rubbed his jaw. "I'm afraid I do."

"She doesn't take arsenic," Miss Marsden said. She looked at each person in the room. "Could it be arsenic that poisoned Persa?"

A horrible weight slammed into David, squeezed his chest and made him burn. He pinched his lips closed to keep the stream of curse words inside. Persa poisoned and then Charlotte? He didn't believe in coincidences like that.

Another occurrence burst in his head like ignited gunpowder that left him dazed and off-balance for a moment. The man who'd rammed into her, the man who'd stolen her reticule and was chased away by Persa...he'd left her with massive bruises. The bastard had *wanted* to hurt her. Now he wanted to kill her and had nearly succeeded! The dark knowledge exploded in David's chest, sent a geyser of boiling fury up his neck and into his head. The force of it locked his jaw and nearly leveled him. His temples pulsed under skin tight enough to split like sizzling sausage and spew boiling blood.

Christ! He dragged a hand down his face and fought against releasing the roar he barely constrained. He'd find the bloody bastard and give him a sample of the way a soldier dealt death. As good as he'd been at killing—striking hard, with aggression and precision—he'd never enjoyed it. This killing—because, God help him, he *was going* to find and kill this arsehole—would be different.

The wide eyes of Bliss and the maid brought him back to the business at hand. From their expressions, it seemed likely his twisted smile was worthy of an actor portraying Richard III.

He hoped his quarry would find it as frightening.

CHAPTER TWENTY-SIX

David lifted the spoon of mud-like, red-brown pulp to Charlotte's lips. Her drowsiness was another consequence of the arsenic poisoning.

"Please, sweetheart," he urged.

Thick, dark lashes swept up, her eyes found him, and she opened her mouth. He slid the hydrated sesquioxide of iron into her mouth. Her nose wrinkled and her mouth turned down, but she swallowed. Thank God she was cognizant enough to understand she needed one tablespoon every five to ten minutes. Bliss had assured him she couldn't get too much of the antidote. They were to force the rusty concoction down her until they saw improvement in her symptoms.

Once Bliss had made the stunning diagnosis, he'd written out instructions for the apothecary and one of the footmen had been sent. The sesquioxide of iron was more efficacious when freshly prepared, so Bliss didn't carry it in his bag.

David sent word to Chetney that he'd be gone the rest of the day and insisted on taking the first stint with Charlotte. He wanted to be with her, wanted to touch her and care for her with his own hands. Bliss had made it abundantly clear there was no guarantee she'd recover, even with the antidote. The poison had already been working on her system for two full days. They could only wait and see.

He rested the spoon in the bowl of medicine. Maybe it was merely his imagination, but he thought he could see a bit of improvement in her. He'd been at this for three hours. Inside he felt in danger of snapping, but he forced himself to remain calm and collected on the outside. Charlotte needed him to soothe her, to direct her servants and oversee her care. He'd make sure everything possible was done for her.

The solid sound of a man's footsteps made him turn. Charlotte's father had finally arrived. David's note had been dispatched hours ago.

To give the man credit, he looked worried. He also looked surprised to find David at his daughter's bedside. He positioned himself on David's left and picked up Charlotte's hand. "Charlotte?"

Her droopy eyes fluttered open. "Papa."

Tears filled her eyes, and David's ravaged heart took another crushing blow. If he hadn't already acknowledged his love for her, this situation would have left him in no doubt of his feelings. The overwhelming worry had him nearly insane. He hadn't felt so helpless and enraged since the day he learned he'd never again stand on his feet.

"I'm here," Shelby said, but her eyes closed before the words were out.

Intense, dark blue eyes appraised David. "What are you doing here?"

For a moment, possessiveness rose and swamped David's other emotions. Damn it, he wanted to tell Shelby he was her lover and he had the right to be here. But common sense prevailed. Charlotte wouldn't want him confronting her father with that fact, so he kept his tone mild and his eyes steady.

"She asked for me."

He scooped up another spoonful of the rusty mush and fed it to her. Frowning, Shelby moved around the bed and stood across from him. When David set the bowl down and looked up, Shelby's hands were deep in his trouser pockets.

"I was at one of my factories," Shelby said. "It took a while for your note to reach me. Thank you for sending it."

Charlotte's father's explanation seemed reasonable, but David couldn't help his flash of resentment. Since he'd met her, he'd seen and heard enough to know this was yet one more instance of her father not being there when she needed him. Of course, in spite of the man's poor showing as a parent, Charlotte loved him. So David nodded and proceeded to tell Shelby everything he knew of Charlotte's condition.

Shelby's face grew tight as David talked. "I may have my physician up," he said when David finished.

"I'm sure Bliss would be happy to speak with your man. I assure you, Bliss is a brilliant physician."

It was time for another dose of the antidote. *Please, God.* David couldn't seem to get out any more of a prayer than those two words, but with each spoonful he added the silent plea.

Shelby pulled a chair from the corner and sat down. "Why are you doing this?" He waved his hand to indicate Charlotte, David and the medicine.

So, Charlotte's father wasn't satisfied with the answer given him when he first arrived. Not surprising. No unrelated man, even one who was a good friend, belonged in a woman's bedroom, much less sitting watch over her. So, well…so be it. David glanced toward Miss Marsden, who sat in the corner, and lowered his voice.

"We've formed an attachment. No one other than her servants will know I've been here, and Charlotte trusts them to be discreet."

Shelby's eyes narrowed, and a vein at his temple began to visibly pulse. "I don't care what your connection is." Spittle flew with his emphatic words. "You don't belong here."

Blast the man. This wasn't the time for a confrontation, but nothing and no one was expelling David. "I don't intend to leave until she's better."

The two men stared at each other. No doubt Shelby's severe, thin-lipped look of displeasure made his subordinates hie to attention, but David had other worries. "I'm concerned how Charlotte ingested the arsenic," he pointed out.

Shelby's gaze darted back to his daughter. "Has she been able to tell you anything?"

"No. But there's evidence. She was someone's intentional victim."

"Evidence?" Shelby's gaze, sharp and analytical, returned to David.

"First the footpad's assault, then Persa's poisoning, and now this."

Shelby's chin dropped. "Slow down, Scott. You'd better back up and tell me everything."

David expected a man with Shelby's intelligence to be a little quicker putting things together, but perhaps he hadn't realized the severity of the injuries Charlotte suffered in the assault. And he might not have heard about Persa.

"Just last week her dog was poisoned and nearly died. And Charlotte sustained unnecessary injuries when her reticule was stolen."

"I didn't know any of this."

"I thought you sent the candy because of the assault."

Shelby's face grew even grimmer. "I didn't send any candy."

"Miss Marsden," David called. "Lady Haliday brought some candy home the night she got sick. Do you know where it is?"

The maid hurried to the fireplace and retrieved the tin from the mantel. Carrying it as though it might explode, she brought it over and opened it. It looked as though several pieces were gone.

David took the tin and raised it to his nose. It smelled the way it looked—like it was full of rich, fruity candy.

"Has anyone else eaten it?"

"No," Miss Marsden said.

Mind reeling, David closed his eyes. Charlotte had joked how unusual it was for her father to send candy, and her instincts had been right. The fudge would have to be tested to confirm the presence of arsenic, but David's gut told him they'd discovered how the poison was delivered.

He pushed aside his rage long enough to feed Charlotte another spoonful of medicine. "A servant delivered it to the office saying it was sent by you."

A red flush spread over Shelby's face and neck. "First that damnable tale of Vivian Garret's two years ago, and now this. I'll tell you one thing, Scott. Charlotte didn't earn or deserve any of it."

David leveled his gaze on Shelby the way he'd once sighted down his Enfield. "I imagine you have a few enemies. Is someone trying to get to you through Charlotte?"

Shelby almost growled. He crossed his arms and for a long minute looked toward the window. With a quick shake of his head he stood, pulled his watch from his waistcoat pocket and opened the face cover. The click as he snapped it closed seemed to spur him to action.

"Sometimes business dealings give rise to hostility. If this is the result of some sort of misplaced revenge, I'll know soon enough." He strode for the door then turned. "You'll send word if her condition changes?"

The man had shifted from outrage at David's presence to assigning him guardianship? David almost laughed. Yet, why should he be surprised? The little bit he knew of Shelby, this wasn't a man to sit vigil at Charlotte's bedside.

"Of course," he said. "Could you also make a report to the constable? Someone needs to do so, and it would probably be best if it were you."

Shelby gave David a nod and strode from the room. By attacking the mystery of Charlotte's poisoning, Shelby would feel as if he were doing his duty as her father. It would also conveniently rid him of the expectation that he be present at his dangerously ill daughter's side. His departure was a relief.

David cupped Charlotte's face and brushed his thumb across her cheek. After the last time they made love, he'd kissed her there, stroked her satiny flesh, and she'd turned her head and sought his mouth. Now he was rewarded by the lifting of long eyelashes and the slight curve of her lips. Recognition lit her remarkable eyes. Although he'd been able to rouse her sufficiently to get the sesquioxide of iron down her, she'd remained lethargic, weak and confused. This was the first time she'd smiled at him and really appeared present.

"Hello, sweetheart," he said, his own smile stretching his tight face. It felt as if he hadn't smiled in years.

Charlotte curled her hand around his, first weakly, then with growing strength. The painful knot in his chest eased, and in its place relief produced a sort of deep trembling.

"You're here. You won't leave, will you?" she asked.

"I'm not going anywhere."

She sighed and her eyes drifted closed. Her fingers relaxed. "I love you," she murmured.

David froze. His heart surged to his throat.

"Bluebell?"

She'd fallen asleep. He wanted to wake her and demand she repeat what she'd said, confirm not only that she knew what she'd told him but that she meant it. Because, God help him, despite what he'd said, despite what he knew would be best for them, there was nothing he wanted more than Charlotte's love.

#

When she opened her eyes, the first thing Charlotte saw was David. He slept in his wheeled chair, one shoulder burrowed lower than the other, head tipped back and to the side, lips parted. She'd never seen his hair so mussed, as if he'd been pulling it in fifty different directions. It made her want to comb her fingers through the glowing locks. Red-gold stubble covered his jaw, and the faint lines that had bracketed his mouth now scored his cheeks. His loosened tie, wrinkled shirt and unbuttoned waistcoat hung limply. He looked exhausted, uncomfortable and thoroughly rumpled.

Charlotte skimmed her gaze over David's long legs. His trousers hid the lax and somewhat shrunken appearance of his lower legs and left thigh, while the fabric conformed to his noticeably larger, well-muscled right thigh. When they'd begun their affair, she'd been afraid to touch his legs—had feared hurting him, feared how touching the appendages might make her feel. That had lasted until the night he woke in agony with a muscle cramp in his calf. Alarmed, close to frantic, she'd tried to knead the knot from the muscle, and when his moans of pain turned to groans of relief, she continued massaging his limbs and found them warm and dusted with the same red-gold hair as his forearms. He could move his feet and toes a little, and once she understood he enjoyed her touch, her fear disappeared. She loved touching him—all of him—and after that night she'd regarded his injured legs as just another part of him.

The weak light flooding through the east window told her it was morning, but she had no idea how many mornings had passed while she lay abed. She thought perhaps more than two. She licked her tongue over her lower lip and discovered it dry and chapped.

This morning she seemed able to think, and her stomach had settled, but she felt heavy, as if leaden air pressed her body deep into the mattress. She raised her arms and found them impossibly weighty. Just that small exertion made her heart quicken, her breath come faster, and her thoughts and memories spun in a confused whirl.

She remembered pieces of the past few days. She'd been poisoned. Perhaps nearly died. During it all, she'd hung on to David. David, gentle and ever-present, with his calloused hands, with his fierce, watchful eyes, their depths overflowing with concern. Whenever she'd felt as if she were drifting away, he'd pulled her back and anchored her.

Tears filled her eyes. Persa had been poisoned, too. Someone would kill her dog to cause her anguish? How could someone hate her so much? She'd been told she was sent fudge laced with *arsenic*. The cruelty terrified her.

She felt fragile, as if even the mildest vexation might break her into pieces. She'd been just this hollow sitting at her mother's bedside and awaiting her mother's last breath. She'd been the object of cruelty then, too, when her father's indifference stole her mother's last precious hours. For years the sound of a clock in a quiet room could take her back to that day, how the tick of that clock interspersed the slow cadence of Mama's labored breaths.

Charlotte had known her father sat behind her, his mouth tight, his wooden ladder-back chair tilted against the wall. She'd felt his gaze when it came to rest on her back.

"It's time for you to go, Charlotte," he said.

Disbelief, rage and hurt had boiled up from her core, mixed with the pain she'd borne the past five days as she sat vigil, melded into a toxic mélange. How could he make her leave for school *now*? She'd convinced herself he wouldn't really do it, even as she pleaded, begged, and watched his eyes harden and his mouth grow tight.

"I spent a bloody fortune and called in favors I curried for years to get you in this school. And in spite of all that, if you don't arrive by their specified time they'll give your spot away."

His terse words were too harsh, too loud, and not to be questioned—though she knew the school didn't want her. Mrs. Brewster's School for Gentlewomen was a boarding school for the aristocracy. Daughters of noblemen lived there and learned the skills necessary to become wives of dukes, earls and marquesses. Her father must have given them a great deal of money to convince them to accept the twelve-year-old daughter of London's most prominent common-born industrialist. He'd certainly gloated when she was granted admission. The finest school, the finest young ladies in England, and she'd be among them. But obviously Mrs. Brewster hadn't *wanted* her. She'd included a stipulation with the offer of admission: If Charlotte didn't present herself by six o'clock, she needn't bother presenting herself at all.

"You can't expect me to leave now, Papa." She'd struggled to get the words out without breaking down. Tears wouldn't sway

Papa, they'd make him angry. Proof of female weakness, he called them. They'd only increase his impatience.

"We've been over and over this, Charlotte. Don't pretend you're shocked." His face could have been hewn from rock. "You know I'll send word when she passes."

She'd turned back to her mother, who was pale, her skin moist with cold sweat, her slight form barely lifting the covers. Mama's normally pink lips were an unhealthy purplish color. This illness had struck with the fierceness of God's hand, and Mama had succumbed to insensibility within three days. The physician Papa called had explained the congestion of the lungs was due to a weakness of her heart. He advised they pray.

Charlotte had. She'd pleaded and bargained, but God remained silent and distant, just like her father. As the hours passed, an unwelcome knowledge took root: There would be no miracle.

Mama. The youngest child of an impoverished baron, she had always been reserved and soft-spoken, given to a deep-seated shyness. Her father had overcome his reluctance to allow her an alliance with a man not even a gentleman because Charlotte's papa offered enough money to repair Grandpapa's estate and pay all his bills. Charlotte's papa had made no secret of the pride he'd felt, obtaining Mama's hand with the same brute force he utilized in his business deals. Mama provided him the entrée he sought to aristocratic society.

Charlotte had inherited her mama's refined features and admirable form, but her bold coloring was her father's. He'd often commented that she got her brain and stubbornness from him, too, although those characteristics didn't always please him—like when she'd wanted to stay and he intended to make her leave.

"Mama needs me." If she left, Mama would have no one with her who loved her.

Papa's front chair legs had hit the floor with a thump. "She doesn't even know you're here, Charlotte. Now say your good-byes. You know she'd understand."

That much was true. No one understood Papa like Mama. She'd always tried to give Charlotte an extra measure of love to make up for his absence and his remote manner, so how could Charlotte leave Mama as she passed from this life to the next? She couldn't!

"I'm not going." He'd have to carry her out.

He stood. "Yes, you are."

The hard certainty in his voice had made her quake inside. As much as she struggled to hold back her tears, they clouded her vision. The cold, brittle emptiness that had sat in her belly for days got colder and sharper and filled every part of her. If she refused to walk, would he truly carry her out? Would her father really do that to her?

She'd stood, stroked Mama's hair for the last time, kissed her cheek and tried not to listen to her rapid, raspy breaths. Mama's eyes, barely open and frighteningly blank, were glazed. Could she see her? Hear her?

"I love you, Mama. I'm sorry. I don't want to go." And then Charlotte had collapsed, shaking with silent sobs.

Papa wasted no time. He'd picked her up and carried her to the carriage.

CHAPTER TWENTY-SEVEN

She hadn't thought anything could ever hurt as much as her father carrying her from her mother's bed to his carriage. So far she'd been right. As bad as being poisoned was, it was somewhat better than that skirmish with Father. Charlotte had lost that campaign against him and survived; she could survive this.

After her husband's murder, when she'd come out of mourning and returned to London, she thought herself a woman tempered by fire. She'd overcome the devastation of her mother's death, her husband's betrayal, and scandal. She'd borne her father's lifelong indifference. What more could the world throw at her? She'd vowed to live without the benefit of a husband or her father meddling in her affairs, to lead a life of independence. She'd been smug and satisfied. But this attack changed everything. Instead of strong and independent, Charlotte felt tenuous and vulnerable. When she searched herself, she found fear and loneliness.

She looked at David, asleep in his chair. No, that wasn't right. She didn't feel alone. Frightened and confused, yes, but not alone.

David had watched over her. Every time she opened her eyes, David was there. She suddenly remembered looking at him and realizing she loved him. Did she also remember telling him she loved him? Could she have done that?

She plucked at a nightdress button with a restless finger. Was it possible to love him if she didn't trust him not to hurt her? She closed her eyes. David had far more capability to hurt her than Haliday ever had. David could hurt her as deeply as her father had.

That thought, coming out of nowhere, stunned her.

Her *father*?

Yes. Because the pain of her father's lifelong dissatisfaction never stopped hurting. And because somehow, in spite of everything, the tiny flicker of hope she carried deep inside had never been smothered. Part of her loved him and still yearned for his affection in turn.

It felt secure and right when David wrapped his arms around her. She loved to rest her head on his shoulder and run her fingers over his curly chest hair. She'd follow its tapering trail down to his taut abdomen and slide her hand around his narrow waist, and she remembered how it had felt when he was deep inside her, sighing and murmuring her name, his blue eyes shining with a light that left every part of her glowing and open and connected to him. *Yes*, she felt more for David than she had ever had for her husband. Far more.

But if she let down her barriers and allowed herself to trust him, how would she ever remain independent? She'd vowed to never again be subject to the whims of a man. If she put her trust in David and he didn't love her enough in return—or if he stopped loving her—how would she ever survive the loss?

She wouldn't. So it would be even worse than the betrayal of her father.

A pulse of pain spiked in her temple. Wonderful. Her headache was probably returning.

She placed her hand atop David's knee and squeezed. When she said his name, he woke. Initially startled, he quickly straightened and then smiled and took her hand.

"Good morning, Bluebell. You're looking better. How do you feel?" As tired as he looked, his eyes were smiling.

"The nausea and headache are gone, I think."

"Good. How would you like a cup of tea? Doctor Bliss left instructions for when you felt able to eat."

"Tea sounds good." She'd wait and see how the tea sat before trying anything else in her stomach, which at present felt like an empty cavern. "David, how long has it been?"

He brushed a lock of hair away from her face, securing it behind her ear. "Four days."

Right now she didn't want to think about how she'd lost so much time. The last day she recollected somewhat clearly, but the days prior held only fragmented memories. "How long have you been here?"

"Three days." He lifted a small bell from the bedside table and rang it. "Have you heard bells ringing in your dreams? They gave me this so I wouldn't have to move away from you if I needed to call for help."

"Three days." She considered his red-rimmed eyes. "Have you eaten or slept?"

His brows bunched together and he gave her an exasperated look. "Yes, I've eaten. And slept as much as I needed to. It may not look like it, but I even washed and changed. I commandeered one of your guest rooms."

From the look of him, he hadn't done much sleeping, washing, or changing, but she wasn't inclined to argue with him.

Rebecca came in. "Sir?" Seeing Charlotte awake, the maid smiled and stepped closer. "My lady, you're awake?"

"She is," David said, "and she wants tea."

"Right away, sir. Excuse me for saying so, but everyone will be right glad to hear it."

Rebecca's happy face had the abrupt effect of stimulating Charlotte's emotions. She pressed her fingers to her leaky eyes until she was certain she'd stemmed her unwanted tears and said, "Please tell the staff I'm feeling much better."

"And tell Cook if Lady Haliday does well with the tea, we'll be wanting a custard next," David said.

Charlotte raised her eyebrows at him.

"Doctor's orders."

A second cup of tea followed the first, and suddenly Charlotte couldn't get enough to drink. In spite of how heavy her arms felt, she refused to let David feed the custard to her. After her abbreviated meal, he disappeared and left her to Rebecca, who gave her a thorough wash and changed her nightdress. By the time David returned—shaved, changed and smelling of soap and his own masculine essence—she was propped against fluffed pillows, her hair neatly braided and feeling weak but comfortable.

Dr. Bliss arrived a short time later. She didn't remember much from his previous visits, but she liked his no-nonsense attitude.

"You're going to feel weak for some time. Just how long, I can't predict. You must resume your activities slowly and take care not to overdo."

Under the covers, she clutched her hands together. "Will there be lasting effects?"

He pursed his lips and considered her. "I wish I could assure you, but I can't. Arsenic affects all the major organs. You're recovering rapidly, which is heartening. You could well recover without permanent damage. I'm encouraged enough to believe that will be the case."

David smiled, nodded, and pressed his thumb and index fingers to the inner corners of his closed eyes. "That's the best possible news."

It was. Just hearing Bliss's optimistic prediction made Charlotte feel better. It was even time for her to show a little pluck and let David get back to his normal routine. She'd noticed the neat stacks of correspondence sitting on her desk and recalled David mentioning he'd advised her father on her progress and directed Chetney on what to do in his absence. The poor secretary must be beside himself.

She didn't recall seeing her father, and the knowledge of his absence was hard and hurtful—though no surprise. Father couldn't stand lazing about a sick room. He was too much a man of action. But, then, David, in spite of his physical limitations, was no less a man of action. His intelligent mind was constantly evaluating, planning, dreaming, *thinking*. David didn't like being idle, but he'd stayed with her, guarded her, *cared for her*. Her father navigated life with his mind. David's compass was clearly his heart.

She looked at him, shaking hands with Bliss and bidding the doctor good-bye. A horrible certainty welled up inside her. Her time with David was near its end.

David deserved a woman who could make a full commitment, a wife who would trust in his love with an unshakable faith. She loved him, and yes, she trusted him for now. But how could she trust that he'd never change? That his love would always be steadfast? That he'd never hurt her? After the actions of her father and Haliday, she just wasn't capable of such blind belief. Not even with David.

He'd said he wouldn't marry, but he should. He should have a wife who would bear him children. A sharp pain pierced her heart and she tensed. How beautiful and bright David's children would be, and how well-loved their mother. Such a fortunate woman, but not meant to be her.

Oh, but how I wish I were that woman.

If she insisted, she knew David would marry her. She could convince him. But then he'd be married to a woman who might never bear his child, a woman touched by scandal. Worst of all, he might realize she wasn't capable of a love great enough to overcome her fears. That wasn't what she wanted for him. She wanted him to have so much more than she could ever give him.

Perhaps, if she wasn't monopolizing his affection, he'd be open to falling in love. Did she have the strength of character to emulate David? When he'd been awarded the Victoria Cross he'd told her he was no hero, but she knew better. Courage resided in David's bones, coursed through his blood. Could she be brave enough to turn him away? She would then have to face an unknown enemy without him. Perhaps, if she thought only of what was best for him, she could.

He was back. She tried to guard her expression and smoothed her hand over the colorful, intricate quilt that covered her.

He reached out, and his finger stroked the slope of her nose. "Your busy morning has tired you, hasn't it? Would you like to sleep a while?"

She nodded. What a miserable coward she was. She couldn't give up David. Not right now. She hoped when she recovered she'd be strong enough to overcome her selfishness and do the right thing. But not now.

He smoothed the covers around her shoulders. "All right then. I'm going to leave for a bit. Rebecca will be here should you need anything."

He rolled himself to the door. Charlotte watched his powerful back muscles bunching beneath his coat as he did. Soon she heard voices in the hall: David's, Boone's and her footman Beckham's. She heard Boone and Beckham lift David and carry him downstairs. Given his dislike of dependence on anyone or anything, she knew he must hate being carried above all things. And yet he'd come upstairs for her.

She rolled over and picked up David's carving of Persa from the bedside table. The care he'd taken with it made the figurine that much dearer. She brought it close to her chest, held it and listened to the sounds from downstairs. As David left, the house returned to quiet.

#

In response to his note, Wakefield appeared at the Fund offices by late afternoon.

His friend strode in, and a quietness settled over David. He didn't care if Wakefield's attraction to Charlotte or his loyalty to David motivated his help; David knew he could depend on Miles. He also owed it to his friend to tell him he'd laid claim to the lady's affections. And he needed to confront the busybody about the way he'd warned Charlotte off.

"Where have you been?" Wakefield asked. "You haven't been home, at your club or at work, and no one would tell me a thing." He dropped onto one of the chairs in front of David's desk, folded his hands across his belly and stretched out his long legs. The military image was gone. In its place was a sophisticated gentleman of discerning taste. The dark gray frock coat and pinstriped trousers appeared both expensive and finely tailored.

"Were you in need of something in particular from me?" David asked.

"Hmm. Not really." Miles's eyes narrowed. "So, where were you?"

"With Lady Haliday. Someone tried to kill her."

"What?" Wakefield shot up in his chair and bent forward. "Good God, man. Is she all right? What in holy hell happened?"

"Arsenic poisoning—enough to kill. She's recovering, but it took a substantial portion of antidote. Her physician is encouraged she'll make a full recovery."

"Thank God she's all right." Wakefield tugged off his gloves and slapped them against his thigh. "It's hard to believe. You mean someone *intentionally* poisoned her?"

"Someone pretending to be her father sent her candy and loaded it with arsenic. Shelby knew nothing about it, of course. Charlotte's dog was poisoned and nearly died, too. At the time we thought it accidental, but now I don't think so."

Wakefield stood and began pacing. "What do you want me to do?"

"Shelby's taking a hard look at his business associates. Given their past...I need someone to watch Lady Garret and ask some discrete questions about her."

Wakefield stopped and faced David. "Lady Haliday suspects her?"

"No," David said. "Or she hasn't said as much, but *I* suspect her. Poison is the weapon of a woman. I've seen the two of them, and the baroness hates Charlotte. Charlotte doesn't know why Lady Garret would want to kill her after all the damage she's already done, but perhaps the woman's truly unbalanced. Perhaps she's still obsessed and jealous. Jealous enough to do more than send you and I copies of her novel."

"She must be mad." Wakefield dropped back onto his chair. "Haliday's been gone two years."

"I know. It makes no sense, but Charlotte can't think of anyone who would wish her dead."

Wakefield leaned back against his chair and studied him. "*Charlotte?*"

David hadn't used her given name intentionally, but it was best to get this over with. He dipped his chin in a single sharp nod.

Wakefield's eyes narrowed. "And she calls you David, does she?"

"She does."

Wakefield hung his head, then raised it and shrugged. "I suppose you know I acted the mother again."

"Yes, and you left her in quite a state, too. You've got to stop, Miles. If I need help, I'll ask."

Loose-lipped, Wakefield blew out a gusty exhale. "I know. I'll do better."

For a long minute they took each other's measure, then one corner of Wakefield's mouth edged up.

"Well, it seems you claimed her before I even had a chance—but since it's you, I can accept it and even be happy. Am I to congratulate you?"

David found himself wordless. He had no reason to feel shame, but he had to struggle to meet Wakefield's eyes. He snapped his mouth shut, swallowed, and tried again.

"No congratulations warranted."

"She refused you?"

He couldn't bring himself to tell Wakefield he hadn't proposed. "Neither of us wishes to marry. We're agreed in that."

Wakefield frowned. "Arc you."

David held his friend's gaze, and finally Wakefield's eyebrows rose and he shrugged. He stood and said, "Well, I'll spy on Lady

Garret—and I might have a word with Radcliffe. He escorts her everywhere."

"Thank you, Miles," David said.

Wakefield left, and David turned his attention back to his desk. Chetney had held things together and moved appointments, but some things he had to attend himself. One of those was a letter to Sidney Herbert explaining his need to remain largely absent for a while. He would spend the morning working like a demon to clear away the things that couldn't wait and be back with Charlotte by evening.

#

"Mr. Scott. Sir, might I have a word?"

It was Eleanor, the eldest Butler girl, the one Charlotte had taken in. Part servant, part philanthropic project, she stood with hands clasped, looking nervous.

David held back his sigh. Perched between Boone and Pickett and held aloft by their arms, he'd only just entered Charlotte's home. Beckham was halfway up the stairs with his chair.

"Why don't we talk upstairs? Is it about your brothers and sisters?"

"Oh, no, sir. It's about Persa. Lady Haliday said I should tell you."

The girl's tense face and the slight tremor to her voice called his intuition to attention. He'd learned to trust his gut. Eleanor was going to tell him something important.

He nodded to encourage her. "Very well."

"The day Persa got sick, I left her with a lady for a few minutes," Eleanor said.

A ravenous predator snarled in the pit of David, and his blood hummed like that of a dog on the scent. *A lady? She's the one.*

"Come up right behind us, Eleanor, can you?"

It seemed to take forever to get upstairs and into his chair. David barely managed not to snap at Boone and Pickett to hurry, and finally they had him situated.

"Let's talk out here in the hall, in case Lady Haliday is resting." He forced a brief smile and hoped it would put the girl at ease. "Now tell me everything that happened."

"I took Persa for a walk and a woman—she looked to be in service, sir—started chatting with me."

"Looked to be in service?"

"Her dress was plain and dark, sturdily made. And she wore a cap."

David nodded to urge the girl on.

"Well, we got to talking about my situation, sir."

"Your situation?"

"About my place in Lady Haliday's house. I'm so grateful, Mr. Scott, but I miss my brothers and sisters so much."

"She encouraged you to talk about it, did she?"

A relieved sigh escaped the girl, and her shoulders relaxed. "Yes, sir. She did."

"Go on."

"She said I should get another position—one that pays enough so I could provide for all the kids and we could be together. She said she knew of an open position just down the street."

"And she offered to hold Persa for you?"

"Yes. That's exactly what she did."

"How long were you gone, Eleanor?"

"Only a few minutes. I couldn't find the house she described. I was nearly back when I saw her waving. She tied Persa's leash to a bush and left. Do you think that woman poisoned her? Did *she* send the candy to Lady Haliday?"

"She very well may have. I hope she did."

Eleanor's eyes widened. "You do? Why?"

David could see he'd shocked her, so he gave her a reassuring smile. "Because with your help we might be able to find her. I want you to think about her. What color hair she had, how old she was, how tall she was—anything you can remember."

Eleanor's face lit up. "Her speech was coarse, sir. And she had gold hair."

"Good girl. Now, what else?"

CHAPTER TWENTY-EIGHT

Vivian accepted Radcliffe's assistance as she alighted from his brougham. He turned and spoke to his coachman, telling the man to wait. Evidently he intended to go home once he'd seen her inside.

She waited and looked at the trees and flowers that decorated her neighborhood. It gave her a moment to puzzle on Radcliffe's behavior. He'd taken her to a new art exhibit but had been exceedingly quiet. Several times she'd had to speak more than once to engage his notice. When she questioned that, he blamed it on a headache and suggested they leave. His inattention and grim mouth worried her. They weren't like him.

If she hadn't paused to wait for Radcliffe, Vivian wouldn't have seen the girl. What drew her gaze to the coach waiting across the road she didn't know, but she just caught the glint of spectacles and the small face of Charlotte Haliday's servant in the coach window before the girl ducked out of sight and the coach drove away.

Vivian's body grew hot and then cold. She couldn't think. Couldn't move. Helpless, she peered at Radcliffe.

"Vivian?" He grasped her arm. Even that much support was a relief. "Are you all right?"

He frowned, let go of her elbow and wrapped his arm around her back.

"Radcliffe." She grabbed his lapel. Oh, Lord. Was she going to faint?

A tiny part of her mind recognized Radcliffe's confusion as he looked down at her hand. She held on for dear life, scrunching and pulling at the fabric of his coat. Then he urged her forward and her feet began to move. She didn't take in much else until she found herself in her sitting room, seated beside him, a glass of sherry—no, brandy—in her hand.

"Drink," Radcliffe commanded, and she obediently lifted the spirits to her lips. It made her cough a little, but its burning heat streaked down, settled in her stomach and roused her.

"A little better?" he asked.

She nodded and took another sip.

"I'm sending for a doctor." He rose and strode toward the door.

"No. Please, Radcliffe, that's not necessary. I'm fine."

Head cocked, he studied her then ambled back to her divan and retook his seat. His intense gaze belied his relaxed posture, his arm stretched along the back of the settee. "What's wrong then?"

His long-fingered hand dangled near her face. It would take very little to lean her cheek against it. Vivian wanted to. But as much as she wanted him to share her burden, she couldn't tell him what she'd done. That would risk too much. Radcliffe even found gossip distasteful, let alone actual scandal. It still amazed her that he'd chosen to overlook her somewhat notorious past enough to take up with her. A few times she'd caught a look of regret on his face and wondered if he was thinking about the future.

Radcliffe was only the third man she'd lain with, but she realized he meant more to her than a thousand men could. Each day she measured her happiness by how much of him she saw. Sometimes, after they engaged in lovemaking and he left her, she lay and wondered what might have happened if she hadn't had such an open affair with Haliday. He cared deeply for her. She thought he might have proposed if her life had gone a different way.

"If you're not ill, then what is it?" Radcliffe repeated, and she realized he still waited for her answer. Perhaps she should lie, tell him something that might explain her behavior and resolve his worry.

"I thought I saw someone watching me, and it discomfited me a bit is all."

"Watching you?"

"I believe Lady Haliday watches me. She's wished me harm in the past, and I'm not sure but she still doesn't."

Radcliffe straightened. "You saw Lady Haliday watching you? Just now?"

Something about him made her uneasy. Why had she said such a thing? Why hadn't she just pretended to be ill? "I'm not sure, but I think so, yes."

He stared into her eyes, and she couldn't hold his gaze. She shifted and smoothed the pleats of her skirt. He'd never looked at her like this. He had a reputation as a shrewd politician and negotiator, but she'd never seen that steely side of him until now.

"Has she ever threatened you?"

How could a voice so low peal like a warning in her head? Then Vivian remembered Lady Elliott's ball. Charlotte *had* threatened her. "Yes. Little more than a month ago she threatened to destroy me, though I have no idea what she meant by that. I wouldn't put anything past her."

A shadow seemed to fall across Radcliffe, turning his face bleak. A monstrous feeling grew from Vivian's core. "Stephen?"

He stood and strode to the window where he stood looking out. The fingers of one hand tapped against his thigh. His posture, so stiff and upright, frightened her.

"Stephen."

He turned. "What have you done?"

The question came slow and sharp and edged with horror, and her heart lurched. "What?"

"Lord Wakefield came to see me last night. You're acquainted with him, aren't you? He's a friend of Lady Haliday's. He served with David Scott. But, then, you'd know that. You know everything having to do with her, don't you?"

She had good reason to know all about Charlotte Haliday, but Vivian saw it was too late to take Radcliffe into her confidence. She doubted he'd understand, anyway. She'd been so foolish, allowing herself to fall in love with him.

Should she act outraged or puzzled? Oh, she couldn't *think*.

"*What* are you talking about?" she said instead.

"Lady Haliday was poisoned with arsenic and nearly died, and Wakefield and Scott suspect you. You're the only person who has a contentious history with her."

She nearly died. Those words battered inside Vivian like storm waves pummeling the shore. She bent her head and shielded her face with her hands, unsure if she could bear the hurt, the disbelief and anger in Radcliffe's voice.

He rejoined her on the divan, took her wrists and pulled her hands away. She'd always feared losing him over this, but she'd tried to keep him separate from her dealings with Charlotte. Oh, it wasn't fair to have Radcliffe taken away along with everything else. Hadn't she given up enough?

"Stephen, it's true I have a grudge against Lady Haliday, but do you honestly believe I'd kill her?"

He studied her intently. "Did Haliday mean that much to you, that you wanted to elicit some kind of sick revenge? Was that it?"

He still held her wrists, had shackled them with his hands. She hated constraint of any kind and gave an ineffectual pull that only made his restraint feel more rigid.

"Let me go," she said, tugging. "*Let go.*"

She yanked hard, and he released her suddenly, holding his hands up and spreading his fingers as if he were the one breaking free. She surged to her feet and growled, "Get out." She dashed at her wet cheeks. "Go on. *Get out.* You don't believe in me. You automatically assumed the worst."

He wavered for an instant. She saw it in his face but then his determination was back, his mouth and shoulders set, and he was leaving.

In the doorway he spun and stalked back. She'd never seen the relaxed, confident Radcliffe like this. Jaw tensed, teeth clamped together, face dark and fierce. He didn't stop until he was close. Much too close.

"Did you do it?"

The wave of conflict and anger radiating off him hit Vivian like the burning heat from an unbanked fire. She took a step back. And waited. Everything in her waited.

All emotion fell from his face, leaving it blank, empty and so sad. He turned and walked away. A moment later Vivian heard the noise of him leaving, the front door closing, and inside her chest cracked like an egg and a horrible pain exploded. She sank down onto her settee. She'd believed so strongly in him, yet he'd judged her before asking a single question. Then he'd convicted and sentenced her. And left her.

#

Charlotte wasn't sure what her condition would be without David's steady presence and care, but he would see her through. The antidote had taken hold, and the pain, vomiting, and confusion subsided. Two days of rest and doing her best to eat the sick foods her cook tried to make appealing had her feeling well enough for conversation and thinking about the bizarre turn her life had taken.

Today David looked more rested. He'd continued to work from her bedroom desk, but last night he had gone home to sleep. And he'd finally relented, agreeing she was well enough to hear the details he'd been piecing together.

"I believe the woman in the park poisoned Persa and poisoned you," he said. His steady, straightforward manner gave Charlotte the courage to ask a question she wasn't sure she wanted an answer to.

"Was it Lady Garret?"

"I think so."

Ever since David posed the possibility of the baroness being her poisoner, Charlotte had been unable to get the woman out of her head. "Is Eleanor all right? She must blame herself."

"I assured her she'd been tricked by someone very smart and determined. You and I were fooled by the candy, which I think helped ease Eleanor's guilt. Plus she's remembered enough details of the woman's appearance to make it very possible she was Vivian Garret. We'll soon know for certain. I've got Wakefield and Eleanor in his carriage, waiting outside Lady Garret's home. They'll make sure Eleanor gets a look at her."

"Then what?"

"Then we let a detective inspector do the rest."

Charlotte smoothed the shawl she'd thrown over her legs. This morning she'd insisted weakness wasn't reason enough to stay in bed, and David and Rebecca had relented. Rebecca had ensconced her in a chair near the open window.

"I just can't believe she tried to kill me."

"Did you ever have a confrontation with her while you were married?"

"No. We were never friends, but once she published her novel and I learned of her affair with Haliday I never spoke to her again. Not until the night I met you. I've never written or received a letter. Before that I'd stopped accepting invitations. I stayed home while Haliday spent his evenings by her side. When I encountered her by chance, she just smirked and laughed."

The angry glitter in David's eyes eased the pain of those memories a bit. It still hurt Charlotte that so many had believed Lady

Garret's lies and thought her a woman of spiteful, even cruel character, but she no longer cared that Haliday had loved Vivian Garret. That excruciating heartbreak had healed. Her husband's death now truly seemed a just if tragic liberation.

"Did either of them try to hurt you? Try to physically hurt you, I mean."

"No." Neither had injured her body. They'd struck a higher prize: her spirit.

David rolled forward, closing the few feet between them. "Tell me everything you remember about how he died."

"Haliday? What are you thinking? Surely you don't suspect—"

"I don't suspect anything right now. I just want to hear about it."

He took her hand. It amazed her, how much his touch affected her. Warm and strong, his palm and the pads of his fingers, rough with callus, his hand comforted and reassured her to a degree all out of proportion to the small amount of physical contact.

"David, I'll help in any way I can. But I don't see how Haliday's death could have anything to do with this."

"I can't say that I disagree, but for some reason my mind keeps wandering there."

Charlotte sighed. Since beginning work at the Patriotic Fund, her thoughts rarely strayed to her husband, for which she was thankful. She'd spent the last two years thinking about his betrayal and unnecessary cruelty, grieving the death of her innocence. Her dreams. Then she'd become determined to forge a new life.

She let her head fall back so that it rested on the chair. "The police believed the man who killed Haliday intended to rob him."

"Were they able to find any association between them?"

"No. None. Haliday had been playing cards and had just left his club. Those inside heard the shot."

"One shot?"

Charlotte nodded. "Haliday made a habit of carrying a small pistol in his coat whenever he played. He was accustomed to carrying large sums of money on those nights."

"He shot the thief, then."

"Yes. Apparently they scuffled first. They both had some scrapes and bruises on them. The police believed the robber threatened him with a knife. Haliday shot him, but the man was close and didn't go down. He was still able to stab Haliday in the chest. They believed the robber acted alone because Haliday's money was still in his coat pocket."

"Wasn't anyone near? Where was the club footman?"

"Evidently Haliday intended to engage a Hansom. There was one just down the street—mere yards away. The footman said Haliday sent him back inside and started walking toward the coach. But the night was dark and the coachman wasn't aware anything was amiss until the gun fired."

"I find it remarkable Haliday wouldn't just hand over his money rather than put himself in jeopardy," David said.

"It would have been the cautious, wise thing to do, but Haliday was an arrogant man. He never believed anyone could best him."

"I don't imagine the robber was expecting him to resist." Charlotte could see David thinking. His gaze sharpened on her and he added, "It must have been a very difficult time for you."

"I don't know what I would have done without Lady Etherton." She hesitated but actually wanted to tell him. Her chest grew hot, the compulsion to reveal all building like a kettle on the verge of a robust boil. "Jane's compassion helped immensely, even though I couldn't share what a burden was lifted by his death."

David's thumb caressed her hand. "It must have been a huge relief, knowing his outrageous behavior with Lady Garret and the gossip would finally stop."

Charlotte shook her head, finding solace in David's accepting blue eyes, and she forced the words out. "That wasn't why. The one thing he still wanted of me was a son. That's what made his death a relief. It left me free of his soulless bedroom visits."

"My God. Why didn't you leave him?"

The pain on David's face made Charlotte close her eyes. "My father refused to give me money. He wanted a titled grandson for his heir, remember. Father said I'd been obtuse. That loveless marriages were common enough, and if I would produce an heir everyone would be happy. He promised that once I did he'd open his purse strings. Haliday didn't want to give up, either, and he promised if I gave him a son he'd give me the freedom and money to live as I chose. I could live at Hazelton Park for the rest of my days. He even said I could raise the child. He hated that he'd set his estate to rights with my money and had no heir."

Charlotte opened her eyes. David's body seemed to have grown larger. He leaned forward, muscles rigid. His nostrils flared.

"Bloody hell."

"I realized he'd pretended to be a different man in order to win my dowry and my father's favor. The man I fell in love with didn't exist. Once he was flush, he tired of his charade and revealed his cruelty, arrogance, and selfishness. He didn't care what I thought or how I felt."

"Couldn't Jane have helped?"

"Yes. She would have helped me." Charlotte paused. Could she make David understand, or would the truth disgust him? "But I got angry. Very angry. I'd been duped. He'd stripped everything from me." *Please, please understand.* "Everything but my desire for a child. I thought I deserved something, and I thought I could bear his bedroom efforts." Oh, blast. Her voice was starting to shake. "I prayed I'd get with child."

With his thumb, David rubbed away the wetness under each of her eyes. "I'm so sorry, Bluebell."

Really? But could David know the worst of her and still want her? She had to know.

"When we began our affair, I told you I was pregnant at the time Haliday was killed. And that after his death I had a miscarriage."

David nodded.

"I was sure I was with child, but I didn't tell him. As much as I wanted the couplings to stop, I didn't want to make him happy." She took a deep breath and tried to steady herself enough to finish.

"I-I thought I wanted a child," she stammered, "but once it happened I began to wonder if he'd use the child to control me. To make me do more things I didn't want to do. To hurt me. I knew I couldn't trust him, and I wished I'd never consented. I wished...oh, David! When Haliday died, I was *happy*. My child would be *mine*. And now I fear God made me miscarry that innocent soul to punish me for my wickedness."

With a couple of deft moves, David aligned his chair with hers. She went into his arms, and he lifted her onto the armrest then over. Nothing had ever felt so right as sitting on his lap, his firm arms wrapped around her. His hands lifted and cradled her face, and his warm lips nuzzled her temples, her eyes, then the corners of her mouth.

"Bluebell, don't torment yourself so. God didn't take the child to punish you. Haliday was a bastard. Anyone would be glad to have his abuse stop."

She held him so tight she could feel his heart beating against her chest.

After a long minute, David eased her away. Charlotte sniffed and wiped at her eyes, strangely unembarrassed. David's smile somehow pulled at her own lips and made them curve the tiniest bit. He pushed a loose strand of her hair back and slid his fingers down the thick braid that rested against her shoulder and breast.

"You don't deserve what's happening now, either," he said. "I promise it's going to stop. Whether it's Lady Garret or someone else, I'm going to stop them and we'll know why you've been targeted."

It helped to have him turn the subject. She gave him a quick thank-you kiss, but his hands tightened and pulled her back for a slower one that left her wanting more. Much more.

"I'm well enough to visit Rose Cottage," she whispered.

One corner of David's mouth, which she'd been admiring, pulled up in a lopsided smile. "Nearly well enough. I want you strong *and* safe the next time you leave home."

The distant noise of an arrival at the front door floated up the stairs. Then came Eleanor's and Wakefield's voices.

Charlotte stared at David. They got her back to her chair just in time.

CHAPTER TWENTY-NINE

At last. Jane, turned out in the very latest and most complementary fashion, glided through Charlotte's sitting room door. So much had happened since the last time she'd seen her friend. They'd corresponded during Charlotte's short convalescence, but it wasn't the same as being together and Jane's failure to visit sooner seemed odd. Jane had written that she and Etherton were talking, but something about Jane's words had sounded wrong. Finally, Charlotte could find out exactly what progress her friends had made in repairing their breach.

As soon as Charlotte stood, Jane was there hugging her. This was the best day she'd had since becoming ill. She would spend the morning with Jane, and tonight, for the first time since her poisoning, she'd be at Rose Cottage with David.

She released Jane and started to smile, but the instant her eyes met her friend's Charlotte's stomach fell. She pulled Jane down onto the settee and guessed, "Something's wrong."

Her friend smiled—a quick, false sort of smile—and looked toward Beckham, who was preparing to serve tea. Charlotte understood. As soon as they had their cups and saucers in hand, Charlotte dismissed him.

"What is it?" she asked.

Jane's chin quivered. "Phillip's left me. He's gone to Friar's Gate. He told me I'm not to go there, and I'm not to expect him here."

"Jane." Charlotte took her friend's hand. "You said you were talking. I never dreamed you weren't resolving things."

Jane's eyes pleaded for understanding. "I can't accept that I won't bear Phillip an heir. He said he was shocked I'd have so little regard for him and our daughters, to demand to risk my life with another pregnancy. And he said I was being cruel, expecting him to deprive his son of his father's love and attention. I…I corrected him and called the boy his bastard. I couldn't stop myself. And Phillip exploded."

What a disaster. Charlotte had never known a couple more in love than Phillip and Jane, and now their marriage had degenerated to the point they were living separate lives. How could the situation have come to this? Didn't this call into question the nature of all romantic relationships? Was all such feeling so transitory?

"Do you still love him?" she found herself asking.

Jane's head jerked, as if the suggestion shocked her. "Of course I still love him. But…I've lost faith in him."

Charlotte wanted to grab her friend and shake her. "Lost faith? I don't understand how this affected your trust. Phillip wasn't ever unfaithful to you."

"He loves this boy. He sees him and his mother every day he's at Friar's Gate. He kept them a secret from me for *eight years*. How can I trust him after he did that? And when I say I need to give him a son, he loses patience." Jane held out her hands, palms up, entreating. "Not producing an heir is an unforgiveable failure."

Charlotte shook her head. "Phillip never said that. He'd never even *think* it." She was beginning to sympathize with Etherton, actually. Her friend could be so stubborn. "Did you consider *me* a failure when I didn't give Haliday an heir?"

Tight-lipped, Jane shook her head. "Haliday didn't deserve an heir. Phillip is completely different, and he won't even listen when I tell him I want to try again for a son. He said I'm crack-brained jealous. He said he'd kept them a secret in order to protect me. He didn't want to hurt me." Jane's hands fisted. "He doesn't understand why his loving the boy pains me."

"Jane." Charlotte tried to keep her tone level and reasonable. "What is the boy's name?"

Her friend blinked. "What?"

"What's his name?"

"Francis."

"Have you met Francis?"

Jane's expression grew mulish, as if she knew what Charlotte was about to suggest. "No. I haven't."

"You should meet him. If they're both part of Phillip's life at Friar's Gate, you should meet his mother, too. And you must talk to Phillip again."

"He said he's done talking."

If someone had told Charlotte that Jane could pout like this, she wouldn't have believed it.

"Well, you know Phillip's temper never lasts long."

Jane's lips parted. "You're defending him. You're taking his side."

"I wasn't aware it was a contest. A battle of wills, perhaps, but not sport."

"Believe me, I don't consider the state of my marriage a matter of amusement."

"Neither do I," Charlotte said. "And I'm not supporting Etherton. I'm very angry with him, in fact. I don't like him hurting you for any reason. But Jane, I think you've hurt him, too."

Jane looked down at her feet. She appeared miserable, but her husband loved her and was faithful. Charlotte kept a tight hold on her patience. Her friends had some family changes to adjust to, but Phillip had always been devoted to Jane and they would triumph. If *Charlotte* could believe in Phillip, why couldn't his wife? Jane had been so relieved to have a love match in the first place.

"Does this have anything to do with your parents?" Charlotte guessed.

Jane frowned. "What? How could it?"

Jane's parents led separate lives and were somewhat notorious. When Charlotte and Jane had been in school together, Jane had complained bitterly about her parents' dalliances. Her father had a number of illegitimate children he supported, several of them living on his estate. Her mother had lived on the continent for years.

"Growing up, you rarely saw them. When you did see your father, he included his out-of-wedlock children in your time together. Because you lived at school, he spent more time with them than he did with you."

Jane shook her head and crossed her arms. Her lips tightened.

"Your parents don't even pretend to have a harmonious marriage. Your father showers love on his illegitimate children." Charlotte didn't want to hurt Jane, but who else would tell her the hard truth she needed to hear? "Couldn't some of your anger be due to your seeing similarities between your parents' marriage and yours? Or fearing there are similarities?"

Jane's mouth dropped open. Then snapped shut. "No." Her eyes glittered. "You're very trusting and forgiving when it comes to my husband. You defend him and criticize me. Yet there's not a man on earth you would trust for *yourself*, is there? You don't even limit it to marriage. You don't trust love."

Charlotte said nothing. Her friend might as well have ripped out her lungs and wrung them.

"You're just like me," Jane whispered. "Your father's at the root of your fear."

Deep inside Charlotte, Jane's words vibrated like the air after the strike of a great bell. Her friend was right, and this revelation had been coming for some time. Father hadn't loved Mother, and he didn't love Charlotte. He loved himself. His wealth. His power. Haliday had convinced her she was loveable because she'd wanted to believe it, but he'd lied and the world came crashing down. They were just two men out of many. Why did she think everyone would be cast in Father and Haliday's mold? She believed in Phillip and Jane's love, so why couldn't she believe in David?

Annoyance gripped her. He'd never done a single thing to make her doubt his loyalty or his honor. Could she even imagine David being unfaithful? No. Just posing the question made her feel ashamed, and she shifted uneasily.

Yet, his past actions were no guarantee of the future. Hadn't Haliday proven that? Weren't most men damaged, able to throw off the promise of faithfulness without hesitation or guilt? She'd seen it happen again and again. Society teemed with examples. Yet she acknowledged Phillip as an exception, didn't she? Wasn't David as well?

Charlotte took a big breath, the air hurting as it rasped deep. If she trusted, if she let herself believe in David's love and she was wrong… She had that little book buried in the bottom of her clothing chest as a tactile and visual reminder. The pain of such a mistake was great. If it happened again, she wasn't sure she'd survive. Especially not after all she'd known with David.

"I'm sorry," Jane said.

Charlotte dragged her attention back to her friend. Jane's spectacles were off, her eyes wet, and Charlotte nodded in response.

"I know. I didn't mean to hurt you, either. But I'm glad you said that. I need to think about what you said."

"Me, too," Jane said. She stood, moved to Charlotte, bent and hugged her. Charlotte grabbed her friend in return, warmth spilling into her chest.

Jane sat, picked up her spectacles and shoved them back on her face. "Have you heard from the detective inspector?"

The change of subject felt awkward, but they both wanted to move past the distress to focus on less tumultuous topics. Charlotte offered Jane a selection of small cakes and answered, "The hunt intensified after Eleanor identified Lady Garret two days ago. Mr. Ridley stopped by this morning. He says the baroness knows they're pursuing her. She hasn't been home, and Lord Radcliffe hasn't seen her."

Jane selected a treacly spice cake. "Could Radcliffe be protecting her?"

"I don't think so. He came here and spoke with David and me." It had started out with all of them rather uncomfortable, but Radcliffe's sincerity soon became apparent. "He confronted her. I felt badly for him. He seemed...devastated."

"He went into that association with his eyes wide open," Jane said. "He should have known better."

"I think he's regretful now, although when he met her he couldn't have realized just how corrupt the woman was. I just wish they'd find her." For many reasons. David had made Charlotte promise not to leave the house without two footmen in attendance. "It's been difficult, not letting thoughts of her maliciousness torment me. It'll be a relief to get back to work. Dr. Bliss, my physician, says I can return next week."

Jane smiled. "God bless Dr. Bliss."

#

David turned away from the coach window and smiled at Charlotte as they pulled up to the front door of Rose Cottage.

"Finally," he huffed.

Charlotte laughed. Damn, it was good to hear her laugh.

"You couldn't be as anxious as I am," she said. "I've been confined inside my house for two straight weeks."

"And I stood guard for two weeks, eyes glued open lest angels try to steal you away."

A smile touched Charlotte's eyes and mouth. She leaned over and kissed him. That first spontaneous touch was maddeningly erotic, but he ignored what his body begged for and enjoyed the lush fullness of her lips. He let her control the kiss and breathed in her enticing scent, imagining that the ambrosial fragrance held a bit of her spiritual essence. He wanted to nuzzle into that spot he loved below her ear and slide his tongue over her pulse. It had been so long since he'd tasted her sweetness.

Her mouth opened, her lips firmed against his, and her warm flavor beckoned his tongue. A great spear of joy shot through him. He'd never thought to feel such pleasure again. Not after his injury. He'd hoped to regain satisfaction and pride, but never such sweet passion and searing anticipation.

Their kiss grew in fervor. Some corner of his consciousness warned him Boone would be opening the door at any moment and unless he dragged his mouth away everyone would be embarrassed, so David ended the kiss and contented himself with an up-close contemplation of her amazing, bright bluebell eyes. He wanted to spend his life looking into them.

The revelation snapped his mind to attention. His *life?* Something must have shown on his face, because Charlotte's expression became curious.

Before he could collect himself and make a remark, Boone opened the door. Having waited patiently at their feet, Persa launched herself out the carriage door.

It was just going on dusk, and the cook-housekeeper Mrs. Penny was finishing dinner preparations. At the start of their affair, Charlotte had felt self-conscious in front of the servants, but now she was comfortable. David poured them each a glass of sherry to enjoy until the meal was announced.

"I love the informality here. The peace and privacy."

Charlotte accepted the drink but set her glass down, came behind his chair and leaned over David's back. She pressed her cheek to his and slid her hands down his chest. Heat and desire congregated low in his pelvis and manhood, and he hoped he made it through dinner without having to drag her away from the meal.

"What's this?" She'd found the small, hard bulge in his waistcoat pocket. She delved inside and withdrew his keepsake. She held the token on her flattened palm and inspected it. "Is this my button?"

He grinned at her surprise. "Mmm. Yes, I'm afraid it is." He plucked the purple-blue button from her hand and fingered it. "I found it on the floor of my office the day your reticule was stolen."

"What's it doing in your pocket?"

She reached for it, but he snatched it away and returned it to his pocket.

"David?"

He hesitated. He'd never said the words, but he thought she knew he loved her. He'd never had the courage to ask her if she loved him in return, as she'd said while she was sick, but still their feelings for each other seemed somewhat clear. His explanation shouldn't seem peculiar. "I like keeping a bit of you with me."

He *had* surprised her. Her smile grew, and her cheeks blushed a deep pink. She whirled around his chair, sat on his lap, and pressed a quick, firm kiss to his lips.

"I understand," she said. "While I was recuperating, holding that little carving of Persa made me feel close to you."

"Yes." Deep satisfaction overtook David. It was so wonderful to have her well again. He felt as if he were made of sunshine instead of bones and sinew.

"I love you, Bluebell. You know that, don't you?"

Her eyes filled. Her smiling mouth began to quiver, and she blinked rapidly. Then she nodded.

"I told you I loved you when I was ill, didn't I?" she asked. "I've been so afraid your knowing would change things."

"Yes, you told me," David said. "But I wasn't sure you meant it."

"I meant it."

She looked too serious and solemn, but her lips were warm. Her tongue touched his and reawakened his hunger before she pulled away. He thought he might metamorphose into steam.

They embraced, pressed cheek to cheek, heart to heart. After a long minute, David ran his hands down her back and gripped her waist, which was narrower than before her illness. He eased her backward in order to see her face.

"There's no reason for anything to change." He studied her. "Unless you want more than what we have here...."

What would he do if she did? His views on marriage hadn't altered. He was a man in love, but a crippled man. He couldn't imagine a future without Charlotte in it, so as long as she didn't want to marry they'd be fine. A lover wasn't expected to protect and defend a mistress the way he would a wife, and his many restrictions wouldn't matter to the same degree since they wouldn't truly be sharing their lives. He wouldn't have cause to disappoint Charlotte. Would he? His heart was still wrestling with that logic.

"Sir? My lady? Dinner is ready."

Mrs. Penny stood out of sight, beside the doorway of the small room where they took their meals. Very diplomatic of her.

Charlotte stood and preceded David into the dining room. He liked that she didn't attempt to push his chair; she knew he could easily manage himself and preferred to do so. Of course, she hadn't responded to his comment about their future, and he needed to know she was still happy with their arrangement. He'd ask again when they were private.

Mrs. Penny carried out the main course, and the sight and smell of crisp, browned duck surrounded by turnips made David's mouth water. Charlotte had gotten lucky when she'd found Mrs. Penny. He suppressed his unsettled feeling, as no doubt he had nothing to worry about.

He tucked into the superlative fare, reconsidering a notion he'd been chewing on for the past several days. The longer he'd pondered, the more likely the connection seemed. He'd just never brought it up to Charlotte. "Has it occurred to you that your reticule theft might be related to the poisonings?"

Charlotte set her fork down and took a sip of wine. "How could that be?"

"It's too much of a coincidence that three such dramatic occurrences happened within a few weeks of each other. On the surface they don't seem related, but my instincts tell me they are. I've thought it possible from the beginning. Now I feel pretty certain."

"We know Lady Garret wants to harm me, but why would she want to steal my reticule?"

"The man knocked you down—hard—and there was no reason for it. He might have done you more injury if Persa hadn't run him off." Persa, lying in the corner with her muzzle on her front paws, lifted her head at the sound of her name before David continued. "I don't think his primary intent was theft. He wanted to hurt you."

"If Lady Garret hired him…that seems even more diabolical."

"Oh, she's serious, and this is very personal," David assured her. "She disguised herself to get access to your dog then mixed up a batch of your favorite fudge to poison you. How could it be more diabolical than that?"

"She must have discovered it was my favorite candy while sleeping with my husband."

David understood Charlotte's bitterness. "Will you ever eat it again?"

The bleakness of her face made him think she wouldn't. Then a thin smile curved her lips and she shrugged. Her perseverance humbled David.

"I admire your attitude. Very much."

Her eyes widened, and the sharp little catch of her breath was audible. Her cheeks turned that lovely color again. He hadn't realized before how easily she blushed. How easily *he* could make her blush.

He looked at her half-eaten meal. The last little while she'd been pushing it about with her fork. "Are you finished? Because I'm anxious for dessert."

CHAPTER THIRTY

Charlotte must have seen desire in his face and understood what he was about, because she stood and moved toward the bedroom. David followed on her heels, watching the gentle sway of her hips and skirt, and once closed into the bedroom he matched her garment for garment. They made the bed at roughly the same time, only his small clothes and her chemise remaining.

She tugged off his undershirt and ran her hands over his shoulders and down his arms. Her sound of satisfaction and the admiring glint in her eyes made his chest swell. Damn, but he burned for this woman. She unfastened his drawers and slid them over his buttocks. By now he knew she had a liking for his bum, and her lips parted and the tip of her tongue slipped upward to wet them. The seductive look made David groan as she peeled his drawers off his legs.

He pulled her down and grasped the hem of her chemise, raising it while his hands brushed her sweet, feminine curves. His hands skimmed the sides of her hips then angled in to her narrow waist. Fingers spread, he slid them over her ribs and stroked the full undersides of her breasts with his thumbs. Pushing the finely woven white fabric up to her throat, he revealed her. No, he would never get his fill.

"You're so beautiful," David murmured.

She had the whitest skin, without a freckle or a blemish. He was hard, aching, his bollocks drawn tight. The cadence of her breath quickened, and Charlotte bowed her back the tiniest bit. Her tight, rose-brown nipples jutted out, beckoning, and she moaned as he drew one into his mouth.

Her incredible responsiveness enchanted him. It always had, making David's own desire burn even hotter. He sucked until she squirmed, laved her breast with his tongue and then withdrew his mouth and captured the tip with his fingers. He had to go back to her mouth, had to take it with his tongue. Oh, God, he wanted to devour Charlotte, sink into her, thrust into her, until all semblance of sanity was lost and only feeling and his beloved remained. For her, he wanted to make fireworks detonate.

But not yet. Not yet.

He nipped and sucked the soft crease of her neck, her plump earlobe, the elegant sweep of her shoulder. Her hands stroked his shoulders, his arms, his chest, until he burned to possess her. She moaned and murmured his name. She tilted her pelvis as she thrust her fingers into his hair, and he knew she wanted him. That knowledge fired his desire even hotter, and he swore. She looked at him knowingly and smiled.

He played with her nipple, tugging and rolling, listening to her breathy exclamations of pleasure. He couldn't stray far from her mouth, returning again and again, as each contact fueled his passion. He slid his fingers between her oh-so-feminine and secret folds, and he found her heated and slick with honey. Hot and wet, she pressed against his hand as her tongue mated with his.

"David...please come inside me."

He closed his eyes, relishing her desire. He was thick and hard as a pike. Everything in him—every part of him—wanted Charlotte Haliday with a fierce desperation. His brain, his bone, his very sinew throbbed.

She gasped and clutched him as he pressed into her. His body took over then, the surging rush barely held at bay as he stroked, but hold it off he did, the feel of her at once solid and ephemeral and incredibly good. Somehow he had enough sense left to make sure he was hitting against her mound, against that most sensitive bundle of feminine flesh. There couldn't be anything in the world better.

They were gasping, slick with sweat, moaning, and then her body went taut and her channel clenched. Her lips fell open in an endless cry, and her arms tightened about him—then tightened even more as the rest of her began to relax. Her passion had peaked and was now ebbing, and instinctively David knew she held him with a complete wholeness of feeling. With love.

He let passion take him then, and in the rush of feeling as he flew apart and his fluid pulsed into her he anchored himself to her with his arms. Everything that made him who he was, he silently offered up, and as awareness returned he tightened his hold even more, nuzzling into her neck. Feeling her body move as she breathed, feeling her soft sigh. Knowing when she smiled. Loving when her fingers furrowed into his hair and kneaded the back of his neck.

She'd nearly died. During those uncertain days while he watched over her, he'd refused to even consider the possibility. Once he knew she'd survive, he hadn't been able to think of anything else. He was indeed the luckiest man on earth.

He was too heavy to remain relaxed atop her like this, but he didn't want to move; it was too good, this intimate exchange and each tiny movement. Finally, however, he rolled them to their sides. Her knee nudged between his, and Charlotte positioned herself to allow his top leg to be supported by hers. It had become their way.

"I should go check on Persa, make sure she's settled in the kitchen," Charlotte suggested, yawning.

David tucked the covers around her shoulder. "I'm sure when we didn't come back Boone took care of her and doused the lights."

"Mmm." Charlotte snuggled closer. Her naked upper body pressed against him, her slim arm curved around him, possessive yet relaxed. He hugged her in return and luxuriated in utter contentment.

#

"Good morning, Lady Haliday."

George Chetney stood as Charlotte entered, a huge grin making his face appear even more boyish. Persa scampered up to him and was rewarded with a brisk rub.

"Good morning, Mr. Chetney." Charlotte pulled off her gloves and removed her bonnet. "I believe today may be the day I finish catching up with my correspondence." She'd returned from the poisoning to find a mountain of letters and other business awaiting her. "I'm so grateful for your help. I wouldn't have been as efficient without the benefit of your system of arranging things in order of importance."

Chetney's cheeks reddened. He held back another smile but still managed to look pleased. "You're very kind, my lady. You received several new items in this morning's post. They're on your desk."

The sounds of his arrival preceded David, who came through the door looking more splendid than any man had a right to. Sometimes it felt as if he carried a bit of the sun with him in that bright red-gold hair. Why did men wear hats, anyway? Charlotte wondered. David was altogether pleasing without one. It still amazed her how intelligent, steadfast, handsome and yet humble he was.

The nervous awareness she'd once had of him no longer plagued her. Now it was the memory of his strong arms and the heat of desire that afflicted her.

She must have worn something of her thoughts on her face, for he looked at her with amusement glowing in his eyes, one eyebrow lifted in question. "Good morning," he said. "You both appear eager as dogs with meaty bones."

Persa barked, dashed over, and leapt onto David's lap. He laughed, petted her, and she settled across his thighs.

"And that's pretty eager, isn't it?" he said to the dog.

Their day began. One of Charlotte's duties was writing to widows who received money from the Fund, evaluating their situations and needs, and she was eager to get back to that. She and David also planned on working late today, and Charlotte hoped to clear her desk.

At midmorning, David sent Chetney to Wandsworth Common with a note for Mr. Myers, who was in the middle of constructing the Royal Victoria Patriotic School; building had begun and was proceeding at a remarkable pace. Chetney was nice enough to take Persa with him, knowing she'd love running about the common, so Charlotte was uninterrupted and wholly engrossed in work when a movement in the corner of her eye caught her attention. Vivian Garret stood in the office doorway.

Charlotte shot to her feet. Her nerves quivered like clattering tambourine jangles. "David?" she called.

The baroness wore a black gown adorned with glittering jet buttons and satin trimmings. A delicate white lace collar, cuffs, and gloves turned the otherwise unrelieved black into an elegant frame for its wearer. But in spite of her sophisticated appearance, Lady Garret looked ill: face pale, mouth thin and tight, dark shadows under her eyes. Those eyes glittered with pure, unadulterated malice.

She edged into the room and angled her back to the wall. "You shouldn't have called him," she admonished, raising her arm. She held a pistol aimed straight at Charlotte.

Dear God. Charlotte's legs quivered. She grabbed the edge of her desk. "Don't. Don't do this. Hurting me won't change anything."

A thin smile curved Lady Garret's lips. "Oh, I wouldn't dream of hurting you, Charlotte," she said with a warm honey voice. "I intend to kill you, but if you're lucky you won't feel a thing."

Charlotte's mind foundered, buffeted by a wild sea of disbelief. Her insides quivering like a wobbling jelly, she gave her head a little shake. Devil take it, she needed to stay sharp, yet she couldn't even comprehend that *Vivian Garret held a pistol aimed at her chest.*

David rolled through the door suddenly and turned his chair to face the baroness. He looked unfazed. Relief swept through Charlotte in a rush and helped anchor her. Some of the wobbly jelly in her legs firmed.

"Come here, Charlotte. Stand behind me," he said.

His steadiness pulled everything into focus. Charlotte obeyed and clasped the hard, unyielding lifeline of his shoulder.

Gaze fixed on Lady Garret, David tilted forward, his hands curled around his chair's wheel rims. "Give me the pistol, Lady Garret."

He sounded so calm, his voice so even and reasonable. Charlotte settled a bit more. David had faced hundreds of guns. Thank God he was here.

Lady Garret laughed. "Do you really expect me to? I'm sorry to disappoint." Her pistol waggled between David and Charlotte and then settled on Charlotte. "He can't protect you. Although, I suppose you could crouch down behind him."

Charlotte straightened. Being behind David, she couldn't see his expression, but when he shook his head she knew he'd sensed her movement and was telling her to stop making herself a bigger target.

"Ah. Have I offended you? Well, I'm glad you refuse to hide behind Mr. Scott. Although I suppose I'd best kill him as well. This pistol's a double-barrel, and things will be much less complicated if he's not left to tattle."

"You don't want to do this," David said. "Even if you kill us both, the police will know. The other office is full of workers. They'll hear the shots. The police already know you poisoned

Charlotte. Killing her would make Newgate a certainty. You could even hang, and it would all be for nothing. This won't bring Haliday back."

Lady Garret's smile twisted. "You pride yourself on your intelligence, don't you, Major?" She stuck out her lower lip in an aggravated pout. "How sad. I know you've been puzzling on this and you're not even close to the answer." Her lips pinched together. "I didn't love Haliday, I used him. He was arrogant, ridiculous, and incredibly easy to manipulate."

Charlotte blinked. These words made no sense. "Used him? If you weren't jealous, then why did you do so much to hurt me?"

"Hurt you? Two years ago I wanted to ruin you. Wanted to *destroy* you. Now that's not enough. I want you dead." A short laugh burst from the baroness. "Your husband provided a convenient way to harm you. I didn't intend for him to die, but in the end it was his own fault. The ruffian I hired was supposed to rough him up and say something to implicate you, Charlotte. Only, your husband, the fool, fought the man I engaged. They weren't supposed to kill each other." Her voice broke off in something that almost sounded like a sob.

"You hired someone to attack Haliday?" Each revelation added to Charlotte's confusion. "The affair, the novel to impugn my character, everything you've done—if it isn't jealousy, why are you attacking me?"

"Yes, why does Charlotte matter so much?" David asked. "At first you were trying to hurt her, and now you want to kill her?"

Lady Garret's gaze dropped to him. "She's no more than a means to an end. I wanted her father to suffer. Shelby knew he was to blame when his daughter's marriage and reputation were ruined, so for a time I was satisfied. But then Charlotte came back to London ready to begin again, starting life over and probably glad to be rid of Haliday. I realized hurting her wasn't enough. When I kill her, Shelby will feel the ultimate pain—the pain of a parent losing a child."

"Father knows? What does Father have to do with you?" Charlotte clutched both David's shoulders. "What are you talking about?"

Vivian's eyes flared. "I'm your *sister.*"

CHAPTER THIRTY-ONE

Charlotte gasped. A panicky breathlessness squeezed her lungs. David's hand reached back and she grabbed on. Vivian Garret— Charlotte would never again think of her as Lady Garret—was her *sister*?

"That's...that's not possible."

She'd know if she had a sister. Wouldn't she? Even though Father was no man to share his feelings or his memories, wouldn't she have at least heard rumors? Charlotte had never heard even the whisper of another daughter. Or of Matthew Shelby having a mistress.

Vivian stiffened and her gun bobbed. "You think I'm lying? I always wondered if Shelby—our father—told you. Evidently he did not."

"He knows?"

"He's always known."

Sharp and lethal, a dagger stabbed Charlotte's heart. Father knew Vivian was his daughter? He knew Vivian had a far different reason than crazed romantic jealousy for what she'd done? Those days of misery, while Charlotte's marriage crumbled, Father's knowledge would have helped her. The months when Vivian flaunted her affair with Haliday and made Charlotte the object of rumor and innuendo... How could he have withheld what he knew? If he'd had even the slightest suspicion that Vivian's parentage could be even partly responsible for her actions, he should have told Charlotte.

The dagger twisted. He'd also known when she was poisoned, and he'd stayed silent.

Her eyes grew hot and she blinked hard, staving off the looming tears. This was not the time to cry. Her pounding heartbeat filled her ears. The gun kept drawing her gaze, making it hard to think. The air in the room seemed too thin to breathe, and she tightened her grip on David's hand. Had he felt this kind of fear and confusion during battle? Or when he'd contemplated life in a wheeled chair? The thought that he had—and mastered it—steadied Charlotte and helped focus her thoughts.

Was there any resemblance between them, anything to physically support the woman's claim? Vivian was near her height, but their coloring was very different. And Charlotte's finger lifted to her mouth and pressed against her full lips. She didn't need a mirror to confirm Vivian's lush mouth was all too similar to her own.

"Father *knows*?" She'd already asked and been answered, but she still couldn't believe the affirmative answer.

"Our father seduced my mother, that's what happened," Vivian snapped. The pistol dropped a bit as she leaned forward. "She was innocent and he ruined her. She loved him. She expected to marry him, but her father was a mere knight and Shelby intended to marry higher than that. The arrogant weasel. He may have been well on his way to being rich, but he was *common*.

"He married *your* mother—a baron's daughter—almost immediately after seducing my mother, who had no recourse when she found herself pregnant. She begged him for enough money to support herself and her child. He laughed. *Laughed*. Said he didn't need a second family to generate gossip and impinge on his growing acceptance by society. But he gave my grandfather enough money to provide her with a generous dowry, and that worked. The dowry enticed the eldest son of a baron. A very proud and pious son of a baron. When I was born early but fully developed, he knew I wasn't his get and he'd been cuckolded."

Vivian's flushed skin gleamed with moisture. Her fervent speech, rather than dissipating her strong emotions, appeared to be making her even more volatile. Her eyes had the wild, panic-stricken look of a bee-stung animal, and she brought her other hand up so that both hands wrapped the pistol grip. The barrel angled down, though, as if the gun had become too heavy for her to hold level.

"The man preferred to punish my mother through *me*. I grew accustomed to the taunting about my parentage, but eventually my quiet humiliation wasn't enough to satisfy him. For even the smallest offense, he..." Her head shook with her emphasis, and her amber eyes glowed with the intensity of burning coals. "He *whipped* me.

He was careful not to scar my skin, but oh, he left mighty scars upon my soul."

Vivian paused and gasped in air. Inside, Charlotte cringed and grappled to comprehend. This woman, who had always appeared utterly self-possessed and powerful, stood threatening her with a shaking pistol. Vivian Garret. Her half-sister.

"He said I'd been created in sin, and it was his charge from God to beat the sin out of me." Vivian stopped speaking and advanced two steps. Her lips thinned. "Lord Garret was seventy-eight years old at the time, but he offered my only way out." She spat the words as if they tasted foul. "He wanted a young wife to care for his eighteen children, and he didn't mind one in his bed, either. I was seventeen. I comforted myself that I was finally safe, the wife of a baron."

"How do you know the man...the man who sired you...that he was my father?" Charlotte had many questions, but this was the one she needed answered the most.

"Once, before Mother died, we saw him on the street. She pointed him out as the man who'd fathered me—Matthew Shelby."

Charlotte's small hope that it wasn't true wilted. "I'm sorry, Vivian," she said.

"Are you? For what?"

The question stopped Charlotte. Did she really feel sorry for Vivian, after everything the woman had done? "For...for the abuse."

Vivian's shoulders slumped. She seemed to be calming down. "You needn't be sorry for that. At least, not for Garret. He gave me George."

"George?"

"My son."

"Oh. Of course." How could she have forgotten that Vivian had lost a young child to consumption? It had happened several years prior to the affair with Haliday, but it was generally known.

"When Garret died I was left with next to nothing. His oldest son, Frederick, got everything—not that Garret had much—and Frederick had eighteen of his father's progeny to provide for. George was one of them, but the stipend we received was modest. Until Georgie contracted consumption, it was enough.

"When Georgie became ill, I needed money. There was a new treatment, and it was working. I had no choice but to go to Shelby and beg for help. For what he'd done to Mother—and indirectly to me—I'd always hated him."

Oh, dear God. Father hadn't refused to help her, had he? He couldn't have been *that* cruel.

"You went to Father?" Charlotte said.

Vivian nodded. "He's one of the richest men in London. The amount I needed was nothing to him." For the first time since she stepped into the room, her expression conveyed pain. "I should have believed Mother when she said he was unfeeling. He certainly felt nothing for me. Nothing for Georgie. And no remorse or responsibility for all I'd experienced." A series of fluttering blinks softened her expression. "He refused me. I needed money *to save my son's life*, and our father didn't care." Vivian emitted a strangled sound. "He sired me, and bloody hell but I'd earned that money."

A cold frisson slashed down Charlotte's spine like a crack down an icy puddle. She shivered, and David's fingers, still wrapped around hers, tightened.

"I couldn't afford the new treatment, and Georgie...died." Her last word became a tortured wail. Tears streaked down Vivian's face. "I wanted Shelby to hurt as bad as I did, and for him to know *why*. Only...how was that even possible?" She took one hand away to swipe at her cheek. "Then I realized. *You.*"

Vivian jabbed the pistol in Charlotte's direction. "He spent his life making sure you had every advantage. He built his empire for you. He wanted his grandchildren to be aristocrats. So I seduced Haliday. I ruined your marriage and reputation. I made a pariah of you. I didn't mean for Haliday to die, but when he did, Shelby's plan for a titled descendant died, too." Vivian rubbed the back of her hand across her mouth. "And Shelby knew it was all because of him."

David released Charlotte's hand and rolled forward an inch. "Put the gun down. Haliday's death was an accident. If you kill Charlotte, you'll hang."

Vivian shook her head. "It's the only way, now. Before, making her life a misery was enough. But when she came back she was different. Confident. You became lovers." She waved the pistol toward David. "I couldn't let her be happy. I...could...not!" she finished, yelling the last word.

"But it's Shelby you want to hurt." David's chair inched forward. "You have no reason to kill Charlotte. *She* didn't hurt you. She had no idea of your connection."

Charlotte looked at David. He was so calm and collected. But then he'd looked down other gun barrels.

"An eye for an eye," Vivian shrieked. "To his misfortune, he has only one child he acknowledges." A harsh laugh erupted. "If Charlotte dies, he'll have no one. His dedication to work, his money and power. All pointless." She brought her other hand up and steadied the pistol. "*This* is the way to make him hurt."

"Vivian," David snapped. "You know the police are looking for you. They'll know you did this."

"They haven't caught me yet."

Charlotte stepped out from behind David. He gave her a startled look, tightened his mouth and rolled his chair forward, ending up a bit closer to Vivian.

"Vivian." Charlotte focused on the woman's red-rimmed eyes. "This won't bring Georgie back. And Father won't hurt the way you did, even if you do this." She wasn't sure she could say what needed to be said, even though in her heart she knew it was true. "He doesn't love me like you loved Georgie."

Vivian's chin dropped slightly and her eyes widened. Then she shrugged. "He's a man with a stone for a heart. No matter. Whatever caring he's capable of, I know he holds you most dear."

David suddenly bent forward and gave his chair a mighty push, barreling straight toward Vivian. "*Run,*" he shouted at Charlotte.

The gun cracked, and smoke exploded from the barrel. David plowed into Vivian. He lunged from his chair, taking the woman to the floor. His wheelchair crashed onto its side.

"David!"

He couldn't expect her to run and leave him like this. He lay sprawled across Vivian, who struggled to unpin herself. There was something—it was *blood!*—on the woman's hands and bodice, and Charlotte realized it was coming from David.

"Oh, God!" It was a wail, a curse, a prayer. Then David moved and Charlotte breathed. She stepped forward, but David and Vivian began grappling and forced her to step back.

The blood came from his head, Charlotte saw, and it was obvious he was greatly affected. Vivian pounded on his back and shoulder with her free hand, but David ignored her and appeared to put all his effort into gripping the wrist of her gun hand and pinning it to the floor.

"Charlotte, get out of here," he roared.

He wanted her safe, but she couldn't leave. He needed help.

Vivian's fist bashed against David's bloody head. "Ungh." His hands loosened and the baroness jerked her gun arm free. She struggled out from under him and sat up, aiming the pistol at his head.

Noooooooo. Charlotte sprang forward and kicked at Vivian's chest. She connected, hard, and it felt good. A fierce satisfaction overrode Charlotte's panic as her enemy fell back. Not giving her time to recover, Charlotte kicked again, aiming this time for Vivian's ribs. The woman jerked, gave a thin cry, and raised her hand in a protective motion.

Charlotte jerked the pistol away. It was heavy, unfamiliar and frightening, and she stared at the first gun she'd ever held. Thank God she had it, though, and not Vivian.

She's not going to get it again, Charlotte vowed. Then she dropped to her knees at David's side.

"David?"

His stillness scared her. *Settle down. David's depending on you.* Charlotte forced a shaky breath deep into her lungs, but the sharp smell of gunpowder filled her head. He still lay prone atop Vivian's lower legs. Vivian groaned and clutched her side, but she didn't attempt to move or get up. Charlotte stuffed the pistol into David's coat pocket for safekeeping then pulled him off of her.

He was heavy, but she managed. As gently as she could, she rolled him onto his back. His legs didn't quite come with the rest of him, so she turned them and positioned them naturally. Blood ran down the side of his head. Charlotte grabbed up a handful of petticoat and pressed it to his wound.

His moan filled her with relief. She stroked his hair away from his face.

"David."

Hadn't anyone heard the gunshot? There were workers in their front office, although they were separated by two heavy doors and a long hallway. And what about the office above them? Yet if they'd heard they would have come. It was growing late in the day, so perhaps the workers were gone. Blast! She needed help. If only the overdue Mr. Chetney would return.

Vivian moved, snagging Charlotte's attention. Her half-sister seemed to have gotten her breath back and with a moan rocked onto her hands and knees and slowly rose to her feet. The snood that had confined her hair was gone and golden curls hung to her waist. Bloody hell. Charlotte didn't want Vivian to get away, but she was *not* going to leave David. She wasn't about to threaten her with the firearm, either.

Her half-sister staggered to the door and leaned against the doorframe, facing away. David's hand lifted. Charlotte grabbed it and held on.

"David?" she said.

He opened his eyes and blinked. The dazed look passed, and his blue eyes regained their usual sharpness.

"Are you all right?" he asked.

Charlotte nodded. "Vivian shot you." She felt like her throat was full of prickly bramble stems, and her rough voice quavered. She swallowed angrily. She had to get hold of herself. There was no one else to help them.

David grunted and looked around the room. "Where is she?"

Charlotte glanced around. Vivian had disappeared from the doorway.

"Gone, I think. Her gun is in your pocket."

David grimaced. "Charlotte, try to speak up. My ears are ringing from the gun discharging so close. I can barely hear you."

"You saved my life," Charlotte said loudly. She peeked under the wad of petticoat to check his wound. As soon as the gash was exposed it began bleeding anew, but the flow had slowed, thank God.

David pushed her hand away and felt the wound. Above his temple, the bullet had torn a furrow from the edge of his forehead through his hairline and along the side of his head for more than a finger-length.

"David, stop fiddling with it. You're making the bleeding worse." Charlotte pulled his hand away and pressed her petticoat back atop the wound. In those few moments, her tension drained away. She wanted to hold David, wanted to feel him warm and alive against her.

"What the devil?"

It was Wakefield, crouching beside them, examining David's wound, stripping his tie from his neck and folding it into a neat pad. The relief of him taking command left Charlotte struggling to maintain the appearance of someone capable of providing David with assistance and comfort, though. She braced herself. She wouldn't let him down.

"I come by to see if you've heard anything from Detective Inspector Ridley and find you've engaged Lady Garret yourselves, eh? At least I assume it was the baroness who shot you." He'd dispensed with Charlotte's bloody wad of petticoat and had David holding the pad made of his tie. "Can you sit up?" he asked, putting a hand behind David's shoulders.

Charlotte had been glad to see Wakefield, but what was he about now? Making David hold the pad to his injury himself, and wanting to sit him up? She laid a staying hand on David's chest.

"Lord Wakefield, please. I think we'd best summon a physician before he's moved."

Wakefield and David exchanged a look. David sat up.

"Wakefield, give me a hand, can you?" David asked. His friend righted his chair.

Ire rose like a fountain in Charlotte at their off-hand manner. Persa ran in, barked twice, and began scampering around the room, sniffing David, Wakefield, Charlotte's petticoats, and the floor. Mr. Chetney's sudden appearance right behind Persa was a relief. She could count on Chetney to be level-headed.

"Ah, Chetney," Wakefield said. "Just in time. Let's give him a leg up, shall we?"

Without hesitating, Chetney took the other side of David. A moment later the two men had hefted him up and set him in his chair.

"*Now* may I summon a physician?" Charlotte asked.

They ignored her, and Wakefield began giving Chetney a summary of events. David's face softened and he held out his hand to Charlotte—right in front of Wakefield and Chetney, who'd wiped their hands on her ruined petticoat but still had streaks of blood on them. Charlotte didn't hesitate, and the warm, familiar feel of David's hand provided a huge measure of comfort.

"I don't think I need a surgeon," David said. "Boone can take care of this. Chetney, if you'll send a message to Boone and have him bring my coach 'round? We'll go to Lady Haliday's home. She can change her dress and Boone can look after this wound. Wakefield, if you'll be so good as to find Detective Inspector Ridley and give him a report, he can attend us there." He looked at Charlotte. "We'll ask your father to come, too."

Her father. Yes, they had a lot to discuss. With all the turmoil she'd temporarily pushed what Vivian revealed to the back of her mind.

"Evidently Lady Garret is my half-sister," she explained to Wakefield and Chetney. "Everything she did to me, she did to hurt our father."

The men exchanged surprised looks, and then Chetney went to his desk to write the note to Boone.

David took Vivian's pistol from his pocket and extended it. "Take this with you."

Wakefield slipped the gun into his coat pocket. "Anything else I can do before I track down Ridley?"

David shook his head. "No. But thank you, Miles. This isn't the first time I've been wounded and you've acted in my interests."

Wakefield winked. "You've applied a few battle dressings to my sorry ar—" He stopped and shot a look at Charlotte. "Well. It was about time I returned the favor."

Charlotte recalled it had been Wakefield who David saved at Balaclava, and afterward Wakefield had gone back to search the battlefield for David at first light. She could imagine both men behaving in the same commanding way they had acted today, making sure the needy got help and were properly cared for.

Her irritation at their cavalier attitudes drained away.

CHAPTER THIRTY-TWO

The intensity of David's headache increased while he and Charlotte answered Ridley's questions. Then he waited with her while the detective inspector questioned her father. Now his head pounded like a cannon firing with every heartbeat.

Boone cleaned his wound, put a few stitches in to hold it together, and dressed it as tidily as any he'd done in Her Majesty's service. David's ears still buzzed and probably would for another few hours. That meant he had to listen carefully to what was being said, and concentration wasn't easy with his head taking artillery fire.

There was one more conversation he intended to be part of—the one between Charlotte and her father. Matthew Shelby could practice his overbearing, superior manner on someone other than his daughter. David wasn't going to let him lord anything over Charlotte tonight.

He watched her pace back and forth across the foyer, her gaze locked on the sitting room door. Ridley had left and Shelby waited inside.

Charlotte strode to the door, stopped, and put her hand on the knob. She looked at him, eyes huge and apprehensive, and he pushed at his wheels.

"Can I come in with you? Be your watchman?"

Charlotte's stiff shoulders relaxed. "Yes, please."

He rolled across the foyer and gave her a cheeky wink to bolster her spirits. She leaned down, placed a soft kiss on his mouth, and he wrapped his hand around the back of her neck. As she eased away, he pulled her back for a longer, firmer press of lips. He drank in her smell, that lovely scent of roses and jasmine that was so uniquely hers. When he released her, he was happy to note she looked distracted. The reaction of certain parts of his aching anatomy left him less happy.

"Thank you for being here," she said.

He looked at her, absorbing the marvel that was Charlotte. He said nothing.

Her brows furrowed. "Did you hear me?"

"I did." It was just that she took his breath away.

She bent closer. "Must you go home tonight? I'm sure Boone is a wonderful attendant, but he's not me. I know I won't sleep for worrying about you and wondering how you're faring. I want to be near you."

"Shall we go to the cottage?" David asked. While she watched over him, he could then take care of her. Once she spoke with her father, he suspected she was going to need a great deal of tenderness. He wanted to be the one to whom she turned.

In answer, she gave him another too brief kiss and a firm squeeze of the shoulder. Then she straightened, took a deep breath, and opened the door. He followed right on her heels.

They found Shelby pacing the length of the room, much as David had watched Charlotte doing a few minutes ago in the hall. The man stopped, strode over to them and took Charlotte's hand. Deep grooves bracketed his mouth and scored his forehead.

"I'm so sorry she sought her revenge through you."

The man never looked less than commanding, but today Shelby looked at least ten years older than the last time David had seen him. His eyes held great weariness.

David ground his teeth and tried to ignore the pent-up urge to throttle the man. *I hope you're feeling every bit of the shame you deserve.*

"Can we sit down?" Charlotte asked. Christ, but David was proud of her. Was there another woman who could do what she'd done today and then be calm and levelheaded as she answered Ridley's questions and confronted her self-absorbed bastard of a father?

Shelby dropped her hand and led them to the cluster of chairs and divans. Beckham maneuvered David next to the seat Charlotte chose, and David requested liquor, tea and sandwiches—in that order. He felt wrung out, and though Charlotte's posture was as correct as always, she had to be feeling much the same. They both needed sustenance.

Beckham nodded and moved to the sideboard. A minute later they each held a glass, and the servant slipped out the door.

"Charlotte, I'm going to make sure that woman—"

Charlotte interrupted. "Vivian said you wouldn't help her son. Is that true?"

Shelby scowled. "Her son?"

"She blames you for his death. Did you even show her the least bit of kindness? She grew up being taunted and whipped. Did you know that? It's no wonder she's deranged. She had no one to turn to, no one to help her. *I* might have helped her, if only I'd known."

Shelby stiffened. "When did you become an expert on Vivian Garret's motivations?"

"Perhaps when she held a gun on me and I *listened* to her."

David tightened his lips to keep from smiling as an additional measure of pride speared through his chest. He needn't have worried about Charlotte standing up to her father. Not anymore. Shelby was an intimidating man and she had spent most of her life under his protection and following his dicta, yet she faced him here straight and steady-eyed, with the kind of mettle David had wished for in the troops he commanded.

An almost comical look of bewilderment appeared on Shelby's face. "I gave serious consideration to her request for funds to pay for that Prussian sanatorium. After consulting my physician, I determined I might as well throw the money away as give it to her."

Charlotte slammed her empty sherry glass down on the table. "Her name is *Vivian*."

"Bloody hell. What makes you think I had no feelings for her? I did. I especially did for her mother—whose name was Amelia, by the way."

Lips parted, Charlotte stared at her father. "I... Vivian said her mother was a mistress you discarded."

"If she were, that wouldn't make me any worse than hundreds of other men. But I didn't discard Amelia. She wanted to marry a title. We were both unmarried and wanted the same thing, you see. We understood each other, which made me like her even more. Our liaison was brief and ended by mutual accord. When she realized her condition, she asked for money enough to attract an aristocratic husband." For a moment David saw Shelby's eyes grow distant, and his mouth softened. "She never wanted me."

"Vivian told a very different story."

Shelby shrugged. "Either she lied or Amelia lied. But I've told you the truth."

The tea arrived, and they all fell silent until they'd each been served and Beckham left the room again. Charlotte spoke as soon as the door closed.

"What really matters is that Vivian wanted you to acknowledge her and help her."

Shelby opened his hands as if pleading for understanding. "I couldn't do that to you."

"To *me*?"

Shock had transformed Charlotte's face. David knew enough of her relationship with her father to know she protected her feelings around him, but right now her face—and, he suspected, her heart— was laid bare.

Shelby rubbed his hand across his mouth. "Giving her such a sum of money…if anyone learned of it, she could have made me, and by extension, you, the object of gossip. You had just married. I couldn't jeopardize your marriage and your life that way. I knew Haliday. It would have disgusted him." He picked up his teacup then set it back down. "And my decision was right. She went on to ruin your marriage and publish lies about you. Such a person doesn't deserve to have me champion her. Once I realized what kind of manipulator she was I knew I'd been right not to submit to her demands."

Charlotte shook her head. "Haliday would have been disgusted?" Her angry tone slid toward incredulity and her lips thinned. "You're renowned for your brilliance, Father, but in this regard you've been obtuse. Why didn't you tell me? Surely, since it affected me, I should have been consulted. We might have had a private relationship with her. Did it ever occur to you that I might have wanted to know my sister? And my nephew?"

"Perhaps I should have informed you, but the boy was already lost and I saw how jealous Vivian was. How bitter. Even if I'd given her what she wanted, I think she still would have attacked you. If I'd known the extent of her madness, that ultimately she'd become capable of murder, I would have done anything to appease her and protect you."

Eyes wide, Charlotte stared at Shelby. She said nothing.

"Charlotte? Surely you know that."

"I…I've not always been sure that you loved me."

Please, go to her. Take her in your arms, David though. He waited, silently urging, but Matthew Shelby didn't move. Instead, the man's brows snapped together.

"I can't imagine why you'd assume anything else."

David grabbed the soft pink shawl draped across the back of Charlotte's chair and wrapped the garment around her shoulders. She turned her head as he tucked it under her chin, and her love and gratitude hit the center of his chest with the force of a physical blow, making warmth unfurl and spread through him. This was Charlotte. Even in dire need of comfort herself, she filled him with gladness.

He trailed his finger along the edge of the shawl, gently brushing her neck, and the corners of her mouth edged up. He'd managed to assuage some of the hurt Shelby's callous words had created, thank God, so he did his best to conceal the animosity he felt toward the man, but he doubted he kept all of it disguised.

"It would have helped Charlotte to know why Vivian was so focused on hurting her."

Shelby bowed his head. "I'm sorry. I didn't know whether or not to tell. If I'd thought there was any possibility she'd put Charlotte in physical danger, of course I would have warned her."

And yet, the man had stood over his daughter's sickbed when she was poisoned and not said a word.

David clamped his teeth together. Accusations would only make her feel worse.

"All the hurt she caused when Haliday was alive… I should have known then." Charlotte gathered the shawl tight and straightened. "She subjected me to scandal. It hurt when society believed her and ostracized me. You keeping quiet only kept *your* name from the gossipers' lips."

"Hurt?" Shelby scoffed. "I don't believe that. Not seriously. I watched you. I was proud of the way your poise never flagged. You're like me—too smart to let anyone else get the upper hand. I knew by the way you conducted yourself that Haliday and Vivian's actions didn't really matter to you. Not at all."

Charlotte looked as stunned as David felt. How was it possible for Shelby to have such little understanding of the person his daughter was?

She sagged a bit. "You don't know anything, Father."

David took her hand, and she squeezed his fingers. He didn't give a damn what Shelby thought of the open act of caring.

Beckham entered, pushing a cart loaded with sandwiches. Shelby stood, irritation and impatience in his expression and every motion. "I'm going to eat," he said, "and then I'm going home. And, Beckham, I intend to drink scotch, not tea."

He did just what he'd said. In a matter of minutes, Charlotte's father had consumed a collection of sandwiches, downed another scotch, and left.

David looked at Beckham. "We don't need anything else right now. Please close the door and make sure we're not disturbed."

Charlotte's brows lifted. "You'll have all the servants gossiping."

"As if they aren't already." He took her hand and pulled her toward him. "Come here."

She set her plate on the table and let him guide her onto his lap. Once there, she didn't require any further encouragement. Her open mouth matched his for urgency.

There were so many emotions he tried to express, but their kiss quickly turned into the kind normally reserved for the bedroom: deep, consuming, a kiss to get lost in. A kiss that made him want to possess her *now*.

They broke apart, panting. Her cheeks were as pink as the shawl about her shoulders, and her eyes shone like faceted jewels. David took a deep breath and let it out slow. He'd been a fool for a long time, but no more. How had he ever gotten so lucky to earn the love of this woman? She saw the imperfect man he was. He knew himself to be as flawed on the inside as his less than perfect body, yet Charlotte loved and desired him. Down to the center of his soul, he believed his infirmity didn't matter to her. They made each other happy. And there was *more*.

His crippled legs hadn't prevented him from supporting and reassuring Charlotte while she'd suffered the effects of that poison, nor from directing the search for the person responsible. When she'd been out of her head, he was the only one who could get her to take the medicine. Today he'd stopped a bullet meant for her. So he'd protected her. Protected her as well or better even than an able-bodied man might have. But again, there was more.

In time he would have discovered his crippled legs didn't stop his being a physical, capable man, but one important thing would never have been realized without Charlotte's help. She'd taught him to open his heart. To believe himself deserving of love and equal to the challenge. Now he believed. He felt more a man than when he'd stood on strong, steady legs. He just needed one answer for everything to be perfect.

He cupped Charlotte's cheek. "I love you, Bluebell. I want to be able to hold you every day, not just when we go to the cottage. I want to be there every time you need me. I want to start every day with you, and end every blessed day with you." He looked deep into her purple-blue eyes and smiled. "Marry me."

She drew in a sharp breath, blinked and inched backward, creating a space between them. The shining, open expression in her eyes disappeared, and a gossamer curtain dropped, hiding her feelings. David's stomach flipped. A thin blade of fear pierced his core, and his confidence began bleeding away.

"I thought you didn't want to marry," Charlotte said. "We agreed about that."

"But that was before we fell in love." He remembered. She didn't think herself able to trust and considered it essential in a marriage. "You *know* me, Bluebell. You know I'd never leave you or intentionally hurt you."

He ran his hand up her arm, searching for her familiar, lithe softness. Oh, God. There were tears in her eyes. How could that be? A moment ago they'd been so happy.

"How can you just…change? When you were so positive? So certain. I even tried to convince you that you were wrong, and I couldn't." Charlotte eased off his lap as if she thought he might break. Her face still glowed with a flush from his kisses. "I feel like I don't know you." She pressed her hands to the area just above her waist. "Why didn't you tell me you were reconsidering our decision?"

David shook his head. "It's not that simple. The bedrock of a person doesn't change. You thought you stopped believing in a steadfast love, yet we found it together. Somewhere inside you there was still a seed. It grew and flowered. I thought I was too broken to be a proper husband. It's your unfaltering acceptance of me that's made me believe in myself again. I've loved you, championed you and protected you, all while I didn't think I could ever again be lover, champion or protector. I became those things because of you. They were always in me, but I couldn't believe it until your eyes showed me a true reflection of myself. I wasn't hiding anything. I just realized what I wanted."

Charlotte slid onto the chair beside him. He wanted to reach out and pull her back, but her face made him hold off.

She folded her arms across her waist and leaned over them. "I love you. I do. More than I ever believed it possible to love someone. That makes me *want* to trust you, but it doesn't make it easier. The people I trusted—my father, my husband—had secrets. Secrets that concerned me. Terrible secrets that affected my life in a profound way. And, until I found them out, I *trusted* both of those men. Even Etherton, my friend Jane's husband, held secrets from Jane, and that was in spite of loving her dearly. Now those secrets are causing her pain and ruining her marriage."

David's stomach twisted. "I'm not your father, Haliday, or Etherton. I haven't lied or hidden any secrets."

"You're not listening," Charlotte half-shouted. She unfolded her arms and gripped her hands in her lap. "If I marry you, if I decide to *trust* you, I'll be completely vulnerable again." She took a deep breath and rubbed her forehead. "I've lived half my life in an invisible cage. I love you, but how can I trust you'll continue to love me forever? I need to know that if anything happens I'll still be free."

"I believe in *your* love," David offered. Desperation made his voice strained. "I trust it. Trust it will last. Despite what your father says, he's never shown you love. Haliday should have loved you, but he was full of greed and debauchery. I doubt he was even capable of love." He squeezed his chair's armrests. "Deep inside, I think you wonder how I could love you when they couldn't. But I do. So much. I understand why it's difficult for you to trust the feeling again, but I'll help you. This is different. This is *me*."

He slapped his palms to his chest, but no. Oh, no, no, no. She was shaking her head back and forth.

"I can't marry again, David. Not even you." Her eyes closed, and she bowed her head. "Especially not you," she whispered. "If it somehow went wrong, I don't think I'd survive."

Her words speared him like a Cossack's *shashka*. He'd been crushed beneath a thousand-pound-horse and it hadn't hurt like this. His heart plummeted into an empty pit and kept falling. He wondered if it would ever hit bottom.

Then anger spurted through him, turned him forge-hot. This wasn't right. Charlotte was not being true to herself.

He grabbed her arms and gave her a little shake. Her head jerked up, revealing lashes spiky with tears. "Damn it, I love you! You're not being honest nor fair. After all we've been through, you're going to let your fear of what *might* happen stop us from enjoying happy, full lives?"

She pulled away and he released her arms. The sound of their rapid breaths filled the silence.

"Not us, David. Me. By refusing you, I'm depriving myself. I'm not meant to marry. Trust makes us vulnerable and gives someone else the power to hurt us. I'm too frightened. The woman you marry should be your match in strength—in *all* your wonderful qualities. As much as I can't bear to think of you with someone else, I know it's best. I intended to tell you so. I'd already decided."

He hardly knew what to say. "What kind of nonsense is this? You're destroying me now to save me later?" A grim, choked laugh escaped him.

She stood and gripped her hands together, the knuckles turning white. He felt her withdrawal and despair crowded close. *Convince her, man!* He had to make her understand they could weather every challenge.

"You're exactly my match, and you'd make a very fine wife. I admire so much about you, but how can I convince you? Do you think I've never been frightened?"

She blinked as if he'd surprised her.

"I've been riddled with fear, stinking of it more times than I can count. I understand fear, and I understand hurting. Let me help you, sweetheart."

Misery twisted her face. His love did this to her? He'd thought he knew her so well, yet he hadn't expected this. And wasn't that what she feared—that she could never really know the person she loved? If she put her faith in him, it left her vulnerable to exactly this kind of hurt, a hurt only he could inflict.

Christ!

"I don't know what to say, Charlotte, except that you're hurting now. Not marrying hasn't spared you."

"Yes, it has," she murmured. "It would be so much worse if you were my husband. David, I *want* to trust you. If I could trust anyone, it would be you." Tears ran down her face. She pressed a handful of the shawl to her eyes.

Ah, Bluebell, how have we come to this?

He had to see her face. He grabbed her wrist and pulled her hand down. He'd looked into her eyes as he thrust into her body, and he knew she loved him to the rock-bottom of her soul. So he said, "You're wrong. All you have to do is let yourself. Let yourself trust me."

Tight-jawed, she shook her head.

David wasn't sure what she was disagreeing with, and he didn't care. If he didn't leave right now he was going to break down or smash something. He released Charlotte and gave his wheels a mighty push toward the door. With his hand on the knob, he turned back. He struggled to keep the bitterness from his voice and said, "You know, it's not just me you have to believe in. It's yourself, too."

He opened the door and barked for Boone, who came running. The man took one look at David's face and wheeled him out the front door.

CHAPTER THIRTY-THREE

Charlotte stumbled into her bedroom. For a minute she stood adrift, no landfall in sight. Then a noise drew her to the window. David was leaving.

She went and watched as he arranged his sling and hauled himself into his carriage. He'd discarded Boone's bandage upon his head. His bright hair stood out like a beacon in the dusk. Why had he removed it, though? Was he hurting? Dizzy? She should be with him, she knew. She should be taking care of him.

Behind her, the door opened. "Lady Haliday?"

Charlotte didn't turn from the window. She had to force in two deep breaths before she was able to speak. "I won't be needing anything, Rebecca. I'd like to be left alone."

"Yes, my lady."

"In fact, I don't want to be disturbed again tonight."

Charlotte heard the rustle of the maid bobbing a curtsy and leaving, then the click of the door. The events of the past several hours, and most especially of the last hour, had battered her to insensibility. She tightened her shawl—the shawl David had wrapped around her shoulders—and wondered how could he want to end everything they had by pushing for more. They'd always said they didn't want to marry. So, what right did he have to be angry with her? He'd been so very angry. Yet *he* was the one who'd made the unnecessary proposal. She hadn't been able to terminate their affair, even though she knew it was for the best, so they could have gone on just as they were…at least for a while. Instead, on this god-awful terrible day when she needed him more than ever before, he'd left her. And he blamed her, saying she couldn't believe herself capable of standing strong in her love.

Was that it? She did trust David, of course she did. But if that trust was challenged, would it collapse? If put to the test, would it sustain? Worse, would she erode their love with constant doubts and reassurances?

As David's carriage pulled away, Charlotte pressed her forehead against the window. Her entire life, her father had hidden the existence of a daughter, her sister. Her marriage—no, her entire association with Haliday—had been defined by his duplicity. Was it any wonder she doubted her ability to wholly trust anyone? And most painful of all, hadn't David just ended their association in spite of his vows of love? It was exactly what she'd feared all along, just early.

There'd be no comfort tonight. Nor would there be any tomorrow when she saw him at the Patriotic Fund offices. How ironic that she would yearn for the solace of David's arms to save her from the pain of his abandonment. However would she bear it?

She stood at the window long after David's carriage turned the corner, even until the streetlighter passed.

#

Charlotte gave Chetney a quiet greeting as she entered the Royal Patriotic Fund's administrative area and moved straight through to her own office, but Persa stopped to give the secretary a quick, more enthusiastic greeting. Charlotte removed her hat, listening. Chetney chuckled, and then the tinkle of claws on marble sounded, marking the dog's hurried steps into David's office.

He was here, then.

She'd barely seated herself at her desk when David rolled in, Persa ensconced on his lap and looking quite pleased with herself. Frowning, David nudged the terrier off him. She leaped to the floor and sat.

"What are you doing here?" he asked. "Didn't you get my note?"

Charlotte lowered her hands to her lap where they were out of sight and clenched her chilled fingers together. She had gotten his note. The one that politely informed her he didn't expect, under the present circumstances, for her to continue working for the Royal Patriotic Fund. He'd urged her to take some time to completely recover from her recent medical and situational crises; he'd fill her position and when she was ready provide her with a recommendation to help her secure a post with another government agency or charity. After receiving that letter, she'd wanted nothing more than to wallow in misery. Over and over she'd recalled yesterday's events, as well as every private moment and conversation she'd ever had with David.

Her stomach cramped, and she wished she'd eaten *something* this morning, but she'd only gotten a couple swallows of tea down. "I don't need a rest. I prefer to work."

Surely he was the one in need of rest. He'd been shot yesterday.

A muscle in his jaw bulged, a jaw that looked hard and sharp as chiseled granite. "I've already sent out the notice. I'll be interviewing applicants for your position."

"That will take weeks, and there's too much to do. I'll work until you hire my replacement." Charlotte paused. She understood. Of course she did. He was hurting, just as she was. Working in such close proximity would effectively pour salt in both of their wounds. "I'll stay out of your way, I promise."

She'd keep her door closed, update him via memorandums. Chetney could be their go-between. Perhaps that way she could do what she had to do and survive. Because she wasn't leaving. Not yet.

David's shoulders drooped, all rigidity gone. He closed his eyes and scrubbed his hands over his face, and when he looked at her again he exuded weariness. He rolled forward until the toes of his shoes touched the front of her desk. For a minute he let her see the sleepless night, the misery, and the determination.

"I don't want you here, Charlotte," he said, at once firm and quiet.

Don't cry, she willed herself. *Whatever you do, do…not…cry.*

She couldn't bear to look in his eyes, so she stared at the masculine dent in his chin, made her voice no-nonsense brisk. "I have an appointment with Edith Carroll at the end of the month. I'll stay until I've concluded my business with her."

He'd been so grateful the day she'd agreed to attend to his good friend's widow. The meeting had been postponed several times, and Charlotte couldn't leave him to face the woman's animosity.

His low, vulgar curse shocked her. She jerked her gaze from his chin and saw that, hands fisted, face flushed, he fairly radiated outrage.

"Chetney!" he roared.

The secretary arrived so fast he might have been discharged from the muzzle of an Enfield.

"Take me back to my office, and see that Lady Haliday's appointments are moved to my calendar. Then get her a hack."

Chetney, eyebrows at maximum loft, looked back at her as he wheeled David away.

"The hack can sit out front all day," Charlotte called after them, barely resisting stamping her foot. "I'm not going home. And I'll be back tomorrow and every day after that for two weeks."

Even from the confines of his office, it wasn't difficult to hear David's angry voice. "She's going, Chetney."

The secretary exited David's office. He stood and gaped at her.

"I'll say a prayer for you, Mr. Chetney," Charlotte said and closed her door.

#

Setting the traveling bag at her feet, Vivian flexed her fingers. Stuffed with her maid's clothes, it was heavier than she'd anticipated. Mary must have been thrilled when she'd found her employer's entire wardrobe abandoned in exchange for a few of her own simple dresses.

Vivian looked down at the well-worn jacket, skirt, and sturdy black shoes she wore. She'd tinted her hair with a henna rinse and dressed it in a simple, low knot. Most of it was tucked out of sight under Mary's navy bonnet. Her ticket, and what money remained after purchasing her passage to America, were in the nondescript reticule she carried. Her jewels were secured in bags and sewn to her petticoat. Withdrawing money from her bank had been out of the question, which meant there wasn't much for starting life over, but this was all she had.

It would be enough.

Finally she was on the quay, milling about with the other passengers waiting to board. Just a few more hours and she'd be safe gone. The wind had even picked up, as if to blow away her doubts.

Four days ago, when the ship's agent asked her name for the *Telegraph*'s passenger manifest, she'd panicked. He frowned when she hesitated, and she blurted out, "Amelia."

Her mother's name.

He'd waited. Looked up from the manifest. "Well?"

"Endsley. Amelia Endsley." Oh, what had she been thinking? She'd given him Radcliffe's family name. How could she have done that? *Why* had she done that? Her face had burned with fiery heat. Mercifully, within a few minutes she'd paid and collected her ticket. The agent hadn't questioned her name or purpose.

She found a room in a hotel near the dock. The establishment was full of hopeful immigrants waiting to sail, and she became just another. Several of the women she met were joining husbands who'd shipped before them. Their men had gotten jobs, places to live, and had accrued enough money for their wives' passage. It was easy for Amelia Endsley to be just another wife headed for a reunion with her husband.

"Vivian."

As quiet as the voice was, she nearly jumped out of her skin. "Radcliffe."

Grim-faced, he wore what might have been his man of business's casual dress. He looked finer than the men crowding around them but coarse enough to pass for a clerk or surgeon, and his hand clenched about her arm. His other hand scooped up her traveling bag. He began pulling her away.

"Wait. Stop. What are you doing?" She resisted, even when his hand tightened. Was he turning her over to the police?

He stopped but didn't loosen his grip. "I'm not actually sure what I'm doing. I've been looking for you for days, but what I intend to do now that I've found you I don't know."

She'd never seen him looking this way—his face bristling with golden whiskers, his brown topaz eyes somber. Creases scored the skin on either side of his mouth.

Her throat tightened into a painful constriction. The sudden weakness of her legs made her glad for the steely constraint of his arm. "I'll be boarding soon. I shouldn't leave."

He glanced around them and led her a short distance away, to a less congested area where a wagon sat. He released her and tossed down her bag, removed his hat, and blew out a long stream of air through loosely pursed lips. Then he ignored her, stared over her head and thumped his hat against his leg.

Vivian stayed quiet and waited, drinking him in. This final look would have to do for the rest of her life.

Glinting eyes suddenly focused on her with the concentrated intensity of a lighthouse beam. She couldn't have felt any more exposed if she'd stood in the all-revealing glare of Leasowe Lighthouse's lamp.

"Are you all right?"

She couldn't answer. She blinked, sniffed, searched in her reticule and up her sleeve for a handkerchief.

"Here."

A square of snowy linen was thrust into her hand. She pressed it to her eyes and nose and closed her mind to the scent of soap and starch and tobacco that clung to the cloth and made her want to bury her nose in his neck.

"Now answer me. Are you all right?"

She nodded. She wasn't all right, but there was no repairing what was wrong. And that wasn't what he meant, anyway.

"I knew I'd find you. I've been staying at a nearby hotel and searching the docks. The police are looking at inns on the roads leading away from London, and at train depots." A harsh laugh broke from him. "They've even watched my home."

"How did you know I'd be here?"

Finally, he looked at her. "I didn't, really. But I thought, maybe..." He seemed uneasy, not at all like his usual confident self.

"What now?" He'd found her, but he could barely look at her. Did that mean he intended to turn her in? Surprisingly, the thought didn't fill her with anxiety.

He lifted his hat and turned it round and round, smoothing the brim. "I don't know why I'm here. I suppose I wanted to see if you needed any help."

"To get away, you mean? You're offering money?"

Flinty eyes locked onto her. "No." He dragged air in, huffed it out, scraped his fingers through his hair, and jammed his hat on his head. "I don't know. I just had to see you—see that you're all right."

Now it was her turn to look away. There was too much emotion in his face—emotion she'd never seen at any ball or dinner party or poetry reading, or even making love. This expression, she knew, would haunt her.

"I don't deserve to get away, but it appears I'm going to. I'll be boarding soon."

He nodded.

"You should go," she said. *Please go.* Before she asked him to hold her once more. She wanted to feel his arms hard around her, to nestle her head on his broad shoulder. She wanted to wrap her arms around him, smell him, taste him. Just one more time.

He nodded.

She knew. There was to be no embrace, no last kiss. He straightened, adjusted his hat, started to turn away.

He might have planted his heel to her heart, the way it split open then. "Stephen." She grabbed his arm. "Why aren't you turning me in?"

He turned back, hesitated, then stepped close. A gust of wind blew a few dangling strands of hair across her face. She lifted her fingers to brush them away, but his hand intercepted hers. He brushed her skin as he gathered the strands and wrapped them round and round his finger. His eyes narrowed before he slowly withdrew his finger and let the burnished strands fall.

A funny, sad kind of smile quirked one corner of his mouth. "I've got sleepless nights ahead no matter what I do, but I can't turn you in."

This time she didn't call him back when he turned and strode away.

He *loved* her. Oh, dear God. She'd been wrong when she assumed he couldn't overlook her past. What if she'd known he could? What if she'd known he'd be able to love her? Her eyes filled, and she angled her face into the wind. As much as she hated the wrenching pain, feeling this deep, cutting emotion brought a measure of relief to her mind. She'd committed violent acts— poisoned a woman, shot a man—without feeling much of anything. Only a lunatic could do such things and remain impassive. Only a lunatic would let anger and revenge dictate such heinous actions.

She'd been so very afraid for so long that she was in the grip of insanity. But surely a madwoman wouldn't feel such devastation when her lover walked away? Or feel soothed by the simple act of turning her face to a gusty ocean wind?

An increase in dock commotion pulled her from her bewildering thoughts. The *Telegraph* was boarding. Very soon now she'd be away, and she'd have weeks to face into the wind.

CHAPTER THIRTY-FOUR

Charlotte gathered her completed letters and stood. After a week mostly closeted in her office, even the few yards to Chetney's desk provided a welcome change. Working without seeing David, knowing he sat in the next room, was the most exquisite torture. Two weeks remained until her appointment with Edith Carroll. After that, she wouldn't even have the occasional, indistinct low rumble of his voice.

She turned the letters over to Chetney just as David's door swung open. Persa dashed from her place at Charlotte's feet, past Wakefield standing motionless in the doorway, and gave a flying leap onto David's lap. David laughed, gave Persa a vigorous rub, and Charlotte's heart took the smashing blow of a blacksmith's hammer.

David's head jerked up as a soft exclamation of pain escaped her. The soft amusement fell from his face and left it grim. Their eyes met. David didn't move, didn't blink. His blank eyes held steady. Hard. Not even a glimmer of tenderness shone in their cold blue depths.

The horrible pinch and tear of scavengers' beaks attacked the inside of Charlotte's chest, and she had to put her hand on Chetney's desk to steady herself. She couldn't do this. Could. *Not.* She whirled and hurried back to her office, collapsing into the nearest chair.

"Are you all right?"

Wakefield. He was crouched beside her. She sat open-mouthed and gasping, her hand pressed to her chest.

"Can I get anything?" Chetney. He hovered behind Wakefield, hands twisted together so tight his knuckles gleamed white.

Breathe, Charlotte told herself. *Breathe.*

"Charlotte?" Wakefield asked. She shook her head. Wakefield looked up at the secretary and jerked his chin. "Nothing, Chetney. Just close the door behind you."

She felt his soothing hand on her back and managed to drag in a little air. Then a little more. What a kerfuffle. She'd shown them all what a ridiculous, heartsick woman she was, and all from just one look into David's remorseless eyes. She needed to pull herself together.

She started to straighten, to compose her features, but one look at Wakefield and she lost all desire for pretense. He'd know it was nothing but false bravado. So she slumped back into the chair. "He looks so..." Not exactly angry, but... "So ill-tempered."

"Ill-tempered?" Wakefield huffed out a laugh devoid of humor. "If you'd call a rabid hound ill-tempered, then I imagine Scott's mood could be labeled such." His eyes narrowed. "I'd be more likely to call him enraged, with more than a little despair and anguish in the mix."

No mistake, his tone held a measure of accusation.

"You know?" Charlotte asked.

"That he proposed and you tossed his offer back in his face?"

Wakefield was angry. At *her*. The concern he'd shown as she gasped for air seemed to have drained away.

Her own temper flared. "We were fine. We were *wonderful* as we were. We had an agreement, and I didn't want anything to change." She hated her defensiveness but couldn't help herself.

Wakefield stood. "Oh, it's Scott's fault, is it?"

He leaned forward, back rigid, jaw clamped, and Charlotte drew away from his hostility. "This is what he wanted."

Wakefield's nostril's flared. "You crushed him," he roared.

The door flew open and banged into the wall.

"Enough."

David rolled partway through the door, and the ferocity emanating from him shook Charlotte. Oh, God, what had she done to him? This was not her David. His eyes held a feral gleam that frightened her.

"David?"

He ignored her whisper and stared at Wakefield. The men glared at each other before Wakefield made a frustrated noise and stepped forward. David rolled back enough to clear the doorway, and his friend strode past. Wakefield continued through the reception area, his heels resounding against the marble floor. After he pushed through the outer door, silence fell.

Charlotte found herself on her feet, facing David.

"Enough of this," he said. "You're leaving, or I am."

"David—"

"No."

She shivered and folded her hands over her chest. Seeing him like this filled her with razor-edged shards of ice so biting cold that the deep, deep ache nearly overcame her. She moved one step forward, but he raised his hands, palms facing out, and stopped her.

"You. Or me."

The sharpness made her wince, but somehow she held her emotion at bay. Her eyes grew hot, but she suppressed the powerful urge to blink. David's face bore a weary droop, new lines, and dark smudges under his eyes. She couldn't bear to look at this evidence of distress, so she gazed past him and regarded Chetney…only to wish she hadn't. Chetney was doing nothing to hide his dismay. David had meant his ultimatum, and she couldn't let him leave the Royal Patriotic Fund. He was the executive committee chairman.

She whirled, retreating back to her office, then stopped and turned her head just enough to address him over her shoulder. "I'll be back for Edith Carroll's appointment."

She heard him grunt, and the sound of his chair moving away.

He wasn't arguing with her over that, at least. A sign of how much he wanted to avoid his old friend's widow.

This was it, then. She no longer belonged here. Charlotte closed her door and managed to get around her desk, where she sat and gathered Persa into her arms. Held close, her dog's body warmed her and brought a measure of comfort. In a few minutes she'd call Mr. Chetney in and give him her last instructions. She'd be back for Mrs. Carroll's appointment, but she might never again see David.

#

Jane entered Charlotte's sitting room with the energy of a small whirlwind. For a moment Charlotte could only stare at her friend's disturbing appearance. Face pale, eyes red-rimmed and glittering with a hard light, she gave the empty chairs a dismissive wave and paced the room, skirts swirling.

"I thought you were at Friar's Gate," Charlotte said.

Jane's last note had said she was taking Charlotte's advice and intended to keep a cool head and explore the possibility that the faith she'd lost in her husband and her marriage could be restored. All week Charlotte had imagined Jane and Etherton together at Friar's Gate and refused to consider any but a happy outcome. She'd welcomed those moments when pleasurable thoughts of her friends supplanted the emptiness that now filled her days.

"I came back and brought the girls with me. I don't plan to go again."

"What? Jane, you can't mean that. What happened?"

Her friend wheeled and faced her. "I met his son and mistress, that's what happened."

"Former mistress," Charlotte corrected. "Now, sit down." She grabbed her friend's hand and urged Jane to sit beside her on the settee.

Jane sat, looked at her, and dissolved into tears. "I don't think I can bear to be with him anymore."

Oh, no. How had the situation deteriorated to this? How could Jane and Phillip let it?

"Jane…" Charlotte wrapped her arms around her friend's bent shoulders. Jane grabbed on and hugged her back.

Her friend pressed her lips together. "I couldn't sleep. I couldn't stop snapping at him. I've become this person I don't even know."

This truly wasn't like Jane. She was one of the steadiest people Charlotte knew. "What did Phillip do when you told him you were leaving for good?"

"Nothing. He looked like he wanted to murder me, but he turned and stalked out the door. Left me standing there, screaming at his back."

Jane, screaming at Phillip? Jane never screamed at *anyone*.

"I just couldn't stop myself. I can't bear it, knowing his former paramour and their son Francis are living nearby. Phillip and Francis ride together every morning. Phillip bought him a pony. He adores the boy more and more every day."

"Jane, does that surprise you?" How could it? Hadn't Phillip's innate decency been what attracted her friend in the first place?

Jane sighed. "No."

"Then why are you so upset? I know you wouldn't want any boy to grow up without knowing his father, especially when the man is as wonderful as Phillip. Your jealousy seems extreme. And uncalled for."

Jane blotted her eyes with the crumpled handkerchief she held clenched in her fist. In spite of her tears, her face looked steely. "How can my concerns be unreasonable when Phillip prefers the boy's company over mine?" Her face turned bright red. "We haven't been intimate since we first fought. And when I told him I was leaving, Phillip said, 'Good.'"

Charlotte shook her head. "I can't believe he meant he *wanted* you to live separate lives. He probably took your leaving as an ultimatum and got angry."

Jane bounded to her feet and resumed pacing. Dress wrinkled, hair falling from the knot atop her head, and with her spectacles contributing to the hard, glassy look of her eyes, she presented an image at odds with the woman Charlotte had always known.

"Why shouldn't I give him an ultimatum? Don't I have that right? Don't I have more say than a former mistress and a bastard child?"

Stymied, Charlotte searched for soothing words but nothing occurred. "You said the boy's name is Francis? What happened when you met Francis and his mother?" She had truly thought meeting the pair might help Jane.

Her friend turned. "He looks exactly like Phillip, excepting the red hair and freckles he got from his mother."

"Did you meet her?"

Jane resumed pacing. "A good mother to the boy," she admitted begrudgingly. "She's to marry Loyal Gibb, the miller."

"So, she…doesn't inspire the same worry? Phillip's never broken your vows," Charlotte pointed out. "Don't you think, over time, you could accept the boy?"

"You don't understand!"

Saying so, Jane threw up her arms. She returned to the settee, sank down and covered her face with her hands. Charlotte drew Jane's twitching fingers down, cradled those newly short-bitten nails, and saw her friend's lovely eyes were steeped in pain.

"He wanted to tell me before we married, but he asked my mother's opinion first. She advised him not to."

Jane's mother would have known Jane had no tolerance for bastard children.

"Can't he love you and your daughters as well as Francis?" Charlotte asked. She silently begged her friend to be forgiving.

"He shares a bond of blood and forebears with Francis. I am a mere wife. Of course he loves our daughters, but they'll marry and leave. I reminded Phillip that Francis won't share his family name or inherit his title. Only *our* son could do that, but he treats Francis as if he has all the rights and privileges of a child of mine."

"Jane…" Her friend had always been a bit possessive, but never to this degree. Jane's misplaced jealousy even made Charlotte think of Vivian before she'd understood her half-sister's mental disturbance had a much deeper, darker root. It was nothing short of unnatural for Jane to be so extremely envious of the boy. Was there something more at work here? Was it not the fact that Jane was still reliving the mistakes of her parents? If it was…

"You need to reach deep inside and believe in your and Phillip's love. Believe in its strength. In *your* strength," Charlotte declared. "You have an abundance of love in you, Jane. Don't stifle it. Don't let other people's mistakes ruin your marriage—your entire life. If you do, you have no one to blame but yourself!"

As soon as the words left her mouth, they rebounded and struck deep like sharp-bladed arrows. Wasn't she letting her father and Haliday's mistakes stop her from attaining happiness with David? David had never given her reason to doubt him, only reasons to have faith. How was it she could advise Jane to believe in Phillip when she withheld her trust from her own perfect man? She'd told David that independence—freedom—was most important to her, yet her lack of faith had kept her shackled to Haliday's betrayal all this time.

As surely as she knew Jane had hurt Phillip, Charlotte knew she'd inflicted a mountain of pain upon David. Their lack of faith must have crushed the men they loved. It had ended her love affair with David, and it might yet deal Jane's marriage the final killing blow.

Anger fired up inside Charlotte, but this time it was anger at herself. She'd acted like a ninny, refusing to look beyond old hurts. The past week had been complete anguish. She was better than this.

Stronger than this. She knew her heart belonged to David. That had never been in question. David held it in the palms of his hands, and he would never destroy it. He'd protect and care for it. *If she let him.*

David's love was as solid and steady—and as fierce—as he was. It was time for her to let the past go, to believe in herself as a woman worthy of his love and capable of returning it. As certain as she felt right now, she knew there'd be times when she'd need encouragement and reminding, but David had offered to help her and she trusted him to do that.

She'd been so frightened of being vulnerable. All because of the actions of Haliday, a man she'd conjured and who hadn't really existed. She'd been young and impressionable and trusting without good reason, thereby giving the real Haliday the opportunity to do immeasurable harm. She'd trusted Father, too, even after a lifetime of proof she should not. But David had said she knew him. And she did. She knew the bedrock of him.

Jane's tears had nearly dried, and as difficult and hurtful as this conversation had been, Charlotte thought her intelligent friend would benefit from it. Eventually she would surface from her sea of anger and despair and reason her way through. Charlotte would be there to give whatever support she could.

Her friend was quicker to rational thought than she'd expected. Jane raised her head and said, "I can see that my parents probably contributed to my feelings, but there's something else I haven't explained." Her look—almost one of embarrassment—heightened Charlotte's interest.

"Phillip was the third son. He never expected to be earl. And you know how brilliant he is."

Charlotte nodded.

"He became a civil engineer—a railway engineer and railway bridge designer—because he wanted to work where he could do the most good. He envisioned spending his life in countries that desperately needed railways and lacked men with the education to build them. He loved the travel. Loved finding the best route for the rail, cutting tunnels, designing and building bridges. He loved opening up remote areas and bringing new opportunity to the people who lived there."

Charlotte nodded again. She knew Jane had met Phillip after his father and two older brothers unexpectedly died of cholera, requiring him to return from his work in South Africa and assume the title.

"Phillip gave up the work he loved when he became Earl. He explained how he felt before he married me. He didn't love me—not then—but he liked me more than any woman he'd met."

"Because you are as smart and serious and generous as he," Charlotte suggested. Their union might not have started as a love match, but it hadn't taken long for passion and a profound caring to grow. It certainly wasn't one-sided. Charlotte was positive Phillip loved Jane just as deeply as Jane loved him.

Her friend smiled. "He hadn't wanted to be earl, but since he was, he intended to be the best one he could. He took his responsibilities seriously and spoke frankly before we married. He wanted to know if I'd be willing to have a large family. He wanted sons to secure the title, and he wanted to be involved in his children's lives. He said he hoped he wouldn't make too boring a husband. He had no enthusiasm for being Etherton, but he intended to do his duty."

Charlotte's friend squeezed her eyes shut. When she blinked and drew a deep breath, the look she wore begged Charlotte to understand. But Charlotte was uncertain.

"Don't you see? If I can't give him the son he needs, he'll have given up his dreams for nothing. And it'll be my fault!"

What could she say? Leaving Phillip without a legal male descendent was more to Jane than simply failing the law of primogeniture. It was failing to make Phillip *happy*. Charlotte could see how that would cut so deep.

"Have you told Phillip how you feel?"

Lips crimped together, Jane shook her head.

"You need to. You might find Phillip has an opinion on the state of his life and his dreams that's different than what you imagine. You've always said he's the best man you've ever known. And the smartest. The man's marriage is in shambles, but the truth might be the solution. Don't you think he deserves to know what's really going on inside you?"

"I don't need empty reassurances," Jane snapped.

"What makes you think they'll be empty?" Charlotte replied. She wasn't about to let Jane make the same mistake she'd made with

David. Jane needed to be honest with her husband and tell him what she really feared, and a sudden impatience surged in her like the burst of water from a pump. "He deserves another chance. You'd better give it to him, or you'll have me to contend with in addition to everything else. Just go back. Leave the girls at your townhouse with Nanny and Miss Edwards."

Jane stared into Charlotte's eyes, a little less rigid. "I may have expected him to understand what I was feeling without my explaining. He thinks I'm jealous and angry that I haven't produced an heir. He doesn't understand why I can't accept the thought of his cousin inheriting."

"You need to explain it to him just the way you did to me. I know Phillip must be as devastated by this split as you are."

"I've been so angry, I haven't really thought of his feelings," Jane admitted. "I haven't really let myself." A quavering smile tilted her lips. Then she and Charlotte exchanged hugs and Charlotte escorted her downstairs.

At the front door they found Mr. Chetney dropping off what papers he had for her. Charlotte quickly introduced him to Jane, who then left. But Charlotte was still aflutter. Her earlier thoughts of David had stirred a warring mix of emotions inside her. Excitement was uppermost, but, like Jane, she felt fear and regret, too. What if David was disgusted by the way she'd acted and no longer wanted her? That was extremely possible.

"Well, thank you for these," Chetney said, holding up the letters she'd had waiting for him in return. "I'll take them in tomorrow morning. I'm for home now."

"Has Mr. Scott left the office as well?"

Surprise flashed across Chetney's face, closely followed by a frown. "I'm afraid not. He's been keeping rather long hours of late. It's not good for him, either."

Already tender inside from sharing Jane's distress, this blow stung. "Is he ill?" Charlotte asked.

"No, not ill. He's..." Chetney paused and looked away. His complexion had a distinctly flushed appearance. "Let's just say I've seen him look more rested."

David had looked exhausted her last day at the offices, and that had been four days ago. Worry welled up in Charlotte with the pressure of a boiling kettle capped with a tight-fitting lid.

As soon as the door closed behind the secretary, Charlotte raced for the stairs. A mere ten minutes later she was on her way. She hugged Persa and marked each street they passed, and for once she beat her dog out of the coach. The driver tipped his hat and drove off, while Persa whined and scratched at the front entrance of the Patriotic Fund office building and gave Charlotte a pleading look. Charlotte gripped the handle and swung the door wide.

CHAPTER THIRTY-FIVE

David lifted his head. The sun had set, and his small lamp just lit the top of his desk. He barely had light enough to make out her figure, but he knew. He could *feel* her presence. Bittersweet hope lanced through him and whirled his soul into such a tangle he feared he might burst apart. He clamped down on it, hard, and clenched his teeth together.

He scarcely noticed when Persa launched herself onto his lap. He rubbed her ears, his eyes straining to make out Charlotte's face. Why was she here? There was nothing left to say. A week and a half ago she'd left his heart, mind and spirit gravely wounded, and he doubted he'd survive if he let her do further damage.

She strode forward, her face full of anticipation, her lips curving. A mere three paces from him, she stopped abruptly and her expression crumpled. Whatever she saw in his face, it had shaken her.

He marshaled his will and battened down the longing that lashed his core. Christ. Why was she here? He nudged Persa from his lap.

"What do you want, Charlotte?" Please, please, let her get it quickly and leave.

"I...I... Are you all right?"

Anger began to trickle through his defenses. He closed his eyes. Why couldn't she stay away and leave him in peace? It was already nearly impossible to get up each day. To dress, work, and eat. He didn't need the additional burden of this fresh encounter, the reminder of how she looked and sounded. And smelled, he thought, as he caught a whiff of her alluring scent.

"Why are you here?" he asked again.

She came forward. Slow, slow, slow. Closer, closer, closer.

She was flushed, her bosom rising and falling with rapid breaths. Her tongue stroked across her lower lip, and he reacted with a small jerk before he could stop himself.

Charlotte stopped right next to him, gazed at him for a minute and then dropped to her knees to wrap her hands around the arm of his chair. He drew his arm in, away from her. His discomfort increased tenfold. Whatever she meant to say, he had a feeling she'd leave him far worse off than she'd found him.

"David, I've been such a fool."

"What?" Charlotte was no dithering miss who changed her mind at every turn, especially not when the importance of the choice was momentous. "You can't mean to retract your refusal."

She grabbed his arm. "Yes. I was frightened. Stubborn. You love me, and you'd never do anything to hurt me. I *believe* in you."

Her eyes gleamed like purple stars, and the urge to believe her—to accept her—rose in David with a power unlike anything he'd ever known. He held it back, just barely. Pressed it back with a paralyzing fear of his own.

He managed to force a few words out. "What changed your mind? Why so suddenly sure of me?"

"I spoke with Jane." Charlotte shook her head and made an impatient gesture with her hand. "Everything between her and Phillip is in a muddle. Perhaps unfixable. It's all unnecessary and very dangerous to their marriage. I realized I've been as foolish as she has." The pleading expression she adopted nearly broke him. "I was rash. And stupid. Being apart from you is worse than any of the fears I imagined."

She leaned forward and pressed her mouth to his. Her open mouth.

A hard shudder tore through David, and he pulled her tight against him. Palming her head, he held her in place and devoured her mouth, stroked and thrust with his tongue, and wished he could mirror the movement inside her body with his suddenly stiff cock.

He urged her onto his lap. Her tongue twined with his, she unbuttoned his waistcoat, and right through the linen of his shirt he felt her hot ungloved hands moving over his chest. He tasted her, breathed her in, tilted his head and deepened the kiss even more. Her curves were just as womanly as he remembered. Her breast filled his palm, her waist so slender his fingers spanned from navel to spine.

Frustrated by her layers of clothing, he pressed his face into her neck, below the angle of her jaw. Her head fell back as he mouthed her. Desire blazed. Incandescent and pure as the sun, it burned away every other thought.

Until she made a small noise.

As if rousing from a daze, he pulled back and looked at her. Her half-closed eyelids nearly hid her eyes, but he saw a narrow rim of purple-blue color circling those huge, dark pupils. Swollen lips, red from his kisses, and with high color marking her cheeks, she was beautiful.

She cupped his face. "I'm so sorry."

Then he remembered.

"You believe in me…," he rasped, repeating her earlier statement. "Believe in my love, I presume?"

She nodded.

"And you know I'd never hurt you." The fire that roared through him just moments ago had turned to cold ash in his belly. Lack of love had never been the problem. There was a greater darkness here.

"Does this mean you trust me now? You're not worried I might change someday and leave you with an unpleasant stranger for a husband? This means you can enter our marriage heart-whole, without doubts?"

She stiffened, and her eyes lost their slumberous look. A guarded expression stole over her face and a crease appeared between her brows.

"You're not concerned I might be concealing my true nature? Just as Haliday did?"

"No," she said with intensity. "There's not another man hidden inside you. I hurt you by not believing in you, but I believe in you now."

Anger built inside him, crowding out the warmth and hope. He loved her, but—*damn it!* The past two weeks she'd put him through hell! And now she was to say sorry and he was to forget it all?

"So you're not afraid I might change. Not worried I might grow tired of you. What makes you so confident I'll never feel different than I feel now? I'm a completely different man than I was five years ago. Or even one year ago."

A whine drew his attention to Persa, who sat looking back and forth between them, a distressed expression on her canine face.

Charlotte slid her feet to the floor and inched upward to stand at her full height. The look in her eyes sliced open David's chest, and for a moment he had to look away, to steel himself. He didn't want to do this, he really didn't. But since the day she'd refused his proposal, anger and skepticism had extinguished the dream he'd had of them together.

Her silence confirmed it, too. She didn't trust him. Not wholly.

"Will you watch me?" he asked. "Question me? Every time I lose my temper, will you lie awake and wonder if I've changed? Will I have to live with your doubt? Is that what a true marriage is based on?"

"You said you'd help me."

"I wonder… Do you realize my faith has also been broken? I've trusted the love of two women in my life. You and Lydia. And you both tossed me away. Now I'm supposed to shrug, smile, and forgive? Welcome you back with open arms?"

Charlotte backed away, tucking her shaking hands behind the folds of her skirt. David hated himself in that moment. Christ, what a sorry bastard he was! Charlotte was a strong woman, yet he'd managed to beat her down. Yet, what if she was no longer capable of trust? Shelby and Haliday had certainly been awful.

Her skin had turned white, as if he'd eviscerated her and drained her of blood. That didn't stop David from pushing farther. This had to be said.

"You say you believe in me, that your fear is gone. But how can you love me with a full heart if you don't trust me?"

"I love you."

That simple answer made stars shoot through his blood, but David squeezed his eyes closed. She didn't look like a woman declaring her love. She looked desperate and hurting.

She took a step toward him. "I realized today, *that's* what's important."

David felt a madman's howl building, and he wasn't sure he could hold it in. Was she right? Could she truly dismiss her concerns regarding trust and be happy regardless? His answer to her words ripped free of him in an agonized burst.

"I love you, too. But we're not satisfied with each other. I can't live with you doubting me. And you still do."

His words hung between them. Lips parted, Charlotte stared. He couldn't bear to look at the pain in her eyes—the pain he'd delivered—but he wouldn't let himself look away, either.

Thank Christ, she whirled and ran, Persa scampering after her. God help him, Charlotte and everything he might have had with her was leaving. He'd have to satisfy himself with work, friends, and his brother's family. Before he'd met her, when he was struggling back from seeing himself as a cripple, such an existence had seemed like a good life, a full life. Now, it stretched before him like a dead husk.

#

David heard Wakefield being admitted and looked up from his correspondence. The past week he'd worked all day at the office then continued to work all evening in his den. It helped subjugate his anger and keep his mind off his misery—and he was still catching up on the work he'd let fall behind while Charlotte was ill.

He'd last seen Wakefield the prior week, when he'd invited Miles to dinner and confronted him about his behavior to Charlotte on her last day in the office. Miles had *yelled* at her—another example of his bloody overprotectiveness, which they both knew stemmed from the guilt Miles felt. Even though David hated it, Miles couldn't seem to stop. Well, he'd told the man again to cut it out, and to apologize to Charlotte.

His friend strode in but didn't present the appearance David expected. Miles carried an odd-looking saddle over his left forearm, and he laid it atop David's desk.

"Special delivery, Major."

David immediately understood the unusual alterations that modified the item. The length of the flaps had been increased, and three leather straps were attached to each. Why had this never occurred to him?

"Will this work?" he asked. If the excitement rumbling through him was any gauge, if—*when*—he actually got on the back of a horse he might well fly apart. Or fall apart. For certain, when he dismounted he wouldn't be the same man.

"I don't see why not." Wakefield's hand smoothed over the fine leather. "You sat every mount before like a burr stuck to the horse's back. Secure your legs with these straps, and I imagine you still will."

"Miles, I don't know what to say. Is it your design?"

Wakefield dropped into the chair facing the desk, stretched out his legs and crossed them at the ankles. "I had nothing to do with it."

David looked up from his study of the saddle. "You didn't?"

"Lady Haliday gets the credit. I saw her yesterday and apologized for shouting at her and sticking my nose where it didn't belong. As requested."

The saddle was from Charlotte? David rested his hand on the cantle. "How was she?"

Wakefield grimaced. "Rather distant but gracious. She asked if I'd deliver the saddle to you. There's a letter goes with it."

Still sprawled in the chair, Wakefield pulled an envelope from his inside coat pocket and held it up. David stared.

His friend leaned forward, dropping the missive within David's reach. David scooped it up, opened it, and withdrew the letter before second thoughts could stop him. Charlotte's elegant script covered half the page. The paper shook, and David realized his quivering hand caused the movement. Which was odd. He wasn't a man who trembled. Ever.

Once he started reading and realized the letter had an impersonal, business-like tone, he relaxed. She hoped he'd accept the saddle and ride again. She thought he might mount the horse much like he entered his carriage.

"She was afraid you'd reject it if she had a servant deliver it to you. She thought, if you were angry, I could calm you down and convince you to accept it. You're not going to return it, are you?"

David shook his head. Just the thought of getting on a horse again... Of all the things his injury had stolen, this was the one he most longed for. He imagined Charlotte for a moment, conversing with an unknown saddlemaker, the air redolent with the smell of leather. She'd have been excited and impatient at the wait until she could give it to him.

Today she was probably relieved Wakefield was presenting it rather than her. The moment was bittersweet for him, too.

"We can give it a try tomorrow morning. Have you a mount for me?"

"You've seen the bay, haven't you? He's a goer."

David folded the letter. Looked at Wakefield. Breathed in. Had to ask. "How did she look?"

"Not as bad as you."

"Christ." He shouldn't have asked.

"Have you looked in the mirror?"

His appetite had deserted him, and try as he might he couldn't sleep. He looked like a man subjected to nonstop cannon fire for days on end—completely drained. But, enough. "We're not talking about this."

Wakefield slowly gathered himself and stood. He put his hands on the desk and leaned forward until he was inches from David's face. "Don't let her go."

He'd told Miles that when he proposed she refused and in addition ended their affair. He'd been so disturbed that it poured out of him, but he hadn't shared anything after that. Wakefield didn't know Charlotte had tried to repair their rift, and that David had rebuffed her. He could barely manage his own anger and hurt; he couldn't deal with Wakefield's too.

He leaned back and pinched the bridge of his nose. Damn Wakefield! He had no intention of telling Miles anything more.

He sighed and let his hand fall. "Drop it. Please."

Wakefield straightened, and his mouth took on an exasperated slant. "Is she completely finished at the Fund?"

"No."

Wakefield's look of annoyance turned to one of surprise. He slid his hands into his pockets and rocked forward and back. "No? She told me she wasn't going to the office any more. She knew it would be uncomfortable if she did, so she asked me to bring the saddle."

David clamped his back teeth together. "She's coming back next week for one last appointment. With Edith Carroll. Unless she's changed her mind."

Wakefield dropped back into his chair. "Edith Carroll is coming *here*? What for?"

"She wants to make a donation. I asked Charlotte weeks ago if she'd see her for me. The meeting kept getting put off."

Wakefield's gaze drifted away and then homed back in upon David. "Will you see her?"

"I don't want to. I don't want to drag that pain up for either of us. That's why I asked Charlotte to see her." Peter's image rose up before him. Those proud shoulders. That wide grin. He'd been a leader, a man who inspired others. In no small part, Peter's ghost had been responsible for David rejoining the living after his injury.

He gave Wakefield a look. "But I think Peter would want me to see her."

Miles nodded. Quiet settled in upon them for a minute.

Wakefield stood. "I can be here if you like. He was my friend, too."

But it was David's promise Peter had asked for. David had vowed to look after Edith if Peter fell, but Edith hadn't let him keep his promise. And so he'd all but given up.

He sighed. "Not necessary, but thank you."

"You remember the stable I use? I'll see you there tomorrow? Early."

David looked at the saddle. "I'll be there."

Wakefield turned at the door. "She wouldn't have given you the saddle if she didn't still care. Go see her. Thank her for the saddle. *Talk to her.*"

The quiet camaraderie of moments ago vanished. The choking mass of doubts that had tortured David since his dismissal of Charlotte rose and filled his chest. The failure of his broken promise to Peter swirled into the miasma. The best way he knew to get rid of the pressure was to spew it at Wakefield. He was certainly finished with Wakefield's well-intentioned advice.

"We did talk," he bit out. "She changed her mind and revoked her refusal. I told her I'd changed my mind as well."

Wakefield's eyes went wide. "What in hell were you thinking?"

The patience David had used to hold himself together evaporated. "That's not your concern. I'm done with your mothering and coddling. I'm done listening to your opinionated courtship advice." He felt a bit wild, out of control, and the shock on Miles's face confirmed that he was. "Go. Get out."

But Wakefield, damn him, wasn't going. His mouth curved into a satisfied smirk, as if he were pleased he'd gotten a rise, and all David's pent-up fury turned his arms to piston rods as he pushed his chair wheels as fast and hard as he could around his desk toward his friend. His exhausted brain could barely think. Only his resolve had kept him going, and he didn't know how much longer he could last, constantly re-examining his decision. Maybe razing Wakefield like a skittle pin would help.

Evidently, his former comrade-in-arms didn't expect David to actually hit him, because he waited until the last second to jump aside. David missed him by a hair's-breadth. One more word, David vowed, and he wouldn't miss.

"I told you," he growled, "I don't want to talk about her."

Wakefield reentered the office, and again he dropped into his chair. David started to say more, but his friend's stare arrested him. The man's eyes were dark with compassion and sadness.

David closed his eyes and rubbed his forehead. The tension drained out of him. "She doesn't trust me. And I don't think I could bear it if we married and she still didn't. How can we commit ourselves if she can't trust me? How can anyone commit like that?"

"I'm sorry," Miles said, "but you'd better not give up. I've never yet seen you do so, and you'd better not start with Charlotte."

He'd never given up? Was that right? David did try to face things head-on. As an officer he'd certainly never turned away from his duty, even when it meant facing nearly insurmountable odds. It had taken him some time to accept that he'd spend the rest of his life in this chair, but once he had, he'd risen up against the multitude of challenges his injury brought. So, could he find a way out of this? The goal was certainly worthy, only how could he convince Charlotte to trust him?

He looked at Wakefield. Nodded. "All right."

"Is there any way I can help?" his friend asked.

"Make sure I don't do something foolhardy tomorrow on your bay."

He was only half joking.

"And just how do you expect me to stop you? If I managed to quash your injudicious deeds that somehow masquerade as derring-do, it would be a first."

Good. They were back on familiar footing. Any additional soul-searching he would rather accomplish in private. "Well, being as we're in London, you needn't worry overmuch. An early gallop is all I intend."

He did plan to set a good pace.

"I've already got a pulley and rope waiting at the stable," Wakefield said.

"Pretty confident I'd accept the saddle?"
Wakefield grinned. "Never any question."

CHAPTER THIRTY-SIX

The day of Edith Carroll's appointment dawned with dark skies and a downpour of rain. Charlotte asked herself if she was being wise to follow through on her promise. She supposed there was no other option where she maintained her honor.

David's door was closed when she arrived, but somehow she knew he was there. She *knew.*

She left her umbrella in the umbrella stand in the outer office and focused on Chetney, whose expression seemed to offer both sympathy and welcome. His eyes swept down her, and his smile grew bright. Judging by his reaction, she'd been right to combat the gray day and her morose state of mind by wearing something new and pretty. It wasn't the kind of dress she'd normally wear to the Patriotic Fund offices, being as she'd ordered it with Rose Cottage in mind. Beribboned bouquets of red roses danced upon a cream-colored skirt. A robin's egg–blue jacket, trimmed with matching rose fabric and crocheted lace, topped the flouncy skirt. It was a dress made for laughing and kissing, and she hoped David got a look at her in it. It would serve him right.

As a kind of rebellion, she left her office door open. She wanted to see him even though the possibility made her belly somersault. He'd been horrid the last time she saw him. Unfair, angry, even cruel. He'd broken her heart.

He wanted her to say she trusted him completely and without reservation? The way he'd acted had only proved she *couldn't* trust him. Hadn't it?

The inside of her chest was actually sore—a constant reminder of his rejection. She knew she'd hurt him as well. First when he proposed and she refused him, and then again when she'd professed her love but not her trust.

After Wakefield took the saddle to him, she couldn't help but hope David would contact her. She hadn't even received a note. That disappointment heaped an additional measure of despair on her, and another round of wretched sobs commenced.

But that had been the last of her waterworks. The past few days she'd spent thinking about Haliday and her father. About Vivian, who'd completely disappeared. And about Jane, still at Friar's Gate. Yesterday's letter from her friend had delivered a bright shaft of joy. Jane had taken her advice and shared her feelings with Phillip. The two were finally talking honestly and repairing their marriage.

All will be well, Jane had written. Thank God for that.

Charlotte removed her bonnet and considered her desk. Chetney had left enough work to keep her busy until midmorning, at which time Mrs. Carroll was expected.

She had a hard time concentrating, straining her ears each time Chetney opened David's door. Until their rift, David had rarely shut his door. Now, rather than calling out to Chetney when he needed him, David rang a bell that was easily heard through the wood. Whenever the bell jingled, Charlotte's head jerked up as if she'd been trained to respond to its peal. Knowing he'd sequestered himself in his office to avoid seeing her made her chest ache, and she willed Mrs. Carroll to arrive before the tension became intolerable.

By the time Chetney announced her, Charlotte was more than ready to get their business done. Edith Carroll appeared attractive and composed, with glossy auburn hair, a fine figure, and aloof green eyes. Once past their introductions, she didn't waste any time.

"I believe you're aware I'm an army widow," Mrs. Carroll said. "Peter was a captain in the Eleventh Hussars. He fell at Alma."

"My condolences, Mrs. Carroll." From what David had told her, this woman had dearly loved her husband. "It's very kind of you to consider a donation to the Royal Patriotic Fund. The Patriotic Fund coffers can't ease the loss of a husband or father, but they help alleviate the strain of lost financial support."

"This is a worthy cause, and Peter would have wanted to contribute. Some of your recipients might have been family to men under Peter's command."

"So many families are struggling," Charlotte replied. "Your gift will be appreciated."

"You get money from the Treasury, I believe?"

"We do, but we need donations, too. We've made a great difference in many lives."

Mrs. Carroll nodded. "I want to be part of that." She opened her bag. "A bank cheque is acceptable?"

It took only a minute. Once she'd handed the cheque to Charlotte, the lady made ready to leave.

"I appreciate your cooperation," Mrs. Carroll said. "Regarding my desire to avoid Mr. Scott, I mean."

Charlotte clamped her lips together. She shouldn't comment. David certainly wouldn't want her to. He wouldn't welcome her interference. But what was wrong with Edith Carroll? When David told Charlotte about the destruction of his friendship with his old friend Peter's wife, his hurt had been palpable.

"You were good friends once, weren't you?"

Mrs. Carroll waited so long to answer, Charlotte wasn't sure she was going to. The widow linked her fingers in her lap and gazed down as her thumbs rubbed against each other. "Yes. They were three best friends in the same regiment. Peter, Major Scott, and Major Lord Wakefield. Scott and Lord Wakefield often joined Peter and myself at home. I considered both of them my friends, too."

She took a large breath, her shoulders rising and falling. "That is, I *thought* Scott was a friend." Her hands stilled. She raised her head and looked at Charlotte. "But he's the reason Peter's dead." Her words drifted, soft and easy like blossom petals falling. "Peter intended to sell his commission but Scott convinced him to stay."

Charlotte nodded. Big, slow nods. "Mr. Scott told me your husband was a good officer. And he loved the army."

Mrs. Carroll blinked like she was throwing off the last traces of a dream. "Scott made Peter feel guilty for wanting to leave." The soft quality of her voice altered, becoming firm with an underlying nuance that sounded like agitation. "Peter wouldn't have died if not for Scott. And it's not as though Scott didn't know the risk. He knew." Mouth tight, the woman paused for a deep breath. "I know my husband wouldn't have liked it, but I can't forgive Scott."

Cold wafted through Charlotte. She shivered and fisted her chilled hands, but she said nothing.

Mrs. Carroll stood, ready to leave. Charlotte hurried over to Edith and got close. Close as an intimate friend. She covered Edith's clenched hand with her palm and said, "I know Mr. Scott. He's fiercely loyal. The finest man I've ever known. The kindest, the most principled. He wouldn't have tried to sway Peter for his own gain. Nor even for the good of the army. I know he listened to your husband and advised him. Advised him to follow his heart."

She squeezed Edith Carroll's hand, and the woman's lips rolled inward. The widow closed her eyes and dropped her head. Sniffed.

Nodded.

When Edith's head came up and their eyes met, Charlotte's throat grew tight.

"He would have been alive and happy *enough*," Edith whispered. "Sometimes I think it's God's justice that Scott was crippled."

"Sometimes I think so, too," David said. He sat a few feet beyond the doorway.

Edith gasped and whirled to face him.

Charlotte hadn't known David was there, and her hungry eyes absorbed the man before her. Her David, with shoulders back, head up, forthright and ready to face whatever came. His hands gripped his chair wheels, knuckles white.

"We should talk, Edith. It's what Peter would want."

Thank God, Edith nodded and followed David into his office.

#

Two hours later, David waited in Charlotte's drawing room, blind to its agreeable accoutrements. In response to the overwhelming urge to pace, he tapped the arms of his chair.

He'd spent the days since Wakefield's visit considering how to belay Charlotte's fears. The only answer he'd come up with was time. In time she'd come to trust her belief in him, and he was going to be patient if it killed him. He was going to crush his stupid pride, which had been offended that Charlotte didn't see him as the one man above all others she could trust. What crazy madness had made him spout that ultimatum? It had been pure, angry nonsense, saying he couldn't accept her love without immediate and whole-hearted trust. Arrogant nonsense, built on resentment and overwhelming his common sense. When she couldn't offer her whole, unrestricted heart, he'd lashed out.

A week of missing her had righted his thinking. Humbled him. He had no choice but to be patient. And he would be. For as long as it took.

What better way to build her trust than loving her, actually? By living with her, showing her every day the man he was. The restrictions that hobbled her would drop away in time. He trusted that would happen.

He'd never been so proud as when Charlotte described him to Edith. *The finest man I've ever known.* That gave him hope their rift could be repaired. Without knowing any details of his and Peter's friendship, Charlotte had believed David wanted only for Peter to be satisfied and happy, which was the truth. Her defense had shown she trusted the man he was today and the man he'd been in the past. One day she'd trust his future self as much as she loved him now.

Charlotte walked in. Last week she'd been willing to take a leap of faith and marry. She'd put all her reservations aside, convinced their love would see them through. David hoped she'd still be willing, but if his stupidity had made her hesitant, then he would be patient. This time, he wasn't giving up.

She hadn't changed her dress after work. Her cheeks were rosy, and she looked beautiful. Persa scampered past her, raced to David, and leaped onto his lap. David rubbed the terrier and let her settle. He never took his eyes off Charlotte.

She nodded to Beckham, and the footman closed the doors, leaving them alone.

"What happened with Mrs. Carroll?"

David felt a flush of pleasure. Of course her first concern would be his lost friendship with the woman.

"If Peter is looking down, I think he's pleased. We talked, and Edith accepts that I just encouraged Peter to follow his heart. She knows how much I miss him, and that I will shoulder some blame for the decision he made. But none of us took the risk of military service lightly, and Peter loved serving. I think in her soul Edith knows he wouldn't have been happy doing anything else."

"She stopped blaming you? Or if she couldn't do that, did she forgive you?"

"She forgave me as much as she was able. And she's agreed I might stay in contact with her." It felt good to say that. "I'll be able to abide by my promise to Peter. To provide advice if she asks, and any assistance she's in need of. To make sure she's safe and feels secure."

Charlotte sat on the settee, laying a book beside her. "I'm glad. For both of you."

David rolled forward until their knees touched. "It was your conversation with her that opened the door. I'm grateful. I feel as though a bit of wrong in my world has been righted."

Charlotte's lips curved. "I'm glad."

The two of them fell silent.

"Have you tried the sad—?"

"I'm here to ask your forg—"

They spoke together, breaking off mid-sentence. David gave Charlotte an encouraging nod.

"Have you used the saddle?" Her expressive eyes shone eager and full of hope.

"Every morning since Wakefield delivered it. I'm indebted to you."

"Does it work well? How does it feel to be riding?"

"Like food after a two year fast. But I didn't come to thank you for the brilliant saddle or for your intervention with Edith." He reached out, captured her hand, and cradled it. He raised those elegant long fingers and kissed them. "I'm here to apologize and ask if we could go back to the day you told me you loved me and wanted to marry. Please say we can go back."

Her lips parted. She turned her hand until they were palm-to-palm, fingers interlocked. "I feel the same. Exactly the same." She was beginning to smile, actually. "Are you saying…? Tell me what you're saying."

He tightened his fingers. Kissed the back of her hand. "I'm sorry. I've been crack-brained. I'm ashamed to admit it, but my damaged pride was to blame for my idiocy. I hope you can forgive me. If it's any consolation, I've been the most miserable man in England."

"I'm rather…stunned."

"Stunned in a good way, I hope?" Her smile was full and beautiful, her face alight, so he went on. "Missing you made me see reason. I want to take that leap of faith with you."

"I love you, David. So much. Will that be enough for you?"

"Yes. It's more than enough. If someday you're able to give me your whole heart, it will be a great treasure. But I don't care when that happens."

"You're sure?"

"I'm positive. I want to marry you. As soon as you'll have me." He dragged in a breath. "It will be my everlasting shame that, for a while, I pushed you away."

"I admit I prefer when we're pulling together."

Charlotte's voice held an underlying tease. David's throat grew hot, and he knew things were going to be all right.

"If you're worried I'll give up on us," he said, "don't. I'm not a man who gives up, and I'm not giving up on you, Charlotte. Not ever again. And if you're worried I'll become impatient, complain or criticize, I promise I won't. Or I'll be eager to work to fix that."

She scooted to the edge of the settee and leaned toward him until their foreheads met. "There's something I want to do."

She moved back, stood, and picked up the book she'd brought with her. He noticed what book it was. Charlotte went to the cold fireplace, knelt, and opened the novel's cover. David wheeled closer. One after another, she ripped out pages and tossed them into the fireplace just as he'd dropped identical pages into his brass waste receptacle weeks ago. He went closer, close enough to touch her, until he could see every nuance of her expression and the tiniest shimmer in her eyes.

She tore out the final page and held it aloft, her face confident and determined. The cover she tossed into the firebox. She stood, picked up a waiting match and striker, and passed it to David.

As she rolled the page, he struck the match, and when she held the paper tube out he touched the flame to it. The paper kindled and she raised it, the licking flame blackening and curling the edges, producing a thin column of dark smoke and a flood of charred paper smell. She dropped the burning sheet into its waiting bed, and the mass of paper caught, crackled and sang as flames rose and began to consume the entire heap. Its flare dispelled the shadows and set purple glints alight in her eyes.

David set his hands on her hips and guided her onto his lap. She twisted so she faced him, and he grasped her waist.

"I'm proud of you for burning that bloody book."

She put a hand on each of his upper arms. "It was a reminder of how trusting someone makes you vulnerable. I haven't forgiven Vivian, but I understand how despairing she was. I don't want a reminder. I don't want anything that might keep me apart from you or happiness. I don't want to be afraid. I want to be free to love and trust."

He traced her lips with his thumb, and her mouth opened just enough for the tip of his thumb to slip inside. Her lips pursed around it. He felt the gentle pull as she sucked it deeper, then the warm brush of her tongue as it swirled around the end of his thumb and pushed it from her mouth. His entire body went hard.

He wrapped his arms around her. She was warm, fragrant, and when he kissed her it was all he'd been yearning for. He tasted her wet, delicious mouth and asked for more. She answered, pressing harder, her tongue growing bolder.

When they broke apart, gasping, her smile grew huge and happiness spilled from her sparkling eyes. His own smile couldn't stretch any broader, and his body thrummed. Even after being left for dead on the battlefield, waiting all night for daylight and rescue, breaking dawn hadn't felt this good. He gathered Charlotte close, suffused with the most intense happiness he'd ever known.

"Will you be my friend, Bluebell? My love, and my wife?"

"Yes," she said, and kissed him.

EPILOGUE

Four years later

Charlotte looked up, surprised but delighted as David came through the door.

"Papa!" Three-year-old Margaret ran across the room, her fingers holding in place the newsprint hat Charlotte had just made and put atop her head. Brown curls danced as the child climbed onto her father's lap.

"What's happened to my girl?" David asked. "Has she become a sailor?"

Margaret gave him an exuberant kiss, which earned her a grin, then nodded solemnly. "Yes, but Mama's going to make a crown next, and then I'll be a princess."

"I see. I suppose that would make me king."

Margaret laughed. "No, Papa. Kings wear crowns, and you don't even wear a hat."

The child patted David's bare head, and Charlotte smiled at their antics. David still eschewed headgear. She recalled Wakefield's long-ago description of David, the way he'd been before his injury. He'd become that man again. A man of laughter.

She watched him give his daughter a big hug before letting her feet slide to the floor. Then he rolled toward Charlotte.

"How's little Julia?" He glanced toward their four-month-old's cradle.

With the birth of their second child, Charlotte and David's joy knew no bounds. Whatever had caused her failure to conceive and carry a child for Haliday, she'd had no problems bearing David's.

"She's sleeping. What are you doing home?" On the days Charlotte didn't accompany him to the office, she didn't expect to see her husband until dinner time.

David rolled his chair close. "Something came in the mail today." He pulled an envelope from his coat's inside pocket and held it out. "It was addressed to both of us. I told Eleanor and Chetney to carry on, and I left."

Eleanor had recently begun working at the Fund, and already the young woman was a valued addition to the growing staff.

Charlotte eyed the envelope and the postmark. Margaret had returned to the newspapers and was busy fashioning a three-year-old's creation. Charlotte's home and her family looked just as they had a moment ago, before David had pulled the letter from his pocket.

Her husband's blue eyes held steady, a smile deep at their center. He responded to her unasked question.

"It's from Vivian."

"Did you read it?"

He nodded and extended it to her.

Charlotte curled up on his lap, wrapped her arms around his neck and laid her head on his shoulder. "Just tell me what it says."

He hugged her close and she closed her eyes. "She's in America. She likes it there and she's trying to make up for the wrongs she's done in the past."

Charlotte opened her eyes and studied her husband's chin. She slipped her fingers down his waistcoat until she found the little bump in his pocket. Her button.

David continued. "She doesn't ask for forgiveness. She knows she'll never deserve it. But she wants you to know that you need never again fear her. She intends to remain in America." He tossed the envelope onto a nearby table. "She played a part in two deaths and tried to murder you. She can't come back to England. But I think she's truly contrite as well."

Charlotte raised her head. "Do you have to go back to the office?"

David brushed his mouth across hers. Twice. Then his lips settled, and he delighted her with slow, lazy kisses.

Wherever Nurse had got to, she couldn't have chosen a better time to be absent.

"Papa?"

At Margaret's little voice, David broke off their kissing. "Yes, Poppet?"

"Why do you kiss Mama so much?"

David looked at Charlotte and grinned. "Because my legs are hollow and Mama's trying to fill them up with kisses."

She loved this man. Charlotte cupped his face, kissed him, and whispered in his ear.

"Will you be able to walk then?" Margaret asked.

"I don't need to walk. Why walk when I can soar?" David said.

ABOUT THE AUTHOR

After a satisfying career as an Emergency Room nurse, Sheri Humphreys closed the book on her diverse nursing experiences and followed a lifelong love for writing and historical romance to a new vocation as a writer. She lives with a Jack Russell mix rescue, Lucy, in a small town on the central California coast.

Did you enjoy this book? Drop us a line and say so! We love to hear from readers, and so do our authors. To connect, visit www.boroughspublishinggroup.com online, send comments directly to info@boroughspublishinggroup.com, or friend us on Facebook and Twitter. And be sure to check back regularly for contests and new releases in your favorite subgenres of romance!

Are you an aspiring writer? Check out www.boroughspublishinggroup.com/submit and see if we can help you make your dreams come true.

Made in the USA
San Bernardino, CA
31 July 2016